FOR D…

K…

— HUGS

— PETER
+ MARGARET

PHOTOCREDIT: Julia Maria Seemann, 2008

Marco Sonzogni is an award-winning editor and poet. A widely published academic, he is a lecturer in the School of Languages and Cultures at Victoria University of Wellington.

from Christine 09

A VINTAGE BOOK published by Random House New Zealand
18 Poland Road, Glenfield, Auckland, New Zealand

For more information about our titles go to www.randomhouse.co.nz

A catalogue record for this book is available from the National Library of New Zealand

Random House International, Random House, 20 Vauxhall Bridge Road, London, SW1V 2SA, United Kingdom; **Random House Australia Pty Ltd**, Level 3, 100 Pacific Highway, North Sydney 2060, Australia; **Random House South Africa Pty Ltd**, Isle of Houghton, Corner Boundary Road and Carse O'Gowrie, Houghton 2198, South Africa; **Random House Publishers India Private Ltd**, 301 World Trade Tower, Hotel Intercontinental Grand Complex, Barakhamba Lane, New Delhi 110 001, India

First published 2008

ISBN 978 1 86941 969 1

Cover design: Sarah Laing
Text design: Elin Bruhn Termannsen
Printed in China by Everbest Printing Co Ltd

for Bob

SECOND VIOLINS

New stories inspired by
Katherine Mansfield and
edited by Marco Sonzogni

CONTENTS

KATHERINE MANSFIELD'S UNFINISHED STORIES

Introduction

MANSFIELD MELODIES

Observe the young and tender frond
of this punga: shaped and curved
like the scroll of a fiddle; fit instrument. . .
— A.R.D. Fairburn

'To achieve great things', argued Leonard Bernstein, 'two things are needed; a plan, and not quite enough time.' Katherine Mansfield (1888–1923) certainly did not have quite enough time to live, yet achieved great things. Mansfield's legacy as a master of the short story is undisputed — though short stories occasionally seemed even to her 'unreal and not worth doing'.

The short story has proved one of the most elusive forms to classify, with variations from the Bible to Boccaccio to Borges. Mansfield was recognised in her own lifetime as a powerful short-story writer, even in comparison with contemporaries such as James Joyce, Virginia Woolf, Franz Kafka and D.H. Lawrence. Her work was 'a continual and sincere response to all she encountered in her path through life' (lifting the words of E.M. Forster).

Shortly before succumbing to tuberculosis in 1923, Katherine Mansfield wrote that 'after all' she seemed to have 'nothing to leave and nobody to leave things to'. When she died, there were fifteen stories that were not completed but which she had intended for inclusion in her planned fourth collection, called *The Dove's Nest* and published posthumously in 1923.

Reviewing the uncompleted stories, J.B. Priestley said that 'the merest beginnings are capital reading. Even though we never come to the point, and do not know what the stories are about, it does not seem to matter very much' because 'the delicate enchantments of her art are there as of old'. Those stories are published here and prove Priestly's remarks. In addition, their 'merest beginnings' have been handed over to contemporary authors to be taken in a new direction.

Many of the chosen writers have their own connection to Mansfield — for example, being a Menton Fellow, winning the BNZ Katherine Mansfield Short Story Competition or having researched her work and life. All are known for the quality of their writing. Each was given the first paragraph of one of Mansfield's fifteen unfinished stories: not to complete as Mansfield might have intended but to use as a starting place for their own work. Some have followed the brief; some have been creative with it. Vincent O'Sullivan, for instance, has concluded his piece with the initial paragraph; Albert Wendt has quoted it in his second paragraph and Charlotte Grimshaw has pulled out some elements from it and distributed them in her story. And if the first and last stories — by Alice Tawhai and Witi Ihimaera — have sprouted from the same beginning (hence their repositioning to bookend the new stories), the opening of 'A Married Man's Story' has been transformed into a complete story by Annamarie Jagose as well as into an evocative poem by Bill Manhire.

Mansfield's completed stories are masterworks, as immediate now as when she wrote them. This special gift challenged the writers involved. They have responded with sensitivity and individuality — making a nod at Mansfield's stories or life, or exploring the nature of influence and inspiration, or simply letting imagination take the lead.

Hatched from the nest of Mansfield's unfinished work, *Second Violins* confirms Seamus Heaney's belief that 'whatever is given can always be reimagined'.

Marco Sonzogni
Victoria University of Wellington
7 June 2008

A MARRIED MAN'S STORY

— Bill Manhire

One's wife at the rainy window.
She carries the baby. She turns away,
she turns him over on her knee.
He is quick and kissing, he is soft.

The gas jumps.
To call to her and wonder.

\+

For a moment she opened her arms.
I heard voices and laughter.
The evenings entered my room.

I forgot the moon. She drew me to her
like a cloud, like ash! The great flame steadied
as the small flames joined.

+

The golden-haired girl is happy.
She says nothing. She whispers.
How frightened I was!

I was born
long before I could sit,
yet every day my father drank.

On sofa days
I peered through to watch her fingers.
Big coloured bottles by the counter.

The taste of years.
I think she never left her room again.

+

I felt my heart thump, indifferent.
She held the bunched-up pink and purple flowers.
I understood their shaking.

My father was a cork that sits on a step.
My mother moved a little faster in the sun.
Sometimes she nodded, hid in rocky hollows.

I never wondered what to do.
The moonlight was a deserted road,
weak afternoons at the window.

+

Is that you with the black label?
We want to go in, and yet
the dark beach is our bed.

Is that you?
Is that you with the black label?

+

The little bare foot.
The sea.
The lantern.
The signs.

My writing table.

Soft, and almost crumbling,
boats knock against the books.

Outside it is raining: a catalogue.
The bright green glorious voice.
My wife turns round quickly.

Hard, steady drumming.
The small, cold dining room.
Still lakes. All is as usual.

+

Now something that leaps up tempts me terribly.
I lift my spoon. My wife declares
yet keeps a secret. She was always deeply bound.

One day, we say, the surgeon.
One day, the patient's eyes.

+

You sat at a mirror
composed of old reflections:
anticipation first, then great fatigue.

You turned out the gas.
You wrapped away the evening.

Hand on the door.
Hand on the reference pages.

+

But we were never plainly written:
There are people who love the truth
and light a cigarette.

"Do you think I never think?"

She said this cheerfully, certainly —
with dark, distrustful eyes.

+

And now I recall my childhood,
the bell sobbing, and
everything big behind the screen.

Pale stem at the side of my face.
It smells of the shop, of the hillside,
of the corridor where coats still hang.

I am standing again in my corner.
A green cape is coming across
the dark stretches, the blanks.

In the gaslight, I see the wet eye
shrink above me. I was once so small and thin:
a voice in a body in the playground.

Such a Sweet Old Lady

EAST OF THE SUN

— *Alice Tawhai*

Why did old Mrs. Travers wake so early nowadays? She would like to have slept for another three hours at least. But no, every morning at almost precisely the same time, at half-past four, she was wide awake. For — nowadays, again — she woke always in the same way, with a slight start, a small shock, lifting her head from the pillow with a quick glance as if she fancied someone had called her, or as if she were trying to remember for certain whether this was the same wallpaper, the same window she had seen last night before Warner switched off the light.

She was never quite sure what the wallpaper would be like when she woke, suspecting that it did sometimes change from the night before, replacing itself from the repertoire of wallpapers she had lived with in the past, although she couldn't place where or when any of them had been.

Sometimes the wallpaper was emerald green with black tiki. Other times it had brown horses running against a background of orange flowers, or it was just a plain deep pink. Today when she opened her eyes it was black with white daisies. It took her a moment to take it in, because her eyes needed to adjust to the dark, until daylight came slipping in, ashamed to find that Phoebe Travers was awake before it was.

She saw other fluorescent white patterns glowing among the daisies. Maybe they were there, or maybe they were just the ghosts of a dream. There were the bones of an X-ray, the coins and keys from inside Hakaraia's stomach, and the two white rabbits that Warner brought in for elderly residents to cuddle, in the belief that they were calming. As if calm were in short supply.

Phoebe hated being called Mrs. Travers. Inside, she still felt like Phoebe, still felt like a girl. She liked her name because it reminded her of a rubber ball held underwater, bouncing back as soon as it was released, over and over again: Phoebe, Phoebe, Phoebe. She still felt bouncy and full of life on the inside, even if her body wasn't keeping up on the outside. She didn't think she'd ever be old on the inside.

But she did regret the fact that now that she could sleep in for as long as she liked, she hardly slept at all. There wasn't much to be done so early, not until the sun spilled in at the window, like orange juice brimming over the rim of a cup and onto the floor. So she waited in the darkness, searching for clues to her life in the patterns on the wall.

Once she rose, she grew irritated at herself, unable to find her jade earrings, or the black cameo choker she often wore around her neck. She considered blaming Warner, but then again she couldn't be sure. Maybe she had given them away years ago. She missed all sorts of things: bookmarks, lingerie, the perfume that Hakaraia had given her for her birthday.

Some areas of her mind were covered by a very fine mist. It was like trying to watch Earle shower through the opaque shower curtain. She could see bulky shapes and shadows, glimpses of things before they were covered up again, and she felt that if she just stared harder, and tried harder to focus, then her eyes would clear, along with her brain.

She went for an early morning walk, moving as slowly as the rhythm of her heart. Once around the pink weatherboard home for the elderly where she lived at the end of Hakanoa Street. She watched the orange sun rising above the dark jade bush of the mountain. The paua shells around the empty dirt of the flowerbeds made the shape of tiki, still retaining that ethereal pearly green glow that said they hadn't long been out of the water.

Inside, at breakfast, blowflies hung in the air, buzzing around like little pieces of X-ray that had broken loose from the film. Once, she had X-rayed things herself. In her day, girls had been expected to be nurses or teachers, or even just wives. Phoebe had chosen nursing. During the war she'd managed to sneak into radiography, which had suited the side of her personality that needed to be a little bit different to everyone else. She'd enjoyed working in a darkroom, making pictures of white bones on black film. Seeing inside people, where they couldn't even see themselves.

When her son Hakaraia was little, he'd wanted her attention so much that he had swallowed tiny metal objects: coins, small keys, and once even a safety pin, thankfully closed. Begging her to take him to where she worked and X-ray him, so that he could proudly bring the pictures home and pin them to the wall, black squares on a background of orange daisies.

The safety pin incident was the last time he'd done that. The doctor had insisted that it be removed, and Hakaraia had spent weeks in hospital, away from home, curled up in a little ball. Even when he grew up, Phoebe would think of him walking around with coins and keys inside him.

When Hakaraia had first come, he had clung to her, and when she walked down the hallway he had insisted on crawling between her legs, so that she had to keep them slightly apart. She was always tripping over him.

Hakaraia had come slightly after, even though he was slightly older. She could never tell whether he was quiet and loving because that was his nature, or whether he had quickly realised that the market for loud angry grief had been cornered by Kitten, who would stand continuously screaming in her cot for hours at a time. She refused all attempts to comfort her for the entire first year that she was with them. Phoebe had known that she was screaming with rage at being separated from her birth mother, but she'd always thought that Kitten would get over it.

Kitten had never gotten over it. She had always been angry.

Kitten was her daughter, but recently Phoebe had realised that although she loved her, she didn't like her very much. It was almost a relief, after all those years of trying so hard and never being able to name what was wrong. Now that it didn't really matter any more, she could acknowledge it. She was glad to be in the Hakanoa Street home. She would have been as horrified to find herself staying with Kitten as Kitten would have been to have her. They both felt more at ease with each other at a distance.

When they had adopted the children, Earle had wanted to choose new names for them. He'd wanted to call them Hector and Veronica, but Phoebe had insisted that they keep the names they came with. It seemed cruel that they should lose their names as well as their birth mothers.

Before she'd gone back to work, Phoebe would push her pram with her brown babies in it down into town, and people were full of wonder at their big dark eyes.

Phoebe had a shameful suspicion that she enjoyed being the only one to have brown babies, the only one to have Maori babies. She'd always liked to have what no one else had. Her distress at not being able to bear her own baby had been heightened by not being able to have what came so easily to others, even when she wanted it so badly.

Eventually the children had noticed their skin. Kitten had handled things by under-achieving, and Hakaraia had handled them by over-achieving. Phoebe had had many fights with Kitten about trying to do better at school, because Phoebe knew she could have. Those fights had always ended with Kitten shouting, 'I don't want to be what you want me to be!' Phoebe had tried to explain that she didn't want Kitten to 'be' anything. She just wanted her to do well.

Hakaraia had grown up to be a lawyer, and the chairperson of an urban iwi committee. No matter who asked, Hakaraia always gave of himself, to the point where he had nothing left to give himself. Phoebe thought it was because Hakaraia was still so desperate to be good enough to be loved and wanted. Although she had always loved and wanted him.

Kitten had told her she didn't know whether she was Maori or Pakeha. In the end she'd hedged her bets, marrying a white Maori from Dunedin and having three children with him. Kitten had blamed Phoebe for never taking her down to the marae, but Phoebe hadn't known how to go down to the marae.

Phoebe was the one who had chosen to adopt Maori babies. Earle had never stopped being uncomfortable with the fact that everybody could tell that Kitten and Hakaraia weren't his biological children. People who didn't know their story would look at them sideways, and Earle told Phoebe he could see them thinking that the children might belong to her and some other man.

He had felt it diminishing who he was. And to console himself he had a succession of office secretaries who offered a little more than they were paid for.

Phoebe went from having what everyone seemed to want, to wishing she could have something other people seemed to have.

Sometimes, when she looked at Warner, Phoebe thought

she could see Earle's face. She often confused Warner with other people she had known.

Warner's name reminded her of the cartoons at the movies she had gone to with Earle. The trailers before the feature film. Warner Brothers cartoons, disappearing into big, fleshy pink concentric circles. 'Tha', tha', that's all, folks!' How funny that they should be sharper in her mind now than what she had had for breakfast.

Just to test this thought, she tried to remember what she had eaten. Warner had been there, but she wasn't sure if this was a memory or not, because Warner was always there. Warner was a fixed, constant thing. She wondered if this was because Warner fed them, and she thought of Warner in the way that a cat always recognises the person who spoons the food into its bowl.

At lunch Warner had the plates out on the table, waiting for them. Today there were pink lamingtons and strips of bacon. Everything was as cheap as possible. The lamingtons were left over from yesterday, sent over by the bakery, bare of coconut where thumb and forefinger had placed them on the plate. Bright pink, and bleeding inwardly into the sponge. Warner wore a heavy black apron, possibly as protection from radiation.

The bacon consisted of off-cuts from the pig farm. There were red marks on the fat of the meat, written in butcher's pen. They made patterns that may as well have been Arabic, sliced from its original context. This was how Phoebe's thoughts were. Sometimes they sliced away from where she had first thought them. They floated free, slipping and escaping, and she could never be sure of finding them, but sometimes she encountered them unexpectedly.

Warner was loud and cheery. Phoebe felt sorry she'd spoken so loudly and cheerfully to those elderly patients she'd had to X-ray. Now that she knew how irritating it was to be treated like an idiot.

Every day after lunch Phoebe played the piano and sang for everybody. Just one song, before she got too tired. Every day she considered what she might sing. Billie Holiday's 'Strange Fruit'? Holly King's 'Slave to Memory'? Goldie Tween's 'Slow Train'? Today she chose Sarah Vaughan's 'East of the Sun'. She heard Warner muttering that she chose 'East of the Sun' every time. Phoebe was sure she'd chosen something by Ella Fitzgerald yesterday. Maybe every day that seemed different was actually the same. But that was better than the other way around.

Phoebe had always thought that her children would grow to be like her, and she was surprised to find that even though they were the people who were most familiar to her, they remained the children of strangers she had never met, no matter how much love she gave them. But then maybe that was how all parents felt, even the people who had made their own children.

Kitten had an overt sexuality that Phoebe had never understood. It wasn't what she wore, or what she said, or what she did; it just was. It was a part of her that every person who came into contact with her instantly knew. Phoebe had spent her life covering up every aspect of her own sexuality that might be visible to outsiders, worried that they might see through her clothes and down to her skin in the way that she could look inside other people and see their bones. But she couldn't cover up Kitten.

Kitten could sing. Her sound was sultry, smoky and big-voiced. Note-rich and perfect. If she chose to sing. Which she didn't. Phoebe, who could sing well but fell just short of being good enough to have real talent, would have given all the teeth in her mouth to be able to sing like Kitten. She couldn't contemplate how Kitten could have something so special and want to throw it away.

Kitten didn't come to see her. Maybe she was still down in

Dunedin. Or maybe she did come and Phoebe just forgot.

After lunch Phoebe walked around the grounds again, this time in reverse. The black buildings of the rest-home contrasted with the beds of orange marigolds. They were edged with the ocean-jewelled eyes of paua, and looked like traffic islands on the dark green lawn. Sometimes when she blinked she saw the flowers as X-rays, as delicate as black chiffon. It seemed to be a trick of the light, only lasting for as long as her thoughts did.

Some things were fixed, like the sun, and other things came and went, revolving like planets. Phoebe disliked common sense, which, if she knew no better, would say that it was the earth that was fixed, and the sun that came and went. She thought of a song she used to sing. Something about the sun and its direction.

She was ashamed that she had worried about Earle when he was with Kitten. Kitten wasn't one of Earle's secretaries. Phoebe had no idea how or when it had started, but a bad feeling had come to her when she saw the two of them together.

She remembered waking early one Christmas morning, which was unusual, because generally she cursed having to wake early on that day or any other. She hadn't been able to place her unease, but she'd felt the urge to get up and check the house. She remembered that the wallpaper had been bright green with black daisies. It was the background to Earle and Kitten: Earle back home from his office party and smelling of whisky, and Kitten on his knee.

They were laughing and giggling and fully clothed, and what happier picture of a father and daughter could there have been on Christmas morning, but Phoebe had lost everything calm about herself.

She could still hear herself, screaming at Kitten to get back to bed, screaming at Earle for being home so late. That had been a very strained Christmas, with everyone except Kitten putting on a brave face for Hakaraia, who took such pleasure in giving them all the gifts he had made.

When Earle had died, it had put him out of the reach of the secretaries for ever. And it had put Kitten out of his reach.

Phoebe sat down on a bench and looked at the turquoise green weatherboard building. It doubled, trebled and quadrupled on itself, every wing the same as the last. She was reminded of the wallpaper she'd woken up to that morning: same pattern, but different colours. Or maybe it was a much longer time ago. Perhaps it was her mind wandering and seeing wallpaper everywhere, her real life becoming papered by living, breathing strips of it.

And it really did seem to live and breathe. The sun burnt down as orange as a child's crayon. The pink daisies rose higher, and the green grass grew to waist length, whispering and rustling as it softly caressed itself. Small sandy rabbits with night in their eyes and white under their tails looked out from between the blades.

And for a moment, out of the corner of her eye, Phoebe could have sworn she saw a lion in the meadow.

She had no idea how long she sat there before it faded, and the daisies folded up flat again. She often misplaced the stick by which she measured time. It may have been minutes, or it may have been hours.

Warner shut the curtains. They were a deep plain pink against the green wallpaper, with its large silhouettes of black tiki running in alternate lines. Or perhaps they were rabbits. Warner straightened Phoebe's blankets, and for a minute Phoebe thought that she was Kitten, and that Warner was her, Kitten's mother, checking on her, making sure she was safe and secure. She wondered if Warner loved her. Had she loved Kitten? She thought she had.

She admired the black cameo necklace clasped around Warner's neck. The white profiles on the black marble were like X-rays of all the faces of all the people she'd ever known. How funny that Warner should have everybody wrapped around her neck. What were they doing there? Earle, Kitten, Hakaraia, her singing teachers, all of Earle's secretaries, and her own mother and father.

The lightbulb was a glowing orb above her, too bright for her eyes. She heard the faraway sounds of a song she thought she knew. 'East of the Sun'. If you were east of the sun, then the sun was in the west, about to sink. Flaring solar brilliance, about to be permanently dimmed. What had once been so bright was going to descend into blackness, leaving only an empty space where it had been, seared and burnt onto the dark X-ray film of memory. Nothing else left.

Warner turned off the light.

A Married Man's Story

KITTENELLE

— Annamarie Jagose

It is evening. Supper is over, we have left the small, cold dining room. We have come back to the sitting room where there is a fire. All is as usual. I am sitting at my writing-table, which is placed across a corner so that I am behind it, as it were, and facing the room. The lamp with the green shade is alight; I have before me two large books of reference, both open, a pile of papers much scratched through and rewritten and a double tot of brandy that Deidre has slipped me. While Mrs. Bethell has me in her rheumy sights, I content myself with surreptitiously wafting the cup behind my papers, its resinous toffee bouquet a relief from the curds and cabbage farting of the sitting room after supper. I think better on a drink. These days it is hard to have a clear thought, something singular and distinct from the shaggy herd of half ideas that hoof about ceaselessly on the prairies of my skull, their dull rumble the better part of my proof that I still have, as we liked to say, a 'consciousness'. The things we used to talk about. There was some conference, wasn't there, or perhaps an airport bar afterwards. A tubby fellow, British, I think, bloated on his footnotes and coming at me full performance volume so the others could hear, pretending concern that I perhaps had not fully understood Professor Garter's point. Garter, was it. Or Garton. Names are the worst, the first to go. They just aren't there, leaving behind a bit of nothingness that holds their shape a moment, like the stale smelling earth where a house has been lifted off its stumps. Gordon. And here's something, they come back when you stop trying to remember. Professor Ian Gordon. Meanwhile Billy Bunter's holding the floor, smiling as a hare would, toothy and pursed at the same time, worrying the difference between consciousness and subjectivity. He had an aggressive lisp, one of those speech impediments English academics acquire with their college colours. It was all a question of consciousness apparently. *Conthithnith*, as Edie said afterwards, making me snort my nightcap out my nose, the hotel sheets still smelling agreeably of Scotch the next morning when the shutters were opened onto a postcard avenue of gold and red trees crowded behind with fresh snowed mountains.

Mrs. Bethell's eye has turned up in its socket, showing white to the room. A feint to my mottled brown Waterman fountain pen and I have palmed the dose of brandy, glanced curtly about the room from under my halo of lamplight and, with a quick chin chug, it is down and the cup tucked expertly under the yellowing leaf of a potted fern for Deidre to collect later on her way back to bed. It must be more than fifty years old, my Waterman, its nib no longer as crisp, the ink sometimes gobbing a clean page of notes, although it looks as good as new. The same can't be said of my writing hand, once trim and tasty enough to be sighed over and one time even pressed the length of an astonishing crevice in the ladies room of the British Library, now scaled and purple as a rooster's claw. One thing about ageing, it happens entirely on the outside. If you think otherwise, just wait. As well to remember this in the sitting room after supper where my companions, dentures loosened, stockings adrift, sleep and wake in the competing flicker of the gas fireplace and the television set. Mrs. Bethell plucking at her crochet lap rug with dreaming fingers; Mrs. Woodifield, deaf as a doorbell but ever hopefully calling What? What? like a marshbird; Miss Brill and her powdered fox fur with its leprous snout; Mrs. Buckingham with the talking clock; Mrs. Haggie, goitered and gartered. All ladies except for Mr. Queet, who takes early to his bed to listen in the dark to National Radio.

The circle of light from the green-shaded lamp falls around me like a mosquito net, the rest of the room turned down to a distant whine. I sit immensely still and wait, as a hunter waits, as waiting waits on itself, unmoving, the steady core of a whirl of expectation. The print on the page snaps into a sharper focus. Something impossible is heaving itself out of the morass of detail. I don't have time to explain: just understand that there is a pattern I have been pursuing for some time across these various papers. Like a hand of patience, it is not easy to say whether it will come out true. For the last few months, as the days have grown shorter and colder, I have been chasing down the facts, pulling together evidence from the archival clutter. Tonight, though, something shifts and attaches in a new figuration to something else, this slight modification freeing up other possibilities previously beyond my consideration. Perhaps I have been taken in by the usual scholarly dating of the friendship and the falling out? Such a simple thing and yet how consequential it might turn out. However irrelevant I must seem, bundled up in a peggy-square rug stained with the yolk of someone's breakfast egg, it might yet be that my name, silver-plated by the admiration of my peers, is passed onto the next generation of scholars. Barely a thought, I dare not put any weight on it. This is how it was in the months after I lost my leg and what could be called, I suppose, my will to live. I was always falling down and hoping to be allowed to stay there. O Edie. The afternoons in Bandol, your shoulders strewn with new freckles and the sound of lunch time cutlery through the party wall. But here's the squeal of the medicine trolley with its gimpy back wheel coming down the corridor from the infirmary. To keep the shape of the thing, I write myself a hasty note —*1917? 'she seems to have gone every sort of hog'* — and then the staff nurse is on me with her deserts of vast eternity and an unpoetic handful of zopiclone.

'Working late again, Professor.' It is Barbara Bruden, RN, going by her name badge. She flares her nostrils professionally, catching perhaps a whiff of the brandy or that more troubling smell of corruption that I associate with my stump, although when I hoist it horizontal to the mirror it never presents anything other than an inoffensive nubbin of loose flesh. I know how unlovely I must look, a great whale of a woman wedged behind this writing table, fat beyond even my own comprehension and pointlessly old. Barbara Bruden is in her late thirties, perhaps just the far side of forty. She has thick, short hair cut blunt at her nape, the squared-off nails of the health professional and, since I am not blind, firm, pear-shaped breasts with an acceptable bounce. I make no sense to her. She would sooner tolerate in me a catheter bag and a rubberised cushion protector than my notecards and indexes and my endless scuffling through the same drifts of paper. Shortly after I first came here, there was an incident or, at any rate, an event that Barbara Bruden wrote up in something called the Incident Log. It seems after three incidents you can be put under restraint, which sounds intriguing but means I take absurd care with my brandy, not to mention Deidre's visits. I had a cough I couldn't shake and the doctor was called to my bedside, Barbara Bruden hovering implausibly as my chaperone in the doorway.

'What seems to be the problem, Mrs. Meadows.'

'Doctor,' I said.

'Yes,' he said, not seeing we were at cross purposes. 'Yes?'

'She's a doctor too,' said Barbara Bruden, hurrying forward to make amends. 'A university doctor.' She offered this last as if I were a particular order of maniac, one that took humoring. It would be a simple matter, I thought, to explain myself. A doctor, even a medical doctor, might be interested to know of breaking developments in literary scholarship. Probably he has even read the better known of Mansbury's work. Masephipp's. Fuckity fuck: has there been a worse moment? Mangleton. I had a violently detailed vision of my brain hollowed and oozing as a honeycomb and suffered further the exchange of knowing smiles between doctor and nurse. Middlefield. Marbridge. I swung my good leg over the edge of the bed and, being unable to do more, relieved my feelings by snatching up my bottle of black ink and smashing it against the far wall.

No doubt it is on account of this incident that Barbara Bruden approaches me these days with such care. She holds my drug chart up as if it were a tiny shield and takes a tentative step toward me, arm outstretched, shaking my pills in their tiny crimped paper cup to show she means no harm. I give no trace of agitation although, like Coleridge, I am held from the pleasure-dome of my papers by some dull plodder while the milk of paradise turns cheesy. As if she is the one kept waiting, Barbara Bruden lets loose an impatient sigh. I throw the pills back, tucking the small white one with the red logo high into my top gum to give to Deidre later, and Barbara Bruden wheels herself off, satisfied. She was not so sloppy the morning of the incident, so-called. With the ink still dripping down the wall, she had me on my one good hip, a shot of horse tranquilliser buried in my arse.

'Mansfield,' I cried, so happy to have the name restored to me I barely minded the commotion. Katherine Mansfield, born Kathleen Beauchamp, 1888–1923. Up to her elbows in girls at boarding school and dogged about the world ever after by Ida Baker. Gonorrhoea at twenty, tubercular eight years later.

Coupled with John Middleton Murry, Wig to his Tig. Lover of Virginia Woolf for six secret months. It was then, improbably then, as I lay upended on my bed, the doctor and Barbara Bruden with their ink-smattered backs to me tutting and tsking over the damage, a breeze from the corridor cooling my bare rump except where the needle jab still burned, sending out a little shower of sparks into every particle, into every finger and toe, even those five toes I never expected to feel again, that I saw the blossoms of ink, saw them budding and blooming in late Victorian fashion and knew at once, even as I passed into oblivion, that Mansfield wrote for goatish Virginia when she described *the sticky, silky petals* of the poppy wallpaper in 'Prelude', *the rough leaf and the tight glazed bud.*

I woke some hours later to the stink of fresh paint, the sunlight angling differently into the room, my prosthetic leg, still in its brown hose and polished shoe, leaning against the bureau in the corner. Tucked so flat to my bed I might have been in winding sheets, my head was all I could easily move. I still felt radiant, lit from within as if I had swallowed a silvery pear tree in full flower, and there, on the far wall beneath the new coat of paint, an inky bruise showing through in the shape of Australia, quite perfect, right down to the hanging saddle of Tasmania, Edie's birthplace. So I drifted the downstream day, sleeping on and off, the sheets tucked as hard against my ribs as Edie's horseriding thighs until I was pricked out like a stallion. My papers could wait.

Some days I give myself goosebumps thinking how my studies have taken off, more progress in the last year than across my entire career. True, my brain is curdled by the drugs but a welcome side effect is this gift for lateral thought, fresh ideas springing thick and green as from a pruning cut. I have grown almost accustomed to the tooth-rattling inspiration that reliably strikes around eleven in the morning and again after supper, the kind of meaty possibility that might have kept me going for a year, now shunting into view twice a day with the regularity of a commuter train. Unlikely as it seems, I work here undisturbed. No one else lays any claim to my writing table. It sits here like a piece of specialist equipment, uncovetable as a dialysis unit. My setting myself up every morning after breakfast is tolerated with the same cheery indifference as Miss Brill's daily announcement that she will be taking lunch in town today so please don't set a place for her. Only a couple of books and an armful of papers; no access to a library, no computer even, no more sweet Edie coming up the stair to rub my neck and take me out before dark walking the dogs. Nothing to protect me from the rough interruptions of various staff wanting to set me upright on my doughnut cushion or wheel me aside so as to get the vacuum cleaner into the corner, the television left to run the whole day, its braid of voices rasping away at my attention, and, every now and then, visits from the feeble-minded occupational therapist with her coloured fabric scraps and wicker baskets.

Sometimes when Mrs. Buckingham is throttling the robot voice out of her talking clock every quarter hour and the plates are rattling down the corridor on the breakfast trolleys, when every call button on the nurse's station is red and blinking and Mrs. Dove has got out over her cotsides and is raising hell, I make myself remember how little headway I made all those hours uninterrupted in quiet archival spaces, calling up folders and files from soft-shoed attendants, or holed up at home with copies of various letters I had begged or, in one instance, stolen. Back then there was next to nothing, so much unpublished and Mansfield's extraordinary handwriting giving little away. Now every second post-doctoral fellow is a Mansfield scholar on little more than a snouting acquaintance with the major biographies and the collected stories. Their yackety-yak turns my stomach. They have no feeling for her; their Freudian allusions and deconstructive parentheses could just as easily roost on someone else. You couldn't get on in the old days with some limp-dick notion of the phallus. Around the anniversary celebrations, so much rubbish was spouted that I gave up on conferences altogether, never attending another. And the camel's straw, the rising star brought over from England to give the plenary address, 'Mansfield's Hunger and the Maternal Symbolic' or some such. The detail is gone but the gist of it was that the many references in Mansfield to hunger, each tediously itemised from the podium, were evidence of the author's psychic resistance to being a mother. Nothing to do with the venereal disease that pulped her uterus like fallen autumn quince? Or the wartime food shortages that had Ida Baker eating the raw oatmeal intended for face packs at the beautician's where she worked? At least this is how I remember my interjection but I am historian enough to admit to the possibility of inaccuracy, since every face swung my way like dandelion heads turned against the wind and the speaker, lips pressed together in a bloodless seam, said nothing while I was hustled from the lecture theatre by my Head of Department, who the following Monday morning wrote a disciplinary note against me to the Dean, quaintly citing 'blue language.'

I can't claim my career was a success but I showed early promise. My first research trip was a sea passage to Southampton. It was my first view of England whose grass as green silks newly washed. A cunt of a country, as it turned out, but it looked pretty from the passenger deck, all smokestacks and cobblestones. I lugged a typewriter in my suitcase and on the strength of my letters of introduction visited anyone prepared to talk who wasn't already worn to a thread by surviving Mansfield, or Kittenelle, as Virginia liked to call her. It is not widely known that these two were on together for one half-year. Hampered as it is by inane interruption — *Keeping yourself busy, dear?* — my recent work suggests this was most likely sometime in 1917, possibly when the Woolves were arranging to publish 'Prelude' and Mansfield lived in a studio in Chelsea on Old Church Street, alone for the first time unless you count Ida badly concealed behind a curtain in the balcony over the bedroom. An idyllic affair, I imagine, despite the pinch of wartime, cut short by Mansfield's pleurisy and her retreat to the south of France in the New Year. Sometime that year, perhaps even regularly, I believe the two met for calisthenic afternoon sex in the upstairs rooms of a club on Gerrard Street in Soho. As a modernist love token, Mansfield slips a lewd description of the bedroom wallpaper into the story she was writing for the Woolves and Virginia, working then on the first draft of *Night and Day*, replies by having the paper in Mary Datchet's no-nonsense rooms sprout a pattern of *swollen bulbs blush-tinged by inner flame*. She edited this out before the novel's publication (but recall, please, the famous sapphic line in *Mrs. Dalloway* that has *a match burning in a crocus*), although as tribute to their dalliances on Hampstead Heath she kept the bit about *sofas resembling grassy mounds*. All anyone remembers is Mansfield's dismissive review of *Night and Day* when it was finally published a couple of years later, the scholarly position being that these two didn't much care for each other, given their professional rivalries. As if envy ever got in the way of good sex.

They get under your skin, the writers you make your study. After decades awash in their words, your own thoughts are shot through with their voices: it turns out that Mansfield's is light and clipped as though her teeth were polished pearl buttons she might swallow in her haste to give up her secrets. My life work, unfinished, was a complete concordance of her writings including all the variant manuscripts. I was two-thirds of the way through, having just finalised the *O* section, when a budget crisis forced my retirement. My department hosted a party to mark my passing into oblivion. They would as happily have fired me from a cannon. An early evening event, it was held in the grim little seminar room with the tables covered by hired linen and huddled together as if for a wedding dance. How many deadborn papers I had been pleased to present in the same room over the years. Knowing now how things lay with Mansfield and Virginia, my best ideas, once magpie shiny and fresh minted, can seem rubbed flat and dull as an old coin The new professor, hired only two years previously and yet to speak to me directly, gave a speech. A difficult task, I appreciate: he concentrated on the satisfactoriness of my teaching and the sheer number of years I had stuck with it. Edie was beside me at the top table, already tunnelled with cancer although neither of us knew it. The previous week, the library had declined to accept my papers. At twelve linear metres, the letter from the Head Librarian read, they put an undue strain on available resources. Having been measured like calico, my papers never seemed quite themselves again. I got no further than *Q*. After Edie died I had the last dog put down and buried him Viking-style at her feet. When it became clear I couldn't manage the house much longer, I put aside a few of the most important documents and paid the neighbour's boy to lug the boxes out to the garden where I set fire to the lot, the flames leaping to the dry hedge and from there to the clothesline next door before the engines came, the weird chatter of burning paper still audible over the clamour of the sirens.

The scrap of paper I'm looking at now was spared the conflagration on account of its being in Mansfield's original hand. I am not able to say quite how it came into my possession but it was held by a former friend of the companion to Mansfield's husband's fourth wife. Clearly Mansfield's handwriting, there is nothing else clear about it. Perhaps a scrap of dialogue being worked up for a story, at first I could only make out three words for certain: *My*, *all* and *is*. Mansfield's writing is famously difficult. Even Murry didn't always get it right, his definitive editions riddled with error. Consistency is minimal, the angle of her upstrokes and the detail in her baseline varying from day to day. It is easy enough, for example, to find a lower case *p* with a bold upright separated from its rounded face in one entry and on the page opposite the same letter tricked out as two continuous curlicues. And then her looping horizontal style encourages individual letters to merge indistinctly with their companions.

Over the years I have perfected a battery of techniques to decipher her scrawl. My first approach is always the quick once-over. I approach the work in a relaxed fashion and read it as if it were typescript, expecting full legibility. Sometimes a few extra letters can be persuaded into plain view. *My god, all something something is something something.* Then I take a more forensic approach, holding the page up to the light to determine what is a surface mark and what, if anything, an impurity in the paper. With a magnifying glass I go over each pen line, determining the weight of the stroke, where the pen has broken contact with the paper and so on. I don't have my magnifying glass in here but the lenses of Mrs. Bethells' spectacles are so fantastically thick that I have made good use of them more than once. There are more capital letters than might be expected: the initial *M*, of course, but the fifth word and the last two also begin with capitals. Someone's name? It could be *P* or *B* and then *D* or *R*. Perhaps Bruce Richmond, the editor of *The Times Literary Supplement*? But the second word is considerably shorter than the first. I wipe what looks like sausage fat from Mrs. Bethells's glasses and bend the frame a little to make them more fit to the task. Only a small adjustment but I am afraid the arm snaps clean off and will have to be planted in the laundry if suspicion is not to fall on me. At four times magnification, the letters show their lunar surface, pocked and uneven. The ink quality itself is very poor, faded back to the page in places, which dates it to October 1917 when wartime restrictions reduced Mansfield to an inferior batch of ink. A capital *R*, I think; it might be *Road*, a street address. Next I clip the page to a stand and attach a cardboard frame over the passage to be got out. Long hours I have sat like this until the page pulses like a heartbeat, the inked marks ratcheting in and out of focus, but tonight it tumbles out quickly. *My god, all of London is something Road.* My *London A-Z* would make quick work of this. *Pelican. Paragon.* I have it. *My god, all of London is Paradise Road.* 34 Paradise Road, Richmond. Hogarth House where Leonard and Virginia Woolf lived from 1915. And then without even thinking I read it true: *My goat, all of London is Paradise Road.*

Wheeled back to my room for the night, as I am wheeled back every night, the rubber treads biting into the groove of my hundreds of previous passages along this same stretch of petunia-patterned carpet, the world seems crazily new, dripping with promise. Even the nurse aide with her high-school tattoo and acned chin is wise, smuggling into our ordinary conversation an intelligence exquisitely fragile as a chandelier.

'Feels like a Sunday, dunnit,' she says, easing my leg off and then, wrestling my head through the neck of my nightgown so vigorously I feel toothpaste grit grinding between my molars, 'A quiet night's a good night, but.'

I say nothing and, saying nothing, learn there is no need for this richness to be spoken. *My goat, all of London is Paradise Road.* Deidre calls by once my light is off, although it seems I myself am tossing off sparks, a fizzing radiance as if I were the wick of a Catherine wheel. She fetches up the pills I have saved for her across the day and feels with a practiced hand for my stump under the counterpane. It is our nightly ritual. She rubs the loose skin until it feels human again. Sometimes she lets me call her Edie. I lie awake in my room at the end of the corridor, single and silent, the only person in the world with this bit of knowledge, so tremblingly new, like a lapful of raspberry jelly, it can scarcely hold its own shape. Outside my window the rustle and creak of the night nurse having a quick smoke under the mad lick of the milky way.

The Doves' Nest

THE OLIVE GROVE

— Charlotte Grimshaw

Larry told Emily, 'The universe is expanding.'

In the hours before dawn, when thunder cracked in the mountains and still there was no rain, Beth's voice came out of the dark. 'Are you listening? Have you heard a word I've said?'

Sometimes Emily could hear her parents laughing. Beth would sigh in the morning. 'Per makes so many jokes, I can't get to sleep.'

Long nights. Forked lightning through a crack in the curtains. There was heat and distant storms, no rain.

The darkness was gigantic and had size and weight. Emily felt she was pressed into a tiny space. Everything was in the ear. Voices. Silence.

She lay in the dark, thinking. Before Beth and Per there was no Emily. Emily was Nothing. Then there was the Big Bang (ha ha, the big old double bed creaking in the night) and Emily began to be. Before Beth and Per, there was no family. No Emily Larry Marie. The family began: a small, tight nucleus, full of packed energy. Years passed, eons of notimetime, of crowdedtime, of allclamouringatoncetime. And everything moving out across the vast emptiness, always spreading outwards. One day there would be no Beth, no Per . . .

The Big Bang was not an explosion, Larry explained. It was a slow, cold expansion.

The card had arrived last week — a postcard of three dancing figures by Matisse. Emily brought it to her mother, who was sitting as usual on the balcony admiring the garden. 'It's from Javine,' Beth said, turning it over. 'She's coming to stay for three days. Do you remember Javine, Milly?'

Emily thought. 'No. Yes.' She made a face.

In the garden by the olive grove, sunlight on grey stones. Emily, hiding in the long grass, spied on her mother through the wire fence. Beth held Marie by the hand. And she said, 'Marie, pick those ones. They're fresh. No, those ones have had it.' (The petals overgrown and limp.) 'Chuck them away. They're going to go brown!'

Funny little Marie, with her blonde hair. She threw the dead flowers in the air and watched them scatter. Petals stuck to her hands.

Perhaps the universe was like a flower. Starting from a bud, losing its tightness as it spread outwards. Would it wither and die? She went to Larry, who turned the pages of his book with one finger. He sighed importantly.

'When the universe is ready it will start to shrink again, back down to the first pinpoint.'

'How do you know?' she asked.

'I just do.'

'How will it know when it's ready?'

Was the universe like a balloon, blowing up, deflating? Was it like lungs?

'Go away,' Larry said, propped in bed with a stomach bug, his head in a book. He burped horribly, to make her leave. The sun made a dancing white star on his bed cover. She left a trail of petals on the floor.

Emily slouched down to Madame Olivier, who let her feed the two elderly sausage dogs that lolled on grimy cushions in her kitchen. Madame Olivier gave Emily greasy snacks that did strange things to her stomach.

'I'll have to start boiling the drinking water,' Beth said.

In the flat Emily had her own bedroom with a window that looked over the olive grove. She sat on a table on the balcony, playing ludo against herself. Beside the building the path ran down the slope, through a tunnel under the railway line to the harbour. The waterfront was beautiful; it ran along the bottom of the Old Town and around the shore towards Monte Carlo. The town lay in the curve of the coast, its orange buildings and tiled roofs rising up the slopes of the steep hills. In the marina were lines of boats — launches and yachts, their tall masts clinking and jinking. The sea was blue and sparkling with a milky haze on the horizon, the beaches were sheltered by stone breakwaters, and along the seafront the palm trees whispered and clattered in the breeze. Behind the town rose the grey mountains and, way up high, were the twin tunnels of the autoroute that ran through the ranges into Italy. In the winding lanes of the Old Town the houses were ancient and crooked; the paths between the houses ran steeply up the hill to the graveyard; in the dead hours of the siesta, under washing strung on lines beneath the houses, there was shade, silence, sometimes the strong waft of primitive drains. Emily and Larry walked to the graveyard and watched the funerals; in the bright air under the cypresses the tiny black-clad widows, their absorbed, inward faces.

They lived in a large, ornate, white block of flats. There was a white gravelled courtyard and a grand front entrance. In the mornings the courtyard blazed with colour: bright flowerbeds, palms, rock gardens sprouting spiky cacti. On one side of the building was the path that led to the school, a large old house with green shutters and bullet holes in the walls. There were two classrooms — one for Emily's class, one for Larry's. The playground was a shady circle of concrete with a tree in the middle. The toilets were in a wooden outbuilding — little cubicles with a circular hole in the concrete and two footprints to stand on, one on either side.

Beth sent Emily to school in new clothes — a skirt and a matching tartan jacket. Emily was furious. She hated skirts; she loathed anything that matched. The girls in the playground asked, 'Tu veux jouer?' She nodded but dropped out at first, unable to understand the rules. There were red beetles in the stone walls. After school Emily collected some and stuck them alive to a cardboard card. They waved their legs, drowning in the white glue. Ashamed, she hid the murdered beetles down the side of her bed.

That night there was thunder, and in the morning, in the tunnel under the railway line, she and Beth and Marie came upon a gulping mass of toads. All morning in the classroom Emily wanted to go to the toilet but was too embarrassed to ask. Instead she drummed her feet on the floor, tap tap tap. The teacher told her to stop the racket. '*Pas bon point*!' She frowned. If you earned enough *bons points* you got a prize, usually a pretty little card, *une belle image*.

That week, let out the gate early, Emily turned to go home, thinking it was lunchtime. But the teachers laughed and pulled her back, and led the children down the path to a bus. They drove to a medical centre and were stripped to their underwear. They stood in a line and were pushed forward, one by one. A doctor poked a cold metal stick in Emily's ears. He covered her eyes one at a time and asked her what she could see on a coloured chart. She knew the French words for all the pictures, but wouldn't say.

'How old are you?'

She whispered, 'J'ai cinq ans.'

The doctor splayed his fingers. 'Yes. You are *fife*. Good girl.' He laughed kindly, reached out his finger and pinged the elastic on her underpants. She backed away. She felt that what he had done was terribly wrong.

They rode back on the bus, and this time she was allowed to go home for lunch. But in the afternoon she was caught scribbling in pen on her hand. The teacher grasped her blue and red paw and held it up to the class. '*Pas. Bon. Point*!'

That evening Emily fished up the cardboard card from the side of the bed. The red beetles had turned brown. There was a faint smell. She pushed the card back down. Next time she went to look the card had gone. No one said anything about her crime.

Larry went on being ill. He refused to get up.

'Perhaps it's culture shock,' Beth said. She boiled water and set pans of it on the bench to cool. She told Emily to drink from the pans only, not from the tap. Emily drank from the tap anyway, when no one was looking.

Larry lay reading, or staring at the ceiling. Beth called Per into his room. 'Look at this.' She held up Larry's hand. The skin on it had begun to peel.

'How weird,' Per said, perplexed.

'I'll have to get a doctor,' Beth said.

The doctor came, breathing fumes of garlic and wine. 'A virus,' he said.

'And the peeling hands?'

'A side-effect. Give him fresh air.' The doctor sniffed. 'Try boiling the drinking water, Madame.'

Per came home for lunch. Emily got a great surprise when she saw him. His front tooth was missing. He'd bitten a piece of French bread and felt a jolt ('like being socked in the jaw!') and when he'd looked down his false front tooth was stuck in the sandwich.

Emily stared at the new Per. The previous winter Larry had read a book about androids. Emily had got an idea fixed in her mind: perhaps Per was a robot. She had watched him for signs. Was he real? How could you tell? In France Per had grown his hair and beard long. Now, with his wild hair and missing tooth, he looked like a pirate. Perhaps he was a criminal, with a band of men.

Madame Olivier was scandalised — a missing tooth, *tiens*! For her, the beard and long hair were shocking enough.

Emily fed a piece of salami to the elder sausage dog, Agnes. She said to Madame Olivier, 'My father has a gun.'

'A gun?'

'A pistol,' Emily said. 'This long.' She held out two hands.

'Get away,' Madame Olivier said calmly.

There was a football field below the olive grove where local games were held. When there was an important match a line of police was stationed in the olive grove to stop people watching the match for free.

On a hot, still day Emily listened to the crowd singing: *Allez Menton, Allez Menton, A-Allez.* Hunting alone for lizards, she came to the line of police. She spied on them from behind a tree until one of them saw her and nudged the others. They glanced, shrugged and turned away. They were watching the match. The one who had seen her beckoned. Emily held her hands cupped in front of her. The policeman ambled through the grass and asked what she had in her hands. He was young, with a smooth brown face and black hair. He had a tiny chip out of his front tooth. His cap was shiny, his uniform exact and neat. Slowly she opened her fingers and showed him the grey lizard, motionless in her palm, its throat throbbing. In a quick convulsion of its whole body it rushed up Emily's arm, fell off her elbow and disappeared into the long grass.

The policeman turned his mouth down in a sad face, like a clown. He parted the grass with a stick, trying to find it.

'No, it's gone,' she said. Then she saw it. She pounced, and picked it up by the tail, but the tail dropped off and lay, wiggling horribly, near Emily's foot. The policeman made an expression of disgust. Together they leaned down, peering. Emily got it between her finger and thumb and the young man made such a face they both laughed.

On the bank the other policemen raised their arms and shouted. Goal! His superior called roughly, telling him get back. He clicked his tongue, threw the stick into the brush and jogged away, turning once to smile over his shoulder. Emily could hear him being lazily told off.

She roamed through the sun-striped grass, savagely thinking. She liked the policeman terribly. The grass was dry and brown, the paths were dusty. Everything was still in the midday heat. The sky was blue patterns through the lattice of branches, and the leaves had that graceful grey feathery sheen that made the light in the olive grove so dreamy and soft. A wizened grandfather and grandmother took turns to wheel a pram up and down under the trees. The baby thinly wailing under its cover. They leaned close and made cooing, clucking sounds. '*Po po po*,' said the old man.

Emily drifted near to the wire fence. Madame Olivier's dogs set up a yapping in the basement. The old woman cursed them and banged her shutters. A train rumbled by.

And in the garden, Beth was calling, 'Marie, Marie'.

Javine wandered out onto the balcony and stood running her hands through her yellow hair. Her breasts bulged over the front of her tight top. Her neck had three little bulges of fat, like rings, on which her gold jewellery rested.

Marie pointed up at her. Javine waved her pretty-coloured scarf. 'Hello down there!'

Javine had brought wine for lunch. It was too hot to eat on the terrace. They sat at the wooden table inside, in the shade. Javine leaned back and put a cigarette to her red lips;

Per started forward and lit it. She blew out a long grey stream of smoke.

'I am working in London. These last four months I am all alone. No friends, no family. But that is the way to work. An artist must be alone. I am working on a new idea. Somesing crazy, somesing to *catch* you by the breath . . .'

Per gazed out the window. A blush had spread over Javine's throat. 'This light,' she said fiercely, pointing to the terrace, where the spiky cacti stood in their pots, cutting green shapes out of the sky. 'This Mediterranean glow. It is incomparable. These blues and greens. These oranges. These reds and blues and . . .' She shook her head and smiled simply. No, it was . . . impossible. Words failed her.

'Yellows?' Beth frowned.

A flash of laughter across Per's face.

Javine tossed her head. 'These turquoises. Especially so. I know that *you*' — she leaned toward Per — 'are sensitive yourself to these *sub*-tleties, these storms and changes of light. You bring them to your work in a way that is . . .' She crinkled her eyes, as if she were tasting something delicious. 'It is . . . genius,' she whispered.

Per cleared his throat. 'No no,' he said with a boyish laugh — he felt suddenly clogged, drowsy. He traced a pattern on the table with his forefinger.

Beth laughed strangely. Javine looked at her without expression. She tapped her fingers on the table and breathed in through her nose. 'I must see where you work, Per Svenson,' she demanded. 'Your lair, away from the noise and bustle. Your *fictory* of ideas.'

'Of course,' Per said, glancing at Beth. He had the use of the Villa Isola Bella, as part of his Katherine Mansfield fellowship. 'It's not far away,' he said. He began to clear the table. Below the window the gardener cleared his throat and hoiked. Madame Olivier shouted at him. The dogs yipped and yapped.

Emily, on her best behaviour, fetched her colouring-in book. She had been working on a page of geometric shapes, making a complicated pattern. It had taken her hours; her felt pens were nearly dry.

Javine leaned over. 'Ah, what are you doing with these little shapes?'

'Colouring in.'

'But why do you not draw your own pictures? Why do you colour these little diamonds and triangles? You could make your own pictures, express yourself, see?' She turned to Beth. 'All children are natural artists. But we force them into these little boxes, into other people's *black lines*. To stifle the creativity, so.' She crushed her hands together, mangling something between them. Beth and Emily saw creativity slide out like a squashed beetle and fall to the floor.

'We're not very good at drawing in this family,' Beth said.

'But this is the mistake. Everyone can draw; true expression, it is the thing we must find!'

Beth half closed her eyes. Her shoulders drooped, but she rallied. 'Shall we go for a swim?' and she left the room to gather up the bathing suits and towels, and to check on Larry. She peeped in and saw him studying a book on geology, the windows open and the palm tree waving against the bright sky. 'Should we make him get up?' Per had wondered, but Beth was against it. She felt she understood Larry deeply. She might have done the same if she could. To rest and dream and read in the sunny quiet — what luxury. To escape from this ravening Javine!

In the sitting room — bright silence. Javine smiled at Per, her head on one side, as if they could both hear, but only just, the most beautiful, distant music . . .

Emily stolidly coloured in: a diamond, a triangle.

On the table in front of her the solid metal boule Per used as a paperweight was struck by the sun, making a little dazzle of silver light. Emily put her hand on top of it. The curve of cold steel. She rolled it until it was at the edge of the table. It was terribly heavy.

Javine swished close, trailing her scarves. Resting her hand on the table she crooned, 'Give me your pen. I will show you how to draw a cat. A pretty little pussycat.'

Emily handed her a pencil. Javine began to draw in quick, clever strokes. 'We make our own picture, see. Not other people's lines.'

Silence. The scratch of the pencil. Emily gave the ball the tiniest push. Down plunged the heavy object — *thud.*

Javine gasped. She screamed. Emily shrank down quick-small in her chair, clenching her fists. Javine crumpled, making a strange sound: *Grrrrnnnnnn.*

Beth rushed in. She and Per knelt over Javine, who was hunched on the floor, gripping the damaged foot in both hands.

'What happened? The boule? How awful! Do you think she's broken? . . . I mean . . .'

And Per, hovering, trying to be helpful: 'Could you hop to the couch?'

''Op?' Javine almost shouted. 'Oooooh.'

They pulled off her pretty sandal. Emily looked over the edge of the table at the damaged foot. It *was* an odd shape. The funny square, blunt toes had little hairs on the knuckles. It was a fascinatingly ugly sight. Already it was swelling, the circular bruise growing dark.

Per helped Javine over to the couch. Beth hurried to find some ice.

Emily looked at the cat Javine had drawn. He was walking along a fence, the line of his body just right as he balanced himself, placing one careful paw in front of the other. It was clever, Emily thought, to get the sense of him *just* keeping himself from falling. But there was a hole gouged in his head and at the tip of his nose lay a broken pencil lead. The pencil line veered away from the hole, across the page. The cat had been shot in the head; the pencil lead was the tiny bullet . . .

Emily drifted toward the couch, holding the drawing. 'I'll colour him in,' she offered, far too casually.

But no one was listening.

'Right,' Per said, 'it's time you got up.' And he banged the shutters.

Larry poked his legs over the side of the bed. He was so thin. But Per had been skinny all his life. In fact when he'd reached twelve stone he'd joked to Beth that he'd finally Achieved Fatness.

Larry peered up at his father through round spectacles. He had buck teeth, tiny vulnerable shins, small tentative hands.

Per hardened his heart. 'Fresh air, old chap. That's what you need.'

Larry drooped about, languidly picking up clothes. 'Use both hands,' Per said. And as the shirt slipped out of Larry's grasp, 'Get a hold of it. Hang on to it, can't you? Use your *fingers.*' Per hustled him into his sandals and marched him out. 'Right. Where's Milly? Milly!'

Javine lay on the couch, her foot wrapped in a flannel and resting high on a cushion. She shot a plume of grey smoke into the air and tapped the cigarette on the side of the ashtray. Per saw himself wheeling the couch to the edge of the terrace and tipping her off into the rock garden. But she'd been very good about the accident, very forgiving. And she was rather fetching, lying there; she looked — he searched for the right word — rather beautifully *palpable* . . .

Larry had slipped away from him. But not back to bed — he emerged from his room with a notebook and pen. He looked fresher already, resolute. Per cheered up. 'Go out and play,' he said. He looked at Larry's thin shoulders and felt a rush of love for his poor sensitive boy.

He watched from the terrace as the children opened the gate and went out onto the path. Larry was explaining something. He paused, showing Emily his notebook. She looked up at Per. Her face was a mask.

It was the hottest time of the day. All was still. Down the side of the building a tap was dripping; water plinking onto cool stone, in the trench of shade. The sky had a sheen over it, a mesh of light. Insects zoomed and hovered over the bright flowers. In his mind Per sought out cool places — the ivy-covered wall by the pedestrian tunnel; the path up to the graveyard, smell of waxy flowers, cold concrete; the path between the cypresses; the long grass at the top of the olive grove where the road ran under high banks, through striped, tawny light.

Beth came out and stood beside him.

'Are you going to show her your little *fictory*?'

'I don't think she can walk,' he whispered. He moved close to her. He could feel her laughing.

Emily and Larry sat on a wall watching for cars. Larry took notes. When a Ferrari or a Maserati throbbed past he recorded the make and model and the number of exhaust pipes. The record for exhaust pipes was six: three on each side.

Emily stared up at the grey mountains. The sky above them was intensely dark blue. She was yearning to go to the beach. She loved to climb on the breakwater, to stare down into the deep water. There was a whole landscape down there in the green swirl — mountains and valleys in rippling strands of light, schools of tiny fish flying through them, their silver sides flickering as they turned and turned.

Larry saw a sports car pulling in to the kerb along the road. A couple got out and walked away.

It was a Lamborghini Mura. A beautiful specimen. Larry lingered over its shining flanks. It was green — no, blue — a bright iridescent blue, the colour of a scarab's wing. He sketched it, showing Emily, pointing out the extraordinary dashboard, the chrome racing steering wheel, the plush interior.

But soon, too soon, the handsome man returned and shooed them away, and stood polishing a speck on the door with his sleeve as his companion swayed along the pavement on her heels. They got in and sped off in a series of jerking, throaty blasts.

'They are the Rich,' Larry said solemnly, and Emily saw the Rich careering through, across a red landscape in mad, bright cars with fantastic shapes, a crowd waving tiny flags . . .

'Watch out,' Larry shouted, too late. Oh horror, the most terrible stack of dog shit. She had ploughed right into it. They wandered along to the marina, Emily scraping her sandal along the pavement.

She pointed into the water. 'Look at that.'

Swimming just below the surface was a strange tubular creature with a red head and white frills undulating out of its body.

'What is it?'

He didn't know. They crouched down. She said, 'It looks like those things you play that game with. Babmington.'

It did look just like a shuttlecock. But it was alive, the white frills pulsating in little feathery bursts as it propelled itself along. They couldn't catch it or poke it with a stick: the boardwalk was too high above the water. Larry fetched some small chips of stone from the beach. He dropped one down, right on top of the creature. There was a rapid swirl and the feathers of the shuttlecock splayed out and then closed, drawing the stone inside.

'It's sucked it in,' Emily shouted. 'Look, the stone's inside it.' The creature was see-through. They could see the dark shape inside the body.

'Let me do one.' Emily dropped another stone, but missed. Larry let fall a twig and again the creature swirled its tentacles and drew the stick inside itself; they could see the shape inside the body, next to the stone. Emily tried again. With a little twist and flurry the creature absorbed her stone. It slowed, the dark shapes jumbled inside it. The little feathery quills flickered. They dropped a few more pebbles. The creature began to sink, the quills trailing after the body as it drifted down. Larry thought of a drowned swimmer, arms and hair waving in the swirl as the bubbles rose . . .

'We sunk it,' Emily breathed. She looked at Larry.

The creature was a white blur under the water. Then it was gone.

'It's hiding.' Troubled, Larry took off his glasses. The world jumped nearer, and the distance was a silvery blur, like water.

'Do you think it's dead?' Emily persisted.

'No, it'll spit the stuff out.'

'We've killed it.'

'No. It probably eats stones all the time.'

'Eats stones all the time!'

They crossed the burning road. The light struck off the cars. Below the road, beyond the marina, the beaches were dotted with hundreds of brightly coloured umbrellas. There were boats far out at sea, little black dots on the quivering horizon. A grey heat haze lay over the mountains, and the houses on the hillside were bright blobs of colour. In the gardens the flowers hung on juicy creepers and the cactus plants curved their cruel spears against the stonework, shadows like scimitars. Grey lizards, little dragons, lay motionless in the sun, scurrying into cracks as they passed. A woman scolded a cat and put it outside her door, and the cat leapt onto a wall and eyed them. Emily reached up and stroked its hot back and it rolled over and flexed its claws and looked at her upside down with one evil green eye. Orange and lemon trees in the gardens, a line of tablecloths drying on a line. Scent of dust and cypress and dog shit. Leaning against a wall, out of sight of the sun, a thin woman rifling in her bag, track marks on her arms, glanced at them, gave a blank shrug and shambled on. They climbed the steps, studying the cracks in the walls. Once, on this path, they had seen a pink and red snake curling away through the stones.

It was a hot night. They sat at a table in the square. The cafés were full of people eating the evening meal, children and passers-by milling around the tree in the centre where a singer was performing. The singer had a nervous tic and a high, pure voice. The waitresses pouted and rolled their eyes and scurried around the tables. From her glassed-in niche in the wall above them, the Virgin Mary coldly surveyed the scene.

'I'm absolutely full, and drunk as a skunk,' Beth declared, very satisfied.

'She doesn't approve,' Per said, pointing to the Virgin.

And the Holy Mother gazed back, small and chilly behind her glass. No, not at all, she confirmed in a tiny voice of steel. Emily looked up at the little statue, stiff in her rigid blue robes. There was a wire connecting her light to the wall. The light flickered, neon white. The Virgin had no face, only a rosy pink blob of painted plaster. The rest was worn away.

The children had ice-cream. Marie banged her spoon and a creamy splash shot across the table. Javine rested her bandaged foot on a chair. She smoked cigarettes and drank a thimble of green liquid, like poison. She rubbed her damaged foot.

'I hope you'll be all right to walk back?' Beth asked warmly.

'One must walk. One must exercise,' Javine said. 'As the Zen master says, one must roam around and drop down 'ole.'

'Drop down a hole?' Beth concentrating, polite.

Emily saw that flash of laughter across Per's face, so quick it was like a bird passing the window, a streak of movement then gone, the pane open and blank again.

'*Whole*. You must "Roam around, and at the end of the day: Drop down, whole." It is Zen,' Javine explained.

The Virgin Mary's neon tube gave a little pulse of light. It buzzed. A moth landed flapping on the glass, showing Her its furry underskirts. The singer under the tree struck a last high note, so sweet that the crowd burst out clapping.

Per paid the bill and they made their way through the crowds. Lights were strung between the buildings. Emily and Larry dawdled, gazing at the sugary bright sweets laid out in wooden barrels. But Emily was watching for her enemy.

He was a street performer who painted his whole body in glittering gold paint. Every evening, as soon as it was dark, Golden Guy appeared in the street and struck a pose, as rigid and immobile as a statue. He would only move when a tourist gave him a coin. His antics made the crowd laugh, but Emily knew there was something menacing, a kernel of anger, hidden in every move he made. Emily never laughed at his performance, she only watched, *waiting* for the dark note.

There he was, a small crowd around him. A tourist tossed a coin. Golden Guy broke into a wild jig. The crowd laughed and clapped. And when the tourist turned away, laughing, Golden Guy made his fingers into a pistol and shot the man in the back of the head.

Emily went close. Golden Guy turned his head a fraction and looked at her. His eyes cold in the glittering face. The eyes moved, watching her. He knew her. She was the one who stared and never laughed.

She felt that he was very dangerous. She lingered on this thought: you would not know him without his paint. He could be anyone. She might pass him every day in the street and *not know*.

This was secret knowledge. It was the kind of thing she kept from Larry. The more often Golden Guy saw her watching, the more often their eyes met and something — her knowledge

— passed between them, the greater the danger that he would seek her out. He would be disguised as an ordinary man. She would not know him until he came close and she recognised his eyes. And she couldn't explain it, but she had to stand at the front of the crowd every time, had to wait until she was absolutely sure he *had* seen her . . .

But they were calling, 'Milly, Milly!'

They crossed through the deserted market, leaving the crowds behind. The moon had risen and there was a glittering trail of light across the water. In the dark near a wall a light flared and a group of faces crowded around. Teenage voices, laughter. Girls and boys kissed cheeks — one, two — and rode off on noisy bikes. Above them the flats were lighted islands of lampshades and striped sofas and fringed drapes. The salty scent of the sea, the rustle of the wind in the palms. Javine smoked as she limped, moving her wrist in languid swirls.

Around the corner, by the tunnel, the streetlight made a long oval of light. Two police cars were parked up on the pavement, and four policemen had a teenager against the wall.

The boy was tall and thin, his hair black and kinky, his face angular and dark. His jacket was short in the arms and his wrists were curled against his stomach. He wore cheap cotton trousers with holes in the knees. They were kicking him. He pulled his knee up and curved his hands over his face, trying to protect himself. His movements were gentle, almost tentative.

One policeman wedged his forearm under the boy's chin, holding his head up. Another punched the boy in the face. He punched again and turned. Emily stood still. It was her friend from the olive grove. She had shown him the lizard and he . . . He shook his fingers. Was that blood on them?

Beth clutched Per's arm. 'They can't do that. They're hitting him. Stop them — it's terrible.'

And Per, starting forward, 'Oh no . . .'

But Javine was hobbling away. She lurched, limped,

launched herself furiously at the four policemen. They paused, uncertain, holding the boy.

Unspeakable! . . . Monstrous! . . . Close friend of the Mayor! . . . To beat a child! Official complaint! . . .

Slow and sullen, they loosened their grip. The boy sank down. He flattened himself against the wall and then, delicately, like a cat, extricated himself, edged along the pavement and fled into the darkness.

The policemen faced Javine. For one uncertain moment they were poised, like animals. She drew herself up and glared. Per and Beth hurried up beside her, dragging the children by the hands.

Emily's friend came sauntering, prowling, towards them. She knew him so well. She had thought about him very often. There was his smooth face, his nice freckled nose, his one chipped tooth. But strange, how strange — the eyes were not his. He looked directly at her. He did not see her. He looked longest at Per, turned and said something to the other men. They focused; they came nearer. They were going to do something to Per.

But a noise — the crackle of the car radio — broke the moment. The men relaxed, shrugged and slouched back to their cars. They revved their engines and spoke into their radios. Emily looked through the window as they drove away. One elbow crooked, his chin tilted, he was turning down the rear-view mirror, smoothing his shining hair.

Beth and Per surged around Javine. 'Phew! You were marvellous. I thought they were going to . . .' Per lit her a cigarette, Beth kissed her on both cheeks. Even tiny Marie clapped and laughed.

Suavely, Javine took Emily and Larry by the hands. Her fuming cigarette poked out the corner of her red mouth. ''Obble on,' she cried.

The adults talked. 'Those monsters,' said Javine. 'Pigs.'

'Cochons,' Emily piped up, and the adults laughed. She flushed and giggled. But something happened . . . a different self in her got up and stood apart and knew a secret: that the policeman, too, had a different self. And if everyone had different selves, how could she know which was real?

Beyond the breakwater someone was swimming in the dark. The moonlight caught the shining drops as they flew off the surface. The sea surged, hissing, on the stones. They walked through the courtyard, their footsteps crunching the gravel. The cactus plants made fantastic contorted shapes against the sky, and the moon touched the tops of the olive trees with a silvery glow.

From her lair in the basement Madame Olivier silenced her dogs with chocolate and watched them pass by.

Dark night. Moonlight through the curtains. When Emily closed her eyes her head whirled. When she opened them she saw marbles running slowly from one side of the ceiling to the other, as if the flat were a ship tossing on a rough sea.

'You've got a temperature, Milly.' Beth's hand on Emily's forehead felt like ice.

Emily shivered and shivered and couldn't get warm.

'Another one down,' Beth sighed, and went to get a cool flannel. She sponged Emily's head and tucked her in. She sat on the bed until Emily had gone to sleep, then she went out onto the terrace. Per and Javine were smoking. The sky was full of stars. Per handed Beth a glass. They sat together, talking, watching the clouds draping soft black shapes across the moon.

Emily woke and looked about her. The adults had gone to bed. All was silent. The chair was a black tombstone hung with coiled snakes. The curtains moved in the breeze and shadows shifted on the walls. Standing in the wardrobe was a witch.

Emily froze, froze. Terror stopped her breath. She blinked

hard. The witch was looking straight at her, moving — just minutely. She was smiling. There was something so insinuating, so evil, so *confident* in the smile that Emily screamed.

Beth burst in. 'What is it? What's happened?' Her voice was frightened.

Emily sat up, clutching at her mother. 'There. In the cupboard. There.'

Beth looked all around the room. Then, relieved, 'There's nothing. What a fright you gave me.'

Behind Beth the witch moved, smiled. She was round and solid, her body was heavy.

'There, in the cupboard,' Emily cried. 'A witch.'

Beth crossed the room. 'There's nothing in the cupboard.' She put her hand into the dark space and waved it.

But the witch smiled, delighted at the joke. 'She can't see me,' the witch said to Emily. 'She doesn't know I'm here. But I *am*. And there's nothing *she* can do about it.'

'I'll tuck you in,' Beth said. 'It's only a dream.'

'No no,' Emily shouted. 'Don't leave me with her.'

'Goodness. You're . . . Look, I'll turn on the light.'

But the light only made the witch laugh, and then she showed her teeth. They were jagged spikes. And the smile, so sly and intimate, said, 'How funny. They can't help you. Only we know I'm here. You and I are quite alone.'

Emily threw back the bedclothes and ran out of the room. Beth hurried after her. Lights came on. There were muffled voices. Larry said sleepily, 'What's going on?' From the spare room Javine called, 'Tiens. Who is screaming?'

Beth turned off the lights and tucked Emily into the big bed next to Per. She got in beside her. The child was hot and feverish. She lay on her back staring at the ceiling, her eyes moving as though she were following something up there.

'The ceiling is full of marbles,' Emily said faintly.

'But no witches,' whispered Beth.

They lay awake. Outside, the night was alive. A cat jumped up onto the balcony and walked neatly along the rail. He stopped to wash his paw in the moonlight. Something rustled through the long grass in the olive grove — the cat's ear revolved to catch the sound. Footsteps sounded on the road, and from the mountains came a faint pulse of light and a fainter answering *boom*.

On the ceiling the marbles rolled in streams and turned into cold glass eyes. The Holy Mother flew past the window, laughing in a voice like birds. Over a red plain, past flag-waving crowds, Golden Guy sped in a glittering car. Where had he gone? Without gold he was nothing but eyes. What colour was he really? But she would know him when he came. She would know his eyes. Wouldn't she?

The cat touched the surface of the bird-bath with his paw. He shook the water off and strolled across the moonlit terrace. But Agnes, the old sausage dog, dreamed she was chasing a rabbit. From the basement came a long, low growl. The cat stiffened. His feet splayed out and his tail stood out like a brush. He ran over the rail, lurched sideways, landed in the grass and lay still. Then he got up and sauntered away, as though nothing had happened.

Six Years After

THE ADDITION

— Sarah Quigley

It was not the afternoon to be on deck — on the contrary, it was exactly the afternoon when there is no snugger place than a warm cabin, a warm bunk. Tucked up with a rug, a hot-water bottle and a piping-hot cup of tea she would not have minded the weather in the least. But he hated cabins, hated to be inside anywhere more than was absolutely necessary.

'Wouldn't you rather go up alone?' Her voice lifted hopefully, like a flag in the wind. 'It might be one of those things best experienced in solitary splendour.'

He didn't hear her, or wasn't listening. He'd been very busy since they boarded: busy introducing himself, busy unpacking, busy settling in and chilling out. And now he was busy striding about the cabin, picking things up and throwing them down as if, somehow, they disappointed him. Every now and then he went over to the porthole and gave it a sharp rap as if warning the weather that, as soon as he found his gloves with the special thermal lining, he'd be coming out.

'I can't imagine where they can be,' he said, lowering the

impressive eyebrows inherited from his father, a high court judge. 'It's hardly labyrinthine in here.'

This was true. If you lay spreadeagled in the middle of the cabin, you could almost touch each of its four walls. *Thirteen days*, she thought, a small fist of claustrophobia clenching in her stomach. *Thirteen days, without the chance of walking away.* But the beds — they had surprised and delighted her. 'Bunks!' she had said. 'I haven't slept in a bunk since I was ten!'

Ralph came over to where she was sitting, curled up in the only armchair, and he lifted her feet as if they were a Sunday newspaper. 'Not there,' he mused.

'Perhaps you forgot to pack them?' But this was impossible: Ralph was extraordinarily accomplished at the art of packing, adding small items to growing piles, striking words off colour-coded lists.

Sudden rain racketed against the window. 'It's pouring,' she said, with relief. 'Dinner's in an hour, and I'll never get my hair dry in time.'

'Darling.' Ralph looked at her with pity and affection. 'Aren't you curious to see what's changed outside?'

'I'm always more curious in good weather,' she said. 'Give me sunshine and an Italian city, then I'm a regular bloodhound.'

But Ralph had spied his gloves, half wedged under the miniature closet door. 'There they are!' He pounced. 'You must have knocked them down when you unpacked.'

'No doubt,' she said. It was undeniable that Ralph had been born tidy, and she had not. She watched him wrestle his way into first a large fleece, and then a yellow waterproof jacket. 'Come on, Carson,' he wheedled. 'Before you know it the cruise will be over.' It was clear that he wanted an audience and, until he befriended some other passengers, the task was hers.

Outside, the corridor was empty. Pale green walls met a polished floor, also green. 'Appropriate,' she commented, 'considering we're on an ecological cruise. Being green is a highly desirable quality here.' She laughed and half fell against the wall because of the huge swell. She followed Ralph's rustling back, up some steep metal stairs, flaking with white paint — and then Ralph was pushing through the heavy double doors that swung back and almost trapped her in their rubbery grasp. 'Sorry,' he shouted against the sudden noise. 'Couldn't — hold — them.'

The wind was ferocious. She could barely see; strands of hair whipped her eyeballs, and wool streamed from her rapidly unravelling hat. 'In thirty seconds,' she shouted, 'my hat will join the ranks of the extinct.' But her voice was tiny in the roar of the engines, the waves and the wind; and already Ralph was at the side of the boat, peering ahead, his hand to his eyes like a captain.

She sheltered behind a large metal strut, pressing her face to its cold, damp flanks. 'Almighty God,' she whispered, though she'd been a committed atheist since the age of five. 'Sweet Jesus, Mary and Joseph' (though she'd never approved of asking biblical figures for help).

All she could see was water. The boat was caught, tossing, in a net of torrential rain and rising grey waves. 'What?' She turned to see Ralph, his fish-mouth gaping at her through the spray. 'What did you say?'

He seemed to be shouting 'Magnificent!' but each time, before it could reach her, the word was carried away, up and over the red funnel. Nonetheless, Ralph continued to cry his soundless appreciation, occasionally raising one arm in a boxer's victory salute.

Yet there was nothing to be seen; and how could one consider Nothing magnificent? The world had been obliterated. All that remained were the pitching wet boards underfoot, and the whining bare masts overhead. She glanced sideways and saw the ship's bow pressing against the grey suffocating water-wall.

She had never seen anything so final in her life.

That evening, their first on board, they and six other guests were to dine with the captain.

'But that means that, on the last night, four people will sit with him a second time.' Ralph stared at the seating plan; his lowered eyebrows indicated that this was not quite fair. 'I wonder how they make the final selection?'

'Perhaps the captain makes a note of the best conversationists.' Carson was watching the bearded men and the floppy-haired women parading slightly self-consciously into the dining room.

'You think so?' Ralph straightened his navy blue shirt with renewed confidence.

'No, I was joking,' she said. 'I'm sure it's entirely random.'

Random or not, as soon the soup had been served, Ralph swung into his best entertainment mode. 'I've done the running-with-bulls thing in Spain several times,' he said, ostensibly to his neighbour but loudly enough for the table to hear. 'So, with all that experience of running and wild beasts, I'm considered a good candidate for Mayor of New York!'

A gust of laughter and admiration swept around the table. Ralph's high forehead flushed in gratification. Soon the whole dining room was repeating the joke, and the fact that there was a potential mayor, with humour, in their midst.

Carson turned to the captain, who was surreptitiously scraping soup off his white shirt-front. 'My first time on a ship,' she said, 'and you look exactly as a captain should. A beard, a twinkle in your eye, and shiny buttons on your blazer.'

'Thank you, my dear.' The captain wiped his napkin over his rosy mouth. 'And may I say, you are also everything an old clichéd captain could wish for!'

She demurred: surely, he was being gallant. Her hair was still damp from her time on deck. Her black dress was slightly creased, and the captain had many years of compliment-paying under his belt. But —

'I rarely tell lies,' he assured her. 'And never during the first twenty-four hours of a cruise.'

'After that, you regain your sea-legs,' she suggested, 'and your silver Irish tongue runs away with you.'

The captain chuckled. 'Your husband's a lucky man.'

She glanced at her wavering candle-lit reflection in the window. Admittedly, she looked pretty; perhaps being in the middle of the Southern Ocean agreed with her? 'Thank you,' she said. 'Though Ralph isn't my husband. He considers marriage an outdated bourgeois tradition.'

'Indeed!' said the captain, looking slightly taken aback. A pity, he added; Carson would make a beautiful bride.

Now the main course was being delivered, amidst a clashing of china, and Ralph began gesturing expansively. It was difficult to hear over the rising conversation, but he seemed to be describing the day he was trapped on an ice-shelf in the Himalayas.

'Ralph is a most adventurous person,' Carson explained to the captain. 'Marriage would seem like a cage to him.'

'One can only hope the cruise doesn't prove dull for him,' said the captain politely, accepting a plate of steaming risotto.

Back in the cabin, Carson brushed her teeth at the tiny sink. The food had been delicious, but plainer than she'd expected. Weren't people supposed to eat lobster and salmon on cruise ships?

Ralph looked amused and pointed out that they had set sail on this particular ship with the aim of observing endangered species, not consuming them.

'No whale meat?' she asked. 'Not even a sliver of seal?'

'Seal?' echoed Ralph, looking scandalised.

'I was joking,' she said, for the second time that evening.

Ralph pulled a T-shirt over his head and eased into his bunk. 'I'm feeling a little queasy. I hope it's just the brandy.'

'It's very rough,' she said.

'Carson, you know I never get seasick.' Ralph looked pained, peering out from his neatly turned-down sheets. 'I've been sailing since I was two.'

'Captain Gallagher said the weather will clear.' Carson clambered up to her own bunk. 'Maybe we'll see penguins! I've never seen penguins in their natural habitat.'

'Speaking of the captain,' mused Ralph, 'd'you think he heard my ice-shelf story? I wasn't sure if he could hear. At least I managed to talk to him over coffee. I told him my Ganges story, about sailing in the dinghy. It's a good one.'

Carson leaned out of her bunk on a dangerous angle and reached for the light switch. Suddenly she felt very tired.

'At any rate,' said Ralph's voice through the darkness, 'I'm pretty sure I was entertaining enough to get us invited back to the table on the last night.'

The captain had been right: the weather cleared in the night. For the next few days the horizon lay still and unmoving and the sky was a pale frosty blue, arcing over the ship as it sailed steadily south. Whale sightings were discussed at lunch, and polar-bear stories swapped at dinner.

'But the icebergs!' Carson was amazed by them; the size of small houses, they floated silently at a distance, concealing their blue-veined hearts.

Ralph's adventurous past had won him plenty of admirers, but his particular friends became the Donaldsons, an intense and wiry couple from Vancouver. Every morning the three of them would jog around the upper deck, passing Carson several times as she stood by the railing, mesmerised by the low sun. They circled energetically, discussing their respective professions, their breath pluming in the chilly bright air.

'Vicky is Canada's most eminent geologist,' said Ralph generously, over coffee and port. 'Daniel advises the White House on global warming.'

Vicky passed the mint chocolates to Carson. 'Ralph tells us this is your first eco-cruise?'

The deep creases on her freckled forehead made her look permanently enquiring.

'I didn't want to come,' said Carson. 'I was going to stay home and wallpaper.' She often told unexpected truths in public, as a kind of test to see if she would be believed.

Vicky and Daniel laughed, while Ralph smiled indulgently. 'Fortunately, Carson realised she concurred with St Augustine. "The world is a great book, of which they who never stir from home read only a page."'

'Very true,' said Carson. 'Now I'm here, it's wonderful.'

This was also true. Early mornings, before the deck had been cleared of ice, and early evenings, while the others were gathering for pre-dinner drinks — these were her favourite times. The wide glint of dawn or the bright swinging stars, and always the faraway crack of the ice. She felt herself shrink until she became the nail on the deck, the knot in the wood, the drop of water swinging from the rail.

'One hundred passengers,' she told Ralph as she entered the cabin, pink-faced from cold, 'and fifty-four crew. A boat that weighs two and a half thousand tonnes. Yet we are nothing! Nothing at all, compared to what surrounds us!'

Ralph pulled the laces of his trainers tight. 'Fifty-four crew? Is that so?' He looked interested. 'That's a high ratio of staff to passengers.'

'Jun told me. He has seven brothers and three sisters, and they're all employed on this boat.'

'Jun?' Ralph pulled on his glove-liners. 'Who's Jun?'

'The boy who serves us morning and afternoon teas. And brings you extra hot water for shaving.'

'Oh, the Filipino chap. Should you be so friendly with him?'

Carson stared. 'But we know dozens of Filipino people at home. What about Rosa? And the director of your department?'

Ralph roared with laughter. 'I wasn't referring to his nationality! How could you think such a thing! I simply think it's better to keep a distance from staff.'

'Why?' Carson found Jun far more entertaining than many of the passengers.

But Ralph wasn't listening; he was ready to jog. 'See you at breakfast, darling.' She heard him laughing all the way down the corridor, heading for his morning appointment with the eminent geologist and her beleaguered husband, whose job was an uphill battle and required him to keep fighting fit.

She woke later than usual, with a crick in her neck. There had been the possibility of rough weather in the night and, as a precaution, Ralph had wedged several books under the edge of her mattress, tilting her towards the wall. 'We don't want you falling into the cabin,' he'd said.

But she woke unfallen, the book-barrier still in place, and the sun shining in its circular porthole fashion on the floor. 'Ralph?' she said. But he had gone running already. She tugged a book out from under her mattress. Joseph Conrad, *The Heart of Darkness* — something Ralph always took away with him and never read. Twenty pages, and then she would go for breakfast.

As she climbed the stairs to the lower deck, the noise from the dining room swelled out across the landing like a wave. It was much louder than on other days: perhaps there had been an early-morning sighting of a rarer species of whale? She put a hand on the glass door, and stopped in surprise.

The room was full of people she'd never seen before. They

sat in rows on the banquettes, or perched on dining chairs. Wet coats hung from the tables like vast leaves. Dozens of people who had not been on board when she'd gone to bed, but who now filled the dining area, chattering, gesticulating wildly — and dripping all over the carpet.

Carson knelt down beside the nearest woman. 'What on earth happened? Were you shipwrecked?' The word sounded ridiculous, like something from a boy's adventure tale.

'We hit a barker!' The woman's white hair was dripping, but she sounded more excited than upset.

'You mean a growler,' corrected her husband. He turned to Carson. 'That's one motherfucker of an iceberg,' he explained. 'Ripped a hole right through our hull.'

In the middle of the room, by the centre table, stood Ralph, still in his running clothes, a towel slung around his neck. He was advising a group of women on how to slap their hands on their thighs to get their circulation working.

'They had to abandon ship,' he explained to Carson. 'They were bobbing about in open lifeboats for hours before we picked up their distress signal.'

'Do what the captain says,' hissed one pale-looking woman to another. 'Slap your hands on your legs.'

Carson laughed. 'He's not the captain.'

'Really?' The woman looked disappointed, almost disbelieving.

'I'm not,' Ralph assured her. 'Just someone who knows what to do in an emergency.'

By mid-morning dry clothes had been found for the new arrivals. 'Eighty of them,' said Ralph, who, although he was not the captain, seemed remarkably well informed. 'Fortunately, none of them has hypothermia.'

Most of the eighty returned to the dining room, where they were served vast platters of steaming sausages and eggs.

They ate heartily but a trifle nervously, glancing at the ship's permanent residents, who were taking their morning coffee. Carson had planned to retire to the cabin with Joseph Conrad, but the odd mix of tension and relief in the dining room made it difficult to leave. 'Pastries!' she said, seeing Jun pass with a loaded tray.

'Reserve supplies,' said Jun with a wink. 'Chef thought sugar might be good for the shock.'

'It'll only give you a sugar rush,' said Ralph to Carson in mild reproof. 'No good for long-term energy.'

'I don't need long-term energy,' objected Carson. 'My only plans today were to watch birds and read a novel.'

Vicky appeared in a rush of cold air, her face half hidden by a huge furry hat. She seemed excited. 'I've been on deck,' she said, 'hearing stories from the survivors.'

'Technically,' said Ralph, shifting in his chair, 'they're not survivors, as the accident wasn't fatal. Technically, there was nothing for them *to* survive.'

'A sinking ship is hardly nothing,' objected Carson, through pastry.

'At 2 am they were asleep in their cabins,' said Vicky. 'At 3 am they were ordered to abandon ship. At 4 am they were in lifeboats, watching it sink!'

'At 11 am they were eating our sausages,' said Ralph, a trifle acerbically.

Vicky's face was more than usually serious, but her eyes were almost dreamy. 'I just met the man who stayed on board. He was pumping water until the ship was virtually on end.'

'Yes, I heard the captain almost went down with the ship,' said Ralph, taking a swallow of tea. 'Part of the job description, really.'

'Not the captain,' corrected Vicky. 'At least, not *only* the captain. I meant — him.' She motioned with her head towards the buffet, where a large curly-haired man was loading up his plate with food. He was wearing a sweatshirt belonging to Adam-from-Edinburgh, and some unidentifiable trousers.

Ralph stared at the man's feet. 'Why is he wearing Wellington boots?'

'He lost everything,' said Vicky emphatically. 'Ev-ery-thing. He grabbed the boots from the engine room when he went to help.'

'All the better to wade with,' murmured Carson.

'While other people are bailing out,' continued Vicky, switching to the present tense in the manner of a sports commentator, 'Blake is bailing water! It's Blake and the captain, up against the elements, trying in vain to save the *Crusader*.'

Ralph made an odd snort, as if tea had gone up his nose. 'What kind of a name is that?'

'All ships have stupid names,' said Carson.

'I meant Blake,' said Ralph.

'Perhaps,' suggested Vicky, 'he was named after William Blake, the poet. He does have a touch of the visionary about him.'

Carson watched Blake pull up a seat at a crowded table. His arrival caused a small commotion; chairs were rearranged, plates shuffled, glasses raised, and shoulders patted. Certainly, he was the man of the hour, an unlikely hero in shrunken trousers and rubber boots.

By mid-afternoon a rumour was circulating. The ship would make an unscheduled stop at the port of Ushuaia, where all new arrivals would be able to disembark and, from there, make their way homewards.

'The southernmost city in Argentina,' said Ralph, his eyebrows almost meeting in the middle. 'That's a detour of over four hundred nautical miles. I hope they don't expect us to pay for it.'

Captain Gallagher appeared in the passenger lounge to

formally welcome Captain Yitaki and his flock, and confirm the detour to Ushuaia. 'There is, however, an alternative option,' he beamed. 'The *Explorer* has a capacity of 691 passengers and 214 cabins. Even my admittedly poor calculations can confirm that we have plenty of room. Should the newcomers wish to join our cruise for its duration, they would be most welcome.'

A ripple of pleasure and surprise ran around the lounge. Captain Yitaki, a slim Japanese man, bowed low. 'We are truly grateful,' he said, 'to have been rescued by such a generous captain, and such a substantial ship!'

'It's impossible,' muttered Ralph. 'We have only one staff member for every two passengers — how can their services be stretched so far?'

'They've brought their own crew with them,' pointed out Carson. 'The stewards and cooks were hardly left to drown.'

'Oh,' said Ralph. 'Of course not.' Nonetheless, he pulled out his pocket calculator and began jabbing at the keys.

Captain Yitaki, finishing his thousand words of thanks to Captain Gallagher, turned to the room. 'There is one more person to whom I must express my gratitude. My honorary first mate, Blake!'

There were catcalls, and thunderous applause, and Blake was pushed out of the cheering crowd to say a few words. 'It was nothing,' he said self-deprecatingly. 'I once spent a summer working for a volunteer fire brigade. Ever since then I've been good with pumps.' He shook hands with both captains, and was soon swamped with people from both ships, asking him excited questions.

'Still in his Wellingtons, I see,' observed Ralph in a low voice. 'Affectation?'

But everyone was being hushed once more; Blake had a final apologetic comment to make. 'My Norwegian ancestry,' he said, 'has left me with rather large feet. Until I find a spare pair of twelves, I'm afraid I'll be slopping around in your midst in rubber boots. Or socks.'

The drama and the subsequent bonhomie allowed the two groups to merge quickly. Ornithologists chatted to Texan engineers. Nature-reserve workers swapped tips on solar power with motel owners from Palm Springs. Ralph alone seemed disturbed.

'It's ruined,' he said, lying flat on his bunk, his arms by his sides like a stone knight on a tombstone.

'What is?' Carson was examining the floral dress she'd unearthed from the bottom of her case; it was only a little crushed.

'The ambience.' Ralph's voice was gloomy. 'Everything has become frivolous.'

It was true: things had changed. People spent far less time on deck, huddled in their jackets spotting faraway objects, and more time in the lounge, where cocktail hour now stretched to several hours.

'Nice dress,' said Vicky, eyeing Carson up quite sharply for someone who made a point of meditating for thirty minutes a day. 'But aren't you cold? It's freezing tonight.'

'Not freezing,' said Ralph apologetically. 'In fact it's above zero.'

Blake, who was drinking martinis and chatting affably to Daniel, came over to be introduced. He also seemed to like Carson's dress; his eyes moved over her in an appreciative but non-offensive way. 'Carson?' he queried. 'That's a curious name.'

'My mother was a big reader,' explained Carson, 'and Carson McCullers was one of her favourite writers.'

'Carson is no more curious than your name.' Ralph seemed determined to correct everyone who spoke, although he did so with a reluctance born of a lifetime of courteousness. 'Surely Blake is more often a surname?'

Blake agreed that this was so. He told them he'd been named after the luxury hotel in London, where his parents had stayed as newly-weds. 'I was conceived in the Cardinal Suite,' he added, drifting away to another table.

'Blakes Hotel is unbelievably chic,' whispered Vicky to Carson. 'I once knew someone who had a passionate encounter there with a famous historian.'

Ralph drove a toothpick through his olive. 'Family money,' he pronounced *sotto voce*. 'That explains the air of assurance. Half his life spent in luxury hotels, the other half on cruise ships polluting the high seas. And I'm guessing he never reads, judging by the blank look on his face when he heard the name Carson McCullers.'

After dinner Ralph made a beeline fjor the table where a bevy of admirers was asking Blake for yet another account of the *Crusader*'s last waterlogged minutes. 'Mind if I sit?' he said, not waiting for an answer. 'It's just that your story puts me in mind of the dicey day I once had on a Norwegian icebreaker.'

Carson listened to Vicky and Daniel arguing over when the quality of the *National Geographic* magazine had begun to decline, and she watched the crowd around Blake and Ralph splinter off and float away like chunks of weakened ice. She sighed. Soon Blake was the only person remaining at the empty table, nodding politely as Ralph elaborated on the breadth and depth of his Scandinavian danger.

'Brave man, your husband,' said Blake as he came to bid them goodnight nearly an hour later.

'He's not my husband, actually,' said Carson. After Blake left the bar, she checked her reflection in the side of an ice bucket: she still looked pretty.

They woke to thick fog, pressing up against the porthole, touching the plastic with soft grey fingers. 'I'll read,' decided Carson.

'Good idea,' said Ralph heartily. 'The cabin's the place to be.'

'Oh, not in here,' she said. 'I'll read in the lounge.'

'But *they'll* all be there. The newcomers. It won't be peaceful.' Ralph left the cabin in a flurry of warnings and disapproval.

There were few sightings of Blake that day. Many people asked for him, but he appeared only once, and briefly, to get a breath of fresh air. It seemed he was becoming reluctant to carry the burden of heroism, in spite of his broad shoulders.

Vicky and Daniel had begun to bicker over small things: the origin of the beans used for their after-dinner coffee, the number of nautical miles between Graham Land and the Shetland Islands. Occasionally Vicky would glance over her shoulder and smooth down her wiry blonde hair before returning to the fray.

'I think he's a property developer.' Ralph took a long mouthful of wine, swilling it around in his cheeks.

'Who?' Carson had been looking at the way the fog seemed to sit on the curved windowsill beside her, as solid as snow.

'Blake, of course. He's evasive about what he does, in the way that people working with property and money often are.'

'So you've talked to him today?' asked Carson. She felt a rush of something like irritation, or even envy.

'I asked him to play some table tennis,' shrugged Ralph.

'You hate table tennis,' said Carson.

'Well, we didn't play!' said Ralph, as if agreeing with her. 'He said he wasn't any good at it. He doesn't seem very physical, I must say, despite his size.' He sat back and reached into his pocket as if hoping to find a cigar there, even though he didn't smoke.

'He's physical enough when it counts,' said Carson, a trifle stonily. 'When a ship's sinking, for instance.' She excused herself, leaving Ralph to his brandy, and Vicky and Daniel arguing over whether cognac enhanced the cognitive processes.

As she lay in the dark she could feel the engines throbbing below, powering the boat and its disparate passengers through the fog, carrying them forward into an unknown place where anything might happen. Ralph appeared to have propped up her mattress again. She threw the books out onto the floor and turned on her front to sleep.

She was alone on deck the next morning when Blake appeared, stepping over coils of rope, his cigarette a bright point of orange in the grey light. He started when he saw her. 'Caught me red-handed,' he said.

'I don't think smoking's banned,' said Carson. 'It's just that eco-people usually don't.'

'Neither do I usually.' Blake leaned on the rail. 'To be honest, the attention's getting a bit much.'

'People always need heroes,' she said. 'To take their minds off their own possible deaths.'

'I'm not a hero — that's Captain Yitaki.' Blake shuffled his feet. 'A fine man.'

'Still wearing rubber boots?' said Carson. 'Ralph might have a pair of shoes that would fit you.'

'He's a fine man too,' said Blake, squinting against the reddish glow of the sun. 'He seems to have a lot of adventures under his belt.'

'Adventures are his thing,' agreed Carson. 'His extra-curricular activity.'

'And what about you?' he asked.

'I was going to stay home and wallpaper,' she said.

Blake laughed. He offered her a cigarette, and they stood there, inhaling the smoke and the fog, shivering slightly and staring at the red rub of the sun. 'What do you —' started Carson. But just as she spoke, the sun broke right through the bank of fog, and there was a pounding of footsteps, and three jogging figures rounded the corner of the funnel: Ralph and

Vicky, with Daniel bringing up the rear.

'You won't believe what's happened!' Vicky was flushed from more than the exercise. 'The *Explorer* has its own hero aboard.'

Ralph stretched by the railings, his face turned into the shadows, while Vicky told the story and Daniel added the odd parenthetical detail for extra effect. A small boy (the only kid on board) had gone missing that morning; his father (a single parent) was frantic with worry, and the lower decks had been turned upside down in the search.

'Meanwhile,' said Vicky breathlessly, 'Ralph tried to imagine what would fascinate a young boy the most.'

('The whales,' said Daniel.)

'By the time we emerged for our run,' continued Vicky, 'Ralph had already discovered him, lying behind a coil of rope, under a tarpaulin. He might easily have frozen to death.'

'Had he been missing for long?' asked Carson.

'About twenty minutes.' Vicky seemed reluctant to divulge this information. 'But it might have taken them hours to find him. A child's life was undoubtedly saved today.'

Blake clapped Ralph on the shoulder. 'Congratulations, man!'

Vicky and Daniel beamed at Ralph in a proprietorial way, while Ralph coughed modestly and said he should go below and get cleaned up. But his pleasure appeared to evaporate during the day and, by the time he and Carson were in the cabin getting ready for dinner, he seemed almost annoyed. 'What were you doing smoking?' he asked, brushing his hair with vigorous strokes. 'You don't smoke.'

'Sometimes I do,' said Carson. 'It's a good way to bridge a gap.'

'A gap?' Ralph looked uncomprehending. 'A gap in conversation? A gap in understanding? I'm not surprised you don't have much to discuss with a banker, so why talk to him at all? He's not our kind of person.'

'You were the one who wanted to play table tennis with him.' Carson pulled her hair up on top of her head; it looked even more thick and lustrous than before.

'I felt sorry for him,' said Ralph stiffly. 'He was alone.'

But when they entered the dining room Blake was not alone: he was surrounded by the usual crowd of admirers, including Vicky in a bright blue thermal fleece ('I didn't bring a dress,' she said to Carson, almost accusingly). Blake made a face at Carson, as if to say 'Save me!' But Ralph had a firm grip on her arm, and he led her towards the drinks table, introducing her to the director of an outdoor clothing company that had supplied the latest Everest expedition with undergarments and gloves.

After a detailed conversation about high-tech fabric, Carson heard the welcome clink of a fork on a glass. 'A toast!' she said, sounding a little too eager.

On the podium stood Captain Gallagher, beaming. Beside him was a small boy clutching a large leather box.

'That's Bertie!' exclaimed Ralph. 'The boy I rescued this morning.'

'I'm sorry to interrupt your cocktails,' said the captain, 'but tonight I wish to honour a life-saver, a man who has combined bravery with intuition. I understand that adventurous acts are in his blood, but single achievements are not diminished by repetition.'

Ralph's eyes met Carson's. His cheeks flushed and his nostrils flared.

'We have a tradition in my sea-faring family,' said the captain, 'and it's become law on my boat. We always carry a gift, a trophy — a reward, if you like — to award to any passenger who might have carried out a selfless deed. This is such an occasion. Bertie, the box!'

Ralph smoothed his jacket. 'Do I look all right?' he hissed.

'In here,' said the captain, brandishing the box, 'is a vintage Stanwell pipe. And in here' — he pulled a red tin out of his voluminous jacket — 'is the finest Dutch tobacco I know of.'

'I don't smoke!' Ralph whispered to Carson, his voice flaring with momentary anxiety.

'By now most of you know the man,' said the captain, 'but what you may not know is that his father was the famous Norwegian explorer Knut-Henrik Henriksen, and that the son — also an explorer — often travels under an assumed name to avoid publicity. Without further ado may I present Mr. 'Blake' Henrik Henriksen.'

Ralph appeared the following morning with his bags packed. He sat quietly in the lobby, answering his fellow passengers' queries with regret. No, he had not originally intended to disembark at Ushuaia, but late last night he had received an urgent call; he was needed back at the institute as soon as possible. Yes, he'd enjoyed the cruise, although it had not proved quite as professionally stimulating as he'd hoped.

Carson brought him coffee from the buffet in the lounge. She selected the very largest piece of sultana cake, with plenty of fruit and vast slabs of yellow sponge, hoping to stop up whatever internal wounds Ralph might be suffering. 'You're sure you're okay?' she asked repeatedly. Ralph answered, repeatedly, that he was fine. He was sorry to desert her but he was gaining nothing career-wise by staying. 'Mustn't waste time,' he said, looking around him sternly. 'Life's too short.'

Time was, indeed, short: the ship was now behind schedule, and there was to be no dilly-dallying in the port. Those deciding to leave were asked to report to the purser with their full details, and then to disembark as smartly as possible.

No one but Ralph, it seemed, wanted to leave the *Explorer*. Now, more than ever, it was a ship of good hope, a floating myth, a magnet; it lay there glowing beside the sunny docks, seeming to radiate its own light.

Carson stood on deck watching Ralph walk down the gangway. In his black fleece and white jumper he looked a little like a penguin. Or, in his solitary state, an intrepid explorer? Perhaps a little of both. 'Goodbye, goodbye,' she called.

Ralph turned and raised a hand. 'See you at home' — was that what he said? She waited until he had merged with the crowds, and then she waited longer, watching the distance between herself and the shore stretch. When at last she turned away, the deck was empty. In front of her the horizon was an unending line, leading anywhere.

Daphne

ART NOUVEAU

— *Marilyn Duckworth*

I had been in Port Willin six months when I decided to give a one-man show. Not that I was particularly keen, but little Field, the picture-shop man, had just started a gallery and he wanted me — begged me, rather — to kick off for him. He was a decent little chap; I hadn't the heart to refuse.

Then, with my usual luck, the gallery hit a bit of a snag.

Did I say heart? Well, another part of me might have been involved when I agreed to 'kick off' for Field, as he put it. No, not that part — my head. Even an artist as flaky as myself must use her head. I do have one, never mind my Greta Garbo features, which I'm well aware of. Believe me, I'd disown my cheekbones, my nose, even my deep eyes if I could find my true genius. Or if someone else could find it for me — that would do. Ordinary recognition is something I know little of — I guess that comes from never settling in one place long enough to make an impression, to get myself entered in people's personal files. Blind belonging is against an artist's principles but . . .

I've taken a curious liking to Port Willin and I confess there might have been a secondary motive when I said yes to the art shop man whom I barely knew — a secret craving to become part of this place, one of the elite inner circle? Pathetic. Not Garbo after all, then. I like to be alone while I'm working but soon enough I'm itching for company. It's not as if I've been left off Port Willin invitation lists. Emails turn up in my inbox with regularity, blinking inanely, spitting exclamation marks. I haven't yet convinced the art crowd that I'm not worth worrying about. The jury is still out on that one. I'm hanging in there. I go to everything. I'm keeping an occasional diary now so that I can record days that matter and pin myself down.

Drinks in the landscaped garden of Field's home, a few streets from here, at 6.30 yesterday evening. The occasion was to entertain a visiting friend from Fiji he was sure I would enjoy meeting — a wood carver or some such. The wind was getting up but not enough to prohibit garden umbrellas or discourage *décolletage*. This summer is unusually warm, I've been told. I wore my new green — as near to Prussian as you can get at Kimberleys — and was carefully fifteen minutes late. The guests were mostly teachers and student daubers — one Liverpudlian with an accent and Emma Somebody, wife of a famous portrait painter — must check on the name. Small boys everywhere, swinging on trees and falling in the fishpond — thank heaven I haven't any of that — children, not fishponds. My biological clock has hopefully ticked past that possibility. I had worked out early in my life that childbirth and art can cancel each other out too easily. Fishponds are possibly good for the spirit, soothing as well as inspirational.

I could see no one specially appealing that evening, and no one worth drawing or even drawing out. I got stuck with the sleek wife of a shipping magnate (I think) who hates the Dutch. She had mauve lipstick on her teeth and her dead-in-the-eyes husband wore what looked like indigestion medicine decorating his lip.

'My dear, everything with them is money, money — it's really offal. Offal! I mean, I'm very careful, I always check prices before I buy, but if one needs something one buys, after all!'

They asked me to lunch, these two who hate money, money and the Dutch, insisting I must see their marvellous home inland from the coast, and their expensive art collection. Monday. Field was coming too, and would take me with him in the ancient Mercedes. It had been decided for me. I mentioned this to Field as I was leaving.

'Oh! Well actually, darling, that could be a bit difficult.'

Whoops. His last day alone with the dark boyfriend from Fiji? Johnno was definitely a boyfriend. And anyway, why should little Field want my company all that way up the coast? He was probably planning to get out of the lunch himself. I mean, how could he actually like the 'offal' woman? He had invited the Posners here to his drinks party — but perhaps the husband with indigestion was a business acquaintance he couldn't afford to ignore.

I tripped home in my sandals before the dark set in properly, wondering about the nature of my *faux pas.* Oh dear. So many of my *pas* are *faux* — I shouldn't care. But only famous artists don't care.

I have a stack of paintings in my studio quite suitable for the exhibition, and am still trying to paint one brilliant one. I know brilliance is in me somewhere, straining to get out; I've been told as much, several times in my not-so-long life. There's plenty of time, although my late mother might laugh.

Worked far too long last night on one of my improvisations. I use music for that, matching the pitch of notes to bring out the intensity of colours. The sense of colour is fragile, I've discovered; it can become attached to the wrong things in early childhood and cross over to emerge as shapes and even smells, which is useful for an artist like myself. Some days I'm swimming in it. Last night wasn't good — too much black swallowing the light.

In the evening of the next day I found a scribbled note from Field saying he would take me to lunch up the coast tomorrow — they'd expect me at his place in the morning. Well! The piece of yellow notepaper was sitting on the bottom shelf of my letterbox under the streetlamp and if I hadn't been putting rubbish out late I'd have missed it. He — or they? — must have called while I was on one of my wanders, sieving the city streets for inspiration. Field is allergic to cellphones and emails — or affects to be.

Should I telephone? No, too late for me to let him off the hook. 'We leave at 10.30 latest.' I would have to graciously accept.

10.25 next day I handled Field's iron gate, waiting for the complaining squeak to announce me. He was still in his gardening clothes, with hedge-clippers dangling from one hand and his dropped jaw hanging in a direct line. Johnno, stark naked — sunning himself on the front deck with a book and a glass of whisky — collected his paraphernalia and quietly ducked into the house. I thought — of course, they hoped I wouldn't find the note, since there's no mail delivery on Sunday. However, I had found it, and there I was, summoned up like a bad genie.

'No, no. Of course we want to take you! Is that the time?'

While they were inside the house changing, or arguing, or fucking — time passed, anyway — I sat on the lopsided garden swing, watching the fish in the pond and pretending to be cool.

Johnno insisted on sitting in the back of the Merc, still only in shorts and T-shirt, with bare feet. He would put on trousers and shoes on the way.

Beside me Field drove a little too fast, making clichéd remarks about the way the hills draw blue down from the sky, and picking his nose — a habit I'd never noticed before. Yuk. He made the obligatory references to my progress on work for the exhibition, although I already knew there was a leaky building problem with the gallery premises and a delay was inevitable. The rather good painting of mine he had displayed at his shop was still looking for a buyer. Johnno's voice from the back seat of the car was deep and slightly hoarse, like a badly tuned radio, but mostly it remained switched off.

We arrived at the Posners' 'Palmcourt', an unbelievable art nouveau — nouveau riche? — house with a pillared terrace, in the centre of nowhere, surrounded by grapevines. In the living room a five-tiered fountain with free-patterned green mosaic and immense light globes suspended from newly wrought iron. Arched doorways, of course, and parquet floor, heavy blond furniture so squat and ugly I shuddered inwardly. A couple of rather good paintings, one I'd seen reproduced in a book recently, but nothing I'd want to own myself — and displayed in a stupidly bad light. The only other guests were a 'logistics expert' who claimed to be suffering a hangover, and his limp IT girlfriend with a curvy spine. She sat apart from us, rudely drinking a cigarillo instead of wine and sniffing at the smoke.

'I've swallowed a Dr. Bach but it hasn't had the least effect!'

Neither of these two could face eating at the moment, apparently. The table was awash with food. Salmon eggs and pâté, green salad with squashy strawberries, calamari and mashed kumara. Pavlova, mousse, blueberry flan. Wow. Supposing we three hadn't come? But then three small boys I recognised from the Saturday drinks party sidled into the room and snatched up plates from a tea trolley, swatting off their mother's hectoring instructions like bothersome flies.

The host was less dead-eyed in his own setting than in Field's garden, but no match for Tania, his out-of-control wife with the megaphone voice. It appeared she had asked her spouse to fight some legal battle for her and he had let her down. 'Well?' she demanded, forgetting to pass the pavlova. 'What did you say to him? No, but what *exactly* did you say? And what did he say?'

With one knee Field nudged Johnno, who was yawning deeply. Why not? He had beautiful teeth.

I escaped to find the bathroom and it was dazzling green and gold mosaic with three recessed archways. A great black bath, great black toilet, great black bidet. Yellow sun was raying out in tiles above the bath. I could hardly pee for staring.

We had yet to view the main art collection, wherever that was displayed, but I wasn't holding out any real hope.

Field was quiet in the car going home, picking his teeth now with a long fingernail and sliding Johnno petulant glances. Did I call him a decent little chap? He wasn't behaving very kindly. I could feel there was some sort of lover's tiff going on, but they would have to wait until I'd been dumped before they could get on with it satisfactorily. It could have been my fault, for jostling them into coming here. Surely not. Field had seemed obligated for some reason of his own to view the shipping man's art collection, as if there were a purpose compelling him, although I gathered he'd been there at least once before. He must have known in advance what lunch at the Posners' mansion would be like. No, his mood was nothing to do with me. Actually, people behave mysteriously with me all the time — must be the kind of folk I move among; it can't be my fault, unless there is some genetic disabling feature makes me constantly misunderstand, as Mother certainly misunderstood me and no doubt Father. I'm not deaf, not yet — I'm too young for that. Father explained to me when he was going deaf that there is a kind of elderly deafness that is attributed not simply to the inner ear but primarily to the brain, which begins to have trouble translating the meaning of sounds. Perhaps my green eyes, so overworked at translating colour and shapes for my art, have trouble translating the more simple messages. I will concentrate on enjoying what I understand. I understand art.

In fact the art collection when we got to see it had been a surprise. We were led onto an elevated terrace that was planted in holly hedgerows, close-clipped and designed to resemble a mini maze, something like the famous one at Hampton Court, which I visited as a twelve-year-old. ('I mean, if one needs something one buys, after all!') The Posners obviously had no conception of how the shortage of grants and sponsors, not to mention customers, could cramp a struggling artist such as myself. Did they really need this extravagant foliage? Apparently. And they would need a full-time gardener to keep it up. In fact that was what the legal argument had been about, the garden, I recalled as we picked our way through the looming green passages to a rather disappointing edifice — a Lockwood prefab, perhaps, but spacious enough, as I discovered when we walked through the heavy door. And there it was — whoosh! Genuine art. Magnificently lit by what looked to be a skylight but was in reality artificial lighting as warm and clear as a French summer day. They were familiar works until I looked again and saw the differences. The artists were known to me but these huge paintings were certainly new. Where had they come from? The artists were all dead now. I hardly dare write their names. And that was when the lights went out. We stumbled into each other, complaining, and Tania Posner began shouting abuse.

No wonder Field and Johnno were silent in the ageing Merc as it crawled up the swelling hills, past toiling windmills. Wind-power is admirable but it costs as much and doesn't prevent the power failing at the worst moment. I had painted the drift of sheep on these hills as maggots, once, and later as tombstones, but today my vision reeled and I couldn't make a lot of sense of what I saw framed in the side window. I was more than tired — the visit had drained me.

'It's obscene,' Johnno whispered in his sandpaper voice. 'The woman has no idea, does she? No idea.'

I didn't know if he was talking about me or bossy Tania and I didn't care. I was dozy after all that wine; I lay back in the Mercedes and abandoned them to their front-seat muttering.

I woke up as we reached the downhill stretch of motorway that delivers the rooftops of Port Willin like a tray of jumble-sale items. I felt pleased all over again to be living in this place, and wondered how long before the pleasure gurgled away down the plughole of my life. Or perhaps something could happen to plug the hole this time and allow me to stay. I've noticed and enjoyed the way people here can seem impermanent while at the same time putting down roots. I didn't know how long the money from my inheritance might last. I cleared my throat more noisily than was necessary and Johnno glanced around.

'Nearly there. Okay?'

'You don't have to drop me home. Your place will be fine with me. I like to walk.'

Field said: 'I need to call in at the gallery first and check if a delivery might have gone there instead of the shop. We'll have a coffee and you can see how it's progressing — you'll have to excuse the smell. The leaky wall's at the kitchen end and the decorating's pretty much on track, but the claim inspection — well, there's a queue, so we're not holding our breath. It's some sort of drainage problem — and the owner can't take any short-cuts if he wants to get compensated. A bugger, but we'll get there. You'll be a star, darling. You can help me design a flyer.'

I asked Johnno when he was leaving to go home but he inclined his head and pushed his lips up. So nothing was booked, nothing was certain. Typical.

The new building had been completed only thirteen years

earlier but the floor of the gallery, which was at ground level, had retained the original material so that it was pocked and pleasantly battered. Field had told me it was the best feature of the place.

'It's the new timber that was dodgy. Don't you love this floor?'

I did take pleasure in the glossy floorboards. But Field wasn't asking me, he was asking Johnno, using his round eyes, and there seemed to be a hidden message there, perhaps sexual. I'm sometimes a bit thick on picking up that stuff — something missing in me. Most of my passion has gone into my art — nothing wrong with that.

The walls were white and so clean my eyes saw sharp vertical lines. They needed pictures. But right now I was feeling superfluous. We'd already been through several art magazines and discussed possibilities for the flyer to advertise the opening. Field had to join the digital twenty-first century 'as soon as', Johnno bullied him. I swallowed the last of my instant caffeine and told them I could walk home from there.

I started walking. I passed two Asian eating houses, one used-car lot, and reached the first traffic light before I felt in a pocket for my cellphone to summon a cab and found it missing. Not at the Posners' — I'd been too engrossed at Palmcourt to play with a phone. I guessed I'd left it on the back seat of Field's car and began to retrace my steps. The gallery light was out now but the Merc was still parked outside. So. I couldn't think where they might have gone on foot. I tried the car door, just in case it was unlocked, and then peered in the window of the building to see if there was a light burning in the kitchen space at the back. The blinds were three-quarters drawn but there was no light. Nothing. And then, voices!

Field's camp tones were higher and easier to hear than Johnno's raspy voice, and what I heard kept me riveted to the window.

'Outtage they call it. A stroke of luck, anyway. Didn't want Chillybin getting a closer look.'

Johnno laughed. 'Chillybin! That's good.'

They were talking about me, Hilary Benn, often shortened to Hilly. And it wasn't funny.

I wasn't chilly, was I? Well — I pulled my jacket around me because the wind was starting to bite. But I wasn't unfeeling — I liked to think I was quite sensitive. And it offended me that I could be seen as cold, especially by someone like Field, the nose-picker. Cheek! I missed some of the next bit because I was so annoyed. Anger's a feeling, isn't it? I was hurt. Does a chillybin hurt? I recalled someone telling me once that Mondrian had no feelings, but I didn't understand that at the time and still don't.

I stood there eavesdropping at the window and wondered why Field hadn't wanted me to get a closer look at the Posner art collection. Presumably it was stolen — that would be why they kept it hidden away for select viewing. It made sense. Field was laughing again.

'I felt a tad sorry for the dozy wife,' Johnno growled. 'All that loot the boys would have inherited, and what for? Fakery!'

'You don't mind spending the stuff, I notice. And what's it matter if they can't see the difference? We know the value of art lies in the eye of the beholder.'

'Not to the little boys.'

'Ah, so that's what interests you — the little boys!'

There was a sort of scuffling silence and a giggle in the darkness, bouncing off the shiny timber floorboards that my imagination lit up. Naked perhaps and snarled together like *The Kiss*? A cyclist passing on the street alongside me swerved slightly in my direction as if questioning my position at the shaded window. I started and pulled a muscle in my neck as I stood up and began to walk quickly back the way I'd come. I wasn't going to knock on the door of the gallery — no way. I would have to do without my cellphone.

When I reached the crossing the cyclist was there right beside me in his crimson helmet, waiting for the lights to turn green. He raised his eyebrows and then I believe he winked. Ouch! My cricked neck really hurt.

I couldn't sleep. Except I must have slept because I kept waking. I woke up half a dozen times, sucking from my water glass, rubbing my neck, and each time my dreaming gave me a new aspect of the previous day's trip. 'Chillybin' still bothered me, but the paintings bothered me more. Stolen? Or faked? Or both? It was difficult to believe. And the Posners were weird, really weird — as awful as the sad family I'd run away from.

By the time the alarm clock went off — I'd forgotten to kill it before I got into bed — I was nearly convinced the whole day had been a dream. I seemed to hold the memory of it in a contained bubble in my brain, inflated with gassy white. White like the walls of the gallery that were waiting for my paintings.

After two strong coffees I glanced out of the window. The clouds above the harbour resembled the white muddle inside my own head. I shook it, did a bit of running on the spot and trotted to my studio out the back. It had been a garage but now had mirror glass filling one wall and extending around a corner. I needed to refresh myself with a measured look at what I'd accomplished here in the past six months before I decided what to do. If I had to do anything.

It didn't make me feel any better.

When I turned to go back inside, Field was waiting for me on the porch — a surprise, so early in the day. He'd brought my cellphone, of course, and handed it over with a look of casual distaste.

I asked him what he'd done with Johnno.

'He's gone, darling. I told you he was leaving today. Why?'

'I had the impression he was staying on a bit.'

'He'll be back.' He rubbed his nose. 'Hilly, I need to talk to you about yesterday.'

'You really didn't want to take me with you, did you?'

'What gave you that idea? No, no, it wasn't that. It was just a bit unfair of us not to explain what was likely to happen. And then letting you walk home.'

'I like walking.'

'Not after all that stuff. You do realise they spiked our drinks, don't you?' The way my face looked must have startled him. He stood up quickly and put out a pale hand.

'They can't have! We were perfectly all right.' Then I remembered sleeping in the back of the car, not something I usually do. 'Weren't we?'

'They do a lot of drugs, Hilary. How do you think they make all that money they throw about? Honestly, you have to be careful about this, darling, or you might drop me in it — or get yourself in serious trouble. Don't worry, I'm not mixed up in any of that myself, but the Posners are valuable clients and I can't afford to lose them — *we* can't. The art scene can't afford to lose their patronage, either. Don't look at me like that.'

'So what is it about their secret art collection?' I knew I was looking grim.

'What do you mean "secret"?'

'The building at the end of the silly maze. All those amazing paintings — you know what I'm talking about!'

Field reached out two fingers and stroked the back of my hand patronisingly until I snatched it away. 'I've no *idea*, Hilly. That's what I mean. We all had different experiences yesterday. I know Johnno did. Shall I tell you about mine?'

'No! I don't believe you! I need to talk to Johnno.'

'Of course you can talk to Jo — when he's back. It shouldn't be long. He comes all the time for his work.'

'You told me Posner was a shipping magnate.'

'Shipping? I don't think so, darling. Shopping's more like it. Import export is what Al's about.'

'And Johnno? Wood sculpting? Or what exactly?'

'Can we sit down — do you mind — and have a cup of tea? I've drunk enough coffee. Or do you have something to eat? I'm starving.'

It turned out to be a good idea. I felt better busying myself in my kitchen preparing slab sandwiches with Gouda cheese and anchovies. Cooking and related tasks have always calmed me, rather like mixing colours or stretching canvas. And actually it's not often I get the chance to entertain in my own home.

I made proper tea with loose-leaf Earl Grey and found I was breathing normally. Field complimented me on the unusual curtains I'd cut and hemmed by hand, making the kitchen my own place.

'He does do some wood carving,' he told me after a bit. 'It's good work — no, it is. But he's got involved in something more lucrative lately, and he's planning to bring the business over here. I don't blame him; it's a safer place to be.'

'Something dodgy?'

'Not at all. He's been working in Suva with a bit of a team turning out old masters. I know! Look disgusted if you like, but there's nothing illegal about it — no forged provenance or anything fraudulent. And there's big money. You'd be surprised how many people prefer the idea of a good copy of Rembrandt in oils rather than a print.'

'God! Really? People want that stuff? Knowing it's not genuine?'

'Knowing it's fake. Yes. They do.'

'But you wouldn't sell it in your shop? Or the gallery?' I noticed I was sticking my chin out in that way Father hated and reined it back in.

'Never. Not me. You needn't worry that I'm going to contaminate you, darling. You're the real article. If I didn't know already it wasn't your bag we'd have asked you to join us: we could certainly use you. I do plan to help Jo, but it'll be completely discrete from my own business — or discreet with two 'e's, spell it how you like.'

I had to ask him then — 'So what has Johnno sold here so far?'

'Here? Nothing yet. It's all in Fiji so far. Next year, with any luck.'

I'm not sure why I didn't ask him to tell me, then or later, what he remembered of our day up the coast at Palmcourt. He'd offered to share it with me — 'We all had different experiences yesterday. I know Johnno did. Shall I tell you about mine?'

But he didn't offer again and that was fine with me. It wasn't that I didn't care if he was lying. I cared. I suppose I wanted to believe that those four astonishing paintings were my individual experience and no one else's. The tantalising details, coloured by that curious warm light, lived in my memory, pervasive as the smell of frying onion. I woke each day with a whiff of it in my nostrils. If they existed only in my mind then that meant they were mine, weren't they? I had made them. It hardly mattered that I'd glimpsed them for less than two minutes — I'm an artist and my eyes devour and record in extended play mode. Which doesn't make it easy to reproduce them all over again, but I haven't given up trying.

I've had to go to Websters for more canvas rolls and tubes of top-grade oils for the second time this month, but I'm not worried about money. I knew it was only a matter of time before Field came back to me with an offer of regular employment in his and Johnno's new business — with a confidentiality clause. I'm a whiz at copying old favourites, as they guessed. The business is going well. They understand that I'm only selling my corporeal skills to subsidise my spiritual creative endeavours, but they don't know yet what I'm creating. Time enough.

I'm sitting now at my easel under the north window, and the paintbrush has become an extension of my hand. It's alive. As I stroke and caress the canvas, vermilion flows intently, reshaping what I remember, and my belly tightens — a pleasurable pressure kicks in my pelvis. It's happening. As the picture begins to emerge in surges and troughs I realise this might be something like childbirth: pain which is pleasure which is a doorway to creation. I wonder: could an orgasm be painful? I don't think I've ever had one of those, but you read about them, and about childbirth, boringly over and over. At the end of this I will have given birth to a work of genius, not just a little yelling thing.

That reminds me — tomorrow I begin work on a copy of Munch's 'The Scream'.

Father and the Girls

PRIMAVERA

— *Fiona Farrell*

At midday, Ernestine, who had come down from the mountains with her mother to work in the vineyards belonging to the hotel, heard the faint, faraway chuff-chuff of the train from Italy. Trains were a novelty to Ernestine; they were fascinating, unknown, terrible.

I. The Vineyard

Julia said I was being ridiculous. She said that at forty-five I just wanted to wear short skirts again and chat up boys. She said I was always telling her to grow up, and now it was her turn: grow up, she said.

I said I was trying to, that was what this was all about. I wanted to grow up, live on my own, exist solely off my own income, fill in my own IRD return, for god's sake — I'd never done that, not without endlessly consulting Paul. I'm innumerate, can't make sense of numbers. Not grown up at all.

What about the house? said Julia. Are you going to sell

it now and buy two pathetic little flats, one for you, one for Dad? Or have you got someone else stashed away? Have you been having an affair? Are you moving out to live with some geek in his hideous house? Does he have kids? Or is he some old-boy loser who watches the rugby channel from bed?

No, I said. I haven't been having an affair.

An affair would have been simple. I could have explained an affair to a furious seventeen-year-old whose experience of love so far had pretty much consisted — at least as far as I was aware — of some preliminary fumbling followed by a few months of delirious involvement with a mountain biker named Luke which I presume involved a lot of sex, and then some equally passionate weeks of grief and heartbreak that required long muttered late-night phone calls with friends, recounting the exquisitely painful detail of separation. But that phase ended too, as all the magazines had told her it would, and now Julia was single. Seventeen and single and off to uni in the new year, where she'd meet heaps of new people.

So why are you and Dad splitting up? she said, snapping tiny green bunches of unformed fruit from the stem. She is incapable of talking without fiddling. It drives me mad, the way she sits at a table, fiddling: pouring salt into tiny piles, breaking corks into pieces, piling up the sugar sachets into neat interlocking wood stacks. It has always driven me mad. Just the way I drive her mad by not being able to choose from a menu or trying on three different things before going out. Stuffing around, she says. You know you'll just go back to wearing the first thing you picked out anyway. She doesn't understand the claustrophobia I feel when I have made a decision. I prefer the free-fall when all choices are open. I can breathe as I fall.

She was flicking bitter grapes like green shrapnel into the air. You're just stuffing around again, she said.

And I said Paul and I had discussed it (those hesitant late-night discussions either side of the chilly wilderness that had become our bed) and that we hadn't just decided out of the blue. We had hoped to make a go of it but it wasn't working. And you couldn't say we hadn't tried, I said. We hadn't done too badly. Twenty years of marriage wasn't exactly lack of commitment.

It's not a competition, you know, said Julia. No one's keeping score.

She stood a little away from me among the vines we'd planted around the house back in 1990: a couple of rows of pinot noir and three of sauvignon blanc. Just an experiment to see how it would go. Paul had always fancied the idea of making his own wine, ever since that summer in Italy.

Julia is tall like him, and fair. She was wearing an op shop nightie she had dyed indigo over a flowery frock from the fifties, and her hair was divided into corn rows threaded with ribbons and beads and some smooth brown tubes she had informed me were marine worm casings from Kaikoura. She had held one up for me to examine.

'Isn't it beautiful?' she said. And it was. A tiny perfect tube of finely grained clay, one of those works of nature astonishing in its perfection, like a fern frond or a spider's web.

She stood barefoot among the vines we'd planted back when we had assumed that life could be simple: a simple life of homegrown vegetables and homemade bread on a lifestyle block 10 kilometres from the city. We'd surrounded the house with fruit trees that burst into blossom every spring: apple, plum, quince. The most exquisite of all flowers. I'd made quince paste and jams, like my mother did, only I made them out of choice, not out of dire necessity and the requirement to make ends meet with five kids to feed on a wharfie's pay.

So, why are you splitting up? said my daughter.

Well, I said, reaching in desperation for a handy ready-to-serve cliché, your father and I feel that we have reached the end of the line.

There were other metaphors for what had happened: I could have said that I felt as if I had been bobbing along on the surface of my life for years, the way you might on one of those shingly rivers streaming from the high country, all briar roses and matagouri and skylarks singing, and you are floating on your back letting the current take you, but suddenly there's a chill and you flip over and try to put your foot down to stand and there is no bottom. You are drifting over a chasm and all that will keep you up is frantic movement.

Or I could have said that I had been swept up by a wave of curiosity. I had published a novel, my first, a fantasy about teenagers on an alien planet, and it had had an unexpectedly unsettling effect. I seemed to have unleashed fiction into my system. I found myself making up stories, not just about aliens and teenagers but about my own life. Early morning stories, as I lay in bed looking out the window at the lifestyle block within the barricade of trees protecting us all from the nor'wester. Stories in which I tried on alternative existences the way I tried on clothes; stories featuring a house that wasn't this house, where I listened to music that wasn't the music I listened to in this house, but the music I might listen to if I could choose uninfluenced by anyone else's taste. Paul likes modern orchestral. In this other house, the person who was this other me listened to Emmylou Harris.

I became impatient at the slightest hint of restraint.

There was a dinner party: we were talking about hitch-hiking. We had all done it in our youth — thumb out, catching a ride to somewhere. Across America or from Auckland to Dunedin or, spectacularly, all the way to London from Cape Town. My contribution was the time Paul and I had hitchhiked through France to Italy when I was five months pregnant with Julia. Our last bid for freedom in the spring of '85 . . .

''86,' said Paul.

'What?' I said, my mind busy with the lorry-driver jittery on speed who had nearly taken out the bridge near Lyons, and the way the countryside had fluffed up so perfectly, so beautifully, into pink blossom as we headed south.

'Eighty-six,' he said. Reasonably. 'It was '86. You always get that bit wrong.'

As if I told this story often, as if I had become one of those bores who insist upon repeating stories over and over to whoever might listen, when I was certain I had never told anyone at this table about hitch-hiking to Florence in '85. Or was it '86?

'Julia was born in August '86,' said the voice of calm reason from across the table. 'You must remember that.'

He turned to the entire table and shrugged, as if it were a joke we could all share, a common affection for my little lapses.

'That's our Mary. Good at words but hopeless at dates. When's my birthday, for instance? When was I born?'

I stared back at him blankly. He was smiling: that crooked charming smile with his eyes crinkled at the edges, the smile that enchanted all the first years and had him voted most popular lecturer in the Media Studies Department. I hadn't realised till that moment how much he disliked me. And how much I disliked him. I sat among the tatters of my story floating like torn feathers about my shoulders and managed to perform. I smiled like one of those celebrity co-presenters at the Oscars and came up with the lines.

'The third,' I said, 'of August.' Then I had to think for a second. 1956? Or 1955? '1956,' I said, and Paul said well done, and everyone laughed in relief because they had also seen the flicker of mutual animosity and did not want it to swell and burst and spoil the evening.

But how could I say that to Julia? That I wanted to be able

to sit at a dinner table and tell my own stories, free of editorial input, mistakes and all? How unbearably trivial that would seem. How could I explain how I had begun to look forward to the weeks when Paul was away at conferences, when I could stay up all night if I wanted, reading, going out for walks on dark streets, liking the sound of my solitary shoes on the footpath and the way the streetlights raced up to meet me and flooded away under my feet. I liked sleeping on my own in a double bed, sprawled right across the centre, resenting his return when I must move back to my own narrower half.

I wanted to stay as long as I liked at parties, right to the end, after all the busy people and the people with babysitters have disappeared when there are enough sofas and chairs for everyone who is left to sprawl comfortably about the fire, and someone makes some coffee and puts on a CD they've just bought, some soft subtle jazzy thing they've been waiting to play all evening just as soon as the time was right, and someone brings in some truffles that had been forgotten in the fridge and the conversation is great, after hours of standing about in too-high heels, leaning on bookcases yelling banalities at strangers. That's the part of a party I wanted to be at.

Paul, on the other hand, liked to get up early and go for a long bike ride on Sunday mornings. It was the only chance he had all week, wheeling off toward Little River with a gang of other older riders, spinning along the near-empty roads past the lakes luminous and studded with the tiny black islands that are sleeping swans. He wanted to leave. I wanted to stay. I came to hate the feeling of him, seated with ostentatious patience on a sofa, casting meaningful glances in my direction.

'Just go!' I said to him. 'Just go, I'll get a lift later. I'll get a taxi.'

But he waited. A taxi from Lyttelton to St Albans? My god, it'd cost a fortune! He accepted a brandy, while from the corner of my eye I could see his foot jiggling, signalling in that intricate vocabulary of gesture that all couples devise that he was impatient to be gone.

Try explaining that to a seventeen-year-old. Try explaining the fury engendered by such trivial things when the time comes for explanations: to your husband, to your mutual friends, to yourself.

Not to mention the other more intimate particularities: the frantic searching that is sex when you lie trying to find each other somewhere in this tangle of limbs, the slap slap slap of dead skin on skin, the terror of looking up and seeing no one there, a blank eye where there had been once complete and delighted presence.

In the midst of life, we had found ourselves in a dark wood. I could have quoted the poet I suppose, to prove to my daughter that Paul and I were not alone in this confused state, that it was quite normal, ordinary even, a standard crisis that they knew about even in the fourteenth century, but I doubt that any of that would have helped. Not when the configuration is mother and daughter caught at that frozen moment before a new story breaks out, among vines.

So all I said was that we would be putting the house on the market at Christmas, and Julia said you are just so full of it. Do what you like. And she walked off, tall, fair and full of grief. Pure Murphy. Like my mother stirring jam on the hottest day of the summer, sweat making black patchwork of her floral print.

My mother's stories were all of failure. Men who went to the drink despite every opportunity. Women of indescribable beauty doomed to disappointing marriage to hopeless philanderers. Horses that lost in the final furlong, taking with them the savings for a house. Brides abandoned pregnant at altars. Cars stolen when the insurance had lapsed only a week earlier. The priest cousin who fell spectacularly from grace by carrying on with the housekeeper. The fiancé who had preceded our father (also, inevitably, a disappointment), who had been a brilliant tenor, easily as good as anyone you heard on the radio, but who had contracted meningitis and was left a living vegetable — we imagined something pale as a swede or a parsnip but wearing clothes and sitting in a wheelchair — and a burden for life to his poor suffering mother.

My mother was an Olympic-standard sufferer. It's in the Murphy genes. The Murphys could suffer for New Zealand on the international stage and bring home gold. And I'm not excluding myself from the Murphy Sufferers. I have finely developed skills in that area. It's that dark streak that critics notice in my writing, which makes me drop the characters I have so lovingly created into a hole in the ground.

And that's the unmistakable tone of the other side of the family: from our father we acquired flippancy. When we were small our mother's tales oppressed us with terror, but as we grew older we took on our father's cruel irony. My sister had only to look at me and say, 'And he was a living vegetable!' to reduce us both to helpless giggling.

I was cruel in divorce, though I tried to be otherwise. I was the first to move. I rearranged the books on the shelves to cover the gaps left when mine were packed in boxes, I pinned a poster over the faded rectangle on the living-room wall left by the removal of the painting I had bought years ago when I felt the room needed light and air. A pair of lovers suspended in mid-air above a New Zealand beach. Where it had hung, I pinned a poster of the *Primavera.* Julia had pored over that print when she was in Year 12, seeking the fine detail for her folio for Art and Design. It couldn't quite cover the space. If you looked closely you could detect the rim of pristine Spanish White that had been the room's original tint. Julia made no comment. She knew when she was being fobbed off with a substitute for the original.

She suffered. Not in an obvious fashion. Murphys don't

lock themselves in their rooms or slash or starve. Instead, she met Morgan.

Morgan was forty-two, a sculptor. That's how they met: he was tutoring her first-year class up at Elam and asked her to model for him. They became lovers, I presume in the basement at the art school where he had his studio. She took me there once to see his work. Switched on a bald fluorescent light on the shock of a bronze torso sprawled on a spike, head flung back, mouth open in ecstasy, arms and legs amputated at the joint so she hung like a plucked chicken, insects emerging from her vagina and the spike rising through her torn breast, bearing her dripping heart upon its tip.

'Isn't it cool?' she said, eyes shining. 'Isn't Morgan amazing?'

I couldn't answer. It was beautifully finished. Exquisitely modelled. But all I could see was my daughter's body posed upon that ripped settee among the takeaway coffee cups. And the man sleek as an eel, with his calculated stubble and shaven skull who was moulding her.

Had I helped pass her into his dead hands through my careless self-absorption? Or would she have gone there of her own accord, drawn by some bleak part of herself, that Murphy streak, to the dark prince in his basement and the enchantment of creation: youth and the transience of warm flesh traded for cold enduring metal?

II. The Train

Then there is the train. It's just a detail, the kind of thing that might be overlooked in the wider landscape, like that scrap of scarlet that is the cloak of the hero among towering trees as he struggles toward Elysium, or those tiny legs splashing into the ocean that is the human falling from the sun. The train is the flicker of movement in the lower left-hand corner, like the beating of a foetal heart.

It's not that I am especially interested in trains. For a brief time when I was in the first months of divorce and lacking in discernment, I knew a train enthusiast. Photos of trains were pinned to his bedroom wall: the Iager Drive-in movie theatre on a summer evening back in 1956 when Ogle Winston Link detonated forty-three flashbulbs simultaneously to illuminate a lineup of necking couples in Ford convertibles at just the moment when Time Freight No. 78 roared past on the Norfolk and Western. And next to that, mad-eyed Hester Poulis of Lithia trapped upon her settee while her grandson George waves at steam engine No. 2, Shenandoah Division, all hiss and *chuff chuff chuff*, passing inches from the floral flounces of her lounge-room curtains. This man possessed recordings of steam trains that he played late at night, enthralled by the orgasmic grunting of shunting and coupling. On sunny afternoons he sat on top of a scale model of a Y6 steam engine he had built himself and chugged contentedly around the silverbeet and chrysanthemums in his back yard.

The train enthusiast featured somewhere between a pony-tailed guitarist stuck permanently in the spring of '78 and a man who told jokes, eyes fixed on the ceiling above our heads, his voice taking on a more rhetorical pitch as all the little bouncing conversations about the table were forced to stand aside and wait till the joke had passed like a train at a level crossing, *chuff chuff* to the punchline and that tiny groaning climax that signalled we were free to talk again. As I say, my powers of discernment seemed to have failed me.

Paul, meanwhile, had vanished into the depths of his own forest.

And Julia sprawled in the basement.

Murphys are not good at solving suffering. We make wild swipes and sometimes we get it right and sometimes we miss entirely. I decided to use my share of the proceeds from the sale of our home to take Julia to Italy. I would entice her forth from the dark basement with dancing maidens and Venus drifting on her shell through the dark walls of the Uffizi and that louche pouting David and Brunelleschi's beautiful cupola floating like a bubble above the tiled roofs of the city. I knew it was not sensible, just another expression of that state of mind Julia had so accurately described of regression to short skirts and irresponsibility.

'You'll be renting for the rest of your life,' said Paul when I mentioned my plans to him. 'Do the figures!'

Maybe his caution affected Julia, because she turned my offer down. She was tempted for a day or two, she almost said yes. But in the end she refused. There was to be an exhibition of student work in October. Morgan said she had a chance of a distinction, but she'd have to really work hard this term, put in the hours, so sorry, mum. Maybe another time?

So I went alone. It felt necessary. I was determined to fling myself headlong off the housing ladder into reckless free-fall; I would declare myself to be, once more, after twenty years of caution, a full, card-carrying member of that feckless tribe who blew the savings for a house on a dead cert for the 2.10. I would go, as I had gone twenty years before, to visit my friend Madeleine.

Madeleine lived in Florence. I had met her when I was eleven, in the first week at intermediate school, when we were paired to make scones. Our scones were a disaster — the dough glued to the board — but we didn't care. We would probably never make scones again, ever. She was going to be a world-famous pianist and I was going to be an archaeologist. I had read a *National Geographic* article about the discovery of Knossos. I was entranced by the little goddess who had emerged from her long burial below ground in her beautiful flounced skirt, holding snakes aloft in her bare hands. I was entranced by the slender boys and ribboned girls who leapt over a charging bull.

I didn't become an archaeologist. It seemed to involve an inordinate amount of scrub clearance in pursuit of nothing more exciting than post holes, so I switched to literature. And Madeleine didn't become a pianist. There were so many. The world was crammed with pianists. But she did get a scholarship to go to Italy to study Renaissance music in Florence, where she met a cellist named Gianni. They lived in a flat near the Pitti Palace. It was Madeleine I went to visit with Paul in the year that Julia was born. In '85. Or was it '86?

Hitch-hiking south, following a random path in the big lorries that rumbled down motorways scattering shoals of tiny cars. Nights spent in a tiny tent pitched surreptitiously at the edges of fields colouring up with the tips of new corn. Paul's hand resting on the curve of my belly where Julia already lay curled like a broad bean beneath the skin. The breaking forth from a dark tunnel into an Italy already fluffed up and pink with spring, when we had left London only days before still clad in its stuffy grey winter suit.

'You're not going to stay in a tent,' said Madeleine, patting my belly in welcome as if it were smooth dough. 'Not while you're in Florence.' She had arranged a sub-let from a friend of hers, a sculptor who was away for a few weeks visiting her mother in Tokyo. The flat was only a block from the Duomo. It was cool and shuttered, but the darkness was lit by Akiko's works, vivid structures of fluorescent plastic tubing that glowed in the shadows. We walked out into the city, to the Duomo and the Uffizi where Venus sailed serenely ashore and Spring danced on the flowery mead, and we ate at small restaurants owned by Gianni's friends, and Madeleine took me shopping to buy a beautiful muslin dress and a pair of strappy sandals that threatened to topple me on the cobbles but were infinitely more elegant than my dusty Keevas. And we talked: about work mostly. About her thesis which was on Paolovicino, and mine which was on Eliot and Cornford and the fertility rites that lay at the root of classical comedy, so not that far, really, from the little goddess with her snakes at Knossos.

At the end of the month we went back to London and three months later Julia was born and not long after that, we returned to New Zealand. Madeleine sent a Christmas card every year: Giotto, Raphael, some scene of the maid seated with her baby on her lap among damp rocks and lilies, with a letter and photos of herself, of Gianni, of their sons when each was born, with their serious infant faces and brown eyes of infinite knowing. I sent some antipodean collage of deckchairs and pohutukawa blossom and a scrawled sentence or two, because I have always been careless with affection.

So now, twenty years later, I sat alone on the train to Florence. Its corridors were packed with the bulge and nudge of backpacks, the air was hot and oppressive in a ten-year heatwave, and my fine journey had melted away. It seemed no longer the dramatically defiant gesture of an independent life but silly, frivolous. (Do the figures!) I was travelling for no better reason than that movement gave my life a temporary sense of purpose. I was going to visit a person with whom I had exchanged nothing more than brief clichés for twenty years, out of some bizarre and sentimental notion that this constituted a friendship.

There were two others in the compartment who stayed while others came and went. One was an old woman in widow's black with the big broad hands of hard work who wanted to talk. I did the best I could with some rudimentary Italian, looking at photos of her grandchildren, explaining that yes, I had a daughter. One daughter. I had a photo: Julia laughing, wearing a daisy chain in her hair. The old woman nodded, and smiled and touched the print with a crooked finger. 'Ah, la bella figlia,' she said. As the train neared Pisa, our conversation reached an impasse. I was trying to answer a question. What did I do? What was my impiego? And I could not find the word to reply. What was the word for writer? Novelista? Autore? I mimed scribbling. The other woman in the compartment was Japanese. She had been reading the whole way, deep in her book, but at this point she looked up. 'Writer?' she said to me, and I said, yes, yes, writer. And she translated for me into rapid Italian.

Thank you, I said. I wish I could speak the language as well as you do.

I live here, she said, and I said (because you always think there must be a link, as the child of a small country, even out in the wide world, that you must know the cousin of the man you have just met in New York or the woman you sat next to on the plane to Buenos Aires), 'Are you a sculptor?'

'Yes,' said the woman, looking surprised. And it was true: she was the woman who had owned the apartment we had stayed in when we were in Florence all those years before, though she now lived in Pisa. And she hadn't seen Madeleine in years, both so busy with their lives, and was she well? And I said yes, and that I was going to visit her. So the Japanese woman said, 'Say hello please from Akiko,' for the train was slowing, we were approaching Pisa, and she and the old woman were gathering together their coats and bags. Then the train stopped and they left and I watched them disappear into the crowd. At the gate, Akiko turned and gave a little wave, open-palmed, like a child.

And I was left in the compartment as the train swept on across the country toward Florence, thinking the kinds of thoughts you always have on trains. About chance, and time, and change.

It had not been a dramatic coincidence: not the discovery of a sister lost in the chaos of Auschwitz, or the lover who had supposedly drowned off the beach in Phuket. But outside the window, the world was rushing backwards fast and I was twenty-six again in my dyed cotton smock, my belly curved over my daughter who slept beneath the placental tracery of veins arching over her frail foetal head like a spreading vine. I was twenty-six and all I knew or needed to know was that I loved Paul and he loved me and we were as simple and straightforward as gods, rolling down the autoroute toward the south. I had not yet caused pain to anyone. I had not suffered yet, nor caused anyone I loved to suffer.

I sat on the train, older now but not wiser, thinking of that other self who had become so faint and far away, and I wished with all my heart for fiction: that Paul should find his way through to a gilded shore, that I should swim straight and strong when I hit the ocean, and most of all, that Julia should step forth from the dark basement, barefoot on a flowery mead, with all the flowers of spring tumbling from her smiling mouth.

All Serene!

PERFECT

— Catherine Chidgey

At breakfast that morning they were in wonderfully good spirits. Who was responsible — he or she? It was true she made a point of looking her best in the morning; she thought it part of her duty to him — to their love, even, to wear charming little caps, funny little coats, coloured mules at breakfast time, and to see that the table was perfect as he and she — fastidious pair! — understood the word. But he, too, so fresh, well-groomed and content, contributed his share. Every Sunday he made English Breakfast tea just the way she liked it — not too milky, the colour of pressed flowers — and served it in bone china. The cups were tiny in his hands — he always felt he might crush them just by holding them — but she said that presentation was everything, and he wanted to please her. Every Sunday, too, he placed one of the silver apostle teaspoons on each saucer. They had been a wedding present from his grandmother, who knew he had always admired them, and he far preferred them to the cut-glass platters, the knives, the jagged crystal vases they had received — all those sharp things, all those glittering edges.

He and Helena had been home from their honeymoon cruise for six weeks now, and still they did not know where to put the angular, icy gifts that somehow did not belong in their home; they did not want to spoil the little haven they had made that was so much to their taste.

He remembered how he used to take the spoons from his grandmother's soft, soapy hand when they did the dishes together. They were warm from the water, as warm as his own skin, and he would dry them one by one, polishing the bowls until they shone like the moon, rubbing the little silver figures and their little silver beards and their holy faces, making wishes. Then he would return them to their satin-lined case, which reminded him of the inside of his mother's coffin — he'd seen it by accident, although he wasn't meant to — and he made sure all the apostles were facing the same way, twelve little bodies laid out in their box, and then he shut the lid and fastened the clasp.

'You're named after an apostle,' his grandmother used to tell him. 'Peter was the one who wanted to wash Christ's feet.'

He supposed it was fitting that he should be the hygienic apostle, the scrupulous one. Much later he learned that Peter was also the denier of Christ, but his grandmother had not told him that, and he was grateful to her.

He and Helena had established a routine on the cruise: each day he had let her rise and bathe first, never stirring as she slipped from the bed and moved through the cabin like a spirit.

'I don't want you to see me until I'm presentable,' she had explained the day after they were married, when they were already at sea, and he had laughed and stroked her cheek and said that she would look beautiful in rags and soot, with cobwebs in her hair.

'But you must promise me,' she had said, and so he had

agreed, and really he did not mind colluding in this little daily double act if that was what she wanted.

Now, at home, he had grown accustomed to waiting beneath the covers in the morning, listening to the tiny sounds of her removing the night cream and applying the day cream, and making sure her hair sat just so, and turning the door handle as slowly as an intruder might. She always lifted the hangers in the wardrobe rather than pushing them along the bar, and never needed to switch on any lights — she was as confident as a person born blind, placing her hands on the necessary items without hesitation. Now and then he allowed himself glimpses of her through flickering eyes — a rumpled nightgown, a face creased by the wrinkles on a pillow: little snatches of disarray. And though he would never have said as much to his wife, he loved her unkempt secret self, and wondered if he would ever be able to pull back the curtains one morning and just look at her.

She was wearing her silk kimono on this particular Sunday. Two birds of paradise covered her breasts, their tail feathers spilling down past her waist, their stitched eyes so dark it was impossible to tell what they were looking at. They faced each other across the opening of the robe, mirror images, although if you studied them closely you could find small differences: tiny mismatches that nobody else would notice. On the back of the robe was a snarling dragon but it was covered by her hair, the wavy lengths mostly concealing it, just a flicker visible every now and then.

'She'll be good for you,' his grandmother had said. 'She's a solid, sensible girl.'

'Is she?' said Peter.

'Well, she doesn't seem flighty, does she? Not the sort to go running off overseas on a whim. Not the sort to leave.'

'No,' said Peter. 'She's not.'

Helena sat opposite him as they ate their breakfast, looking neither solid nor sensible in her silk robe, and he was glad he had bought it for her as a surprise when they were on the ship.

'Oh, but it's much too nice!' she had said.

Every so often she reached across the table and touched his hand or his cheek as if checking that he was real. The steam from their cups rose and curled, forming question-marks between them, and they pursed their lips and blew these misty uncertainties away, then took quick little sips, making sure they would not burn themselves.

'Your nose has stopped peeling,' he said.

'Not my shoulders though,' she said.

'A little bit of colour suits you.'

'Remember how my sunshade blew overboard?'

'It flew out of your hand as if possessed.'

'Bobbing around on the waves like some beautiful anemone,' she said. 'I felt quite lost without it. Quite bare.'

'And that American man — remember? He said you don't go on a cruise to sit in the shade.'

'And he offered me his hat all the same.'

They smiled at the memory of that first day on the ship, although in truth they both had felt a little unsettled by the motion of the waves, and by the absence of anything on the horizon on which to focus. They had clung to each other, too shaky to walk alone.

'To have and to hold,' they had said, staggering down the corridors and across the decks, and they had giggled even as they had concentrated so hard on retaining their balance.

'You'll soon get used to it,' the American man had told them. 'My wife and I, we've been doing this for forty years, haven't we, Grace? And it feels just like home.'

After breakfast Peter washed the two apostle spoons and laid them back in their case. The following Sunday he would use the next two spoons, and then the next two the Sunday after that, so that none of them became more worn than the others.

'Which one am I?' he used to ask his grandmother. 'Which one is Peter?'

But they were all the same.

She was aware of his beauty, and never more so than when they were among other women. Conversations faltered, heads turned, eyes tracked him as he passed. There were nudges, whispers, half smiles. And then those same eyes shifted to her and there were fleeting frowns, and snaky glances that moved down her body, swallowing her, digesting the discrepancy between his attractiveness and her own. She remembered the first time she saw him, and how two thoughts had run side by side through her mind, parallel lines that would never touch: *he's beautiful* and *he could never love me*. And yet he had come and sat next to her in the garden, close enough for her to smell the clean, soapy scent of him, and to see the garnet tie-pin glinting at his throat like a red star. There had been starry lights caught in the trees, too, and when it had grown dark they had seemed suspended in the night about the edges of the lawn, defining the boundaries of that little universe. Other women had circled the two of them throughout the evening, advancing and receding in complex, watchful orbits, and he and she had not moved, had remained the only fixed points, the only place that was steady.

'He's very handsome, isn't he?' her mother had said after the engagement was announced, and Helena had known there was another half to that statement: the unspoken half that applied to her.

'Yes, I keep pinching myself.'

They had been sitting in front of the dressing table in her mother's bedroom, comparing samples of ivory silk and lace — little scraps they had brought home from the finest bridal salons. Her mother had held them one by one against the back of

Helena's hand; they had rested on her skin as lightly as moths.

'No,' she had kept saying. 'No, no . . . you're too pale for these.' She had sounded annoyed.

'Sorry,' Helena had said.

'You'll have to keep your eye on him,' her mother had said, smoothing a piece of beaded organza across her own collarbone and regarding her reflections in the dressing table's three mirrors, tilting the sides so she could see herself from different angles, see herself as others would. 'And on your friends. The career girls. That Annemarie, she always got all the boys, didn't she? You'll have to watch her. I know if I were thirty years younger, my girl!'

'I've asked Annemarie to be my bridesmaid.'

Her mother had let the fabric sample flutter to the carpet. 'Do you think that's wise?' She had asked the question to the mirrors, and there were three of her asking the same thing, and Helena had not known which one to answer. 'I don't want to bring up the school ball — the Tremewan boy — and the episode at the lake that year, of course . . . Well, she can't be unasked now, I suppose.' She had swept the silks and laces aside and said, 'We'll go back into town tomorrow. We want you looking presentable, don't we? The grandmother is still very beautiful, I understand, and so was the mother.'

Peter's grandmother had embraced her when they had met for the first time, taking her hands and kissing her on the cheek, then standing back to look at her.

'Well now,' she had said. 'So this is Helena. You're a welcome change, my dear. A breath of fresh air. But come in, come in; it's freezing out here.'

She had shown Helena old photographs of Peter, all arranged in albums and labelled with comments: *Look, no hands* and *Starting school* and *Off to first dance*.

'And that's enough of that,' she had said when the girlfriends had started to appear (*Louise on donkey*; *Louise as Ophelia*).

'Peter, will you come and help with the supper?'

Helena had waited until Peter and his grandmother were in the kitchen, then had taken up the album again, careful when turning the filmy protective layers between each page so that they did not crackle like a fire taking hold. There had been so many girls — lovely creatures in debutante gowns and ball dresses, slender little things with tiny waists and graceful necks. Helena had peered at the pictures in the fading light, trying to discern whether there were any who looked like her. The album had been heavy in her hands, so full of these slight girls, too heavy to hold any more, and she had put it back where it belonged.

'Here we are,' Peter's grandmother had said, placing a tiered cake-stand before her. 'You'll have some banana cake, won't you, dear? And some cream?'

'No thank you,' Helena had said. 'It looks lovely, but tea will be just fine.'

'Goodness, a healthy thing like you? What do young girls eat these days, Peter? How do they ever manage to have babies?'

'Gran, you promised,' Peter had said.

'Just a question,' she had said, patting Helena's knee.

Helena's unmarried friends — the career girls, her mother called them — had always congratulated themselves on their childlessness and called it freedom. They telephoned each other to say how unpleasant other people's children were, how rude, demanding, dirty, selfish. When visiting the homes of these people they picked their way across floors strewn with wooden trains and naked dolls, and they sat on the edges of couches that had been sponged to remove large stains; they eyed pungent bundles that were knotted and waiting heavy by the changing tables; they murmured kindnesses as the talk turned to cracked nipples and uncomfortable stitches.

'Just push those onto the floor,' the people with children would say as they sat down to dine at sticky tables, and they would sweep mounds of toys — eyeless bears, chewed rubber balls, headless dogs — to the swelling tide of casualties below. Vestiges of baby food sometimes smeared their sleeves and would still be visible after several laundry treatments.

'Imagine what's in there,' the career girls commented to one another. 'Imagine what that does to the digestive tract.'

One friend had phoned Helena to cancel a lunch date because she needed to take her son to the doctor.

'They had to drain his ear of pus,' Helena reported to the career girls. 'It looked like melted butter and smelled to high heaven. They had to throw his pillow away.'

They laughed and laughed.

Of course she and Peter had talked about the possibility of having their own children. They imagined it would be something to do in the future, like repapering the hallway; perhaps in ten years, which was so far away it did not seem real.

There had been one young family on the cruise, including four children, and at meal times the tables surrounding them were always the last to be taken. Since Peter and Helena had risen late in the mornings, they had ended up sitting next to them most days. The children had not seemed to like the food, often wanting things that were not available.

'We can't have that,' their parents had said. 'We're on a ship.'

'But I don't like this.'

'Well, that's all there is.'

'I want to go home. I miss Blackie.'

'I'm sure he's having a lovely holiday at Grandpa's.'

'I saw Grandpa kick him.'

'Of course you didn't.'

'I did. It was when Blackie licked his sandwich.'

'I'm sure it was just a little nudge in the tummy with his slipper.'

'No, it was a proper kick, like this.'

'Don't kick your brother, darling.'

One day the little girl had seen the poached eggs on Helena's plate and said, 'I want those ones. Mine are all runny.'

The mother had given Helena a tired smile and said, 'No they're not, they're perfect, look — nice and soft for you to spread on your toast.'

'Hers aren't all runny.'

'I'm sure they're just the same as yours, darling.'

'Are yours runny?' the girl had asked, coming over to Helena and peering at her plate.

'Darling, you're being rude,' the mother had said.

'They're — well, nice and soft,' Helena had said.

'But not runny?' the girl had asked again.

'I don't suppose I'd call them runny, no.'

'See?' the girl had said to her mother.

'Mine are a bit runny,' Peter had said. 'Yum yum.' He had smeared some egg on his toast and eaten it.

'Is he your brother?'

'He's my new husband.'

'Did you have an old one?'

'Darling,' the mother had said. 'Leave the nice people alone. They're in love.'

The girl had not eaten her eggs that morning, but had taken a bite each out of half a dozen different things — pancakes, fruit toast, croissants — before abandoning them on the edge of her plate. The father had kept going to the buffet table and returning with more items for her.

'Well, it doesn't matter, does it?' he had said to the mother. 'There's endless food. And we've already paid for it.'

After every meal the family's table had been covered with unfinished dishes — a nibble taken here, a taste there. And it was true that there had seemed to be an everlasting supply of food on the ship — great platters of glazed pastries, their berry centres shining like jewels; wedges of pale Edam and marbled Roquefort and viscous Brie; glistening mounds of caviar; exotic fruits cut open to display dark seeds and pearly seeds; handmade chocolates in the shape of shells and starfish and seahorses. Peter had kept bringing Helena little selections of treats, new delicacies for her to try.

'I'll never fit into my swimsuit,' she had said, but had eaten the delicious offerings anyway, plucking them from his fingers and letting the flavours fill her mouth with possibility, and they had made her feel different and rare.

For some days Peter had thought that Helena looked a little peaky — although she was as carefully groomed as ever, her eyes were dull and her skin had lost any colour gained on the cruise. He knew her sleep had been fitful over the last few nights, although whenever he had woken and asked if she was all right she had insisted nothing was the matter.

'What is it, my love?' he said at their next Sunday breakfast, and even as he spoke he felt there was someone else in the room, a silent guest at the table.

She fussed with her hair, smoothing back the little curls that always formed at her temples.

'Helena?'

'I was looking for some stamps yesterday,' she said, her knife scraping the thinnest smear of butter across her toast. She was back to being careful about her weight, he saw — careful not to let herself go, as his grandmother would say, which made him think of Helena embracing herself, arms encircling her own body and squeezing tight, holding herself in check.

'There should be some in my desk. I'll have a look after breakfast.'

'Yes, there are,' she said, still scraping her knife, the sound measured and deliberate. He remembered feeding her pralines and petits-fours on the ship, her careful little mouth licking his fingers.

'Oh — well, good then,' he said.

'I was going to send some photos to my mother. Of the cruise. She said she wanted some.'

'That's right,' he said. 'So she did.'

'I saw the picture in your desk.' There was a tiny dab of butter left on the tip of her knife, and she returned it to the dish.

'The picture?'

'The photograph. Of Louise.'

'They're in New York now,' he said. 'She opens at the Met next month — her first performance since they had the baby —'

'Why is she sending you pictures of herself?' she demanded. 'Dressed like that?' She was wearing the kimono again and she pulled it closer about herself, the two birds of paradise meeting across her breasts, each pecking at the other.

'We're friends,' he said. 'That's what friends do.'

'I don't send Annemarie pictures of myself in my underwear.'

'She's not wearing underwear,' he said.

The possible meanings of this statement eddied about them like dust, like something that catches in the eye.

'It's a gauzy nightgown,' she said. 'It has a definite whiff of the boudoir about it.'

'It's a costume. *La Traviata*? The death scene?' He sighed. 'This is a very ugly side of you, my darling.'

'I want you to stop writing to her,' she said, so quietly that he had to lean in to hear. 'I can't help it. I've tried to be reasonable and relaxed about her but I can't. I can't.'

Peter put down his tea and watched her. She smoothed her hair again.

'I'm not like Louise,' she went on. 'I don't stay in touch with old boyfriends. Do you ever hear me talk about old boyfriends?'

'No,' he said, still watching her, letting the toast go cold in its little chrome rack.

'I couldn't tell you what any of them are doing now. I don't know where they spent their holidays, or which films they've seen lately, or how their parents celebrated their golden wedding anniversary. None of that matters, you see?'

'Yes,' he nodded, and he did see, in her overcast eyes and her small sad hands, he did see the same uncertainty he had found so touching that night in the garden. 'All right.'

She looked up. 'All right?'

'I'll stop writing to Louise. No Christmas cards, no birthday wishes. No photographs.'

'Oh,' said Helena. 'Just like that?'

'Yes.'

'But —' She paused. 'Isn't that a little rude?'

'Probably.'

Then she said, 'I think I'm going — I think we're . . . it looks as if we're going to have a baby.'

She had known for three days — she had done a test at home and watched the two little blue lines appear, faint at first, like veins that lie just beneath the skin, and then darker and more definite, an equals sign, the sign that meant two separate elements were now combined. It must have been conceived on the ship, when they were in the middle of the ocean: in no country at all. She had wondered what form it might take, this tiny being swimming in the depths of her, this thing created at sea, and she had imagined fins, and glimmering scales, and big unblinking eyes. It would be nothing like her. She had cleared the test-kit box and the leaflet and the little blue lines away, returning everything to how it had been before, and then she had continued with her usual morning routine. When she had made herself presentable she had tiptoed back to the bed and leaned over Peter for a moment, taking in the sweet, warm smell of his skin, then kissing his hair and pulling the covers up around his chest. She had not wanted to disturb him, not yet.

Her doctor confirmed it for her. It was no bigger than a walnut, he said, and he showed her a model of what it would look like. It was cool and smooth, this model baby, snug in its satiny bed, fitted inside its model mother like a spoon in a box.

'It'll hurt, won't it?' she said.

The doctor smiled. 'You're young,' he said. 'This is the best time for it to happen, as far as your body is concerned.'

After the appointment she sat in the car staring at herself in the rear-view mirror, wondering if she appeared any different. Other drivers sidled up to her and mouthed *Are you going? Are you leaving? Are you finished?* She did not know, and so she waved them on, and she knew she would be late for her lunch date with Annemarie, and Annemarie was always reminding her how she could take only half an hour at the very most.

She decided she would tell Peter at their Sunday breakfast, when everything else was perfect. She would make an occasion of it, and they would remember it forever, and tell the baby about it, and it would become one of their special family stories. She would crochet a bonnet or a pair of bootees from the skeins of silk Peter's grandmother had given her. Then she would wrap the little garment in tissue and leave it — where? On his breakfast plate, perhaps, or tucked into one of the china teacups he so loved using, and he would see it and look up at her with that puzzled smile that made her insides tremble.

She took out the crochet silk and her old book of patterns and decided on a lacy bonnet. It reminded her of the sunshade she had lost overboard, and she remembered watching it fly from her, a spore caught by the wind; it had moved so quickly that she had only just begun to snatch at it when it was already gone. The book said the bonnet should take five hours to complete — plenty of time to have it ready for Sunday, and a useful distraction from the queasiness that seemed to be with her constantly, not just in the mornings; it was as bad as the first day on the cruise.

When she began, however, she found that the thread kept slipping, and the hook kept falling out, and her work was all uneven, and sometimes when she thought she was making a secure knot it did not hold at all, but unravelled to nothing in her hands. The tension was all wrong. She studied the instructions, trying to trace her finger around the drawings of the different stitches, but she kept getting lost and finding herself back at the beginning. She felt sick, and she had to catch up with the career girls that afternoon, and write to her mother, and finish putting away the wedding presents, and all she wanted to do was sleep.

By Sunday morning the bonnet was a tangle in her bottom drawer, a scribbled-out mistake, and she felt so ill she could hardly bear the smell of the toast. She managed to eat one piece, and then — she did not know why; it was as if a sudden gust snatched the words from her — she began talking about Louise, and the photograph she had seen in Peter's desk. She had refused to let it bother her at the time: he had not married Louise, nor any of the other girls in his grandmother's album. And yet, there Helena sat, the jealousy spewing from her, and she hated herself for it. The news about the baby had not come out right either; she had not wanted to deliver it in such a way, on the coat-tails of the talk about Louise. Peter was silent on the other side of the table, and now it seemed she had made the announcement simply because he had agreed to break contact with Louise; it was as if the baby only existed because of his decision, and if he had not agreed to end the friendship, Louise would somehow have taken the place of the child in their lives, jostled it out of being with her chatty letters and her pictures. Helena stared at the table, picking a few toast crumbs from the cloth, straightening the skewed lid on the jam-pot.

And when she did look up, Peter was smiling at her, laughing, rising from his chair and embracing her, nuzzling his smooth-shaven face into her neck. And then he was crouching beside her and placing his ear to her stomach and saying, 'Shhhhh.'

'What can you hear?' she asked after a moment or two.

He closed his eyes. 'The sea,' he said.

A Bad Idea

AT THE EDGE OF THE ROAD

— James George

Something's happened to me — something bad. And I don't know what to do about it. I don't see any way out for the life of me. The worst of it is, I can't get this thing into focus — if you know what I mean. I just feel in a muddle — in the hell of a muddle. It ought to be plain to anyone that I'm not the kind of man to get mixed up in a thing like this.

Deal is, few weeks ago, everything's sweet as. Rico's had his ups and downs, sure, but he's a good kid, as fifteen-year-olds go. And the trucking business is just getting by. Then one day I'm home for a couple of hours, as the truck had to go into the auto sparky's to fix the onboard computer. Soon I'd be off to Wellington with a trailer-load of new tyres. I hear Rico walk down the path to the outside entrance to his room off the garage. I expect to hear him clatter around inside any sec, but there's just a curse and the sound of jangling. Another curse. Doofus. I decide to freak him out, so I creep through his room from this side, stand at the door, hand on the handle. The keys jangle again and I pull the door open. He almost craps himself.

Keys and a takeaways bag go everywhere. There's burger sauce all over his arm, a seeded bun rolls on the path. I stand there laughing, but it dries up when I see the other bag under his arm. Nah, not a bag. A purse, a woman's purse.

I nod at it.

'And?' I say.

'What?'

'What? Shit. Who does it belong to?'

He tries to hide it behind him, like I'm doddery or something.

'What are you doing home?' he says. 'Where's the truck?'

'Never mind that.'

I grab the purse off him, stand there, a drum solo starting inside me. He pokes around in the paper bag and then raises a finger to his lips.

'I found it,' he says.

I nod for him to come in. He sits on his bed, looking down at the floor.

'You gonna go off like a volcano?' he says.

'No. Just tell me the truth. Don't add lying to your Dad to anything else.'

'Stepdad.'

'Yeah. Whatever.' I look at the purse. 'Don't make me find the answers in here.'

But he doesn't say a word, not a bloody word.

Like I said, everything was going sweet as . . .

Hell.

Who am I kidding?

Business is going crap, and I'm going to the wall. Diesel prices have shot through the roof and the black ink on my statements has turned red. The outfits with several trucks can survive, but it's one-truck guys like me that can't. I'm not paying bills and the bank's on my arse. Home mortgage, repayments on the rig . . .

'Rico,' I say. 'Just tell me the truth.'

He stands, goes to push past me. I stop him with a hand on his arm.

'So *now* you wanna talk?' he says, and he spits out 'now' like it's something sharp. 'Every other time you're too busy.'

I let him go, listen to his footsteps up the hall.

I don't want to but I open the purse. Soft leather, expensive. There's a compact with a little mirror, a wallet with some ID cards (library, DVD rental, AA). No ATM or credit cards. A driver's licence in a little window. She looks stunned in the photo, like the photographer sneaked up on her. Red hair, a hint of grey coming. It was issued only last year, so she probably hasn't changed much. Except for the smoke coming out of her ears as she sits now on the phone to the cops, telling them some tosser's legged it with her purse.

Since Ceal left — left me with Rico — we've got by, sort of. He's got in minor scrapes. Tagging, running with wannabe gangstas, but we've worked through it. But now I'm holding some woman's purse in my hands.

There's a little pouch in fancy material. A little black pencil with a cap, lipstick, a bottle of pills that rattles when I lift it up. Her name's on it, a chemist's label. Migraine pills, like Ceal used to take. A diary in a brown leather holder. I open it. On the inside of the first page is her address.

Maybe it's his first. Yeah. Maybe Rico's never pulled shit like this before. Maybe I could just stick it in the post to her, she'd be none the wiser.

Or maybe it's time I searched this room.

He sits at the kitchen table, starts munching on a bowl of cornflakes.

'Where did you get it?' I say.

'In the park.'

'Be more specific.'

'From a car. In the park.'

'And you got in — how?'

'Whatever.'

'That's not an answer.'

'Who cares?'

I drop the photo licence down on the tabletop.

'She does,' I say.

'Who's she?'

'The lady you stole from.'

He shrugs. I lean over the table, almost over his face.

'Say it.'

'What?' he says.

'The lady you stole from.'

He sits back, wipes his mouth.

'Why?' he says, his voice quieter.

I whack my hand on the table. The licence and the woman's face jump, skew across the formica top and clack against the floor tiles.

'Say it!'

'Fuck you.'

I close my eyes. Hear him crunching on another mouthful of cereal. I open my eyes and lash out, send the spoon flying across the room to clang against a cupboard door.

He stands, opens the front door and slams it as he leaves. In his bowl the milk rocks from side to side, then settles.

When I first met Ceal she was taking dancing lessons, after she'd knocked off from her checkout job in the supermarket. First she went once a week, then twice, and more. It wasn't until our third date that she told me about Rico, scared — she said — that if she came right out with it she wouldn't see me for dust. I felt kind of put out. I'm cool, I said, and I was, but part of me was on edge. A kid. He wasn't even hers, not really. His old man — her ex — had buggered off and lumbered her with him. She never said much about it. First time I met Rico was when I picked them up in my Toyota, took them to the park. He stood with her in the kitchen.

'Rico,' said Ceal, 'this is Sonny.'

'Hi, Rico,' I said, and held out my hand to shake. He looked at it.

'Rico?' said Ceal.

'Hey,' he said, and reached for his skateboard.

In the park Ceal laid out the blanket and basket and tubs of potato salad and boiled eggs. Rico sipped from his juice, looked away into the trees. It didn't bother me. My old man had buggered off too, and I guess I sort of carried his face somewhere in me, seeing him going off just temporary like, trying to get things together before coming back for us. Coming back for me. Sure, my folks used to argue a bit, but who doesn't? And that was them, their hassle, not me. I was the kid he used to take to the footy, to the car racing at Pukekohe. All that meant something, didn't it? He'd come back.

He didn't.

After we'd eaten our picnic I grabbed an old Frisbee out of the boot and gestured for Rico to come with me. He sat for a while, then shrugged and stood and wiped his hands on his jeans. I sent the Frisbee over real soft and he fluffed the catch. It sat in the grass. He stared at it, kicked at it with his toes.

'Have a go,' I said.

He picked it up and sent it spinning, straight as, till it veered away at the last second and I had to leg it, dive headlong. I caught it in my fingertips, just before my chin hit the dirt. He stood laughing. I laughed too, got up and dusted myself off. Spat out a couple of grass stems.

'Yeah,' I said, 'but I got it.'

He shrugged.

'Whatever,' he said.

He caught the next one and the next. He caught more than I did, and his arm was pretty true, too. I only had to lunge a couple of times. After a while he began to smile when he was watching the Frisbee fly towards him. Like for once he wasn't expecting it to turn bad. When we were packing to go, Ceal squeezed my arm.

'Thank you,' she said.

I nodded.

Turned out she wasn't taking dance classes four nights a week. The classes were just Mondays. She'd found a sideline — belly dancing done up in full Ali Baba rig, for sad tossers who sat on couches staring at her.

'I don't let them touch,' she said when I confronted her, after I'd seen her go into some geezer's house.

'And that matters?' I said.

She stared at me and I wished I could've taken that back. Of course it mattered. When her bloke had skipped he'd taken everything with him except for the debts. She was dancing on the edge of having her house repossessed, getting biffed out. Rico was all skittery, jagged with the vibe. Except for those moments when we threw the Frisbee. Those moments were free, couldn't be repossessed.

'She's always on my case,' he said to me once, as we were walking out onto the grass to throw. 'She's not even my real mum. She's just a hassle.'

'No she's not,' I said. 'She's *got* hassles, that's all.'

'So have I.'

'I know. But she's busting herself to keep you safe.'

'I don't wanna talk about it.'

So we just threw and caught. And that smile beamed like the path of the Frisbee in flight. Free and strong and without strings.

Jobs were plentiful then. Auckland to Wellington four times a week, maybe a couple of times a fortnight all the way to Christchurch. Five hundred and fifty horsepower down over the Canterbury Plains, often in skies so dark there were no lights other than my headlights for half-hour stretches.

'Don't do the belly dancing any more,' I said to Ceal.

We were sitting in my car. It was a chilly day. She reached out and flipped on the heater.

'I need the money,' she said.

'I know. Can't we solve this together?'

She took a long breath.

'Couple of years ago,' she said, 'I was working for this guy. As his PA. I was handling a lot of cash for him.'

'What line was he in?'

'Doesn't matter. After a while I began to divert some of the cash.'

'Divert it. Where?'

'Where do you think?'

I turned the heater up a bit.

'When he found out he said he wouldn't dob me in. I could just hand in my resignation and walk away, if I paid him back.'

'Okay.'

'And a little extra.'

A couple of hours after Rico ran out and slammed the door, I see him out in the street. He pauses at the letterbox, looks at the house like it's a stranger's place. He stands there for a long time. He watches me walk towards him, one of his legs all twitchy, foot pointed back down the road. I go right up to him and put my hand on his shoulder.

'Come inside,' I say. 'Let's talk.'

'You talk?'

'And you.'

When he's in bed I have a go at a note to go with the purse I'm gonna send back.

Hi there,

I found this dumped in the park. Your diary has your name and

address on it, so here it is, back to you.
Nah.

Hi,
You don't know me. I found this and

Why not just send it, no name?

I retrieve her driver's licence from the floor, wipe some dust off it and look at those greying roots among her dyed red hair. Those licence photos are like laser beams to everything that looks crappy about us.

Screw it. I just close the clasp and reach for the postie bag.

On the table next to it is the latest letter from the bank. Final demand. Truck and house. We're on the way out and there's nothing I can do.

I open the bag one last time, make sure there's nothing that can lead back to us. It has a hundred pockets and in one of them are three Lotto tickets. I take them out. Different dates, like she hasn't got around to checking them. I glance at the pile of letters from the bank. I go to put the tickets away again, but I don't.

Wouldn't hurt just to check. Would it?

I put the purse in the postie envelope but don't seal it. Not yet.

I head south to Wellington. The Lotto tickets have worked their way into my satchel. You get a lot of space to think, out on the road. On the straight stretches when towns or farmhouse lights blink like sleepy cats in the distance. On the Desert Road the mountains rise beneath a Frisbee moon seeming to spin in and out of the clouds. Signposts come and go, road markers, other trucks.

In Wellington I offload, head away to find some tucker and a quiet possie to snooze before I have to reload and head north again.

The Superette sign winks. I'm thinking couple of pies and a takeaway coffee. The tickets work their way into the Lotto gizmo and the dude hits the button.

Not a winning ticket.

Not a winning ticket.

Winner.

Oh, cool.

I reach out for the cash but the guy shakes his head. The next bit's a blur. The rest of the day's a blur.

By Hamilton I'm telling myself you can rationalise away anything.

At home the purse still sits in the postie envelope amid the bills, all of which can be just small change now. I look at that photo again. That hair dye's probably expensive — salon job. She has a fancy necklace on and those earrings cost a bloke like me a week's wages. And and and . . .

I sit staring at the purse.

'Bugger this.'

I jump in my car. Her street isn't far away. I eye each letterbox, counting, then roll to a stop across the road. Ordinary-looking house, not falling down, not a mansion. I sit there for a long time until a car slows and eases into the drive. She gets out and goes to the boot and lifts out of couple of shopping bags and closes the boot. But one drops. An orange rolls out, winds its way down the sloping drive to the footpath and out into the gutter. She puts the other bag down, goes down to the kerb and looks after the orange, gathering speed now where the road steepens. I hunker down a bit in the seat. She puts her hands on her hips, then slaps one against her thigh and walks back up to her car.

'Hi,' I say in the silence. 'Here's your purse back. I kept your half a million dollars, though. You know how it is. Have a nice life.'

I pull out, head back home.

Rico sits at the table. I pull up another chair.

'I'm gonna send that bag back to its owner,' I say.

'Okay.'

'The next time you've got crap going on in your head or you're thinking of doing something dumb, come to me.'

He stares.

'Got it?' I say, harsher than I mean to.

He shies back a bit.

'Rico,' I say, softer. 'Whatever it is, we can do it together.'

He nods.

I lie awake most of the night. I don't mind the dark of country highways, but this dark has shadows that lean over me. I sit up, go and run the cold tap over my face.

I take the purse and drive over to her house again and sit in the dark. At dawn a light comes on, then another. I'm still there when she closes her front door and walks with a briefcase and a travel bag, her car keys in her mouth. She pulls out of the driveway. I lie down in the seat, sit up when she's gone. Her indicator blinks for a moment, then she turns right at the intersection.

The purse still sits on the passenger seat when I ease back into my place.

One day when I came home Ceal was sitting staring out the window. I put my keys and logbook down on the table. She'd had to sell her place and move in with me. We did okay. Spat tacks now and then, smooched and made up. The fights were always about the belly dancing. If I brought it up she'd just cut me off with a slice of her hand through the air.

'Let me go and visit the bastard,' I said. 'Paying off the debt's one thing, but this is blackmail.'

'No.'

'Look, Ceal—'

'No. Stay out of it, Sonny. It's not your business.'

'I think it is.'

'No. It's not.'

'You're a bloody stripper!'

'So? So? Does that offend your delicate sensibilities? Looking down your nose at me, are you?'

'No. That's bullshit.'

'Is it?'

'Yeah. And you know it.'

'You'd rather I was in prison?'

'It wouldn't come to that.'

'You're a legal expert now?'

'No. Look, we could hire a decent lawyer. What he's doing is wrong.'

'Is that what's really bothering you? Deep down?'

'Yeah.'

'You sure?'

I stood with my mouth hanging open. She reached out and pushed me.

'Are you sure?' she shouted.

'Is that *all* you're doing?' I said. 'Stripping? Is it?'

She half sat, half fell into a chair, took her head into her hands.

'Is that what you think?' she said.

I raised my hands and my breath held, like a ball on a cliff face. Like that orange the woman dropped, before it went rolling, rolling away down the hill.

Ceal stood and slapped me across the face and stormed over to the front door and out.

I take a load down to Wellington and sit on the sand at Oriental Bay. Waves roll in, one after another. A grey sun rises. There's only a light dusting of traffic. I get into the truck's sleeper and doss down for a couple of hours and that orange rolls in my dreams, stuck flat to that road, through the dead leaves and chewing gum and cigarette butts and dog shit in the gutter. All the stuff that gets left at the edge of the road.

I've brought the purse with me. I look at her photo again. Guess she'd be about Ceal's age. And I wonder about Ceal, about where she is, how's she's going. I gave up after I'd called the only numbers I knew. The supermarket, the dance school. They hadn't seen her. I never met any of her family, and she never told me anything I could pin down about this creep who'd used her. She still sends stuff — cheques to look after Rico. I deposit them and stand at the teller's window waiting for the receipt, look down at the slip of paper. They ain't much of a trade. A piece of paper for her. For what we could've had.

On the third day after she'd gone I had to sit down with Rico, stop bullshitting about 'Hey, buddy, she's just had to head away to some family thing, be back soon.'

I told him I had no idea where she was, or when she'd be coming home. He turned and looked at the floor, then out the window.

'Everybody goes,' he said.

'Not me.'

'You will.'

I tried to hold him, but he wriggled free and walked out the door.

The weeks went by. I had my sister, Grace, come over to mind him when I was away trucking and she said he just sat watching TV or lay on his bed. She had three kids, two of them boys. Me, I was still fumbling, trying to put a damned jigsaw together that'd had the most important pieces ripped out by that wanker Ceal had worked for, who made her do that stuff. After a while his face faded and my face worked its chumpy way into the frame instead. The face that had shown disgust I told myself I didn't have, as if my disgust mattered one tiny sandgrain against all that was stacked up against her.

On my darker nights on the road I could see my foot pushing her out the door.

I get back home. Music pumps from Rico's room. I knock, stick my head around the door. He looks up from his Gameboy, flicks the pause switch.

'I'm sorry about Ceal,' I say.

'Eh?'

'I'm sorry.'

'What'd you do?'

'Not as much as I should've.'

He turns his chair to face me.

'You've lost me,' he says.

'Never mind.'

The next day I go back to the woman's house. I put the purse under my arm and walk up the footpath. A dog raises its nose at me; a kid stops her trampolining to stare. An old codger looks up from watering his garden. Yeah, you all look, I think, as my footsteps slow and my legs soften. I go to her letterbox and reach out with the purse but before I think straight I'm up her driveway and past her parked car and onto her steps, still carrying it. I press the doorbell.

She opens the door and stands there in old jeans and a faded denim shirt. She has a scarf over her head, a rag in one hand. No words come out of my mouth. I blink a couple of times, then raise her purse and her face brightens.

'Hi,' I say. 'I'm Sonny. I found this. Your name was in the diary.'

'Oh, great. Thanks.'

My voice is like the robot from *Lost in Space*. Loosen up.

'Kids, probably,' I say. 'Rifled through, it then just biffed it when there was no cash.'

'Yeah. I take my valuables with me when I walk. Where did you find it?'

'Under some trees.'

She opens it up, looks through. Suddenly her things seem so much more personal, with her fingertips on them. She opens the clasp to her compact and touches the eyeliner pencil and the little mirror. The purse now has a woman's smell again and I just let it wash over me. She looks in each pocket, then up at me.

Neither of us speaks, then I see her hesitate and her face blanks. The lines at the edges of her eyes grow and she fades back into the doorway just a couple of inches. Her eyes try not to lie but I sense it.

'Were you expecting —' she starts to say but I cut her off.

'Well, I'll leave you to it,' I say.

I step out into the wind, but still keep looking back at her.

'Thanks,' she says. 'Thank you so much.'

I go down the stairs, look once more as her door closes and my bones feel each step as if I'm suddenly the weight of my truck. There, in that second before I started to move away, her posture. Were you expecting a reward? I hear her say, and I see myself in her eyes. Number two buzzcut, biker beard. Tatts on my arms. T-shirt and jeans and workingman's boots.

I get in my car and sit looking at nothing, then bang my hand against the top of the dashboard. People judge you by the way you look.

Arseholes.

Yeah, but you kept her Lotto winnings, man.

The next week I knock on Rico's door.

'School holidays next week,' I say.

'Uh, yeah, Sonny. I know.'

'No, smartarse, I mean you and me, we're heading away.'

'Eh? Where?'

'Down south. Fishing, jetboating, maybe try and impersonate skiers.'

'Bungy jumping?'

'You, maybe.'

He laughs. We fly to Wellington, then Queenstown. The jetboat sends a scythe of white water out over the riverside rocks. Rico tries snowboarding while I sit in the bar, watching.

The next week I get tradesmen in. The bathroom gets wasted, complete new fit-out: shower box, new basin and fittings, cabinets, electric towel rail. Italian tiles on the wall. Next is the laundry. The shine of new paint and tubs almost blinds me. I sit in the evenings, looking at brochures for carpet.

I can't go back to her house, that's for sure, so I follow her, hanging way back. She takes her briefcase and travel bag and drives across town and parks and goes from door to door, selling. The wind blows her hair all tortured-willowish but she keeps knocking. Rain darkens her coat but she keeps knocking. A dog snarls at her but she keeps knocking. On the second day the heel of one of her boots comes loose and she almost topples, steadying herself with a hand on the jagged stones of a rock wall. She raises her hand and tries to shake the pain away and I'm halfway out the door before I realise how smart that would be.

Hi there. I'll be your stalker for today.

I get back in. She opens her car's boot and lifts out a pair of shoes and so help me I want to run my hands over the burning soles of her feet, maybe lighten the ache a little bit. She puts them on, goes back to her door knocking.

The next day I follow her to the supermarket and this time I get out. Inside, I see her a couple of times, then walk past her aisle and mooch over by the egg rack.

'Hi.'

I turn, see her with her basket and my face goes all surprised.

'I thought it was you,' she says, and hesitates, and I'm about to reply when she says, 'Sonny.'

'Yeah. Hi, Claire.'

She seems surprised for a sec that I know her name.

'Do you live around here?' she says.

'Yeah. Waimarama Street.'

'I know it. I've had a few orders from there.'

'Orders?'

'I sell. Sometimes.'

'Business good?'

She looks into her basket. Macaroni, couple of frozen pizzas.

'No,' she says. 'Well, it could be better.'

'Yeah, me too. I'm in haulage. Times are getting tough.'

'You're telling me. No one wants to spend!'

Her hair is still wind wild and she reaches up to straighten it and there are rings of sweat under her arms even though it's been chilly all day. Her toes flex in her open shoes.

'Sometimes I swear I almost creak,' she says, and in that moment I want to tell Ceal that I'm sorry, that sometimes shit happens inside us and we can't help it and that it never mattered, not really.

I dismiss all that, smile.

'There's a pretty decent café next door,' I say.

'I could murder a flat white.'

I carry her shopping bags and sit them next to the table. She stands and excuses herself and when she comes back her hair's straighter and her lipstick's solid again and her lashes are darker but she makes no show of any of it, and I guess then that none of that's for me and for some reason that's warmer in me than the coffee. She raises her eyebrows at my dumb smile.

'What?' she says.

'Nothing.'

I lie awake in bed again. Seems I can only get some real zzzzs in my truck's sleeper. Next day I nod off on a weighbridge south of Tokoroa until an airhorn from a Kenworth wakes me.

I sort the crap out with the bank but still my bed's full of nails. In the back of my eyes I see her leaning against the boot of her car, rubbing her tired feet, I see those sweat rings. I blink them away, go buy Rico a new Gameboy, this one without a piece of masking tape holding the joystick together.

'When does your next term end?' I say.

'Why?'

'How does the Gold Coast sound?'

'Wow!'

I can't park on any street she's walking and knocking, so I head for the park a couple of times, check out what time her car's sitting there. She sits under a tree with her laptop computer, her reading glasses perched on her nose. A pen in one hand, bunch of printouts at her feet, held down by her backpack.

I head home, grab Rico.

'Let's go throwing,' I say.

'Okay.'

We head back up there. Her car's still parked. If Rico recognises it among the others he says nothing. We spend an hour tossing and catching and the sun peers through the clouds, prising them open, so we're in bright light.

'Hi, Sonny.'

She stops next to her car, her laptop bag over her shoulder. I give a sigh of relief she isn't carrying that purse. Rico stands with the Frisbee in his hand.

'This is my stepson, Rico,' I say.

'Oh, hi. I'm Claire.'

He nods, raises his hand in a wave. I help her to stow her gear in. She steps back, smiles.

'I was hoping to run into you somewhere,' she says.

'Oh.'

She reaches into a little plastic holder stuck to her car's dash, hands me a business card.

'Give me a call sometime,' she says. 'Could always murder a flat white.'

'Yeah,' I say, 'that'd be cool.'

She pulls away.

We toss the Frisbee for a little while longer, then head towards home. I pull up at a pedestrian crossing where an old woman limps across the zebra stripes, dressed in a heavy coat against the coming twilight.

'When are you going to tell her about the Lotto tickets, Sonny?' says Rico.

I close my eyes.

'Eh?'

'Trip to Queenstown, next the Gold Coast. Guys in to do up the place. All of a sudden.'

'What are you on about?'

'You think I didn't look in the bag? When I swiped it? You think I didn't look in it again when you had it sitting in that envelope, which you never sent? You think I didn't recognise her car? So when are you going to tell her?'

Shit.

Shit.

Shit.

'So when are you gonna tell her?'

'Look, I—'

'When, Sonny? You gonna wait till you're fucking her?'

I turn, slap him across the face. He bounces against the passenger door, stares back at me for a second, then opens it and gets out. Cars behind beep for me to move on over the crossing. I pull up onto the kerb.

'Rico.'

He keeps walking.

'Rico!'

He doesn't show before I head to Wellington. Back in Auckland the next day I head to his school but he never showed there either. I sit at home, wait for him to come in. When he does I'm at the table, nursing a cooling cuppa between my palms. He goes right past, then turns and comes back.

'All the lectures you've given me,' he says, 'about being straight up. Being a man. What were they?'

'They were the truth, Rico.'

'Yeah.'

'Yes, they were.'

'And what you do, doesn't that mean anything?'

I take a sip of the coffee, tastes like barbecue ashes.

'Sometimes we do things,' I say, 'without thinking. But it's much harder to come back, to put things right, than we imagine.'

'You could just pick up the phone.'

'It's not that easy.'

He lifts the receiver off the console and puts it on the table.

'Yes it is,' he says.

'That's not what I mean and you know it.'

'Why didn't you go looking for Ceal?'

'Eh?'

'Why didn't you?'

'I did. As much as I could. How the hell did we get on to this?'

'You didn't want to find her, did you? You didn't want her to come back.'

'Yes — you needed her. That's a stupid thing to say.'

'No. Not me. You, I'm talking about you. *You* didn't want her back.'

He tries to push the phone into my hand.

'You think I'm deaf too?' he says. 'That I never heard what you and Ceal were arguing about, before she left?'

'That's ancient history.'

'Is it? Call that woman and tell her.'

'Rico.'

'Call her now!'

Claire's business card sits in the little glass bowl with my truck keys. He picks it up.

'I thought about doing it myself last night,' he says. 'But no, I want to hear *you* say it to her. The lady you stole from.'

He pushes the phone at me again and a spark goes off inside me and the inside of my eyes go all white and jerky and I grab the receiver and throw it against the wall. It smashes into tiny pieces. Rico goes to the console unit and begins to dial and I stand and yank the phone out of the wall, drop it and step on it, and he heads for my bedroom, where there's another phone, and I follow him, trip him up. He topples, crashes to the floor. The card goes flying.

'Fucking kid!' I say. 'You'd think you'd be grateful. You know all the stuff I've done for you? You know how much I've shelled out?'

'Well, now you can afford anything.'

He tries to stand but I see my foot reach out, push him sideways against the wall. I can't stop it. In my skittery eyes I see oranges roll through dead leaves, I see Frisbees fall from the air like shot ducks. I see Ceal's face all torn up from the inside before she walked towards that door. I look down at Rico where he has raised himself to a sitting position and looks up at me, breathing in ragged gasps. His nose and lips are bloody and he's holding his chest. I squeeze my right fist into a slab of concrete. He looks at it and a crooked smile crosses his face and I step forward and lift him up with my left hand, a scrunch of his sweatshirt in my fingers and I raise my right hand and smash it against the hallway wall. Once, twice. I pull him towards me, pain rifling through me. I touch his back with my busted right and blood seeps down, drips onto the floor beneath us.

'Why?' he says. 'Why, Dad. Why?'

We get stitched in the emergency room, then I head off south in the truck. My bandaged hand hurts, feels all rubbery against the steering wheel. On a stretch of highway in the middle of nowhere I call home on my cellphone. He picks up, but doesn't answer.

'Hey,' I say.

Silence, then at last, 'Yeah.'

More silence, each second a knife.

'They asked at the hospital what happened. I told them I tripped, if that's what you called for.'

'It isn't.'

I pull over.

'I don't know what to say to you, Rico.'

There's nothing but dark beyond the truck's headlight beams.

'About any of it,' I say.

'When are you going to tell her?' he says, but I'm too tired to answer, to find answers I don't have. I tell him I have to go.

'Everybody goes,' he says.

'But I'm coming back.'

As I roll into Wellington the sun's rising and there are patches of pink sky amid the grey. I pull over and sit, dial the number I've memorised from the card.

'Hello, Claire speaking.'

'Hey, Claire, it's Sonny.'

'Oh, hi.' I can hear her yawn. 'How are you?'

'Good, good. Well, a bit tired. Listen, Claire . . .'

A Man and His Dog

THE PORTFOLIO

— Carl Nixon

I.

To look at Mr. Potts one would have thought that there at least went someone who had nothing to boast about. He was a little, insignificant fellow with a crooked tie, a hat too small for him and a coat too large. The brown canvas portfolio that he carried to and from the Post Office every day was not like a business man's portfolio. It was like a child's school satchel; it did up even with a round-eyed button. One imagined there were crumbs and an apple core inside.

In addition, Mr. Potts had been born with a face so plain and common in its particulars that it was almost immediately forgotten by all who met him for the first time. Somehow, though, through some quirk of temperament perhaps or childhood circumstance, Mr. Potts' shortcomings in matters of taste and appearance had done nothing whatsoever to dint his overwhelming self-belief.

Mr. Potts had spent his entire working life employed by the Post Office Service. His first twelve years were spent at the Sydenham branch; his next eight at the small brick building in St Martins. For the last five years he had journeyed each working day to the middle of the city to the impressive central branch with its clock tower in the heart of the city Square, opposite the cathedral. He made the journey travelling first by tram — the stop was almost directly outside his gate — and then walking some three hundred yards to the marble columns of the post office. Despite a long and unblemished record of service, at the age of forty-three Mr. Potts was still perennially overlooked for promotion and had not risen beyond the role of head clerk. That is to say, Mr. Potts was in charge of the central branch's front counter, with its glass partitions, two tills and brass bell, to be rung by a customer requiring service in the unlikely event that neither of the two counter staff were in attendance.

It was from this counter that stamps were sold to the public and brown paper packages tied with fraying twine carefully weighed. Also, a good deal of money passed over that marble counter. At the end of the working week men brought in brown envelopes fat with wages, to deposit a lesser or greater amount into their savings accounts. The front staff also dealt with telegrams and cashed money orders. The position of head clerk was, therefore, not without gravity or responsibility. It was, however, generally acknowledged that head clerk was traditionally a temporary role: a stepping stone up to the corridors of the third floor, where senior management had their offices. Yet, after a full five years in this role, Mr. Potts seemed to be stuck down below on the ground floor. He was like a poorly addressed letter, which could go neither forward to its intended recipient nor back to the person by whom it had been written.

It was a reflection of Mr. Potts' natural disposition that even his lack of advancement within the considerable bureaucracy of the Post Office in no way seemed to cause him any despondency. It was clearly enough for him that when sequestered behind the front counter of the central branch he was king of all that he surveyed, albeit a somewhat myopic ruler.

Two people had what they believed to be the supreme misfortune of spending their days working directly under Mr. Potts. Mr. Brakeman was referred to by everybody who worked at the central branch as 'Young Mr. Brakeman'. The epithet 'Young' served to distinguish him from Mr. Brakeman in sorting, who, it transpired, was some type of third cousin on his father's side. Young Mr. Brakeman was twenty-two, unmarried, close to handsome in a gangly, long-limbed way, and as fashionable a dresser as could be managed on a clerk's wages. He viewed the front desk as a launching pad into the upper echelons of management. 'But I don't want to get stuck in the postal service. I'll most likely move into some other government department, possibly foreign affairs.' He made this announcement very shortly after taking up the position of clerk.

'Yes, I'm sure you will,' agreed Miss Osmond, who spent her working days at the till immediately on Young Mr. Brakeman's right. Her long delicate fingers fluttered over the pages of brightly coloured stamps as she cast curious glances at her new colleague. She herself had no thoughts of advancement. She was twenty-three and inclined to be shy around people she did not know well. As Miss Osmond's mother reminded her most days over a breakfast of toast and strong milkless tea, she did not want to be left on the shelf after all the other girls were married. It was clear from her mother's tone that each passing day brought that dreaded possibility ever closer. 'Neither of us,' her mother would sometimes add as she saw Miss Osmond off at the front gate, 'are getting any younger.'

Both Young Mr. Brakeman and Miss Osmond found the

days working under Mr. Potts' supervision long and trying. 'To perform a task well is the quickest path to success. Just look at me.' If Mr. Potts uttered these words only once a day they considered themselves lucky.

'Yes,' Young Mr. Brakeman would say quietly, or sometimes, 'I agree.' Miss Osmond would murmur in the affirmative. Really, though, Mr. Potts' pronouncements required no direct response. It was clear that to Mr. Potts his words were as gentle rain sent down upon young flowers. During the course of any given working day he would often emerge from the small office where he had his desk and take up with some earlier lengthy point that he had been making an hour before. Sometimes it seemed as if he began mid-sentence where he had left off. His subjects were many and diverse: plucked from that day's *Press*, which he purchased every morning on his walk to work and kept neatly folded in his ridiculous satchel, or lifted from his own experience.

Although Mr. Potts had never travelled further than a few hours by train in any direction from the city — the same city where he had been born, married, and still lived — he considered himself a man of the world and deeply knowledgeable in all the world's affairs. And it was certainly true that Mr. Potts could talk at length on matters both local and international, exhibiting all the detail and breadth of knowledge of those far more directly involved. There wasn't an issue of public importance on which Mr. Potts did not have a lengthy opinion, or a figure of prominence in any field to whom Mr. Potts did either align himself or categorically distance himself from.

Mr. Potts could only be diverted from these instructional monologues by two things. Firstly by the entrance of a paying customer: he rightly considered it unprofessional to continue talking while Young Mr. Brakeman or Miss Osmond were attending to the needs of the public. His train of thought was also broken when he happened to observe an unfortunate error in the way one of his young charges was performing a task. This occurred remarkably often. Mr. Potts was in fact constantly amazed by the way young people these days could not instinctively grasp the most efficient or judicious way of going about even minor duties. When he saw such an infelicitous approach to the work of the Post Office Mr. Potts would instruct, in detail, Young Mr. Brakeman and Miss Osmond on the best way to proceed. He would then usually take it upon himself to outline the regrettable inadequacies inherent in the current thinking and fads regarding the education of the young. It was a subject upon which, once Mr. Potts had got up a full head of steam, he could easily continue speaking for a full half-hour. At such times Young Mr. Brakeman and Miss Osmond would stand at their places behind the counter and gaze hopefully toward the door for early signs of the next customer.

Mr. Potts took his lunch break each day from twelve to twelve-thirty. Being only a head clerk he ate on the second floor with the rest of the lower-ranked Post Office employees, in what was widely but unofficially called the Rose Room. In days long past the room had been wallpapered in a shade of pale green, against which small red roses devoid of stems floated. Over time these roses had faded to the palest of pink in the sunlight coming through the windows overlooking the city square.

Mr. Potts clearly enjoyed the opportunity that his breaks gave him to dispense his knowledge further afield than the front counter. He prided himself on his ability to find a subject of interest to anyone he was talking to. To a veteran of the recent war he might outline the inadequacies of military strategy during various campaigns. An amateur apiarist of twenty years' experience would doubtless be happy to learn of the most efficient way to extract honey from his combs. It did not matter in the least if the staff member next to him was a railway enthusiast, a dabbler in watercolours, or a follower of provincial-level rugby football. Mr. Potts was always full to the brim with useful information and advice.

For several years it had been fashionable for many of those who shared the twelve to twelve-thirty break with Mr. Potts to take their lunch to the small grassed area at the rear of the Post Office. No one seemed to mind the belching fumes of the postal trucks as they loaded and unloaded from the raised wooden bay. Even on quite cold spring days, or well into autumn, certain staff would huddle in tight groups, close to the wall, round-shouldered and stamping their feet as they scoffed down sandwiches held by gloved fingers or drank tea poured from a Thermos. It was a fashion that apparently no one had thought to mention to Mr. Potts, who could sometimes be seen frowning around at the almost empty Rose Room.

When heavy rain or other extreme conditions forced staff back into the more traditional space, Mr. Potts' entrance would elicit a flurry of hastily finished meals and scraping chairs. In midwinter some staff regularly managed to keep their lunch breaks down to only five minutes. Mr. Potts never read anything into this practice, beyond his co-workers possessing an admirable work ethic and devotion to the postal service.

The notice regarding the staff end-of-year picnic was posted on the Rose Room noticeboard on the first Monday of December. The picnic was scheduled for the Sunday before Christmas and was to be held at New Brighton beach, at a spot chosen for its proximity to both the last tram stop and the wooden pier.

Mr. Potts took the earliest opportunity to outline his reservations about the choice of venue to Young Mr. Brakeman and Miss Osmond. 'New Brighton beach is a poor choice for a picnic at the best of times. Whoever was making the decision clearly did not consider the prevalence of the easterly wind.'

'A breeze can be quite nice on a hot day at the beach,'

murmured Miss Osmond, who had always quite liked the beach.

Mr. Potts turned to regard her with an expression of the utmost incredulity. 'Miss Osmond, I am not referring to a gentle breeze but to the *easterly*, which, you are obviously not aware, regularly rises to fifteen knots. Or more!'

Miss Osmond smiled thinly and nodded. 'I imagine you're right, Mr. Potts.'

'No, we would have been far better off holding the picnic in Hagley Park. That venue has the advantage of convenience, as well as being well wooded and, as such, sheltered from the prevailing wind. I've half a mind to say something to the Postmaster himself.'

'You should,' said Young Mr. Brakeman from his position beside Miss Osmond. 'You should definitely say something to him.' He sent Miss Osmond a look that caused her to turn quickly towards the bag of outgoing mail as if she had just then remembered something terribly important.

'Although I don't suppose it would do any good,' Mr. Potts continued. 'The decision has been made. Surely, though, they must have considered how disastrous blown sand can be at a picnic. Simply disastrous! Sand in the sandwiches — there is simply nothing worse. Nothing!'

'Perhaps that's why they call them sandwiches,' suggested Young Mr. Brakeman to Miss Osmond out of the corner of his mouth and so quietly that Mr. Potts could not hear.

A sudden coughing fit saw Miss Osmond leave the room.

Mr. Potts frowned after her. 'Are you all right, Miss Osmond? You're not choking, are you?'

The departing Miss Osmond waved a hand behind her in a way she hoped would indicate she was not in any immediate danger. Mr. Potts seemed to read her signal correctly. He frowned after her and then turned back to Young Mr. Brakeman. 'Also, it just occurs to me how dangerous the waters can be near the pier. That part of the ocean is full of holes and strong currents. Have they taken that into account?'

Judging from his silence, apparently Young Mr. Brakeman himself had not, and this, Mr. Potts thought, was typical of a member of the new generation.

II.

The day of the picnic dawned cloudless and the promise of heat hung in the air, along with the blackbirds' first chorus. The antipodean sky turned from dark to pale white and then to a vast unsmudged canopy of thrush-egg blue, changing colour only where it dipped down at the distant horizon to mingle with the darker blue of the Pacific Ocean. At the beach the wooden pier pushed out beyond where the waves swelled up and rushed impetuously towards the beach, to break in a jumble of white water laced with foam.

The Post Office memo had stated that the picnic was to begin mid-morning, but on such a promising day families began to arrive at the beach soon after breakfast. They came through the marram grass- and lupin-covered dunes carrying everything they would need for a full day at the beach. The children ran ahead, up and over the last crest of the dunes, exclaiming with delight at the first sight of the sea.

'Look how blue it is!'

'Bet I can touch it first!'

'My feet! The sand is hot already!'

'See how far the pier goes out! When can we walk out?'

'Look how high it is!'

Their mothers followed not too far behind — certainly not so far that warnings and instructions could be ignored. Behind them all came the fathers, wading through the dry sand, weighed down, or listing heavily to one side, with wicker picnic baskets, from which wafted the smells of cooked chicken and fresh December strawberries. They carried sun umbrellas like a knight's unwieldy lance, and folded rugs for laying out on the sand, cricket bats and balls, bags of towels, bathing costumes, and enough spare clothes to allow for any eventuality.

The end-of-year picnic was not only for employees of the central branch but also for a loose confederation of other branches from the south of the city: Sydenham, St Martins and Beckenham. Although it was an opportunity for mingling between staff from the various branches, people generally spread out their rugs close to their workmates. By lunchtime there were over a hundred people. Seen from a vantage point high on the wooden pier, the Post Office picnic was a small archipelago of brightly coloured islands, each one made up of at least a dozen or so picnic rugs.

Within each island nation there were subtle divisions and distinctions. The men with deeply tanned faces and forearms who did the work of delivering letters on bicycle and on foot kept somewhat to themselves; their rugs were separated by thin creeks of sand within the larger groups. Senior management in each branch also kept, almost imperceptibly, to themselves.

The city's postmaster and his family had arrived exactly on time, mid-morning. He was a short man with a stocky frame and was famous for his imposing presence and decisive nature. His hair was cropped to disguise natural curls, which he may have considered too boyish for the leader of such an important institution. The Postmaster and his five children sat highest up the beach of anyone, almost in the dunes. The slight elevation on the sloping beach enabled him to survey the gathering. Occasionally, senior managers straightened their clothes and approached their superior, congratulating him on the perfect, windless day and the exceptional turnout. All agreed that it was a record attendance.

The divisions broke down somewhat after lunch. Some of

the juniors and other younger men commenced playing a game of cricket on the hard sand left by the departing tide. Wickets were pushed into the sand at either end of a makeshift pitch. The scattered seaweed that fringed the beach at the high-tide mark showed where the field ended on the upper side; the ocean itself did that job on the lower side. The loudest supporters were the rowdy seagulls, which had hung about all morning on the edges of the rugs.

Oh, how Miss Osmond laughed to see Young Mr. Brakeman chasing the ball through the shallow water, his trousers rolled up to his knees, water flicking up from his heels and a broad grin rendering his already attractive face, to her mind at least, positively handsome. In the present company Young Mr. Brakeman proved an adept player, and Miss Osmond clapped enthusiastically whenever he performed a manoeuvre of even moderate distinction.

Miss Osmond had invited her younger sister, Vonnie, along to the picnic. Vonnie had just completed her first year at teachers' training college and was home for the summer. Miss Osmond clapped once more and her sister smiled.

'So that is your colleague Mr. Brakeman, whom I have heard so very much about.' A sly grin threatened to break out at the corners of her mouth.

'Oh, Vonnie, not so very much. I may have mentioned him in my letters once or twice.'

'Surely more than that.'

'Vonnie! You are awful. You're teasing me. Please stop.'

They both laughed. 'I think I will go swimming later,' said Vonnie. 'There are some changing sheds up by the pier.'

'Are you sure? The water is too cold for me.'

'Not for me. In fact I like it cold. It's invigorating.'

'The waves are quite big.'

'Good!' And Vonnie laughed again.

They were prevented from saying more by the late arrival

of Mr. Potts and his family. They both heard Mr. Potts before they saw him. As he led his family over the lip of the last dune he was loudly advising his wife on the best place to set up their rug. The merits of this and that location were proclaimed across the sand. Miss Osmond fervently hoped that when Mr. Potts eventually settled on a location it would be far away from herself and Vonnie. When he came into view it was clear that, with regard to his attire at least, Mr. Potts had made no concession to the fact that it was a Sunday or that the picnic was being held at the beach. He wore the exact same suit, hat and tie that he wore to the Post Office during the week. Only his brown canvas portfolio was missing. Miss Osmond would certainly not have put it past him to have that tucked away in the large wicker picnic basket his wife was carrying.

She was relieved to see the Potts family eventually stake their claim on the far side of the group of a dozen or so families of which Vonnie and herself were a part. Miss Osmond could not help but notice how those people close to where Mr. Potts sat frowned slightly and shuffled uncomfortably on their picnic rugs.

It was the first time Miss Osmond had seen Mr. Potts' wife and two children, and she craned her neck for a slightly better look. Mrs. Potts was a surprisingly pretty woman. She had a striking crop of red curly hair, which she was wearing that day pulled back from her delicate, almost elfin face. A plain but not unattractive hat in blue and white sat on top of her head, but even a hat could not hide her hair's natural exuberance.

Miss Osmond hazarded a guess that Mr. Potts' two boys were around eight and ten years old. They were both very pale, as though they never got out in the sun. They orbited their mother, at times actually clinging to the hem of her summer dress, reluctant to set foot off the large tartan rug their mother spread out, as though the beach were as foreign to them as the surface of the moon. As Mrs. Potts unpacked the lunch from the wicker basket she seemed to be listening attentively to her husband as he described, not only to her, but to everyone about him, the dangers inherent in this stretch of the ocean, dangers that were apparent to his eyes only.

'Good morning, Miss Osmond.'

She started slighty and then laughed with one hand in front of her mouth to cover her embarrassment. How silly she was! She had been so preoccupied with studying Mr. Potts' family that she had not been aware of Young Mr. Brakeman's approach. Now he was standing right in front of her, breathing heavily from the game, wet sand clinging to his damp shirt.

'Good morning, Mr. Brakeman.'

'Good morning,' he repeated, looking down at her sister.

'Oh, yes, this is my younger sister, Vonnie. This is Mr. Brakeman. We work together on the front counter.'

'Really? Hello, Mr. Brakeman.'

'Hello, it's very nice to meet you, Vonnie. Please won't you both call me Andrew. It is, after all, Sunday.'

'Of course, you're right. Andrew, then,' said Miss Osmond. 'And you may call me Mary.'

'It's a beautiful day, isn't it? Perfect for a picnic. And not a puff of wind.' These last words Andrew Brakeman directed over the top of the Osmond sisters in the direction of Mr. Potts and his family, but Mr. Potts was of course talking and did not pause in his flow. Even at that distance Miss Osmond could hear most of what he said. He seemed to have taken the cricket game as his cue and was describing the close-to-miraculous skill of a player named Hardy.

'Yes,' agreed Vonnie, 'it is a lovely day.' And then quite unexpectedly she added, 'I do wish I could join in your game of cricket. Do you think I could?'

'Vonnie!' her sister exclaimed.

'Don't be so old-fashioned, Mary. It's just hitting a ball on the beach. Why shouldn't I?'

'I wish you wouldn't, that's all. All the people I work with are here.'

'None of them will mind. Will they, Andrew?'

Mr. Brakeman moved his feet uneasily on the sand. He cleared his throat and looked down the beach.

'Please, Vonnie. You're embarrassing me.'

'Oh, all right then.'

Much to Miss Osmond's relief, her sister slumped back on the rug and fixed her gaze on the end of the pier. There was, Miss Osmond was sorry to see, a sour expression on her sister's usually open, pretty face. But really, how could Vonnie even think of it? And in front of Mr. Brakeman! With the Postmaster sitting just up the beach!

Andrew Brakeman cleared his throat again. 'Miss Osmond, Mary, I was wondering if you would care to accompany me for a stroll along the pier?'

'That sounds very nice. I will, thank you.'

Without another word to her sister, Miss Osmond got to her feet, and, pausing only to gather together some stray items for her handbag, walked off with Mr. Brakeman towards the pier. As they walked over the sand they talked about the weather and their respective plans for Christmas. Miss Osmond thought again how easy she found it to talk to Mr. Brakeman, and now it seemed especially so, away from the demands of the Post Office. Just off the sand near the start of the pier there was an ice-cream seller. His white cart sat beneath a large red and white polka-dotted umbrella. The ice-cream seller himself was a wide-mouthed frog of a man. It was Miss Osmond's fancy that a fairytale frog had been turned into a man but had not entirely managed to lose all traces of his origins. Mr. Brakeman paused in front of the ice-cream cart. 'Would you like a cone? My treat.'

'Oh no, I couldn't let you.'

She knew that Mr. Brakeman was saving all his money for an overseas excursion. He had on one occasion late last summer talked to her about his itinerary. They had been eating their lunch outside at work. Of course there had been other people present, but Miss Osmond had fancied that Mr. Brakeman had directed more than one of his remarks directly to her. How exciting it had been to hear him talk knowingly about cities on the whole other side of the world: places as exotic as Rome, London, Paris and even Barcelona.

'Are you sure you won't have a cone? I'm going to have one.'

'Well then, thank you. That's very kind.'

'Two vanilla cones, please.'

The frog-faced man regarded them with an air of complete boredom. He scooped the soft ice-cream from deep within the ice-filled cavity of the cart, took Mr. Brakeman's money and handed over two cones, all without speaking once.

'Thank you,' said Miss Osmond when Mr. Brakeman handed her the cone, the edges of which were already dripping in the heat.

'You're very welcome, Mary.'

After the soft crunch and slide of the beach, their footsteps sounded loud and slightly hollow on the wooden pier. Families and young couples arm in arm strolled along in front of them and passed them going in the other direction. Miss Osmond and Mr. Brakeman seemed to have come to an unspoken agreement to walk slowly but even so, because the beach sloped away, the pier quickly seemed quite high. Below them the sand gave way to ocean. Miss Osmond resisted the urge to wrap her arms around herself for warmth. Since the end of the cricket game she had noticed how the wind had come up. It was an onshore breeze and quite cool. The wind made her wish she had thought to bring along the blue cardigan she had left with Vonnie on the rug. She looked back towards where they had been sitting and, although she could see the rug clearly, her sister was nowhere in sight.

'I'm very sorry about Vonnie,' she said, turning back to Mr.

Brakeman. 'She gets in these moods sometimes. She always been headstrong, ever since she was a little girl.'

'That's all right, I understand. My younger brother is forever running off in one direction or the other, no focus in his life.'

'Actually, Vonnie isn't quite like that. She's always wanted to be a teacher so it's not exactly focus she lacks. It's just that she doesn't understand why sometimes she can't do things.'

'Such as play cricket?' He chuckled at the idea.

'Anything, really.' Miss Osmond gave a little laugh herself, which for some reason she immediately regretted. 'It's just that Vonnie doesn't see why there are so many limitations on what a young woman can do in this life.'

She had stopped walking as she said this last part, and Mr. Brakeman leaned on the wooden rail and appeared to listen. Miss Osmond regarded the waves directly below them as she thought how to best express what it was that her sister resented. She saw how the water below, dark with churned-up sand, swirled and eddied around the wooden supports of the pier. The waves also appeared to have grown in size, whipped up by the wind.

'Oh no!' said Mr. Brakeman suddenly.

'What is it?' said Miss Osmond, alarmed.

'Potts.'

She looked down the pier towards the ice-cream seller and saw Mr. Potts. He was with his wife and their two pale children. The whole family was strolling down the pier in their direction, Mr. Potts slightly in front, leading the way.

'Quickly,' said Mr. Brakeman. 'He hasn't seen us yet. Let's walk right down to the end. He might not bother coming that far.'

'We mustn't be rude.'

'It's only rude if he sees us. Really, I'm having too good a time to listen to a lecture on the feeding habits of black-backed gulls.'

Miss Osmond laughed and felt a sudden surge of excitement. Andrew was right. Why should they have to put up with silly old Potts? Today of all days! They began to walk towards the end of the pier with quick steps. For a heady moment she felt like a heroine in a movie, hurrying away from the sinister man who was following them. It was an impression that was only strengthened when she stumbled slightly and, in a gesture that seemed perfectly natural in the circumstances, Andrew reached out and took her hand in his.

They walked that way until they reached the very end of the pier. Apparently the increasingly cool breeze had caused many people to abandon the idea of walking out this far, and Miss Osmond and Mr. Brakeman found themselves alone, apart from two schoolboys whose fishing lines angled down into the dark water below. It was only when they reached the end and stopped that Mr. Brakeman released her hand. He glanced behind him.

'Is he still coming?' she asked.

'Unfortunately, yes. We're trapped. I think our only chance of avoiding a lecture is to walk back and say hello, but not stop. I think that would be the best.'

Miss Osmond's eyes shone with excitement. 'Fine, but we must be polite. It would be terrible if he thought we had snubbed him or his wife.'

'Of course.'

They set off back up the pier and had almost reached the point where it would be necessary to make eye contact with Mr. Potts when Miss Osmond fancied that she heard something unusual over the susurration of the ocean. 'What was that? Did you hear something?'

'I didn't hear anything,' said Mr. Brakeman, and then added quietly, 'Come, now, or he'll stop and talk to us for sure.'

'No. Listen. There it is again. Someone is calling for help.'

Running to the rail, Miss Osmond could immediately see the head and shoulders of someone struggling in the white foaming surf: a swimmer who had been caught in a dangerous current. 'Oh no, it's Vonnie!'

It was slightly more than twenty feet down to the water. Almost directly below where they were standing, Vonnie was now desperately attempting to hold on to one of the pier's thick piles. The wood was black with age and covered in barnacles and clusters of sharp-lipped muscles. Even as Miss Osmond watched, a wave picked up her sister and dumped her back into the surging white water. For a moment she couldn't see Vonnie at all and then — there! — her sister's head appeared. A look of panic and dismay was stamped on poor Vonnie's face.

'Quickly, Andrew, you must help her!' But, to Miss Osmond's complete bewilderment, Andrew Brakeman had hurriedly stepped back from the rail. His face had turned the colour of meringue. 'It's too far down. I couldn't possibly. I couldn't jump.'

'She's drowning!'

His eyes darted up and down the pier. 'No. I'll run back to the beach and get help.'

'There's no time!' Already, while they argued, Vonnie had gone under again. 'Please, Mr. Brakeman! Andrew!' She was sobbing now, begging.

'No, I can't. I'm sorry.' And, with one last panicked look at the water, Mr. Brakeman turned on his heels and ran back down the pier.

Up until that awful moment Miss Osmond had been completely oblivious to Mr. Potts. Now she saw him. He had taken off his tie, his hat, his white shirt and his shoes and socks. These things he calmly handed to his wife. Now clad only in trousers and white singlet, he climbed onto the railing and, with no more apparent concern than a man going for a summer dip, stepped out into the air high above the churning ocean.

Miss Osmond leaned over the rail in time to see Mr. Potts hit the water, his legs tucked up under him like a reclining deckchair, two fingers firmly pinching his nose. He disappeared for a few seconds (seconds that seemed longer to Miss Osmond than hours), then his head popped above the water. He had judged his jump well and had landed close to the drowning woman. Mr. Potts set off swimming the short distance to Vonnie with a choppy but efficient overhead stroke.

Miss Osmond saw Mr. Potts grasp Vonnie with one hand under her chin before turning and beginning to swim with only one arm towards the beach, towing Vonnie behind him with the other.

On the sand, people were only now beginning to realise something was wrong. A few of the younger men began running down to the water's edge, scanning the ocean.

Large waves broke and churned over the two swimmers, and each time this happened Miss Osmond gasped and held her hands to her face, too afraid to look. Each time she expected that her sister and Mr. Potts would not be seen alive again, but after the rush of white water there they were, Mr. Potts was dogged in his progress towards the beach.

When at last — at long last — he reached the shallows, Mr. Potts stood. Several of the younger men waded out to him but they were not needed. Mr. Potts supported Vonnie Osmond as she staggered through the shallows and onto the beach. A few feet above the reach of the surf he released her and Vonnie crumpled onto the sand, where she lay, bedraggled and pale with shock.

As for Mr. Potts, it was not very long before everyone from every Post Office branch in the south of the city was clustered around him, eager to shake his hand.

III.

After the incident at the picnic, Mr. Potts' rise within the Post

Office was both rapid and direct. Within a fortnight he had been promoted away from the front desk. His photograph appeared in the *Press* and the *New Zealand Herald*, as well as the Post Office's own newsletter. In a special ceremony the mayor awarded him a medal for bravery by a civilian. Within a year there were only four other men at the central branch who were Mr. Potts' seniors.

Whereas in the past Mr. Potts had been avoided, now he was sought after by everyone, for both advice and information. His knowledge was regularly referred to by other staff in admiring tones as being 'encyclopedic'. 'Ask Mr. Potts' became the common refrain. 'There's nothing he doesn't know about.'

Everyone at the central branch was disappointed but not at all surprised when, the following year, Mr. Potts was offered a good position in the ministry. Only eighteen months after he had rescued Vonnie Osmond, he took his beautiful wife and his impeccably behaved children and moved to the capital.

Miss Osmond saw him there several years later. She was in that city visiting a maiden aunt who was in the last stages of a long illness. By that time she was no longer Miss Osmond. She had been married for just over a year and was of course using her husband's name. So now she was Mary Harbidge. How strange, she sometimes thought when addressed as Mrs. Harbidge. A whole new name and a whole new life. She no longer worked in the Post Office but stayed home and kept house. How quickly it had all happened. She supposed that she would grow used to things, given time.

When she saw him, Mr. Potts was walking towards her down Lambton Quay. She almost didn't recognise him, strolling along as he was in an almost jaunty manner. There was a younger man at his side, a junior she supposed from the ministry, who seemed to be hanging on every word that left Mr. Potts' mouth. Mr. Potts' tie was straight and most likely silk from the look of it, his hat and coat clearly expensive. His suit appeared to be tailored. She noted that he merged effortlessly with the lunchtime crowd of politicians and bureaucrats who were beginning to spill out from the eating houses and side streets, ready to resume the day's important business. Apart, that is, from one small detail. The thing that undoubtedly first caught the former Miss Osmond's eye was the brown canvas portfolio Mr. Potts carried. It was like a child's school satchel. From where she was standing on the street, the round-eyed button winked at her. How she smiled to herself to see that! Despite everything, Mr. Potts still carried that portfolio.

Something made her decide at the last moment not to talk to Mr. Potts. Engrossed as he was in his lecture, he had not yet seen her. As he drew close she turned her head and pretended to be interested in the contents of a bookshop window. Mr. Potts passed behind her, so close that he almost brushed against her. She saw his reflection flicker past in the glass, for a moment melding with her own before moving on. The old familiar voice found her ears and then was gone.

Mrs. Harbidge was running slightly late for a meeting at the house with her aunt's lawyer. There was so very much to arrange. Putting Mr. Potts out of her mind, she turned and set off quickly up the street in the direction of her aunt's house on Tinakori Road.

Honesty

HONESTLY

— Peter Wells

There was an expression Rupert Henderson was very fond of using: 'If you want my *honest* opinion . . .' He had an honest opinion on every subject under the sun, and nothing short of a passion for delivering it. But Archie Cullen's pet phrase was 'I cannot *honestly* say . . .' Which meant that he had not really made up his mind. He had not really made up his mind on any subject whatsoever. Why? Because he could not. He was unlike other men.

At least this is what Rupert Henderson thought. He had been waiting for Archie to get ready for the taxi that was taking them to the airport. But Archie, aka Mouse, had been faffing around, collecting his eyedrops for the flight ('My eyes honestly never recovered from that flight to Noosa.').

'Darling,' Rupert said in a dry voice, 'get your sorry arse into gear or we'll be late.'

Anybody overhearing the two might think they shared only acrimony. The two men had been living together for over fifteen years. They had progressed from being covert lovers who snatched at each other like starving men to the more stately procession of the homosexual couple. Adored for their cooking skills (or rather the cooking skills of Mouse), they featured at dinner parties in the inner city, were alert to the latest gossip, knowledgeable about who wasn't sleeping with whom. About their own lives they kept an open book. They both believed — or rather Rupert believed — in a scrupulous honesty.

'If you want my *honest* opinion,' he would opine, 'males get over initial intoxication quite quickly. There's about six to eight months of endorphin frenzy — followed by a dying fall of affection. Couples stay together out of lethargy. They slump asleep in a legal coma. You have to *reinvent*,' he was wont to say, lifting his hand in a faintly balletic gesture.

Mouse kept quiet during these pronouncements. He looked a little uncomfortable. 'I cannot *honestly* say . . .' he said to himself. Mouse liked inner commentary, that refuge of the oppressed. 'I cannot honestly say I ever stopped loving you,' he would silently address his partner. 'I have honestly followed behind in your wake, agreeing to whatever you say will keep our relationship "fresh".'

There had been no end of saturnalia in this quest. Threesomes, foursomes, odd instruments, blistering honesty. So long as, Rupert said, we tell each other *everything*, keep each other informed and up to date. There were times when Mouse would have preferred not to know *everything*. Like about Zac, the prematurely knowledgeable nineteen-year-old at Rupert's work. Zac and Rupert kept up a texting relationship all through the late hours of Saturday night and into Sunday morning. Rupert aka Bear and the boy would text each other during breakfast, even in the middle of a conversation between Mouse and Bear.

Mouse sometimes dreamt of a room in which he was sitting on his own. The sun was coming in the window. There was no furniture in this room, no paintings, no *decor* at all, as Rupert would call it. (Rupert was opposed to decor. He said it was a clichéd view of a gay man and his interests.) Mouse wasn't doing anything in this room. He was certainly not with anyone. It was a simple form of bliss — just sitting there, in the sun, dreaming . . .

'Darling, the taxi is here.'

Bear's voice had taken on that special note of command.

Mouse dragged the last of his luggage down. The taxi driver was, as far as Rupert was concerned, a disappointing specimen. A prematurely aged Asian, he had the wearied look of a father kept awake at night. And not by the sort of things that kept Rupert awake. The driver checked out his two passengers, diagnosed them as 'no probs' (a New Zealandism he had picked up proudly), and thrust their many pieces of luggage into the boot of his car.

Rupert sniffed suspiciously as he took the back seat.

'Schoolboy vomit,' he murmured to Mouse. 'I bet this taxi took kids to an end-of-year party.' He raised his eyebrows. 'Who knows what happened on this back seat.'

Mouse said nothing, except 'thank you' to the driver.

'The fastest way to the airport, please.'

This was Bear's big mistake, in Mouse's view. Bear should have been more specific. After all, Bear had lived in Auckland all his life. He knew there was no fast way to the airport. But 'in my honest opinion' . . . Rupert thought that the fastest way was the most complex rat-run down back streets, along the sides of the motorway, across industrial sectors and then, at last, parallel to the city's second harbour. A migrant does not have an encyclopaedic overview of a city. A migrant's view is based on fear, and then, only slowly, on knowledge. A migrant goes the only way he knows.

Mouse had that sinking feeling. 'I cannot *honestly* say,' he said to himself in a worried tone of voice, 'that the driver is taking us the fastest way'. Bear was ominously silent. He was tapping his fingers on his broad knee. He wasn't so much looking out the window as glaring.

They were held up at lights. Bear glanced at his watch for the fifth time.

'If you want my *honest* opinion —' he burst out. Mouse felt his heart contract. This hateful statement was always prelude to an attack. 'I believe you're taking us the longest way so that you can get the largest possible fare.'

The driver's eyes appeared in the rear-vision mirror.

'*Which way are you going?*'

Rupert's voice had taken on the precision used by an English speaker to intimate to a non-English speaker that they belong to a lower form of intelligence.

'The way I always go. Is fastest —'

'There's no point arguing . . .' Mouse ventured. Bear studied the wreck of Mouse's face for a long, concentrated moment. He thought to himself how daylight had a way of illuminating Mouse's faded complexion, the lines on his forehead, around his mouth. He was getting older.

'Darling, relax . . .' Mouse murmured to him, grazing his fingers once over Bear's hand. 'We're on holiday, remember. Or almost.'

Mouse had a way of handling Bear. He had to be very careful, however. Bear could never know he was being handled. The moment he smelt it, the game was up.

The blazing argument had happened outside the airport. Mouse had quietly unloaded the boot while Bear and the driver argued back and forth vehemently about the bill. Mouse knew better than to intervene.

'If you want my *honest* opinion, you are a thief, a liar and an incompetent. I'm surprised you even have a licence . . .'

And so it went on. It was all no use, Mouse knew. It was simply Bear expressing his nerves before the flight. It was hard to be homosexual in public. It wasn't easy. If you were on your own, you could get away with it much more easily. You could blend in, or, if you wanted to make a point of it, you could flame away. But when you travelled as a homosexual couple it was so obvious. You were open to the barbs and slings of outrageous prejudice. Like that time when they were coming back from Florida. They had been put right at the back of the plane, by the toilets. For fifteen hours they had been obliged to be familiar with the toiletry habits of over one hundred persons. It was a version of hell. The smiling ticket clerk had awarded them the seats, even though they had checked in five hours earlier than anyone else. She had sent them off to purgatory with a big American smile.

'Have a nice flight.'

Rupert had said, 'If you want my *honest* opinion, she's one of those right-wing Christian fascists. Like Bush. You know — thinking she's doing God's duty. Invading Iraq.'

Mouse tried to say there was a slight difference between consigning two middle-aged homosexuals to the worst seats in a plane and invading an innocent country, but in Mouse's occasionally honest opinion he knew it was better to keep quiet.

Kind people sometimes called them brothers. 'You two brothers joining the bus tour?' a large American specimen might say, thighs rubbing together as she waddled down a hotel passage. It was too difficult, the other option. 'Lovers' was slightly obscene, given their age. It opened up too many graphic images. Partners was consciously 'hip' — too hip for a bus tour, it must be said. Whereas 'brothers' — there was something touching about this — something sweet: two bachelor brothers living together, perhaps waiting for the right pair of sisters to come along. It was engagingly sexless. Neutral.

There is a kind of neutrality in all couples. There has to be, perforce, a neutral zone, like a joint territory where two mutual antagonists agree to lay down arms, co-mingle and even co-habit. This neutral zone may be a bed, or it may be just a few moments snatched in the civil war that is most marriages or relationships. Holidays are usually an enforced neutral zone. Bear and Mouse liked holidays. They had time for each other. Time away from their friends, acquaintances and enemies — not that the categories were that distinct, as friends may be enemies, and acquaintances closer to true friends.

Mouse and Bear had decided to holiday just outside Kuala Lumpur. Somehow a Muslim country seemed to possess that essential '*je ne sais quoi*' of the unique holiday. Nearly every country on the globe had been ransacked by now. Even their own country, famously 'last, loneliest and loveliest' (according to Kipling), had so many tourists these days that not even the smallest hick town was without its specialist in café latte or Turkish bread. People no longer gathered around solicitously at the sound of a foreign accent. 'If you want my *honest* opinion,' as Rupert had announced to his friends, 'Malaysia is the new Paris.'

'But what about terrorism?'

'Oh,' Rupert said breezily, 'Malaysia isn't quite like that. It's sort of Indonesia-lite. Burma without the generals. At least . . . that's what I've read.'

Besides, Rupert had taken the precaution (he didn't tell his inner-city friends this) of booking Mouse and himself into a resort for the first week. 'Till we find our feet.' Mouse anticipated relaxation, swimming in the pool, maybe a few rounds of golf. And then there would be those escapades into the neutral zone. Bear would lay down his bearishness, his defences. Mouse would evade his inner mouse. They would cohabit.

Mouse looked forward to this. 'I cannot *honestly* think,' he thought to himself, as the taxi took them to the hotel (blessedly at a price fixed by the state), 'I cannot *honestly* think when the last time was that Bear and I had time to ourselves.' In Auckland there were the complex strategies involved in 'keeping their relationship fresh'. It had the effect, often, of isolating the two men from each other, even when, ironically, they might be strenuously involved in a new experiment in intimacy. But this was different. A hotel room would be their neutral zone. For a second Mouse thought of that other room, the room in which he just sat, doing nothing. Sun was on his legs, and he was looking up in the direction of the light. The light was pure . . . drenching his mind, blanching away all the feelings he might have . . . feelings of pain, of discomfort, of uninspected thoughts, dark intuitions. That unrecognised Archibald, perhaps — the man who had a mind of his own.

'Now,' Rupert was saying to him, smiling, 'not so bad, eh?' They were following along in the wake of a bellhop. He was a boy of fifteen who yet wore a soft caterpillar of a moustache on his upper lip. The lad had been ingenuously kind. To him the men were not lovers or partners or brothers. They were guests. The customs of the place dictated a form of politesse that would have put Versailles to shame. But Rupert didn't mean only this. It was the *luxe* of the hotel — the Japanese couples going downstairs to the swimming pool. Honeymoon couples with their fingers entwined. It was escape.

Their room wasn't on the sunny side of the hotel, however. Bear suspected it was homophobia in action. But, as Mouse pointed out, it had 'views'. The views were of a golf course that terminated in another world view altogether: a cluster of rusting tin-roofed shacks, a sort of slum town built on stilts over mudflats. Washing was hanging out and Mouse thought he could see rubbish in the mud.

He switched his gaze to the platter of fruit some underling had laid out. There were grapes of unreal plumpness, a banana that had been thoughtfully circumcised, and cheese from a distant part of the world.

'Be careful to wash everything. And don't drink the tap water.'

Bear was undressing. He was never more himself than when he was stripped naked.

He put on a kimono.

'Let's go and check out the talent around the pool.'

It did not matter that neither man was exactly an Adonis any longer. In Bear's mind he was still a splendid specimen. His eyes followed the males at the pool as if they were so many targets.

Mouse instead went *into* the pool. He immersed himself in the shining cube of light. He lay back. He closed his eyes. He dreamt of that silent room, so still, so empty . . . so inviting.

Mouse waited anxiously for that moment when they would both enter the neutral zone. But for whatever reason, on this holiday, Bear was taking time to unwind. Even worse, Mouse realised with a sinking heart, Zac had found that he could text Bear in Malaysia. Different time zones meant nothing to the fervent beat of Zac's unformed heart. Bear had the decency to feel embarrassed by it. He would take his cell into the loo, but even through door Mouse could hear the *bleep* of an incoming text message. Each time it happened Mouse felt his spirits decline. It was as if he could see a graph, like in the sharemarket pages of the paper when the market is in retreat, each fall registering the slump in his spirits.

It was several days later. They had visited museums that illuminated the local art of weaving, bought cloths to astonish their friends back home (but which would quietly reside at the back of the hot-water cupboard). Intrepidly they had even gone into town and had a few meals at local markets. They had sat amid a welter of exhaust fumes and delighted in the fresh produce. They had not yet found the neutral zone. Mouse was surprised at himself. Each time Bear's cellphone bleeped he felt himself grow taut, as if he had been flicked with a wet towel — something that had happened to him with monotonous regularity in the changing sheds at school. He was wounded and ready to wound.

'Can't you turn that fucking cellphone off?' he had snapped at one point. 'I cannot *honestly* say I have ever been more pissed off.'

A master of the passive aggressive, Mouse settled down to sulk. Bear became rather too consciously 'happy'. Mouse caught Bear looking at him almost plaintively, as if begging forgiveness. But Mouse decided not to talk.

Bear got bored talking up the local talent.

'Go off and fuck yourself stupid,' Mouse said sourly that day, following Bear's eye-line. 'I wouldn't mind spending time on my own.'

This seriously upset Bear. He didn't like spending time on his own. His face went pale and his hand went across the table. He stroked Mouse's knuckles.

'Darlink.' (Bear often retreated to baby talk at moments of negotiation.) 'I had no idea you was feeling that way.'

Mouse had quite a few tart things to say but he saved them for his inner dialogue — the one that kept up as brisk a correspondence as the internet on a day of more than usually salacious scandal.

That night Bear wanted to make love — or, as Mouse saw it, Bear wanted to enter the international zone. But the guards would have nothing of it. Mouse pretended to be asleep. Bear turned on his side, grunted. Soon he was snoring. Mouse, however, lay awake. Like the guards, his thoughts kept marching up and down, up and down. This zone was not lit by sunlight. It was lit by night-lights, unnatural and frightening. And Mouse's shadow was strange, fleeting and jagged, as he seemed to seek safety somewhere outside the bounds of the international zone.

It happened the next day. Bear got up and announced that, *in his honest opinion*, they needed to do something really different. They wouldn't go on the bus tour. They would go into town *on their own*. They would do a spot of shopping. Then Bear would take Mouse to lunch.

'I insist,' said Bear, holding up his cellphone. Before Mouse's eyes he switched it off. He slid it into a drawer. Like a man illustrating he no longer carried a weapon, he held his hands up in symbolic surrender.

'I loves you, darlink.'

'That sounds nice.'

Mouse spoke in a deliberately flat voice.

He went away and showered for a long time. At one point he got out and crept to the bathroom door. He was sure he could hear the neurotic little clicks of Bear's cellphone. And there, indeed, was Bear tapping away, a furrow on his brow.

Bear glanced up suddenly.

'I'm just telling him . . . what's happening . . . he might worry.'

The diminuendo of Bear's voice was lost as Mouse stepped back into the shower and turned up the heat.

They certainly caught the bus into town together. Bear would always remember Mouse saying, as they passed a telephone booth strangely isolated at the end of the road, 'That's the booth the 9/11 terrorists used to pass on their information. Not their cellphones. *They* were clever. *They* used their brains.'

'How do you know that?'

It was so like Mouse, Bear thought. At the last moment he could always save the day by doing or saying something unusual. Mouse had depths he had never quite plumbed.

But in the next moment he brooded. It was an odd feeling, knowing the strangely bland luxury of the resort had held within it such a poisoned bulb.

Soon enough the bus deposited them in the city: a city they did not know at all. It could have been a Muslim town in the north of Africa — dry, dusty, washing hanging between narrow buildings. They were the only parboiled-looking people on the streets.

'Darling, I want to do some shopping on my own.'

Bear was surprised to hear Mouse say this.

'I wants to buy my big bad boy a present,' Mouse said, shrugging, half smiling. 'We'll meet — look — over there. In an hour.'

He pointed to a relatively anodyne-looking café bar. Only to Mouse did it look like the sort of place you saw in videos of Bali — before the bombing.

'Are you sure?'

Mouse just shrugged, leaned forward quickly and squeezed Bear's arm.

Forever after, Bear would remember Mouse's last remark.

'Enjoy yourself.'

From the upstairs bookshop — fully air conditioned — Mouse looked down into the street below. It was now fifty minutes past their meeting time. Mouse was one of those people who were always on time. Bear was grandiloquently late as a matter of principle. 'If you want my *honest* opinion, it is only the socially bankrupt who arrive on time.'

Mouse had had the infinite satisfaction of watching Bear lumber by, sweaty and downcast. It was over thirty degrees in the shade. He was carrying two enormous plastic bags filled with boxes of electronic equipment. Bear had told Mouse on the bus how he intended to snap up new technology at bargain prices. He was also looking furtively around: not at the lissome young men who walked by, their fingers intertwined. He was looking for Archie.

Archie had enjoyed himself. He had gone and had a cup of

mint tea on his own. The café was really just a set of plastic milk crates upended on the pavement. But he enjoyed his little adventure of independence. He had gone into a fabric shop and touched the shimmering surface of all sorts of fabric. He had lingered. He had felt the pleasure of being on his own. It seemed the further he got away from Bear, the more at ease with himself he felt.

In his mind, Archie toyed with the idea of life on his own. He imagined himself, an independent-minded tourist, returning to a room in which everything was placed absolutely where he had left it. (Mouse was phobically tidy; Bear revelled in the free form of mess.) He could read that book he'd studied at high school so many years ago. *In a German Pension*, it was called, an enjoyably malicious little titbit. While he read he would eat all the food he couldn't eat when Rupert was around. (Anything with butter was verboten. Bear must remain athletically thin.) Mouse would sleep, be silent, awaken in his own time.

The reverie was soothing — almost as good as the reality. Or somehow even better: because Mouse knew everything had its limits. He did not, for example, consider actually abandoning Bear. It would be too 'dramatique' to go back to the hotel room on his own, pack his bags and shift out. No, it was more pleasurable just to milk the situation for all it was worth. Besides, hadn't Chekhov himself said that patience more than passion was the requirement for marriage? He stayed in the air-conditioned shop a little longer.

Bear had been sitting in the café bar for a very long time. He looked depressed. Every so often, almost in a tic, he would start frantically patting his body all over, as if looking for a cellphone. Then an oddly shamed look would come over his face. He looked wan.

Finally Mouse took pity on him. He went downstairs and walked towards Bear. On the stairs he passed a young man who looked at him with desire — or was it hatred? He may or may not have been a terrorist.

Bear, when he saw Mouse, tried to put on a look of outrage.

'If you want my *honest* opinion . . .'

Then he grew quiet. He looked sheepish and his eyes appealed to Mouse: *Put me out of my misery. Never leave me alone like this again. I love you, Mouse. It is you I always have loved and will love. Forever.*

Mouse saw all this at a glance.

'I cannot *honestly* say,' Mouse said, sitting down and allowing the sun to fall on his legs, 'I have ever enjoyed shopping more.'

'But you didn't buy anything!'

'Oh, I bought a lot of things in my head.'

Bear was about to object. His implacable honesty was rising to the fore. But he bit his tongue.

On the bus going back the two men fell silent. Neither spoke as they went up to their hotel room.

They entered the hotel room, closed the door behind them.

The room was conspicuously silent for a moment. Then a hand appeared. It was that of Archie, hurriedly putting a sign on the door: Do Not Disturb.

Susannah

SHELL PIANO

— Stephanie Johnson

Of course there would have been no question of their going to the exhibition if Father had not had the tickets given to him. Little girls cannot expect to be given treats that cost extra money when only to feed them, buy them clothes, pay for their lessons and the house they live in takes their kind generous father all day and every day working hard from morning till night — 'except Saturday afternoons and Sundays,' said Susannah.

Katherine laid down her pen and returned her gaze to the orange tree below the terrace in the villa garden. There was a pear tree in 'Bliss' that she had used to fine effect. Perhaps these little girls, whom she imagined at first lived somewhere sooty in the north of England, longed for an orange tree. It could be a symbol of their yearning for warmth and affection. She knew, as soon as the idea for the story first took hold, that their mother had disappeared; probably she was dead, but the little girls had not understood that. She suspected nobody had taken the time to explain it. Children were so often kept in the dark, never told about things that really mattered.

Father himself did not make a habit of going to exhibitions or plays or even the moving pictures, especially since Mother ran away to sea. Should she put her mind to it, Susannah would not recall their father going to any public gathering before Mother ran off on her fateful voyage. Most often Mr. Stokes was to be observed behind the polished counter of the shop, with his wares prettily displayed behind him in a honeycomb of wooden shelves, or sleeping in his fireside chair dog-tired in the evenings. He could sleep through all manner of hullabaloo and high-jinks, while the latest cousin or aunt come to help him tried in vain to contain the five little girls who all lived together in the cramped rooms above the shop.

It is true that the little girls were still too young to understand that if their father occupied a different station in life he would go out and about more often. If he were a rough man for example, of the type you saw falling out of the doors of the corner tavern. Or if he worked in a big factory or for the railways and went on the annual picnics. Or if he were a rich man with a motorcar or a yacht on the harbour. Or if he were a church-goer, or belonged to a small businessmen's society, or had joined the Freemasons, or broadened his mind at the Working Men's Institute . . . but Mr. Stokes did none of these things.

The invitation came from the lady herself. She had given it to Father on an oblong of thick cream-coloured card the day she bought the little wooden piano covered over with shells. The tram stop was right outside Stokes Fancy Goods, and that was why she'd come in, the beautiful lady — to get out of the rain that was slanting in under the awning while she waited for the tram. She'd looked at some of Father's pieces — a porcelain-faced doll stiff in intricate folds of Japanese silk, and the little shell piano. From behind the counter, standing on a box positioned so that she could lean against her father's legs, Susannah watched the lady pick up the doll and put it down, and a little later do the same with the piano, pressing on the tiny, mute, carved keys. In between, her pale fingers navigated the pointed bevelled base of a cut-crystal vase and tested the weave of a yellow silk mantle shawl. Father had sighed a little, as had Susannah, because it was painfully obvious that the new signs they'd made with Ethyl's assistance were not doing their job — *Please Do Not Touch* — in their best script, better than any letters they'd formed for Miss Faith at the Infant School.

Since Mother ran away to sea, a month ago now one windy March day, since then, especially since then, it had been difficult to be ready some mornings, and most particularly on the mornings when they were between Cousin Effie and Aunty Fran and Father forgot to get the milk in or the bread from the baker and Susannah would have to be set to stirring the porridge while he flew down the street. If it got to nine o'clock and feet still lacked shoes and plaits their ribbons, Father would be suddenly and silently defeated by it all and disappear down the stairwell to the shop below. That would mean another day at home for Susannah, who had turned eight just yesterday, and Ethylwyn who was six. Yesterday they made the signs, Father's warm hand cupping hers as she formed the cautionary words. Even so, Susannah would have preferred to go to school. There were other words to learn to spell.

The lady who bought the shell piano wore a fur and a close-fitting green hat and had pretty shoes. She was older than Mother, with papery creases around her mouth and eyes, and not as pretty, but then who was? Mother had met a sailor and run away to sea, and although Susanne had never met the sailor, she supposed he was as handsome as Mother was beautiful, and that one day they would sail into port and Father would take the little girls down to meet them.

While Mr. Stokes wrapped the shell piano in brown paper, Susannah leaned against his legs and clutched his fob watch, having dug it from his pocket. She was the only one of all her sisters who knew how to press the little clasp that made the case fly open. It was ten-to-four.

'It's a gift,' said the lady, 'for the people I'm staying with.'

Father might have smiled a little — Susannah couldn't tell because if she tipped her head back she only got the mother-of-pearl buttons of his waistcoat and his pointy-bearded chin. She was sure he would have given the lady little encouragement, because he'd hardly talked since Mother went away, but the lady went on, 'I've just got back from Europe.'

'Europe, eh?' said Mr. Stokes. 'Never been.'

'It's wonderful,' said the lady. 'I wish I was still there.'

'And where would that be?' Father snipped a length of string.

'Rome, Paris, the south of France. My last stop was Fontainebleau for Mansfield's funeral.'

'Who?' asked Father.

'Katherine Mansfield. The writer.'

Father shrugged.

'Have you never read any of her stories?' asked the lady.

'No,' said Father.

Susannah left the warmth of Father's legs and came around the corner of the counter to stare more fully at the lady, who was taking off her soft grey gloves to open the silver clasp of her purse.

'Mr. Stokes,' said she, 'you are missing out on ever so much. And you only a young man with the world at your fingertips.'

'No,' said Father firmly, 'the world's never been there. Where you say.'

'But —' the lady gestured to the shop and all its merchandise as if she flourished at riches, 'you must not deny you have an eye for beauty.'

Father blushed. Susannah had never seen it before. Under the soft brown hair of his beard, which had little clearings in it like an enchanted wood, his skin was pink and his smooth brow flared. He took the coins from the lady's hand and Susannah, who found herself drifting over to the Japanese doll, thought that if his skin were embarrassed then his eyes were angry, suddenly a harder, brighter blue. If tiny unicorns lived in the wood, they would come to drink from the lakes of his eyes.

'Why've you come back, then?' he asked. 'Couldn't the place hold you?'

The lady looked sad suddenly. Her shoulders drooped under the fur, with her pale thin lips drooping in tandem. 'I'm on my way to Wanganui. My mother is ill and my father called me home.'

'All of us have to do our duty,' said Mr. Stokes in a monotone, like the prayers at school.

'Yes.'

'And you were away on your father's account, I'll be bound,' he said loudly, in the same tone of voice he used when the little girls succeeded in waking him in his fireside chair, or were not doing as they were told.

The lady stared at him, her eyes wide. 'That was certainly not the case. Not all the time. I had a degree of success. Here.' She was taking the ticket from her purse. 'And bring your little girl.'

'There's five of them,' said Father, handing her the parcel.

Though she tried to stop them, Susannah's fingers took hold of the silky end of the doll's sash, red and printed over with a flock of black birds, some of them flown entirely over the horizon from her attentions.

'Bring them all,' said the lady.

`Where was LM? Katherine had asked her to keep an eye on the clock and come to her room to tell her when` it was a quarter to. That would give her enough time to walk to the station at Menton-Garavan to meet Jack's train. She would do it, she would walk there and back with a spring in her step, and if she must stop to cough she would, she would not be ashamed or frightened of making a spectacle of herself.

At long last Jack was coming, coming today, and he would bring with him all that the little girls in the story longed for. Warmth and love and news of other people, of places that mattered. Not only that, but money and cigarettes, perhaps some books, the other things she'd pleaded for in her last letters. LM had already been to the market in Rue St Michel for supplies enough to last for days. Last KM saw her she was mopping the kitchen floor with a strong solution of ammonia, which had made Katherine cry out and cover her nose, but then LM had always had bouts of hopeless insensitivity and had to be coached and coaxed through them. One could only hold on and wait until she returned to her natural empathy. It was she who had suggested Katherine rest on the terrace since the ammonia had infected the whole house.

Whatever happened, the dear woman was to be made to understand that she was on no account to accompany Kathleen to the railway station. It was months since she'd seen her Bogey. Months. She wanted the reunion to be as private as could possibly be, given that it would take place on a railway platform.

Setting down her notebook and arising from the terrace chair made her breathless, but she went in at the French windows and called down the hall. 'Ida? How much longer?'

LM put her head out of the parlour. She carried a feather duster, which irritated Katherine. Rather than do it all herself, she should spend the time recruiting a dependable servant of honest character, one that neither told bangers nor lifted the housekeeping money.

'What is it, dear?' asked LM.

'Until I must leave for his train? How much longer?'

'Oh . . . an hour at least – yes, at least an hour.' Ida was determinedly wiping at the grooves in the panelled doors, which did so hold the dust.

It was Susannah's job to hold on to the ticket all the way into town on the tram. Father had his hands full with the baby and Irma, and Ethylwyn was to look after June, who was the silliest four-year-old alive and had already barked her shins climbing onto the tram. He would never have taken them at all if it hadn't been for Susannah, who had put her hand up for the ticket in the shop, since Father had seemed as though he wasn't going to take it. Since then she'd read every word over and over again:

The Auckland Public Art Gallery cordially invites
you to an exhibition.
'Old Europe'
Landscapes and figure studies
By Phyllis Miner.
Saturday 4 pm. Refreshments will be served.

On the tram Mrs. Brodwell from the bakery sat opposite them and Susannah read the ticket aloud to her — not that she appeared to be listening. She was staring at Father sitting in the middle of the row of squirming little girls, and before she got off at the bottom of Wakefield Street she bent to speak to him.

'Why don't you put these poor children in a home? You're making a rod for your back. No man could stand it.'

Father pretended he hadn't heard her. He hooked his arm more firmly around slippery Irma, who looked for a moment as if she would follow Mrs. Brodwell off the tram. Susannah was less perturbed than she might have been, because Mrs. Brodwell had said that before, the first time only a few days after Mother ran away. It made Father sad and weary to hear it, and Susannah made sure to give him a kiss on his cheek just before he got off the tram to walk them up to the beautiful white castle at the top of the hill, with the turret and clock and forest of Albert Park behind it.

How marvellous it was to be with Father, who knew his way around the town. Mother had brought them all here, but further down Queen Street to the port, on the day she ran away to sea. She left all the children on a bench in the ferry building while she walked to the end of the pier. They hadn't known their way back to Stokes Fancy Goods in Dominion Road, so a policeman had taken them in his wagon. Susannah didn't like to think about that day. First there was Mother crying all over them as she sat them side by side with the baby on Susannah's lap, then the admonition to stay there and not move, and then there was the long wait until a kind man took them into his office upstairs and rang up on his telephone for the police. Mother's weeping was the worst of it. It was worse even than what she'd seen from the kind man's window.

There was a lady with a pearl necklace and fur standing just inside the door and of course it was the artist herself, Miss Phyllis Miner, who smiled at them with such warmth and welcome you would think Mr. Stokes and his five daughters were her oldest and dearest friends. Father was blushing again and couldn't seem to think of anything to say, so Susannah took his fingers and tugged him away up the staircase to look at the pictures. In any case Miss Miner was turning the same smile on the next group of people coming in at the door.

The first picture was a big church that melted into the soft blue sky, as if the artist couldn't see the top herself so just smudged it into the clouds. Susannah thought it was very poor form. She would never do that. She'd finish it neatly. The next showed a village, but it wasn't right — it was made of squares of pink and brown, even a cat sitting high on a wall was all made up of corners. Then there was a clearer painting of a fat man with a barrow of apples — *a costermonger*, Father read from a label — and then a painting of a grand house with horses and a carriage waiting in front of it. And then there was a picture that pulled them all up short. Even the baby ceased its damp wriggling against Father's jacket and stared as Father leaned forward to peer more closely at the grey, cold sea with the pier running above it, way out into the distance, somewhere Susannah supposed, in *Old Europe*.

At the far end of the pier was a woman, and from the way her dress moved she was striding, hurrying along as fast as she could go, even though she was only a couple of steps from the end. It was as if she would keep up her pace and step over the edge. There was no sailor waiting below with his ship as there had been for Mother.

All of Father's hands were taken, so Susannah dug into his pocket for his fob watch. She held it to her ear and tried to pay more attention to its lovely dependable tick than to the fact that Miss Miner had come to stand beside them. Her sweet, musky perfume made Susannah giddy, and the fox circlet had a smell of its own of damp and seawater, as if it had been packed away for a very long time. Ethylwyn took her thumb out of her mouth and jabbed at the tiny woman with the billowing skirts.

'Is that our mother?' she asked, but Miss Miner was not used to children and couldn't understand her.

'Don't touch, dear,' she said gently.

There were no refreshments for Mr. Stokes or any of his little girls. They did not even view the remainder of the paintings. Their father had them out the door and down the street to the tram stop and they were all back in Dominion Road by five o'clock.

Upstairs in their little dark kitchen, while Father broke the bread into their plates and poured over milk and sugar, Susannah thought she understood more. There were two kinds of ladies in the world: ladies like Mother and ladies like Miss Miner. Mother had made a mistake because she really wanted to live the sort of life Miss Miner had — she would have liked a fox circlet and a cloche hat and the time to stand her easel on old street corners and pretend the view was different to what her eyes were plainly telling her, and then to put that into the picture in squares and blobs. Sometimes Mother had sat the little girls up at the kitchen table with smoothed-out sheets of butcher's paper, stubs of pencil and an old crust of bread for rubbing out, and sometimes, if they pleaded with her enough, she would draw them a cat or a steeple, but not often. She was up and down the stairs all day between the shop and the five little girls.

'What possessed her?' Mrs. Brodwell had asked.

Thoughtfully, Susannah spooned up her goody and helped June with hers and couldn't help noticing that Father seemed weary, casting his eyes now and again to his armchair at the other end of the room. Without being asked she slid down from her chair and picked up the baby from where he'd propped it between two cushions. Tenderly she wiped its milky chin and the grains of sugar that adhered to the tip of the little nose, and carried it down to the little wooden cot in the bedroom they all shared — though Father's bed, the one he'd shared with Mother, was now mostly undisturbed. He passed his nights in his fireside chair.

Back she went for Irma and June and Ethylwyn, putting a finger to her lips the way the aunts did because Father's head had drooped to rest on his arms. There were breadcrumbs stuck to his elbows. One by one, before they followed one another down the narrow hall, the little girls went close to him and kissed him goodnight in the cool clearing of his beard below his closed uppermost eye.

Katherine supposed she was coming to the end of the story – and there was still no orange tree. The sun encroached into her shade, slanting between the boughs of the magnolia tree and across her lap so that the paper flared white-hot. She had that sensation in her lungs again, as if a furnace burnt fiercely in their damp interiors, bone-melting fires lit by Doctor Manoukhin's magical X-ray cure. If only she could really believe in it. Jack didn't. She shouldn't. Experimentally she took a deep breath – and didn't cough. There, see!

She would go now. Fetch her purse and parasol and walk up the hill and along the street to the station. First it would be necessary to dispatch LM, whose very presence could put a damper on things. In Jack's case a damper could be caused by very little indeed.

The story was bothersome. She would never finish it. Who cared what happened to the five little girls? She didn't – and if the writer herself cares not a jot for the fate of her own then why should anyone foolish enough to read it? It was pap. She tore out the pages, screwed them up into a ball and tossed them onto the tiles of the terrace, where a breeze scooping through the hillside gardens from the sea picked it up and blew it away. If Jack were here he'd tell her off. He exhorted her to keep every tiny jotting, every false start, every notebook, which he kept stored in an old trunk in London.

For once LM, determined spinster that she was, seemed to have some gleaning of the marital need for privacy and promised that she would be finished drudging and gone to her own lodgings by the time Katherine and Jack returned to the Isola Bella. Katherine paused at the door long enough to feel a guilty pang of affection for her: that dear bent head and pair of helpful hands now straightening the books on the mantelpiece.

The trick was to fool her lungs into believing they were still at rest on the terrace. It was a matter of walking as smoothly as possible, as if one were gliding, so that breath came in and out of her chest without opposition from her tread. As she stepped out of the gate the soft Mediterranean air opened and closed around her and the sun was gentle on her bare arms, not yet at summer's height. A young man tore down the hill towards the sea on a bicycle, grinning at her, his hair and coat-tails flying. How lovely it would be to see Jack on a bicycle, legs pumping and colour in those sallow cheeks. He would be weary from his long journey from Paris, more than even she would be from her taxing walk, so it was certain he would pay for a cab to take them back to the villa. After so long a physical absence surely he wouldn't indulge his enraging parsimony.

As she rounded the corner a fit came upon her. Not one of the black fits of old, where hatred of every living soul in the world would consume her for hours, weeks, but the other kind, the new one sent from hell to plague her. It made a mockery of the old fits of passion – This is the indisputable truth, it said. This is all you are – a piece of rotting meat.

There was a fence so she leaned against it, grubbing at the same time for a clean handkerchief from her purse, an old one of Jack's. Women's handkerchiefs were no good for the job. She held it over her mouth, folding and refolding it against each heaving, bloody expectorance, willing the contractions to ease and stop. The station was in sight, the cedar in the grounds of the last villa in the row obscuring the last of the line as it slid into Menton-Garavan.

A little girl had come to stand beside her, staring up into her convulsing face. In one hand she held a hoop and the other a stick, and she seemed deaf to the pleas of another child, older, who urged her away from 'la poitrinaire'. The girls were dressed the same in summer frocks of the same sprigged cloth, and straw hats, and they had the healthy, well-sustained faces of the children of the bourgeoisie. The closer child, whom she assumed was about eight, obeyed only when Katherine took a tentative step away towards the station.

As she walked, she stopped thinking about her husband and all she loved and hated about him and let her mind drift instead back to the story. The innocence and curiosity in the French girl's face was the same that would enliven Susannah's, and how frightful it would be to have to write of the loss of that, to have to describe the child's tears and despair at the father's abandonment of them at the Children's Home. That was the inevitable solution to the poor man's troubles. First his wife flings herself off the pier, then he takes the advice of the baker's wife. Perhaps the baby would be the lucky one, taken in by the aunt she'd named but had never brought on stage. Perhaps she should have made the baby a boy.

The train station was deserted. The observation sent a dart of panic into her burning chest. Had she got the time wrong – was there to be no train at all? As she sank to the sun-warmed flaking wood of the bench against the station wall she dug again into her purse, this time for a notebook, leafing through the inked pages to find the letter she'd folded into it – but it had been superseded by the more recent arrival. That was the letter she carried with her, the fresh one, loving, longing for her, yearning to satisfy her body and soul, but unhelpful to her present dilemma. She took it from its envelope and held it in her hand.

The panic abated, her heart slowed. She wouldn't have mistaken the time of his train, though Lord knows her mind felt fugged after months of only LM for company and the illness. Instead of conversations and parties there had been reading. And writing and reading and letters. And the illness, the illness, the illness. And penury.

She sighed and looked around for someone to ask about the train. A fine patina of coal dust glistened on the platform boards, birds sang in the trees in the hills behind her.

If she hadn't screwed the story up and tossed it away she might look at it again now, while she waited. She would smooth the pages on her knee and have the father keep the little girls – yes, he would gamble for the first and last time in his life and come into a lot of money. He would move the family to a warm, well-built bungalow and have paid help. And the artist – why, of course she would do her duty until her mother died, conveniently quickly, within weeks, leaving a bequest generous enough for Phyllis to make her way back to Europe and a comfortable life.

But by now the story and the lives contained in it would have blown away to be wedged among the stone banisters of the terrace, or among the orange trees and mimosa and lavender of the garden. She could ask Jack to find it for her.

A guard came out of the station and looked along the line towards Nice. Even before she saw the glorious plume of smoke and heard the slowing engine and squeal of brakes, Katherine could feel the tickling rumble of the approaching train through the soles of her feet.

Second Violin

ON A DIFFERENT NOTE

— Vincent O'Sullivan

Paris with someone you really want to be with, even in winter, when the sky is slate grey as though to match the sloping roofs and the trees have been sketched in, the bare bones of them, and couples huddle together against the cold as you first glimpse them ascending from the Metro — that's one thing. You are warm just thinking of it. But to be there alone, things fallen through as we say — well, Rose couldn't think of anything much sadder actually, yet she refused to let disappointment have the last word. And supposing you wanted to add to the irony, it had all been planned at the end of summer, when Bevan first knew about the festival he would be covering in Cologne and it was simply a matter of returning home via St Germain, where they were bound to hear some worthwhile jazz apart from anything else.

Rose was the one who sat at her computer evening after evening, following one lead then jumping to another, while Bevan lay on the rust-coloured settee, his eyes closed, the earpiece of his iPod making her think sometimes of an old man with a hearing aid. Thinking that should have been amusing, but actually it made her want to cry. And she told him so, which was a mistake. He liked to tease her for being sentimental. He said it was all those Beatles songs and the stuff she heard her father play when she was too young to do anything about it and now she could never shake it off, one never can, he said, once songs like that have burrowed into your little old heart. But then he kissed her and drew her down from where she wanted to get on with her computer search, and as the settee was far too narrow for two he knelt in front of her and put her legs to either side of him which she didn't really like, and made love to her like that. It would have been far better to wait until they were in bed, rather than her propped there like a doll. But the next evening when she followed up the Brit Rail website and told him about the Hotel d'Orleans and the deal with Eurostar, and that their Metro station was on the same line as Cité, which was the perfect spot to start exploring her favourite places, he said, without removing his earpiece, 'You plan it, I'll love it'. The look on his face that amused her and melted her completely, the look of a boy who wants to concentrate and can't quite manage, listening to her and smiling and his stretched hand on her knee beneath her skirt, and her thinking she had known from day one she'd never met anyone who needed music so much, needed it all the time.

It was ten years since she had come to London, getting away from a relationship in Auckland that, believe me, was worth getting away from, and six since she took the best job you could ever have, in the art library at the Victoria and Albert. Which was something of a joke, so far as she and Bevan were concerned. He knew as much about art as she did about rock music, but, as he also teased her, get either of us up to scratch with what the other's good at, and there's a lifetime gone already. And, as he told her quite seriously, 'Liking what I like isn't quite the same as liking *me*.'

What's that phrase her mother used to use — 'couldn't get enough of someone'? His hair seemed burnished as she sat above him and he listened to his iPod on the settee and she caught its sheen in the raw light from her desk-lamp. His whole body struck her like that. It seemed to glow from within. She remembered from the school chapel a long time ago, 'My love, my dove, my beautiful one.' It made him laugh when she said so.

'It's the Bible,' she said, 'in case you think it's me.'

He asked her had anybody set it, bringing his head down so his lips touched the spray of freckles on her shoulder and his warm breath moving to her breasts, then their laughing together, his demanding, in what she called his headmaster voice, 'Can't you ever be serious about anything, girl?'

They were good at fooling together, although each of them had said at different times how they were not great ones for laughing with anyone else. She told him as they lay on her futon bed beneath her genuine Japanese prints, in her tiny flat five minutes' walk from Marble Arch, 'I am thirty-two years old and young for my age and rather hopelessly in love, although I fully expect it has no future.'

Bevan sat up against the black pillow with white edging he angled against the wall behind him, and half echoed, 'I am twenty-six and old beyond my years and although I don't say "love" very much, I can tell you hand on heart there is nothing like this in my past.'

They said little else as the late summer evening lengthened, and then it seemed there was ash falling silently across them, and she pulled the duvet to cover her shoulders and he slid down beside her, tossing his pillow to the side of the bed and across the radio that was always set on Radio 4 when he arrived and a popular station when he dressed to leave. It was the strangest, closest feeling these summer evenings when they lay and sometimes talked about home, and the green light at the window facing the square very gradually faded, and the corridor past the bathroom and into the tiny kitchen became dark and lost all sense of dimension. When he said St Heliers and Herne Bay and Beachhaven, it was not in daylight that she thought of them, but imagined they were lights that flickered in the distance, and she saw them from the harbour as she sailed past. Although it was quite different for Bevan, who said he could almost smell the melting tar on the road as he walked down barefoot to the warm sand at Shelly Beach.

Some nights Bevan stayed with her, but most evenings his work took him all over London, to small clubs and student gigs, and sometimes even to Manchester or Newcastle. He wrote on new bands and rock concerts and trends and gossip for several small publications, and occasionally was asked to stand in for a friend who did a column in the *Guardian*. Apart, though, from the big newspaper he was paid sparingly. Once or twice when his cheque was late Rose insisted that she lend him enough to get by, which he paid back on the dot. She asked him once, 'Why don't you ask me to one of your gigs?', knowing as she said it that the word did not sound right.

'You'd hate it,' he told her. 'A lot of it's shit but I'm obsessed with it. That's my only excuse.' But he did take her to a small dark club on the Caledonian Road, where no one seemed to have heard of the new non-smoking law, and his prediction about her not really enjoying it was dead right. He assumed it was the raw funk group that would never get further than it was tonight, the yellow fugged air, the nose-studded clientele. She did not tell him that none of these things actually bothered her. She was fascinated with the novelty of it, the deals that were so blatantly done, the intense inward privacy of wherever it was the musicians entered once they began to play. They were interesting specimens, something she had never really seen this close before, these cool young men with their curved shades, the girls, some of them with shaven heads and sullen remoteness and long black gloves like torn webs. She wondered what they were like, these people, in their daylight working lives. A tall girl with white make-up said to her in the restroom — not to her in particular, it seemed, yet there was no one else facing the dark mirror in front of them — 'Beata. What a cunt of a name.' All that was quite diverting. What bothered her was Bevan as another person, as though a twin she had never met had come in his place. His easy slowness, his thoughtfulness, those things about him that she so liked, replaced by a sharpness, a quick flickery energy as he moved about talking, laughing, offering a cigarette, although she had never seen him smoke, steadying a stranger's wrist with his own hand as he leaned in to a proferred match-flame. Part of the scene. He used words she had never heard as he called out to those who passed their table. When she told him the one group she liked listening to he said, 'Indie rock, Rose, Jesus! If you like that you like anything'. But said it good-humouredly, leaning towards her, placing his lips against her hair. She said when it was already past one o'clock, 'I don't know what I'll turn into if I don't go before the clock strikes'.

'But it hasn't begun!' he said, his hands held in front of him, cowering away, a comic turn of the male hectored by a demanding mate. He stood outside the club with her until a taxi slowed down and coasted in to the kerb. He tapped the roof of the car like a frenetic drummer before it drove off. He stood back on the pavement and raised two thumbs as he leaned down towards her window, and she watched him slide back into the night.

Rose told him several things so it would not become a big deal. She said, 'I'm just too out of my depth to appreciate it, that's the truth of it, Bev'. She said, 'Well, I like reading novels and that doesn't come between us, does it?' She said, 'Our seeing each other is the best thing in my life, you must know that'. And Bevan explained to her this stuff about when he was on the job — it was like dressing up and carrying on when you were a kid, that's all it was. If you wanted to cover the scene that was what you did, or people wouldn't take you for real. 'If they think I'm on something that doesn't hurt either.' Whereas the fact is, he said, the fact is that if you want to write decently about it your mind has to be ice-clear. You listen pure and undistracted. 'I'm getting good at that. Looking one thing, being something else.' He laughed and told her it was no different from a bee-keeper putting on a hood before he went to work, no worse than that. And they began to play one of their games, each saying something even more absurd than the remark before.

'Than an astronaut in that outfit before he takes off?'

'A doctor slipping his gloves on before he interferes?'

'What's that thing?' Bevan's fingers circled above his head. 'A mitre? — what the Pope puts on before he sings "G'day"?'

She was happy then, and they knew they were closer now they understood each other better. It was even exciting to know how the man you liked being with most, who was so content to be with you, could really be someone different with other people. She called him Mr. Kent after Clark in the *Superman* movie, which they had watched together the week before. He phoned her at the V & A and asked for Lois Lane in the library and of course no one had a clue. The woman on reception asked had someone new been taken on? But the six years between them, which meant not a thing when they were together, made her think when they were apart that the gap seemed even more. She dreamed once that she sat in some place like a bare parish hall, her father beside her. They were watching an old minstrel show on a grainy screen in black and white, while a heavy metal band cracked the walls next door, a partition opened, and in the strobe-laced shaft of light a man with a caricature mask and Michael Jackson legs danced and laughed and danced away. As her father used to say at breakfast when her mother recounted a tedious dream, 'You don't need to be Freud . . .'

Rose knew — it was the only point on which she held a high opinion of herself — she knew that she was a realist when it came to matters of the heart. She knew how happy she was when she and Bevan were together, most often at her own place; and even happier those few times in his tiny, brightly painted, extraordinarily neat two rooms above a betting shop in Streatham. As the sky lightened in the mornings she could see from the high window the cranes on the skyline beyond the far stretch of roofs, where work for the next Olympics was under way. On the table beside Bevan's bed were the exercise books where he kept performers' names and details of even the most fugitive of bands. He entered them neatly late at night, which is why he preferred writing by hand than using the computer. His articles he typed up next morning, sometimes before it was even light. He told Rose, and it was utterly true, that she was everything he never met anywhere else. But she was sad all the same when she sometimes saw him only once a week, and thought more than she should have of what, after all, was only six years.

Paris though was entirely because of Bev. He had been asked by *Vox Moderna*, a tongue-in-cheek high-brow rock quarterly founded by two smart-arses from Cambridge, was he willing to cover a rare midwinter festival in Cologne? They would stump up the lot — tickets, hotel, a decent fee, even an expense clause in his contract for what was wittily listed as 'Indispensibles'. As the already clapped-out young editor said to him as they sat in what was not much better than a rat-hole in Dean Street, a signed photograph not of any muso but of Shirley Temple for fuck's sake on the wall above a filing cabinet, 'It's good of you to go. I know people who wouldn't get *into* bed that time of year in Germany for twice the price.' He looked up with wet, shining eyes. He must be the last person on God's earth, Bevan thought, who still wears those squitty John Lennon glasses.

He explained to Rose. 'I'll come back through Paris instead of straight to London — the Cologne fee will more than cover the lot. And if I'm held up or anything, it is Paris after all. Not as if you'll be bored.' Laughing, kissing her, putting the bottle of wine he had brought with him in the fridge, then returning to ease her down on the settee, while he knelt in front of her on the floor. He said, 'You know with that red hair of yours and your perfect whiteness you make me think of a candle in a church. Wonder why I thought of that.' Rose surprised herself, for usually she was not in the least sardonic. She said, 'Maybe you're wasted, love, just writing about music?'

Minutes after she stepped down from the Eurostar, and walked through the crowd in front of the huge *panneaux* where details of arrivals and departures clacked their constantly changing information, Rose stood on the steps at the front of the Gare du Nord, delighted as she had been that morning ten years ago with the man she thought she would be with for the rest of her life. She looked out past the taxi queue and the swirl of traffic to the flinty blue and grey spread of the city, the smudge of bare winter trees, the symmetry and soft-edged precision of the streets. She had been here once since then with her sister, soon after her brother-in-law left his family for a Fijian law clerk. Not much from that time stayed with her. Fiona had hardly been much fun. One evening, though, they had dined at a restaurant in Montparnasse where ninety years earlier a famous Scottish painter watched recklessly handsome women in huge hats, and painted them in bold brilliant colours — a fact she knew only because the week before a reader at the V & A had ordered everything to be had on him. Two pleasant young men had asked them to a football match on a Sunday afternoon, but her sister cried on the train to the stadium and the young men drifted off.

Now here she was in Paris again. Tomorrow she would look

at galleries and stroll by the river and walk, if the weather held, the bald February paths of the Luxembourg, although the carousel she had so loved watching that first time with Eamon would no doubt be stacked away, its gilt-reined horses stabled under canvas. Then in the evening, or even earlier, Bevan would arrive. She turned and walked back through the station and lifted her light-wheeled case as she descended the stairs to the Métro. The names, so familiar once she saw them again, flicked past. Yes, there were the dark blue tiles that spelled out Saint-Sulpice as the train slowed and stopped and started up again, and it was no time at all until she left the train at Mouton-Duvernet. She came up the stairs beneath the green wrought-iron design that surely made you think of Paris more almost than anything else? And there was the hotel she had booked directly across the road.

The middle-aged man at the desk, his bald scalp reflecting the lights above him in two bright dots, leaned towards a screen to check her booking, and handed her a key attached to a strip of brass. She recognised the print of a famous painting as soon as she entered the room. At the long windows that opened to a narrow balcony she moved aside the floor-length white curtains to see it was already dark. In that little time since she had crossed the street. At a window opposite her own, a woman read a magazine beneath a tall standard lamp, and through another window beneath that, Rose made out some kind of office. What looked like piled directories were stacked on a filing cabinet behind an empty desk. She turned to catch the serious, rather attractive woman glancing back at her from the mirror. They said to each other, knowing of course how juvenile they were being, 'I am in Paris, waiting for my lover'.

The message handed to her at the desk had said he would phone at seven. She slipped off her shoes and put her feet on the shiny gold fabric of the bedspread. The low burring of the telephone woke her at seven-thirty. She heard the rush of talk from Bevan's own hotel. She was reminded at once of the night she hadn't liked at the club in the Caledonian Road. There was the same sense of hyped excitement, the words she could not quite follow. He sounded boyish and self-absorbed as he told her how the dude from the *Scotsman*, a famous columnist he was surprised she didn't know, had OD'd the night before — the guy would pull through but would she believe it he'd been offered his column, McLaren's fucking column! He said, 'How does this sound?' He read her his opening par about the disappointment the Germans could always be relied on to provide, and the way a Munich version of Motown (Gott in Himmel, what next?) was saved by brilliant lyrics. Something too about a group whose angst was so infectious he expected they'd all come down with it before the week was out. He had sent it through only minutes before he talked with her.

She asked, 'Did you say another two days?'

'At the outside,' he said. 'A chance like this, Rose — hell!' She thought of the satin underwear she had bought at Anne Summers in Queensway, the black and cerise flimsiness that now made her feel more foolish than disappointed. He said when there was a moment's pause, 'You're enjoying Paris, though?'

'I've just arrived here, Bevan,' she reminded him.

'How could you not, is what I mean. Paris versus Marble Arch. No friggin' contest!'

Rose walked down the flights of stairs to the lobby with its striped yellow silk chairs and the table with the day's newspapers held between narrow strips of wood. She turned left at the doorway, as the concierge had advised her, passing a toyshop and a matronly clothes store, and another shop with a pyramid of books slanted in its window. The canvas awnings of the shops were folded back and made her think of reefed sails on sailing ships she had never actually seen. Gusts of wind tugged at them. No wonder people huddled as they passed her. She leaned forward a little herself against the wind and the skirl of dust it raised.

Surprising too how much traffic there still was — lorries and vans that made her think this must be an important road. She said no, as kindly as she could, to a dark young woman who offered her twists of frail, small white flowers, and then walked on without answering her 'bon nuit'. She came to a café with cane chairs and round black tables inside its long glassed-in veranda that made her think of the deck of a ship closed in like that — she must have seen it in a movie. Then of course as the waiter in his long white apron drew back the door for her and held up his opened palm like a wing, she felt almost as if she did this kind of thing all the time. She was shown to a table drawn so close to another that her thighs brushed against the edges of both as she took her seat. A man raised his head and folded his newspaper in half, edged his table aside. She told him she was sorry for disturbing him.

It was nothing, the man told her — there was always so little room. She supposed he was much the same age as her father. He wore a brown corduroy jacket, and a thin silver pin ran across his dark green tie, just below the knot. There was a small stone in the middle of the pin, like a dark drop of blood. His hair — it was that she supposed that reminded her of her father — was no more than a stubble. As he smoothed his hand across his paper and returned to it, a glint of silver ran across his head.

She ordered a salad niçoise and a glass of Sancerre. As she waited she looked out to the wet street and the naked branches of the trees. Lights beyond them splintered and jigged in the movement from a sudden gust, as though they were decorations on the trees. She thought of Bevan and his phone call. If it ended now she could at least say she was sad and upset but not distraught as her sister had been, but then that had been a husband, and there was no Fijian, surely, holding Bevan up!

Her sister had once told her she was lucky she would never suffer as she did, she was simply that much tougher.

Fiona's way to compliment herself. Then Rose knew that if she didn't think of something else she would begin to cry. The man who looked like her father saved her from the shame. He suddenly stood up, edging as awkwardly between the tables as she had done fifteen minutes before. 'My turn,' he said, 'to apologise, mademoiselle.' He took a folded cap from his pocket. He stood for a moment in the café's entrance adjusting it, before he stepped into the street. He caught her eye through the glass and tipped the edge of his cap with one raised finger.

It was still too early in the evening for the tables to be busy. The young waiter watched her and, as he removed the emptied glass and slipped the coins beside it into a leather wallet, he said to her in English, 'He has gone to watch his dead'.

'I'm sorry?' she asked. She must have misheard him.

Without turning he nodded towards the street. 'But the catacombs,' he said. The waiter's smile was condescending to the man who had left — to herself as well, Rose thought. She knew he expected her to ask him more, which she certainly would not do. She said she had heard of course of the catacombs, hadn't everybody? She knew they were supposed to run for miles under the city and thousands, millions, of bones were stacked there, neat as supermarket shelves, she had once heard someone say. The waiter said not everyone had heard of them. Americans sometimes looked upset and Australians did not believe it. 'Perhaps no one dies in Australia.' He was trying to flirt with her. She told him she was not Australian anyway, and said no, she would not have another glass of wine. Complimentary made no difference. But he seemed not to mind. He held the door open for her as she left and smiled, and told her not to worry. The bones never moved.

Bevan rang again, early in the morning. Was there a time difference, she asked, between Cologne and Paris? As if he'd go to bed, he said, with a scene pumping like this! You just would not believe it. They say Germans don't know how to have fun but holy Jesus, Rose, some of the stuff he was listening to over here! He'd changed his mind completely. Condolezza's Kinder, he said, we are going to hear more of them. Then 'Uno momento,' he said. She heard muffled voices as he held his hand across the receiver. Then he told her there was this guy he'd become friendly with, an Italian with his own byline in *La Tribuna* — not that the Italians are with it, he said, not the kind of grunt going on here. 'Remember I told you a while back about the Libertines? Wrote a piece on them for *Disco*? There's a Berlin group last night'd knock the arse off them.' He explained again how you simply had to be here as long as here decided you needed to be. Oh, she quite understood that, Rose said.

Before he went he asked her, 'But you're having a good time?'

The elderly man in the café asked her the same thing the second evening she went there.

He sat at the table he was at last night. He nodded to her and smiled as she passed; she could hardly be impolite and not take the place beside him. Once again she edged between the tables that pressed against her thighs. The man folded his paper as he had also done the previous night, but once the waiter — a different one, she was glad to see — brought her the glass of wine she had ordered, he asked her politely and in English, 'You are having a good time?'

He was the easiest person to talk with. This surprised Rose a little. She did not think she was good at random conversation. In fact she had brought with her the book of stories she'd begun reading — brought them to the café against this very thing. She liked the way he dipped his head and listened to her, and the way the light moved across the stubble of his head. He told her he had once worked in London, at a place called

Lewisham, did she know it? He asked about her own work and she described her library with more than a million books, many of them on artists no one knew about that only specialists wanted to read. 'So if you have a book about you, then you are probably forgotten?' She laughed and the man smiled, and she told him why she was here, with her friend detained in Cologne. She wondered why she said that word 'detained', which she had never used in her life. Then as he sipped at the glass of red wine he had ordered to follow the first he spoke about his work, which was to patrol the long corridors of the catacombs, whose official entrance, he said, was no more than fifteen minutes from where they sat. Yes, one needed to say 'official', because there were many other ways to find one's way beneath the city. Hundreds of kilometres, he explained, which was like a shadow replica beneath the glittering city, that is how he thought of it. 'I am at home here. I am at home there. It is like having two lives.' He told her the authorities were vigilant to prevent those who also had two lives, but were real to themselves he supposed only when they passed from an ordinary street like the one they looked out on now, and found themselves in the corridors most people feared. They go there for love, he said, for celebrations, for their own curious religions. And those who are most difficult to understand. The ones who choose to walk through the catacombs alone, in darkness, keeping to themselves.

As he talked about where he worked, Rose's attention rested on the stone in his tie-pin. Last night it had seemed black, yet tonight when the light caught it was different quick shades of red. She wondered if she had ever listened to anyone who was quite so casually strange. Strange and yet still nice. Only once did she interrupt him, when he puzzled her with 'celebrations'.

'Parties,' he said.

'Down there?'

He said. 'Drug people, but not always. There are two men who dress as monks and sing the old chants. There are others who rearrange — not with disrespect — the way things are. But even the solitaries, you see, they break the law.' And without irony he said to her in French, as though quoting from regulations, 'It is expressly forbidden to enter without permission'.

He looked at his watch and tapped its glass, and stood up. 'Even so,' he smiled, 'they are not people to keep waiting.' He sprinkled several coins beside his emptied glass. Then as he had done the night before, having taken his overcoat from the metal stand inside the door, he paused to ease a cap from its pocket and adjust it on his head, tapping its sides with his hands. He turned towards her from the pavement and bowed slightly, his forefinger touching the cap's brim.

It was now the original waiter who brought her the simple steak and salad she had chosen. He grinned as he placed the plate in front of her. His hand dipped sharply as he pointed to the floor. 'This very moment, Madame, they are waiting for our friend.'

'That's all, thank you,' she told the waiter. Now that the man who reminded her of her father was gone, she was glad she had brought the book of stories. Not that it was easy to keep her mind on them. It was a book she should have read years ago, when she was at home. They seemed so remote from her, to tell the truth, and quite what they were getting at was not always easy to decide. Some weren't even finished, like lives one knew half of, then nothing of the rest. An image she could not get rid of kept playing in her mind, the circle of her new friend's flashlight hollowing out the dark ahead of him, the vague yellowish stacks at the edges of its beam. She imagined — but of course he had not actually said so — that there was the smell of ash in the air, as there was when you brushed a grate. He had told her there were tablets and slabs of marble over doorways where new corridors began, with different things written on them: bits of poems and words that famous people had said. But what they meant was always the same. It was resentment, he said. That was what they said in different ways.

Bevan said he wished he were there this very minute: he hated not being there. He wished they were lying together in bed while she watched the cranes for the Olympics on the morning skyline, didn't she wish that? Yes, she told him. Tell me then, he said, don't just agree with me, and so she told him what she knew he wanted to hear. First thing, he said, the morning after tomorrow. 'Bugger Notre Dame,' he joked. 'That can wait till the afternoon!' As she talked to him in Cologne, she looked at the Modigliani print on the wall that faced her, the woman slender and inert as a lovely fish.

Rose thought how first thing in the morning she would change her ticket back. It would cost, of course — that was the disadvantage if you changed your mind with Eurostar. Yet how easy it was to do just that, to change your mind. She read for a little, but again the stories hardly held her interest, although she laughed at the aptness of it when one she would never guess the end of told her, 'Winter is all for bones.' She put the book on the bedside table and opened a half bottle of brut from the room's service fridge. She was not in the least unhappy. She supposed he would be angry when he arrived and she was not there. But Bevan was never cross for long. He would always find something to listen to. She phoned the desk and told them of her change of plan. The concierge spoke to her so nicely you would think she had done him a favour.

But the morning was drab when she woke early and felt, before she opened the shutters, that it had rained during the night, and that the temperature surely had dropped. She crumbled her croissant and drank two cups of coffee in the little breakfast room whose yellow matched the chairs in the lobby. The disappointment of it all came in on her. As she crossed from the hotel to the Métro the day seemed so out of kilter, as if Paris had been drained of so much that it was famous for. It felt tired and from another time. There was some incident further up the road where an ambulance and a police car had stopped and pedestrians, anxious at what may have happened, were directed to cross further along. Yes, that was it, she thought, as though it were someone else's eyes that took in the morning, now the sense of expectation was gone that it is Paris' business to provide. A February morning, windy, cold, with chill-looking clouds hurrying over a pale sky and chill snowdrops for sale in the grey streets. People look small and shrunken as they flit by; they look scared as if they were trying to hide inside their coats from something big and brutal. The shop doors are closed, the awnings are furled, and the policemen at the crossings are lead policemen. Huge empty vans shake past with a hollow sound; and there is a smell of soot and wet stone staircases, a raw grimy smell . . .

WHITE PAPER, BLACK PAPER

— Tracey Slaughter

I am cold
bring paper to light a fire . . .
Light a fire
No more fire
Because there is no more fire
white paper
black paper
a list from the Katherine Mansfield Notebooks

The past beats inside me like a second heart.
John Banville

That winter Mr. and Mrs. Williams of The Rowans, Wickenham, Surrey, astonished their friends by announcing that they were going for a three weeks' holiday to Switzerland. Switzerland! How very enterprising and exciting! There was quite a flutter in Wickenham households at the news.

Such a flutter must have its occasions.

So Wickenham households commanded white tables to be laid. Thin glasses to tilt and glitter. Music to trickle through dusk as platters glided through rooms in the clasp of unseen hands. The rustle of the servants' uniforms was lighter than the grazing of snow across the glass. Glinting asymmetries of frost split into tracks like hair beyond the slumped velvet drapes. These patterns echoed in the red cracks of raw work that marked the servants' hands. But no one from Wickenham households detected such traces. Labour took place in a rough world outside their scope, their senses. It was the flutter that they responded to, the bright hiss: oh, Switzerland! Shrill tales criss-crossed the table, loud recountings boomed: feats, delights, ordeals. Wickenham society raised its voices, its glasses, to the vision of a daring couple setting off — stylishly, of course — into the black-veined crests of snow.

Yet it was a different flutter that passed through Mrs. Williams, seated, as she finally was that winter, at the last of the long tables. Mrs. Williams, or Violet to her friends, appeared to be fixed in the act of staring. At the series of white plates. At the white light slithering along the stems of the silverware. Up at the stabs of whiteness spanning from the chandelier's clouded drips and curls.

The slick of tears appeared to be straining to hold to the whites of Mrs. Williams' eyes.

'In Switzerland,' she was heard to murmur, 'all my things must be marked with my own number.' A remark that nobody, except of course her husband, Lawrence, could understand.

'My utensils, you see. My plate and cup, cutlery and such.'

There was still no comprehension from her audience. Although, with the strangeness of her comments, the flutter around the table was felt to alter disconcertingly. It dropped to a hum: heavy, ominous, not at all encouraged at Wickenham social events.

Violet repeated, 'You see . . .'

'Darling,' objected Mr. Williams. Although he himself was gazing downward, deep into the liquid white disc of his plate. He concentrated on tightening two fists, which he lined stiffly either side of his china, concealing the fingernails that otherwise shone with the same clean elegance as his oiled hair. (Even then, Miss Evans, no longer young, was prone to looking for his fingernails. Imagining their fluted coarseness. The silken indiscreet scratch they might transmit along one's spine.)

'Darling,' Mr. Williams urged again. But no one present had ever heard his words involve such choking. Lawrence was a man renowned among other men for speaking with acumen; privately among the women his tones were loved for their sleek disdain.

'Yes. We agreed we wouldn't say. We would call it an expedition, an adventure. But, you see —'

She looked up. Her look made a long tour of faces around the table. At the centre her eyes were emptily black, a hollow in the room's white shine.

'I think this is the fifth — yes, the fifth occasion we've had our lovely trip celebrated. Yet you all know that I had . . . quite other plans.'

Violet's voice shook on, intent. The dire brightness of her gaze had by now numbed the population. Whoever was stroking the piano had somehow had the signal hissed to them to cease.

'It's impossible you don't all know my plans . . . for the nursery.'

Violet's breath was such a contraction that Miss Evans' knife clattered sideways, her hand thudding after it. In the soundless room there was only her quivering apology, her groping along the starched cloth with ludicrous daintiness.

'I've been laying things out there. A long time,' Violet finished in whispers. 'I saw the doctor because this time I believed . . .'

At which point Mrs. Williams began to twitch.

Wickenham households still remembered, years later, even on her return, how that winter Mrs. Williams had raised her hand. How that hand had seemed to manoeuvre, as if by its own will, in jerks around her face. How bubbles were seen to rise and gleam within her mouth, to slip between her lips and pulse. For a shocking instant. Until out through the thin white fingers blood was suddenly launched.

Above the table — for a moment — floated a chandelier of Mrs. Williams' blood.

On her return Violet insisted on walking out into the black arcade of trees. Leaves smothered the distance. Light descended in thin crossings. Unstable traces of shadow and rain slipped and hushed. She bent, unlaced her boots, proceeded, breathing in time with her cool barefoot crush.

Along her way she let fall shreds of note: small cards from Wickenham society declaring itself, regrettably, unable to call.

After three absent years she paused often, listening. Raised her face, let her eyelids close, colour, throb. Leaves made her a black hood. Waste and pollen released, stirred under her fingers. Spores were smeared through her skirts.

Often, she shifted the black box she carried on a black band to the arc of her ribcage. Either side, long tendrils of bone had been sliced through, lifted away.

*

Dunes of snow. Morphine shoved across the heart. Lined, stunned, in our aisles.

Still, I'm grateful — for the sight of the nurse's hand, its task of gripping and wringing. For the low reliable sound of her iron bowl, its surface of loose warped silvers, its drizzled music.

On days, more often, when I don't write, the empty pages slump back and forth through my hand.

The nurses stay unnamed, silently function. Somehow we rattle and drift in our metal beds, to rest, as prescribed, on the balconies. The snow scatters, according to routine. By the evening, shallows of scalding cold glaze our canvas coverlets, glisten in the infinite quiet. But, as instructed, we don't move. I no longer even ask — though I learnt all the phrases so carefully — about the baby, my chances. I know the children's wards are on the upper floors. I imagine them above me. Curled in solace, under this same shawl of cold. They say it's curative.

Above me, in the high ceiling, there's a white sculpted circle. I've had hours to stare up at its wide braided dome. But the electric bulb that hangs from the centre stops me staring too hard at the small healthy angels. Upstairs, like the spinal cases in here with me, there are real children sealed in their own plaster haloes.

Dusk and a death: a close death, in the bed across from me. But barely a disturbance. No throes. Just a life passing with a low liquid moan. We're so obedient now, we don't lift ourselves to soothe or flinch. Instead, we lie back vacant, relieved. Other endings have lingered: death-cool, the corridors hold on to echoes here. There's no way to sleep through that visceral aria.

The nurses circle, drape the bed as dark falls. They've been taught to conceal. But the mountains lean into the ward, sparkling. And this time, besides, the nurses carry a larger pail. We hear them, bathing, unbinding.

Soon, in a room we know exists, there will be the autopsy. With the same dull, clean hands, tomorrow, the doctor is due to examine me. He'll haul the body at wrist and hip, thumb the blue thoracic wound, tap along the wasted straps of bone. But he will be more interested in the dead. He learns more from them: the living withhold answers. Otherwise, he might forget the difference.

Beyond the curtain we hear the woman's belongings packed to be burnt, hear the water's rock and drip.

In the kitchen, when I would watch the maid bathe her baby in the pan on the table, she would hold up the cloth and he would wriggle his fists up to try and grab the clear chain of beads. Each time unable to believe in them dissolving.

Simple rules. Monotones. Snow, snow, the sky crushed with it. The doctor calls this ward his 'absolutes': meaning we're ordered to absolute rest. But we also know what it means. Out on the cure porches we lie, static. Sometimes a breath bursts into the quiet. But mostly we're not evident. Along our bedframes the phosphorescent gravel of the snow.

Tonight the nurses roll the colonial woman into the deathbed's place. As if she were only a sequel to the woman they removed. An exchange of bodies that might pass unnoticed.

Although eventually the chaplain does traipse around to nod at our bedsides. He brings his trim comments on mortality, his rations of psalm. When we suffer, we partake of Christ, *he reminds us.*

So that's what I keep coughing up, the colonial woman says. The chaplain falters, blinks, but lets it pass.

On our lockers he props up small cards of scripture, patting them, instead of us, with his mild, orthodox hand.

Ina, the colonial woman, prone in her bed, receives her card with a snarl that shocks him. Well, whoopee! Coupons for heaven, she says.

I like her immediately.

*

When she walked out from the trees, Violet still cradled the black box. Miss Evans, tilted as primly as she could manage in the sprawling white lawn chair, opened her mouth to enquire. But glanced across at Lawrence. She pressed two narrow, waxy fingers to the nerves of her lips and swallowed the remark. In three years of tests, lapses, pressures, they'd developed a language. Or at least Miss Evans had learnt his: he thumbed his ash aside now, for instance, not with indifference but with scrutiny. There was a tone associated with the angle at which his lashes tensed across his gaze.

Violet advanced, gauntly. She seemed to exert herself just to move ahead through the patterned red ripples of her dress.

'Hello,' said Miss Evans, her pitch too light, fraught. Up close, the shade and bulk of Violet's dress was so unsuitable that Miss Evans felt her own breath as an abrasion. Over the cut-away sections of chest the empty fabric bulged forward like a sling.

'Well, here she is,' stated Lawrence. He knocked away further fronds of ash, staring down at his own deft hand. 'Do you know, Miss Evans, my dear Violet has returned to me no less bloody-minded. She knew you were expected, but declared she wouldn't rest until she'd seen the woods.'

'Oh. Did you?'

'Hello. Yes.'

Violet stared at the third chair but did not sit. The knuckles of one hand she brushed along the threads of white cane until they pressed, with a creak, into the deepest clefts. Cool moist dust was caught in the scorings of the cane.

'Yes. Hello again.'

Tentatively, two long parallels of bone pronounced themselves, slanted, in Violet's wrist. Miss Evans had to look away from the veins' blue fluency.

But Violet's voice had already begun: monotone, drowsing. Miss Evans found it hypnotic.

'I couldn't see any trees from my last bed. When I dreamed them, it was all our trees here, fallen. I'd be walking through them. Back and forth, through all the broken trunks, like a maze.'

Miss Evans quaked sideways in her low chair. She clenched herself and stared down at the lawn. From thoughtless fingers,

Lawrence was allowing his ash to drip: capsized, a beetle struggled beneath a burning frill.

'After a while I couldn't seem even to imagine them properly, to see real living trees. Our ward had only one plant. No one seemed to know what its name was. The top of the leaf felt like oil. The way it feels over skin. And the underside was like chalk. You see?'

Miss Evans, looking aside at Mr. Williams' fingers, did see. For three years Violet had been a ghost, had passed through, paralysed all Miss Evans' embraces. Had polluted each moment when Mr. Williams had failed, covered his eyes, reached. In those moments Miss Evans had almost stepped, almost sunk, into a future. Ties, sorrows, complexities of guilt had almost been undone, exited, as roughly as a dress. But always she'd felt Violet resurface, slide, under Lawrence's grip. Which had, ultimately, wavered, braced — and been withheld.

In Miss Evans' own dreams Violet recurred, seated, at that final table: she did not haemorrhage but placed down a winning hand of cards in a calm red flush.

'Was it a climber?' Miss Evans managed to mutter at the lawn. The cupped clear wings of the beetle extended from the curl of ash with a soundless flap.

'Yes,' replied Violet. But vaguely, as though the sound of Miss Evans had drifted out from her own monologue. 'I think it was. Perhaps that was why.'

'Why what? Darling?' Lawrence, imperative with the term, botched the softness of it.

'Why it always seemed to return my touch.' She moved her gaze to Miss Evans. 'How long have you been waiting?'

'Oh, no. You're not to mind that,' spluttered Miss Evans. She would have loved to be the kind of woman who could give her little gloves a wave, flippantly. Close her teeth on a tingle of dismissive laughter.

'You're not to mind that. Really.'

'No,' said Violet, 'but I understand how hard it is. Waiting. Perhaps you'd think I got to the point where I stopped minding. Perhaps I did.'

There was nothing either querulous or plaintive in her tone. She seemed merely to quote the words.

'But you should mind,' she went on. 'For your own sake.'

Miss Evans watched the knuckles Violet had wreathed into the weathered cane. Woven the same way, the white bassinet had vanished from the nursery, on Miss Evan's instructions. *Out of kindness*, she'd whispered to herself, pausing once, before disposal, to touch its twined lace: for a moment, with her own aches, she'd set it rocking, found herself made cold by its fibrous croon. *Simply, out of kindness.* Looking back to Violet's hand she imagined she could see the durable pulse that tapped, tapped at the base of the bluegreen bones.

'You're forbidden to walk anywhere else today,' broke in Lawrence. 'You're exhausted. I'm forbidding you.'

Violet wandered toward him and tipped, with neither malice nor frailty, as if to nestle his face. Miss Evans observed the box shift on its black noose between them; in the silence its weight circled, creaking. Surely the thing was a relic, Miss Evans thought. Surely she heard it rattle; its lens looked blistered. But one unshuttered eye fixed back on her. Scratched on the glass were sudden harsh crosses of light. And underneath it Miss Evans read the word 'Target'.

She hardly noticed Violet bend to focus the finder on the grass. The insect had kicked from its dome of ash. Righted, it shone like an atom spilled free from her dress.

*

The colonial woman is a photographer. She props her camera on her bed and takes aimless shots, although she can't move to peer into the finder (the nurses have promised confiscation if she does). She takes snow, a frieze of railings, the last blossom dissolving on the ward's only plant. She takes the dip of the needle into her own arm, the kaleidoscope of blood that she coughs into her tray, syllable by syllable. She takes the sudden dazzle of mercury that snaps from a thermometer, metallic syrup rolling into vessels on the floor. She takes the forsaken eyes in the bed beside her. She takes bristles of frosted blood spreading on sheets. But mostly she takes snow, in streaks, shackles, snow in broken garlands, murky spheres.

She's mad, of course.

I suppose she catches nothing but blots of translucence, tangled blurs.

It's as pointless as me writing: snow, snow.

From time to time we hear the soldiers heckle the nurses down the hall. But they're paltry, cracked-up men — do as they're told. We hear their bodies gulping up sputum on rounds, as per instructions: they sound no different to us. The one young man who limped, blinking, into our room seemed to know it too — that there's now so little difference between woman and man. Although history, also, has blasted his face with a raw scrawl of skin. We lay in our racks, looking back at him. I didn't see thirst in him, only recognition: eyes that no longer expected to wake somewhere else. And he didn't say anything; only his ribcage hissed. He simply watched, then withdrew in bent half steps. He was still silent as we heard the nurses scold him — their bright ignorant choir.

Tonight, the lukewarm threading of blood.

I feel it nuzzle between the lips, one bud rising to rest, a pearl, against the pubic bone.

Months, through years, this would happen and I'd be without hope.

Now it is hope itself.

I don't call the nurse.

I lie and try to feel it, along every nerve, its tiny lapping warmth, its tattoo unravelling.

Hymns. Delirium. The frozen room smells of our fevers. The doctor notes down conclusions. The snow, in stars, chalks over them.

On the fresh X-ray the doctor holds up it seems to me that the snow is also transposed. There are the drains. There is the white ghost of the lobes, strewn with black lights. The bones, almost broken free in the place they are freshly eroding, like flakes of snow themselves, are floating.

The doctor shakes his head and gestures back to the X-ray when I ask about a baby. As if my baby is somehow also floating there.

Her ghost, undeveloped.

In my last ward there was a young woman who had been here since a child. From her girlhood ward she said she could stare down into a distant room. She could see the doctor ploughing open the bodies. Some nights there was a queue. She could even hear the knell of his sterilised tools. Her smile, as she told me, was just like the colonial woman's.

But even Ina does not always manage to stay cynical. Yesterday she translated the plea that keeps rising from the dark girl three beds down. The dark girl has a photograph of her fiancé, but by now it's a mesh of fingerprints, her lover seen through smoke. We hear her rosary spin, dangle, the beads almost as large as the joints standing out in her hand. Some of the spinals are only half splinted, but the dark girl seems lodged in a full steel silhouette. Over and over, she groans the same sentence.

She's asking us all, Ina translates, if we will be her bridesmaids.

The disease has begun to spread into dreams. It's taken this long: I used to be well there, whole. But I'm still less broken. The will to touch, to hold, still stirs, unshattered. It's not so when I wake.

Last night, I dreamed the soldier came into my cubicle, his long withered body flapping from the crutches like a wing. He stood and stared at me: longing, mangled. Without hesitation I slid from my bed and joined us in a long bloodshot kiss.

Until a gutter of it ran down between us.

The reality is: if Lawrence stood by my bed now I would fail to respond, to act. I would only stare out at him, from this distance.

I asked to be sent here, stubbornly, to come so far away. If I were closer, if there were a chance of getting home to him, I thought I would be bound to break out, to run away, escape. I thought I would not be able to stop myself.

There was so little need.

Not long ago, my husband, a hero, came home steadily, without question, across a war, to me.

The chaplain, unwilling to let Ina daunt him, reappears today. This time the token he tries to leave her is an image of Christ, strung up, pierced. She falls silent, eyes up the wound in his side. It's drawn brightly, a quarry of bruise and pulp. The chaplain, emboldened, asks her how the scene makes her feel.

Well, she drawls, I guess the pneumothorax hasn't been fine-tuned much in the last 2000 years.

Thin as salt, the snow litters our blankets, hardens to a slate. We could scratch our names on it. But we don't.

Perhaps this is despair. But that seems too active, too strenuous a word, too much like a call that still expects to be answered. A cry that imagines it could be consoled. Instead, it is zero, zero that the open eyes show; it is nothing that gapes in the faces.

The woman beside me cries, motionless. Her eyes release a long, fused series of tears. They are incidental and soon frozen.

Body by body we are dyed white, whiter, in our steel groves.

Below, above, there are storeys of us. Ice stretches a ghetto from face to face.

*

'Would you?' she said, and turned her spine, which was already half released from the dress.

Where she stood, the shape of her footprint had stayed, crushed, amassing itself in the fibres. Lawrence had watched it for three years. She used to stand here, sly, on this dulled plush, smiling away from him as she eased from her dress with smooth implication, discarded it with certainty.

'Yes, of course.'

He turned to put out his cigarette. He'd built up shores of ash in their separation, trays cluttered with silt around the house. He liked the act of grinding the thing out: it pleased him to watch the burst of dust in the glass like a small contained explosion.

'I'm glad to see you've put down . . . the artefact.'

He stood behind his wife, began on the dress.

When she'd gone, Lawrence had been advised to burn her remaining clothing. He'd tried, watching it incinerate: sheaths curdled, collars shrivelled into black coils. Silks breathed away their structures — the scent, the print of her instantly undone. She owned nothing shoddy or worn: only her body, secretly fraying beneath it all.

The catches were tricks, made him exhale, grapple. Hoops of shadow marked out the nodes of bone as he worked down the dress.

(Coats turned as if filled with the memory of her, velvets fell and oozed into a broth. Gloves beckoned, crawling inwards.)

'Sorry,' he said. 'Stupid. Stupid of me.'

(Buttons sifted through the drum with the tap of fingernails.)

'Sorry. It's my great hands. They make me quite hopeless.'

He lowered the dress with a scrape.

'Hopeless.'

She turned. Waited.

He'd uncovered muscle in narrow strands. Booths of shadow were formed by the subtracted ribs. The scars were silvery in some places, in others still chapped: her breathing set them adrift. For a moment the child she craved seemed to trail toward him through the shallow skin, uncurl, slip. Lacerations flickered with its absence. Against his thumb he felt the beat and brush, as of a fontanel.

'Well. There you are,' he said. 'All done.'

He stepped away, crossed the room.

'Yes. Here I am.'

Lawrence lit a cigarette, concentrated on it. How it charred in intricate waves.

Burning her things, he'd looked down into the drum of her glossy bubbling gowns, and cowered. He'd come to her red dress, held it, hoarded it, unable to complete the task. He'd had to leave the rest of the bonfire to the servants, watching it flare from the windows of the emptied nursery. All that afternoon her grit had mixed with the baby's things, poured away into the trees. Some white gusts were as dense as the shawl he'd watched her unfolding, had imagined her wrapping their child in.

Miss Evans had been there to supervise, of course. She'd been so competent, sorting, directing the servants, standing with such neutrality in his wife's smoke. Browsing through the ash.

When she'd walked back to the house, touched him, he'd felt relief. She had an aptitude for blankness, a method of muting the room with her limited gestures; there was a calming non-entity to her narrow flesh. He relaxed, as if somehow set behind his wartime desk again. Listening to the detached click, the alphabet launched across page after page, impersonal shrapnel, the cool encoded bleeding of ink. Where it had made no difference how the paper he issued might shape events, decide who would come home.

He paused, looked around.

That was where she'd placed her camera. Beside the photograph she'd taken with her: for courage, she said. He watched himself, in uniform, starred, suave, a decorated fraud.

*

Somewhere, they say, there is a rink. The well, the whole, tie on their blades and glide there, cutting patterns into the cold. They are sliding on solid water and do not stop to think of it. They fall and do not drown.

They skate through ghosts: breathing one another's laughter.

I imagine I can hear the sound from my bed. Sometimes I imagine Lawrence there. Scratching his place into the dark ice, dancing with the strong.

Truth: I'm a coward. I look away as they bare and swab the torso of the woman next to me. Her gills — crimped, audible — the twin of my own.

There's the chiming of instruments, strict, wet. There's her iris, swimming up under mine.

If Lawrence were here I'd ask him to finish this for me.

I dream that I'm shaving Lawrence and slice his throat through the foam. There's a scarlet avalanche.

I dream of the tin toy I left in the nursery, Lawrence's toy passed on from childhood. You wind the key and a thin shaking fireman climbs a ladder and down again. I hear the tin man, the brittle circuit, squeal like a siren in a distance I can't reach.

I dream that I'm bathing the maid's baby, and instead of water running from the cloth it is mercury, dripping down in pearls. I can't stop it and this time he catches the cells. They flash and shiver, speeding and bonding on his skin. He closes his hand and smiles at me.

Gloom yellows from a new lamp at the ward's end: we turn our heads for this great event.

Sometimes, down there at the glass panel, they'd hold up the children for the mothers in here, let them wave, if they pledged not to stir, if they swore to be good. So I ask Ina if she'll take a photograph next time. Although it's been a long while since one of these distant visits. Although there's only ever been a ripple, the stain of a face, the limbs faint strokes through glass.

Ina is quiet at first. Then she tells me: because of infection they won't let her send film out.

Spooled inside the box she grips and grips, there is no film.

There has not been for months.

This is what strikes me: not that she's mad, but that I understand her.

Perhaps it's the new lamp, throbbing softly beyond my head. But for a long time I think I can see it pass along the far pane: that wasted trail of light.

Pain, here, is not personal. It is a tide. Each day you feel it filling the room — smooth, shining, lethal. In this ward we no longer try to swim, to cling. We don't even call through the rising current. We lie, soundless, lame, in the rafts we know won't hold us. The wheels quiver, the frames chill and sing, the sheets drag. One by one we slip under, not even watching each other. Until the ward is only a pool, an element. Into which the mountains tilt and brim.

Time elapses, only for more ice to form. I try to let my mind drift. But I can't break it free from the rafters of snow.

All our shadows, unmoving, have nowhere to run but back into our eyes.

The nurses prise white lips, lever in hope in tiny tepid spoonfuls. Rub the vein until it blooms.

Whichever bed they pass to is a dead end.

Faintly, deeply, through my daughter's eyelid there's the graffiti of a single blood vessel.

When she's wet, two symmetrical whorls of pale down shine above each shoulderblade, spiralling outward.

Blue-white, her bellybutton is a frail globe, as wide as a thumbnail, a membrane that quivers when she laughs.

When she cries, her left eye overflows first, always from the inner corner, tracking down to break around her scarred lip (the tin toy, a fall, sprinting through our hallway), to drip into her mouth.

This is how close she comes to me.

Now that I know she is never coming.

The nurses tread, tend, drone. There's the sound of the dark girl's rosary skimming her cage, the loop of her endless whisper.

I long, now, to be her bridesmaid.

*

There were so many ghosts in the woods that at first Violet did not see the child crossing the lens.

The maid's son stomped closer, legs packed into chafed shorts, bulging pockets dabbed with pitch fingerprints. The knobs of his toes pushed up in his wilted boots. The skin beneath his nose shone with a smirch of mucus.

'My mum reckons in them places they tie sick kids into their beds. That true?'

'Yes. Sometimes. Sometimes they do.'

'You wouldn't catch me standing for it,' he boasted with surly eyebrows, chewing his mouth into jowls.

'I see that.'

He nudged aside, waded through the rough slush of flowers, heaved with a foot at leaf-scrap, slime.

'She's out there, waiting, that woman.'

'Oh.'

'My mum says that woman wants keeping an eye on. She's no better than she should be, my mum says. Nor him.'

Scratching through the lull of birdsong, something scuffled in a nest. The boy crouched, peered, gunning his fingers. His lips tucked into a tight bunch over his milk teeth, he made the sound of artillery. The air beyond his face was speckled with bullets of spit.

He shrugged back to Violet.

'My mum knows about them places. She's the only one of her lot it didn't finish off. And she was born in one of them places. They whipped her straight out of her mum and shipped her off. Didn't even let her old sick mum say hello. So that's what she knows.'

Stubbornly, through the water his mother must have applied, his hair had formed reefs of chopped curl. Grime plugged his nails and made thick ditches in the lines of his hands. He fidgeted at his pockets, snug with broken things. He had a habit of gulping away his collar. She could smell him: both carbolic and animal.

'You want to put your boots back on,' he sniffed, an order.

There was scant blue in his eye: the belly of the iris was twilight, the see-through silver she remembered from X-rayed flesh.

She couldn't fend off his beauty. She had to sit down.

For a while the leaves hissed and drowsed.

'Do you know,' she began, to stop him leaving, 'sometimes the children manage to untie themselves. They use the string to tie notes to, to send them down over the balcony. They look . . . like the most beautiful snow. I remember that. Those notes, hanging there. Once, when the chaplain was trying to talk about God, I told him that was God to me . . . all the God I could think of any more. Just the strips of notes. Just those notes, fluttering.'

'What did they say, then? Them notes.' He trooped back and forth again, ransacked his pockets.

'I don't know. I never got to touch them. I'd a friend who

took a picture, though.'

'You write back?'

'Oh. Perhaps.'

'If I'd written one of them notes, you know what it would have said?'

'No.'

'Sod this for a bleeding joke. That's what.' He rummaged again at his collar, squinted. A fleck of sleep battered up and down on his lashes.

'Yes. I think my friend would have written something like that.'

'What happened to her, then?'

Violet watched the reaping movement of his foot through the leaves.

'She . . . was sent home.'

'My mum reckons sometimes they send them home because they've had it. Not because they've come right.'

Violet looked at him, his body soaking all the sky it could through the black aisles of trees.

'Which one are you?'

Behind his head the bark cracked into ripples. In answer Violet raised the black box.

'Are you going to take me?'

'I'll try. Yes.'

The tough face flickered open, spilt along the lens in billows.

*

Straggling through light again today, notes lowered from the children's wing. Maybe they're not cowards, like us — maybe it's their tiny fingers, fitted to scratch open whatever hope they can — but somehow they snip through their harnesses, break each other, in dirty whispers, from their cribs.

Shivering sticks of half word, stammers of ink, crinkled,

dangling. I imagine their breath smudging the scraps, tiny urgent croaks. I see them scribbling questions through icy muscles. Fumbling the knots, slice by slice.

Soundlessly, spine-shaped, the rope of notes hangs, spirals.

The snow turns it to film.

White paper, black paper.

I want to believe that the few words that slip, glitter, from their cord could reach my hand, could be enough.

INTERROGATION

— Albert Wendt

I.

Andrea, my wife, possesses this uncanny, wonderful, sometimes frightening gift of experiencing these uncanny, wonderful, sometimes frightening dreams and then recalling them for only me and Regina, our daughter, in multi-coloured detail and in what she calls 'the dream's language'.

So on that unusually cold December Saturday morning when she woke as usual at 6 am, and deliberately woke me by rolling against my side, and, out of the dim dark, said, with urgent excitement and awe: 'Although it sounded all the year round, although it rang out sometimes as early as half-past six in the morning, sometimes as late as half-past ten at night, it was in the spring, when Bengel's violet patch inside the gate was blue with flowers, that that piano . . . made the passers-by not only stop talking, but slow down, pause, look suddenly — if they were men — grave, even stern, and if they were women — dreamy, even sorrowful,' I knew we were into yet another enthralling interrogation session. It was as if she were quoting from a story written by an experienced writer such as Katherine Mansfield, whose work I'd loved at high school. 'That's exactly how I *saw* that dream and how it wrote itself into my sight,' she insisted.

Our life together has been influenced intensely by the way we interrogate and read her dreams. Even the name of our daughter, Regina, came in a dream the night before Andrea gave birth to her. The dream had also said that the love between Regina and Andrea would be special and would never be broken.

'So shall we interrogate the text you've just described?' I asked, for that was our usual procedure after each dream she considered important. Gently she slid her leg over my stomach, and put her right arm around my chest, her warm nudity and odour of dry sweat and Figiel perfume wrapping around me like a comforting second skin. The centre window curtains were parted down the middle and the summer light was pushing itself through the gap and lying protectively across our shoulders.

'I didn't recognise the street, the garden or the house,' she whispered, her warm slightly stale breath pulsing against the right side of my face. 'But I knew the street is here in Ponsonby.'

We married a few months after we completed our Masters degrees — she in civil engineering and me in architecture — and then, with my parents' financial help, bought this villa that was built in the 1910s, and which I've restored and enlarged, even having it lifted and a double garage constructed under it. Impressed with my restoration, many architectural clients over the years have hired us to restore their villas.

'What about the Bengels?'

'A very striking name. Whatever its origins, I've never come across that name in my life.' I asked her if she'd seen any of the Bengels, and she replied, 'Almost. I think the father — yes, the father was prematurely old and had salt'n'pepper hair, and he wore a black double-breasted suit, like the ones men wore in the 1920s, and his son was the pianist but I wasn't that interested in his age and appearance.'

'What about the music he was playing?'

'It was that classical stuff that I've always found — difficult. But this time I found myself loving it and I wanted to tell you that. It just entered my welcoming eyes and shimmered, like the pianist's fingers, down my throat into my ravenous belly and other vital regions!' Her body trembled invitingly against me.

'Chopin or Mozart or Bach?' I tried the few classical composers I was familiar with.

'Yeah, the first one — Chopin, the music our nephew Rodney plays every time we go to your arrogant sister's house.' I ignored her denigration of my sister because her live twinkling fingers were now playing Chopin, as it were, across my belly just above my 'vital regions'.

'So what about the passers-by?'

'Yes, I saw two very thin middle-aged men wearing heavy woollen overcoats — dark blue, their coats were — stopping at the front gate, and, putting their right hands to their right ears, listened intently to the playing, with smiles radiating across their pale faces, radiating and radiating until they were part of the exhilarating tide that was the music.'

'Any others?'

'Yes, an elderly rotund woman, with a court jester's multi-coloured felt hat — I didn't find that strange, a long blood-red scarf wrapped round and round her throat, its ends fluttering in the breeze that was funnelling down against her.' Andrea paused, pondering, and then, chortling almost inaudibly, she said, 'She stopped, gripped the front gate's handle, but, unable to unlock it, she shook it violently once, twice, three times, said, "Fuck that!" — and that really shocked me because women shouldn't swear in public.' She paused and then said, 'You know, I don't care if women swear wherever and whenever but in that dream that's how I felt about that woman swearing.' Paused. 'By the way, I think the dream is also sexist in pandering to the stereotypes that men assumed "grave, even stern" demeanours, and women "dreamy, even sorrowful" ones when they heard that music.'

'Perhaps it was part of the time the dream is set in?'

'I suppose, so it's dated in that way, the wording of it coming out of the late nineteenth early twentieth century, maybe.'

'And why do you think spring and blue violets in that garden?'

'Perhaps it's because I *love* blue, and randy spring — you know that, darling.' Her fingers were now searching pleasurably through my garden, as it were.

'Do you want to continue this dream interrogation or not?' I insisted.

'Okay,' she said, taking her hand away. She turned onto her back, and, gazing at the blue ceiling across which the morning light was now pushing back the darkness, pondered and then said, 'The piano was a black-lacquered grand.'

And so we continued that interrogation into the eternal question that whole civilisations have tried to answer: where do those strangers in your sleep life come from, and why have they come? A question that Andrea, well before we met, had started living with because of her gift and the circumstances of her life; a question her grandmother had tried to answer years before; and a question that, over the years, has become a binding strand in our marriage.

Andrea was born in Samoa as Autasi Lagilua in the village of Gagaifo, Lefaga. (She changed her Christian name to Andrea, with my encouragement, not long after we met.) I was born in Malie and my parents brought me to New Zealand when I was only five so I was raised here, while Andrea migrated here after she graduated from high school. When we first courted at Auckland University in the late 1970s, she told me that her parents had drowned at sea when she was a toddler and she had been raised by Faivai, her maternal grandmother, who'd believed profoundly in the *truth* of dreams being at the heart of all reality, and because of that you had to learn not only how to live with them and facilitate their entry into your sleep, but how to read them and what they meant for your waking life. For instance, the first of her grandmother's *readings* that Andrea could remember and describe to me, in her grandmother's compellingly poetic storytelling manner, with which I was to become familiar over the years, was this:

In the centre of the silver dark, in the protecting feel of it, is a luminous ocean-green dragonfly, a variety I've not seen before — delicate, with darkly veined transparent wings beating quickly, keeping it hovering, defeating gravity. Then at the rim of the dark I sense a crowd of spectators, their hushed curiosity focused on the wondrous creature. When their faces are lit up by the dragonfly's luminosity I don't recognise any of them and wonder why I don't, and am afraid because they aren't Samoan or Papalagi or Chinese or any other race I know. Before I can identify them, the dragonfly rises up suddenly to the height of our breath and sight. We all sigh loudly in applause. It turns its head towards me and my heart sings with joy as the creature bows, yes, bows once, acknowledging my worth, my value, my existence. And I wake up, weeping, sobbing . . .

Andrea first told me this on a Saturday night on our second date, after we went to the movies — a forgettable thriller — and we were eating at the Ponsonby KFC. (I can still smell the acidic odour of the cooking oil.) I couldn't understand why she was telling me this and why it was important to her. I'd been raised by my deacon lay preacher father and scientifically trained mother to consider such things as irrational, even superstitious. But because I was extremely attracted to Andrea — and had been so since I'd first seen her at our MA anthropology class on Polynesia — I needed to indulge her. She went on relating her grandmother's narration:

For the next few days I tried to decipher that dream. What puzzled me most was this question: how do people and creatures you've never known become part of your dreams? Have we existed before not only as people but as other creatures and things? My beloved, Autasi, that is one of the questions that will be at the centre of your life forever.

Andrea stopped and, gazing sceptically at me, asked, 'You're not really interested in this stuff, are you?' She smiled when she caught my half nod. And immediately explained that her grandmother had believed that everyone and everything was connected through gafa/genealogy right back to the atua, and that gafa was intelligent, and when you *maliu-ed* — moved on — you became part of that intelligence and the inheritance of your descendants.

The rest of that fried chicken conversation amid that invasive cooking-oil smell I can't recall in detail, except that she reached across the table and, grasping my hand firmly, smiled — it was like a beautiful gardenia opening to fill all my sight — and said, 'Don't worry, I'm not crazy, I'm just strange, but you'll get used to that. And I hope you want to get used to it, right?'

I nodded unreservedly, unconditionally, and meant it as a promise.

'Good,' she whispered, 'I want to know you, too.'

When I drove her home that night, the dragonfly continued hovering with all its marvellous luminosity and gravity-defeating flight in my eyes. Holding on to my arm, Andrea slid into my side as I drove.

II.

Andrea jumped out of bed, arms wrapped around her chest. 'Fuck, for summer, it's bloody cold!' she cried, and scrambled into the bathroom and the shower, as she did every morning. She was right: it was crisply cold out of bed, so I put on my favourite dressing gown — the blue-striped woollen one she bought me for my fortieth birthday — and, scurrying down the cold passageway, turned on a few of the heaters. In the quick breakfast routine we'd established over our life together I soon had the electric jug on, the coffee ground, the milk in the microwave for eighty seconds, a glass of orange juice for her, a glass of grapefruit for me, two whole-wheat slices in the toaster, and the table set — even with napkins.

'So how are you reading your dream?' I continued as soon as she sat down opposite me, smelling sweetly of McMullin soap and Daniell shampoo, and in her bright red dressing gown, which was open down the front. I took my first sip of my coffee, eagerly anticipating its hot, addictive taste sliding down my throat and warming up my chest, waking up all my nerves.

With both hands and a thick fluffy white towel, she continued kneading the wetness out of her hair, her face and exposed breasts glowing red from the heat of the shower. How she glowed!

'First thing is: I've never seen violets in any Ponsonby garden. So what does that mean?'

'Perhaps they represent how you felt while in that dream, as you observed the Bengels. So repeat the wording of the dream and we'll see.' After she repeated it, I asked, 'Don't you think there is some sadness in that?'

'Yes, maybe in the way it's worded, but I didn't feel any sadness in the scene while I was there.'

'The piano playing, you know. Doesn't that suggest strange

compulsive behaviour?'

'It may to someone who reads the wording, but it wasn't in the dream. I accepted it as normal behaviour.'

'What did you think of the relationship between the father and the son, if you thought anything at all about it?'

'Normal. Now I'm awake, I could read something else into it, but I don't want to.'

'So, say you didn't wake up at the time you did, and the dream had continued for some length, what do you think would have unfolded, darling?'

'You know I never speculate outside the dream itself!' Her knife crunched across her piece of toast. 'I never unfold a dream outside the boundaries of sleep.'

I knew that, but for some inexplicable reason, for the past few weeks, ever since Regina had rung and told us she and Ralph were separating, I now wanted her to. 'Just indulge me, darling, just . . .'

'Because you're a lit freak who feeds on stories, you want me to do that, even though it's against the rules I've determined?' She took an impatient gulp of her coffee, thrust the piece of toast into her mouth. Her immaculately white teeth crunched down decisively on it and she started chewing rapidly. 'Okay, let me develop the story outside the dream.' Gulped down more coffee, took another massive bite of her toast, thumped down her mug, and, gazing through me, back into her dream, she said, 'The plot line would go something like this: Harold Mansfield Bengel, the father, is a retired bank manager who, five years before, had lost his lifelong, devoted wife, Katherine, to a pulmonary haemorrhage, leaving him to care for their only child, Dyer Beauchamp, who is autistic and a savant.' Paused, deliberately challenging me: so, see what you can do with *that*!

We'd often discussed autism and savants, ever since Andrea had claimed, after excelling in three papers in psychology at university, that perhaps her grandmother had had a mild form of autism and was something of a savant in her incredible gift for remembering and re-singing any music you played or sang to her, and in her mesmerising ability to talk in the accents of the strangers in her dreams. 'Wasn't she feared, considered evil by your village because of that?' I'd asked. Not feared, not evil, she'd replied. 'Hadn't the church condemned such — such behaviour as being part of Samoa's evil pagan past?' I'd pursued her. 'Yes, but when people learned that through her they could connect with their loved ones who'd passed on, and that through her the future could speak to them, they came to love her — but behind the church's back, of course! They especially loved her songs — the songs she fished out of her dreams, which, when I was old enough, she taught me and I taught our village choir. Some of those songs became national favourites and are still sung today.' She listed a whole swag of them, but because I was raised in New Zealand, I recognised only two.

III.

'So, to continue my Hollywood script: With the help of the best psychologists, Dyer Beauchamp is identified as a savant with an insatiable talent for playing the piano. He is given the best teacher' — Andrea refused to slow down as she steered our shopping cart through the crowded entrance into Foodtown in Williamson Avenue, where we shopped every Saturday morning — 'As yet I can't think of a suitable name for that teacher. The teacher *has* to be a middle-aged woman — men are bloody useless at handling autistic kids. She could be a failed concert pianist with the relentless determination to become triumphant through her gifted pupil . . .' In hurrying to keep up to her, in a busy aisle, I bumped into a tall, solid man dressed in a dirty singlet and black shorts and mud-caked sports shoes, who exuded the foulest BO my nostrils had ever encountered.

'Watch where ya're going, chief!' BO objected as I stepped left and out of his way, catching red-veined eyes, a stubbled face, and gaps in his front teeth. I refused to apologise as I hurried after Andrea, who hadn't noticed the incident and was still talking as if I was beside her.

'. . . At the age of ten, Dyer gives his first public concert. It's a smash hit. People especially love his being autistic. Being a very experienced bank manager, Harold Mansfield becomes his son's full-time manager . . .' We hit one of the coldest sections of the supermarket — the vegetable and fruit section. Dressed only in blue cotton longs and a black T-shirt with three red roses stitched boldly across the front, Andrea shivered and started rubbing her hands crisply up and down her goose-pimpled arms. Her long black hair was tied back in a ponytail and her skin glistened with health — she trained at the gym four days a week.

'Darling, how do you like the script so far?'

'It's like the one for *Shine*,' I tried to joke.

'And all the other Hollywood films about autistic geniuses and other "challenged people".' She wasn't joking. 'But darling, it's meant to be that. You're the one who wanted me to go outside the reality of the dream.'

'But not into corny plots!' I tried disguising my annoyance.

Thrusting a package of lettuce into the cart, then a large pumpkin, all the time avoiding my scrutiny, she said, 'Are there any other types of plot, darling? You should know, since high school when you fell in love with Mansfield, the only New Zealand author they taught then, you've continued reading all those *serious* novels and stories.' I didn't know how to take that accusation — yes, it *was* an accusation. 'Isn't there just one major plot line: the hero and heroine are born, they meet, fall in love and if they don't fall out of that, they live happily or otherwise, and then die?' Before I could react, she said, 'Another variation is: the fearless stranger rides into town, which evil villains have taken over, the citizens are too scared of the villains to help him, so alone and with the fastest guns in the west he outguns the villains, and then rides off into the sunset.' She pointed at the potatoes and bananas and automatically, as I did every Saturday, I grabbed a small bag of potatoes and a hand of the ripest bananas and dumped them in the cart.

She started hurrying to the meat and fish section. 'You should know all that from reading Borges, who was once your favourite writer and who you introduced me to.' Why was she being so aggressive, deliberately belittling me? Why was she so bloody upset just because I asked her to go beyond the boundaries of a dream?

I hurried after her as she chose a rack of lamb and dropped it on top of the potatoes. She began again. 'So the plot line for Dyer Beauchamp is a variation of that: genius who uses his major handicap and gift, led by his mentor and manager and utterly devoted mother, to win the world's love for a while, but instead of riding off into the triumphant sunset, he's left with his dying but devoted father in their lonely family home in their lonely street which he fills everyday with his marvellous playing.'

Without waiting for me to answer, she strode to the fish counter, which was misted over with condensation, and, using a small light blue sheet of waxed paper, picked up a whole snapper with silver, bulbous eyes. She held it up to my face as it dripped, asked, 'You want this for dinner?'

IV.

Williamson Avenue was a glittering river of late morning sun over which heavy lines of traffic were running, separating us from Café Oceania across the street. Andrea wasn't deterred by the traffic: she simply stepped off the footpath and, with her charming smile and holding out her right arm, slowed down the next car. Then she stepped through the gap and, stopping at the middle line, again charmed the left-lane traffic to a halt and stepped through. I waited until the traffic lights stopped the vehicles and then hurried after her, my whole being taut with angry tension and trepidation at meeting Regina and her *problem*.

Regina was waiting for us when we entered the café. Most of the tables were occupied, and the fierce sizzling and smell of frying bacon and sausages and coffee saturated the air. She got up and waved us over to her table. It was one of our favourite eating places and we had taken Regina there ever since she was a child. Physically my daughter looked like me — a delicate, slighter, kinder, handsomer female version of me, or so her mother and everyone we knew kept telling her (and me) as she matured, as if I'd find that a hugely uplifting compliment. I didn't — in fact I've always felt anxiously uncomfortable about it. At first Regina had loved it, taking it as a sign that she was 'Dad's girl'. But when — and I can still remember that cruel, painful happening, at her fifteenth birthday party, surrounded by all her awkwardly self-conscious friends — her best friend Tricia said, 'Gosh, Regina, you look just like your Dad!' and Regina declared, loud enough for everyone to hear: 'No, I don't!' A swiftly delivered stab into my heart, wounding the cord of love that bound us.

When we reached her she embraced her mother, kissing her on the cheek. As Regina gazed at me over her mother's shoulder, I once again experienced the startling pain of that stab. 'Hi, Dad!' she said, stepping away from her mother and holding her hand out to me. I clutched it firmly, pulled her in to me, kissed her on the cheek and was hurt when she pulled away swiftly, smiling. 'How are you, Dad?'

'Good, good,' I said, and took my seat. We'd meant, with my parents' enthusiastic encouragement, to have three children, but after Regina, and trying to raise her at the same time as working full time and building our careers, the three children remained Regina, whom Andrea indulged beyond the limits I thought appropriate for a respectful, dutiful daughter.

We ordered quickly and, when the waiter was gone, were left in awkward heated silence, because even though Andrea and Regina found it easy to make small talk between themselves, I've never found it so, and after Andrea's treatment of me in the supermarket I certainly wasn't feeling charitable or ready to lay myself open to a continuation of that abuse.

'Mother, you remember a few years ago you were into the Genome Project and read and talked about it all the time?' Regina asked. Andrea nodded nonchalantly. 'Well, it's completed now — I read it in *Time* magazine.' I caught a short wounded pause in Andrea's manner — annoyance? I was surprised because I was usually the one who under-rated our daughter's intelligence and, by trying to hide my attitude from Regina and Andrea, merely made it more obvious. Before Regina could continue, the waiter arrived with our drinks. I drained half of my beer quickly, the stark cold of the liquid bursting up to the back of my eyes, stinging them.

'Dad, you shouldn't drink cold things so fast!' Regina said, watching the tears brimming from my eyes.

'Actually, darling, the Genome Project was completed three years ago, and their revolutionary findings are already being explored and used by hundreds of scientists and businesses,' Andrea corrected her. I was dismayed — in the past it would have been me saying that. At university and since, Andrea had learned all she could about cells, DNA, genomes, chromosomes and the Genome Project, and had filled our dream reading with that knowledge, transforming her grandmother's belief in gafa with the whole connectedness of DNA and cells. She decided that our past lives and the people we knew then were all contained in and connected through the cells. It made sense to me, and she'd always been patient explaining it all to Regina, but here she was humiliating our daughter.

'How's work?' I asked Regina, and she looked relieved I'd saved her.

She picked up her knife and fork and, looking directly at me, said, 'It's good, Dad. I'm still enjoying it.' Regina was working as a law clerk, a job our company's lawyer had given her, with Andrea's encouragement. I've always been upset by our daughter's inability to hold down jobs for long.

'Darling, you really *have* to complete your law degree if you want to go any further in law,' Andrea interjected, and I caught the wince in Regina's facial muscles. Why was Andrea behaving in this awful way? Regina had spent three years at university but had dropped out after meeting Ralph, to my huge disappointment. Andrea had defended our daughter by contending that perhaps Regina didn't have the ability to get a degree that she didn't really need anyway. I'd reminded Andrea that she herself had come from a very poor aiga in a backward village in Samoa, but through relentless hard work and scrimping and saving every cent she had completed two degrees — and with first-class honours. I also took Regina's 'failure' as a reflection on us as parents and high achievers. 'You're just a bloody snob and tight-arsed father,' Andrea had accused me. 'Loosen up!'

I took a mouthful of bacon and tomatoes. 'And are you still enjoying your karate classes?' I asked my daughter.

Dismayed by her mother's reversal of roles, Regina observed

her warily from the corners of her eyes. 'Yeah, Dad. I should have my black belt by the end of this session.'

Andrea was now into her food, her head lowered, hiding from the inanities my daughter and I were exchanging. I was the one who usually did that.

'Congratulations, darling!' I replied, now deliberately enjoying seeing Andrea excluded. 'I never got mine. Too much other work.' A foolish admission in front of Andrea. So I added, 'Your mother got hers, of course.' We both expected a reaction from her but she continued eating as if she'd not heard.

V.

When Andrea had nearly finished her meal, she glanced up, blinked and then, deep black eyes focused on Regina, asked, 'And how is Ralph?' She'd always admired Ralph and had quickly agreed with Regina's wish to marry him. I'd considered Ralph an unreliable, smooth-talking wastrel and had opposed it. All these weeks since Regina had rung us about their separation, Andrea and I had carefully avoided discussing it, not even in our interrogation of her dreams.

Regina swallowed twice, avoiding our eyes. Trying to smile, she said softly, 'He's okay, he's fine. Yes, he's fine.'

'That's not what we're asking about, darling,' Andrea continued.

'Then what *are* you asking about?' Regina challenged her, and I was glad for her — if a little surprised. She'd never questioned me and her mother in this defiant way.

I saw the trace of a sly, sarcastic grin on Andrea's face as she turned to me. 'Your father didn't want you to marry him,' she said accusingly.

'No, he didn't, Mother. In fact he ordered me not to!' Regina retaliated — and was it satisfaction I was experiencing right then? I caught Andrea staring at me but I maintained my silence, refusing to be party to her unexpected attack on our daughter.

'Yes, he ordered you and you took absolutely no notice of him and now look what's happened.' Controlled but utterly merciless, she stopped her voice from reaching a pitch at which those near us would hear.

Regina caught the encouragement in my demeanour and replied, in the same controlled manner as her mother, 'And what *has* happened, Mother?'

Her remaining piece of crisp bagel crunched as Andrea stabbed her fork into it. Carefully she placed her knife across her plate, straightened up and, rigid face and burning eyes snaring her daughter, declared, barely a whisper, 'What has happened *is*, you're in the shit again!'

Incredible! How could she berate our daughter this way! But before I could react, Regina, tears tumbling down her cheeks, her body trembling, grasped at my aid. 'Dad, are you going to let her talk to me like — like that?'

I reached across, grasped Regina's shoulders and said, 'It's okay, darling, your mother didn't mean it that way.'

'Yes I did!' It was a slicing blow that cut my breath away and severed my daughter's windpipe, left her gasping. I jumped up and, holding Regina tightly around her shuddering shoulders, started steering her out of the restaurant, with people trying not to scrutinise us too openly.

Outside on the busy footpath I continued holding her, waited for her to swallow back her pain. I handed her my serviette, which she used to dry her tears. 'I'm sure your mother is already very sorry about her behaviour, darling,' I tried. 'I don't know why she's behaving the way she is this morning.'

Regina twisted out of my embrace, face distorted into a rage I'd never seen there before. Holding me at arm's length, with my reflection trapped in the centre of her eyes, she declared: 'Dad, she meant every cruel word of it! Yeah, she fucking well *meant* to hurt me!'

'No, she didn't,' I insisted. 'She's never treated you like this before.'

'So why's she hurting me now?' Then, focusing on me, she said, 'All our life together *you've* been the one who's put me down. To you I've been a dumb, ugly person unworthy of being your daughter.' I opened my mouth to protest but she said, 'Don't, Dad, don't! You know it's true!' As she wheeled to flee from me, I tried to hold her arm but she shrugged me off. She paused, and, holding the noonday world's full attention, said, 'And now you've got her treating me the same way. Yes, she came here from a poor aiga in a poor village in a poor country, but she married you and *you* turned her into a pretentious fiapalagi!' She waited and watched the truth gushing up from the unhealable wound in my heart and then said, 'Our aiga reckon you're so Palagi you've only got temporary suntans!'

VI.

Borges, I think, once claimed that we exist only in one another's dreams. As I waited for Andrea to come home I wanted my reality to be that: that Andrea's totally unexpected attack on our daughter had been true only in a dream that I'd wake from. After I'd watched Regina disappearing into Foodtown I'd hurried to the car and driven home, without Andrea, unable to shake off the truth of Regina's accusation that I had never considered her a daughter worthy of me — and that I'd somehow persuaded her mother to believe it too.

'Thank you for leaving me stranded!' Andrea started as

soon as she entered our kitchen where I was sitting having my second coffee. 'I had to walk three bloody miles from the café.' She was always precise about distance.

'Good on yah!' I heard myself saying. 'In the dream we're in, it couldn't have been all that strenuous.'

She dumped her handbag on the table in front of me, her face flushed with anger. 'What the shit are you talking about?'

'You're the one who believes in dreams,' I said coolly. I sipped my coffee. It was turning cold.

She thumped herself down on the stool opposite me, the armpits and front of her T-shirt drenched with sweat. With both hands pressed against her face — a gesture I was so familiar with, she sighed deeply, as if everything was beyond exasperation, and recited through her spread fingers: '"Although it sounded all year round, although it rang out sometimes as early as half-past six in the morning, sometimes as late as half-past ten . . ."'

'Why re-quote me that?' I interrupted her, continuing the interrogation.

As she took her hands away from her face I knew there would be a superior smile there. 'Because, my darling, you and your daughter *need* to be reminded that you can never read dreams.'

'So why are the Bengels and their savant son's music important to us?' I wasn't going to relent this time. 'And why is Dyer Beauchamp's playing so, so sad?'

Widowed

THE HISTORY OF IT

— Fiona Kidman

They came down to breakfast next morning absolutely their own selves. Rosy, fresh, and just chilled enough by the cold air blowing through the bedroom windows to be very ready for hot coffee.

'Nippy.' That was Geraldine's word as she buttoned on her orange coat with pink-washed fingers. 'Don't you find it decidedly nippy?' And her voice, so matter-of-fact, so natural, sounded as though they had been married for years.

The woman who owned the guesthouse, described as 'boutique' in the guidebook, had laid a fire in the grate of their room the night before, so that when they retired from dinner the room was warm from its blaze, even though a hard frost had settled in the paddocks beyond. Two chairs had been set in front of the fireplace, as if she expected them to settle down with the liqueurs she had provided — a Drambuie for Duncan and a Cointreau for Geraldine — while they talked over their day.

'Have you got children?' she asked when she served dinner.

They were her only guests, which didn't seem to trouble her, even though places for another fourteen people stretched away on either side of the vast kauri table. The house had high ceilings, built in imitation of the Tudor style, but more than a hundred years ago, so in a sense it was historic for this part of the world. From the veranda of their upstairs room they saw gently rolling hills and sheep nuzzling close to the fences. On the other side of the house, native bush pressed close to the edge of the carefully cultivated garden where, the woman said, over two hundred roses were planted. If they came back in late spring they could see for themselves the riot of colour they provided.

Geraldine declared the dinner perfect; the woman, whose name was Hazel, had made her own horseradish sauce to accompany the beef, cooked to exactly the right shade of rare. Everything was natural, the vegetables all grown here on the property.

'So how many children did you say you had?' she persisted, when Geraldine praised the food.

'Five,' said Duncan firmly. 'We have five children.' His eyes met Geraldine's for an instant.

Hazel exclaimed extravagantly then over Geraldine's figure, how she had kept her looks, and asked the ages of the children. Hazel herself had a tightly packaged body that suggested constant battles with her weight, short blonde hair styled in crisp upward flicks, her lips a light shade of fuchsia. She could have passed for fifty, but Geraldine thought older, perhaps sixty.

'We've come away to have a weekend off the children,' Duncan said lightly.

Hazel apologised then, said of course, and what was she thinking of, but later when dessert was cleared away she couldn't resist bringing out some pictures of her grandchildren. They were round, cheerful-looking children, photographed beside ponies. 'They come here now and then,' she said wistfully. 'Not often enough.'

'I'm sorry,' Duncan said to Geraldine, when they were seated before the fire. 'My friend recommended it for the quiet — he comes here when he wants to do a lot of reading.' Duncan's friend was a bookseller who believed in keeping up to date with his wares. Duncan managed a research unit in a government department. They had become friends because Duncan spent his lunch-hours browsing in bookshops; reading was his great pleasure, although he admitted to a modest interest in the arts. Mostly he read non-fiction, preferably biography. He had just finished one on Shakespeare's wife that cast her in a more complimentary light than previous biographers. He liked the many details it provided about Elizabethan farming and the making of malt ale. Duncan had considered life as an academic, but it hadn't worked out that way.

'It's perfect,' Geraldine repeated, in the way she had praised the beef, as if stating the obvious, and none of it mattered. She was curled in front of the flickering fire, wearing nothing but a necklace made of fine rolled gold that followed the shape of her collarbone. Her long, carefully crafted hair fell in a mane across her shoulders. She stretched her arms above her head and stood.

'You look like a painting,' he said, reeling off a list of the masters, starting with Rubens. 'Or an Evelyn Page, perhaps — the woman standing in the boat. The New Zealand painter,' he added. He was still dressed, his liqueur half finished.

'All these painters and writers — how can I possibly keep up with them with five children to look after?' she said.

'I shouldn't have said that,' he said.

'No,' she said, 'probably you shouldn't.' She knelt on the chair so that her knees were either side of his. The bed behind them had a canopy of white drapes above it, soft and floating.

'Ravish me,' she said.

He carried her to the bed, and groaned as he undid his clothes. 'I shouldn't be doing this,' he said. 'I shouldn't be here.'

Geraldine reached over to the night table and picked up his cellphone, her fingers travelling over the keys to check that it was switched off.

Towards morning, she got up from the bed and opened the windows because, although the fire had died in the grate, the room was still so hot she said she couldn't sleep. Outside, sheep bleated in long concerted *aaa-aahs* as the beginning of their day drew near.

Geraldine slept then, face down, one arm flung over Duncan's chest, as if she were used to the shape of him in sleep. When she woke up she declared herself famished for more of him, and for the breakfast she could smell wafting up from the kitchen, in that order. When at last they dressed the room was freezing; outside they could see that fog had rolled in, creating a lace-edged blanket fluttering over the paddocks. A strange hush had fallen, so that the sheep sounded muted and far away. Geraldine laughed and stamped her feet and made Duncan hurry his dressing the way she had, in order to get warm, refusing to close the windows or turn on a heater.

After breakfast, when Hazel asked them if they wanted to confirm their booking for the second night, Geraldine said yes, yes, of course that was what they wanted, it had been the most wonderful night and she loved the house, every inch of it. She was still smiling, laughing over some joke Duncan had made, not a funny one really, but as she buttoned her orange jacket, everything in the world seemed amusing and possible. The jacket was made of fine merino wool, meticulously cut, with a Jane Daniels label.

'Perhaps I'll call you later in the day,' Duncan told Hazel. He had taken out his wallet. 'We should check on the children.'

'The children, of course. Five of them. Really, if you're coming back, you don't need to pay me now.'

'Four,' Duncan said. 'Well, two of them are mine,' he corrected himself hastily.

Hazel noticed that he was counting out cash. 'Of course,' she said easily. 'Of course they are.' Something like disappointment had gathered around her eyes. Disillusion, Geraldine thought. Hazel met people like them often enough and was kicking herself for not having recognised them earlier for what they were.

In Duncan's car, Geraldine said, 'You lied about the children — see where that got us.'

'What was I supposed to say?'

'You said five! We have two each. Well, I have two children.'

'It was just a number.'

'Don't you ever use my children as an excuse to change your mind,' she said. The tyres of the car were crunching over frost as they jolted down the rough driveway and out of sight of the house.

'All right,' he said, 'we'll stay somewhere else tonight.'

'Oh, don't feel obliged. I thought you liked last night.'

The car was paused on the edge of the country road as he looked for oncoming traffic. He dropped his head on the wheel for a moment. 'I did. The best time.'

'You think it isn't hard for me too? I'm supposed to be at a school reunion, for God's sake.'

'That woman will have the car's registration.' His voice was morose. Geraldine had suggested taking her car but he thought his green five-door more appropriate. More ordinary, he might have said.

'Oh, damn the car. She doesn't care about it. I don't care.' The bumps had dislodged a miniature soccer ball from under the back seat. He glanced behind him.

'I can't stand things rolling about in the car. Can you fix it?'

'I'm not your wife. I am bloody well not.' They were quarrelling for the first time. Later she would think she should have known then, that in shifting the boundaries of what had gone before, they had begun their descent.

'Aren't you scared? What if you *lost* your kids?' he asked.

'Hardly likely.' All the same, she ran her hand through her hair, clutching it in an anxious knot. 'My children are near enough to grown up.'

'Well, mine aren't.'

'I don't want to talk about my children any more,' Geraldine said. 'Besides, this was about us being together for a weekend. Whoever mentioned forever?'

But for a time, when they had recovered themselves, the idea took hold and enlarged itself. Forever. Perhaps.

A man was stabbed in the city. The police were looking for a youth in his late teens, dark-complexioned, of medium build, last seen wearing a grey hoodie. And a weapon, believed to be a kitchen carving knife. If people were stupid enough to get into fights they got what they deserved, Geraldine's husband said as he glanced over the newspaper. Her husband was an industrial designer whose company exported millions of dollars worth of goods all over the world. He had the competitive edge, he often said, and Geraldine was glad that Duncan couldn't hear him say things like that. Geraldine lived with her husband centre city, in an apartment in a converted warehouse, loft style as if they were in New York, with exposed bricks and giant pipes in the ceilings. They had two Hotere paintings, a McCahon and a Dick Frizzell hanging among their pictures, although Geraldine hadn't mentioned this to Duncan. Sometimes, just lately, it seemed to her that an air of emptiness pervaded the apartment. The boys went to boarding school during the week and came home at the weekends.

'I don't like these things happening in the city,' Geraldine said to her husband with a shiver. 'He was killed for his iPod.'

'They'd been fighting,' Geraldine's husband insisted. 'Another loser.'

'Anyone can get stabbed,' she said. 'I worry about the boys.'

A flicker of concern crossed his face. 'They need to watch out for themselves. Keep an eye on them,' he said, as if this resolved the matter. 'And you watch yourself in town. Don't go out in the mall on Friday nights.'

This was an absurd thing to say because Geraldine didn't go out alone on Friday nights. She would be going somewhere with him, to dinner at a brasserie, or at a colleague's house, or with the parents of their children's friends, occasionally to a theatrical performance of one kind or another. Because her husband was a minor corporate sponsor they had complimentary tickets for opening nights at the ballet. They sat in one of the rows at the opera house reserved for the Prime Minister and the Leader of the Opposition, who came in when the rest of the audience were seated. Geraldine would be wearing something severe and simple with a low-cut back that showed her shoulderblades and a floating stole in a colour to match her dress. 'Hello,' they would say, in subdued intimate voices, and people would lean across the rows to shake hands. 'Good evening, Prime Minister,' her husband would say, because privately he disliked her, although Geraldine would call her Helen, as if they were friends.

They had been in the bookshop where Duncan's friend worked when they met. Geraldine had gone in to buy a guide to the classics for one of her sons, who was struggling with the topic at school. The bookseller had called Duncan over and suggested he was just the man to find something that would help. 'How old is he? Sixteen? He needs Robert Graves, of course.' The shop had got busy and Duncan's friend was occupied, so they searched for the book together. 'Voilà,' Duncan had cried, pouncing on the book and flourishing it aloft, like a scholar who has just made a find. 'Or should that be Eureka?' Afterwards it seemed natural to have coffee. The bookseller, a round man with a beard, eyed them with benevolence when they left the shop, as if he had just arranged something important.

She would wonder if the bookseller had already become Duncan's confidant, if he knew more about him than his tastes in reading. That Duncan was dissatisfied with disposables and weekend sports runs, the badly cooked meals and the way even a good salary didn't seem to run to all the things that families needed these days. These things he told her about later, although in a glancing way, indicating that he knew it was bad form to talk about the wife he was betraying. Not, he hastened to add, that he hadn't known what he was signing up for when he married, it was just the reality that was hard. He'd possibly left his run a little late.

These were admissions he would come to. But on that day, the one when they met, they had simply found themselves laughing a lot over nothing very much, and exclaiming about their chance encounter, and how you never knew what was just around the corner. She found herself saying, 'Have you ever had an affair?' just like that, as if these words were springing from the lips of a stranger. Their laughter became uneasy, her biting her lip and shrugging, looking at him sideways, and him blushing and saying, 'Nothing much more than a bang at the Christmas party,' and God, he could be fired for stuff like that, and anyway it was a mistake and he was sorry it had happened. The woman had left, which was both a relief and made it worse at the same time. 'You know what I mean?' Letting her know that what she was suggesting was not beyond the bounds of possibility.

He didn't look the way she imagined a scholar would look.

He was a lean, closely shaven man wearing rimless glasses, bristle haircut, a slight dimple in one cheek; once he might have been athletic. The bookshop became the place where they met once or twice more before sloping off to Starbucks to drink coffee. She wasn't sure how many times exactly, because when he suggested they drive out in their separate cars and meet somewhere, she had already decided. It was simply a matter of when (although this was not as simple as Duncan had made it sound at first, because he had to organise to have his car on days when his wife was not using it). Summer was at its height, white daisies with yellow eyes filming the hillsides, agapanthus floating like tethered blue balloons above them when they lay down. When they walked back to their cars, they smelled of grass and pollen, semen and heat. Later, after the weather changed, they began to talk of a weekend away, some place where they could sleep a whole night together in the same bed — or, in a reckless fantasy, two nights even. This would take a long time to arrange. In the meanwhile, their meetings were as necessary as eating and sleeping, as nourishing as red meat.

In a way Geraldine supposed that what her husband said about the man who had been stabbed was true. There was a dark side to the town and it wasn't very far away, just up the road and around the corner in Newtown, where people lived cheek by jowl in cramped council flats with washing hung out on the verandas. She had seen them when she took the children to the zoo, glancing out at places where leaks showed in rusty lines down the sides of the buildings, and dusty flights of steps led from the streets up to rooms with torn curtains in limp disarray at the windows. The occupants were often Maori or Polynesian, or men wearing turbans and women in the shadow of their burkhas; others talked aloud to themselves and laughed at nothing in particular, as if, perhaps, they lived in halfway houses.

She had seen some of the low-life that lurked in the shadows as well, some of it up close and far too personal. Of late, she had become more familiar with the area when she made her way to the town belt reserve to park and wait for Duncan in his lunch-hour. Depending on the weather, they made love on pine needles at the edge of the grass, or in the back of her car, their feet awkward against the door. 'We can't go on like this,' they said, all the clichés that people say to each other when they haven't the slightest idea of an alternative. And: 'We can't *not* go on.' One afternoon, when Duncan should already have been back at work, a face appeared at the window, a man with a shock of faded yellow hair and a rough beard, leering and lurching on unsteady feet.

'Give him some money and tell him to go away,' Geraldine said, pushing her handbag along the floor of the car with her toe so that Duncan could take notes from it. He opened the window a fraction and stuffed a rolled hundred through, while Geraldine sat up and pulled her skirt down.

'Cheers, mate.' The man laughed. 'Nice bit of bush there.' He nodded in Geraldine's direction.

'We're going to get caught,' Geraldine said. Her voice was sharp and frightened. 'My picture was in the People's Page in the paper last week.'

Duncan had seen that, of course. Geraldine and her husband had been at a diplomatic reception for successful exporters. 'I doubt if that man looks at the paper.'

'You don't know. Perhaps he sits in the library when he's got nothing better to do. You see people like him there all the time.'

'He won't remember. He's pissed out of his brain. Christ, Geraldine, we can't go on like this.'

'You said that before.'

He sighed then. 'I thought you weren't afraid.'

'Well, I am now. The car — he'll remember the car.'

'He won't have taken the registration.' Trying to make a feeble joke of their earlier indiscretions. Of course the man, pissed or not, wasn't going to forget a flame-red Audi shedding hundred-dollar bills on the edge of the town belt. It wasn't like Duncan's own car, parked further down the road, full of plastic balls and ready to be turned over.

'Perhaps we should let it go,' she said. She was digging her fingers into the sides of the seat to stop her hands shaking.

'Is that what you want?' Again, thinking back, she recognised something almost hopeful in the way he asked the question. Some tired chime that said he was calling time.

'Let's see how it goes. I'll call you soon.' He leaned over and kissed her cheek. 'You're gorgeous,' he said as he slid out of the car.

She didn't care for the way he said this: it was too easy, too pat.

'I can't rescue you, you know,' Duncan said the next time they met, although she had said little about her marriage, simply that at times she was lonely, that she had a lot of money but it didn't really make a difference, especially if you were used to it, as she had been since she was a child. Many months had passed since the beginning of it all. Soon it would be spring and then summer all over again. They had agreed to meet for coffee rather than drive out the way they usually did.

'Are you sure it's not you who needs to be rescued?' Geraldine retorted. Already she felt an ache of loss, thinking back to their first meeting between the rows of spines and dust-jackets in the bookshop, somewhere close to the bestseller stand, the way his friend had thrown them together. As if they were characters in one of the novels he sold, whose lives were ordered to suit the plot.

'Keep your voice down,' he said.

'Since when has that bothered you?'

'Since now,' he snapped. 'Look,' he started over, 'I know this is hard, it's not what I want. But you know what you said: we're going to get caught. Think about it. Let's be careful for a bit.'

Only, she thought it wouldn't happen. When it did, she wondered at her own surprise. People didn't get caught by accident, not as a rule. She had heard this from friends who told how it had happened to them. It was the kind of thing they might tell her after a session at the gym when they were fired up and uninhibited. They hadn't always told her things like this and she supposed that somehow she looked or acted differently, that they noticed the way she lowered herself tenderly onto the exercycle some days, or touched her breasts lightly while she dressed as if remembering a caress. It wasn't necessarily a planned moment, they said — some instant when one or other of the lovers said, 'Now, now is the time to get caught,' but the signals and warnings had already been planted at home. Something has changed. A crisis is about to occur. The messages were as clear as Stickit notes on a fridge door. Listen and watch, and you'll find out. Only fools didn't read messages. And, her friends said, it almost always happened when the love affair was drawing to a close, a message that enough was enough. A phone call overheard, a text message intercepted, a hotel bill or a condom in a jacket pocket. Nothing subtle.

'I'm sorry,' Duncan said when he phoned her, 'I've got no idea how it happened. I didn't mean to leave my phone where she could find it. I wasn't expecting a message from you right then.' There was something accusing in the way he said it.

This was how she came to be standing near the sea at Island Bay on a blustery day in August. She had some books of his. He had a bracelet of hers. They would exchange them at a place where they were not in the habit of meeting. 'Somewhere where I won't be tempted,' he said, only Geraldine didn't believe him.

She sat on the sea wall and smoked a cigarette, her first in years. The wind was a northerly, violent and harsh, flicking ash in her eyes and flattening her hair around her cheeks. The cigarette tasted sour and she tossed it away as she drew her orange jacket more closely around her shoulders. Across the road stood a small low building on its own, housing an art gallery that showed a regular selection of quality works. She had been to an opening there with her husband. For a moment she considered crossing over and browsing while she waited for Duncan, then decided she might be noticed, perhaps remembered. She turned, intending to go back and wait in the car. But the waves drew her towards the edge of the sea.

As she stood there, the elements rising around her, it occurred to her quite suddenly that she was out of it, this situation she had brought on herself, and that she was safe and free again. Some shift was occurring, like a boat slipping its anchor. There had been an expectation that Duncan would change her life, offer some prospect of enlightenment, evidence of things she had glimpsed but not recognised. But all that had really happened was that she was constantly afraid. She thought: I don't even like him. In her head she said to herself: I've had a sheltered life and I'm ready to move back into it. She saw freedom of a different kind beckoning her. There was nothing to stop her doing things that might interest her: going to the theatre more often, learning a language, taking up charity work. She might even take a course in the arts. All of that had been there for the taking, and she hadn't seen this.

Out in Cook Strait a mountainous wave was lifting and rushing towards the shore, causing her to step backwards. A young man, hardly more than a boy, wearing a thin cotton hoodie, hurried along the sand with a stumbling gait. He seemed not to notice Geraldine, stopping close by her and lifting his arm, an object poised above his head. For a moment she thought he was throwing a stick to a dog, but she was close enough to see that it gleamed in the dull light.

The object wheeled through the air, landing close to the edge of the water, and she saw that it was a knife. The young man ran towards the breakers to pick it up and, in doing so almost banged against Geraldine. Water lapped over his sneakers. After an instant's hesitation he turned towards her, the knife raised again above his head, his expression frightened. His face was speckled with pimples and patchy stubble. In spite of his swarthiness she saw a grey pallor around his mouth. She began to run, screaming as she breasted the rise leading to the road. She was faster and fitter than the boy. People who had been browsing in the gallery emerged, rushing towards her. Duncan arrived too, at that same moment.

'Duncan,' Geraldine said, weeping as she collapsed against his shoulder. A man in an anorak who had been walking his dog wrestled her attacker to the ground, wresting the knife from him, using only one hand to break his grip because the young man was weak and pathetic, trying to flee when he saw all the people coming at him.

And, in a short while, the police had arrived too, and Geraldine and Duncan were both witnesses. More than that. Geraldine was now, as the newspaper described her, the victim of an attempted second murder with the same knife that had stabbed the man in the city.

'It could have been worse. The boys weren't here,' Geraldine said. She knew how lame that sounded, but she had to say something, now that truth lay all around her in the silence of the apartment.

'You think they won't find out?' her husband said with deep bitterness. 'Oh, don't be naïve. I don't want their names or mine dragged through the newspapers. I'll get on to a lawyer to get you name suppression. The best money can buy.'

'I was in the wrong place at the wrong time,' she said faintly.

'Quite often, by the sound of it.'

The lawyer came and spoke to her at length. He would support her all the way in court, he assured her. It was difficult to say whether he could have her name suppressed when she gave evidence; it was not as if it were a sexual violation, but he would do his best.

'What about Duncan?' she asked him.

'What about him?' the lawyer said. Geraldine's husband was sitting opposite in a deep leather chair, observing her closely.

'I thought,' she began, in a faltering voice, 'well, because he's why I was there. It'll come out. In court.'

'How many people know about this . . . this friendship of yours?'

'I don't know,' she said, twisting a tissue in her lap. It was a long time since she had been a schoolgirl. Geraldine remembered her headmistress, blonde and elegant, who spoke with a refined and carefully modulated voice. She called her students her 'gels', but when they erred there was no avoiding her gaze. 'The man in the bookshop. The woman at the guesthouse. Her name was Hazel. A man at Newtown.'

'A man at *Newtown*? Who?'

'I don't know. We — well, that is, I — gave him some money to go away.'

A look of dislike settled over her husband's face, the long face with folds at the corners of the mouth, which she had once loved.

Duncan's wife appeared at their apartment. When she announced herself on the intercom Geraldine said: 'You can't let her in.'

'Why not?' her husband said. 'Don't you want to see the competition?'

'She's not.'

'Well, let's take a look anyway,' he said. 'I'm curious.'

The wife was much younger than Geraldine expected. She had a thin, lightly freckled face, a straight bob of fair sticky hair pushed back behind her ears. 'I knew,' she said, 'even before I found your soppy text. I do the accounts, I count every penny. I thought I was helping him, watching the money. His first wife left him over money. Well, I said, I'm a good bookkeeper, I can keep an eye on things. I noticed straight away when he started taking out cash.' She said this with a breathy, slightly nasal twang.

'I didn't know Duncan had been married before,' said Geraldine. Only she did. She understood now.

'I'll make up the money to you,' Geraldine's husband said.

'You will not,' the woman said, lifting her chin. She might look stupid, she told him, but she wasn't.

Geraldine's husband said that no, she didn't look at all stupid to him, far from it. The woman said she came from Taita, she'd lived there all her life until she met Duncan when she went to work in his office. 'I was good at school,' she said, with defiance in her tone. 'I was proxime accessit to the dux.'

'I can see you've got what it takes,' said Geraldine's husband. 'I think it's very brave of you to come here like this. Although I'm not quite sure why you've come.'

'I got pregnant with Duncan,' she said, as if he hadn't spoken. 'Straight off at the office Christmas party. I suppose that sounds real old-fashioned to you,' she said, addressing Geraldine. 'Anyway, I could have got rid of it but Duncan was all for getting married — it was quite a surprise, I can tell you. My mum said it might be for the best — he's got a pretty good job, even if he does throw his money away on tarts.'

'Please,' said Geraldine's husband.

'You can have him,' the wife said to Geraldine. 'I don't give a shit about him. I've got two kids now — well, perhaps you know that — and he's got another one he's still paying for. I'd rather go home to Mum.'

'If I can help in any way,' Geraldine's husband said again.

Another woman came to see them. It was difficult to see how she had found the address, because Geraldine still had name suppression. 'The victim did not wish to be identified,' the newspaper reported.

This woman was overweight and missing some teeth. Her hair straggled over the neck of a red crepe blouse that had seen better days. The defendant in the coming court case was her son. They came from Taumarunui, she said, the centre of the island, near the railway lines. It was a good town; her boy never got in any trouble there, only when he came to the city. That's the way it was with so many of the kids. 'We ask'd him, don't you go away down there. You meet all sortsa rubbish in the city.'

'He stabbed a man,' said Geraldine's husband.

'Mister, they say he did but nobody knows that, eh. Now he's up on this new case, how can he get a decent trial? Look at you,' she said to Geraldine. 'He never even touched you.'

'What do you want?' Geraldine said, much as her husband had to the earlier woman.

'To get him a fair hearing. Drop this case. Someone else give him the knife. He was just getting rid of it for a mate.'

'You should tell the police.'

'Well I did, Madam Muck. They're still doing the DNA — he might be all right if it wasn't for you. You and your boyfriend know he never laid a finger.' The woman began to cry then, heavy tears sliding and gathering into the trail of snot forming beneath her nose. 'He's a good kid. You've got boys?' Her eyes rested on a photograph. A family picture taken at a lake with their boat in the background. 'The legal aid man said he might get out on bail. You got no idea what it's like in jail for boys.'

Geraldine's husband stood to show her out.

'If you said something,' the mother said. 'Like he never

touched you. He told me, he just didn't see you. It might give him a breather.'

Shouting echoed from the lift lobby when Geraldine's husband led the woman out.

When he came back he dropped heavily into his chair.

'Perhaps it's true,' Geraldine said.

'The boy?'

'He mightn't be the killer.'

'For fuck's sake, Geraldine, he was disposing of a weapon.'

'But we don't know.'

'Who cares?' he said. When he had composed himself again he said, 'I loved you. I really did. I gave you everything.'

'Everything? Is that the answer? You just buy things?'

'Well,' he said, 'it's what I had.'

They decided Geraldine would stay. Between them, she and her husband agreed that this was best for the boys. For them all. Things could be smoothed over, they would pass. For the moment her husband couldn't bear the thought of touching her, but perhaps in time he might because, he said, he had always fancied her so much. This admission surprised and pleased her more than she might have supposed. A date had been set down for the trial. Her husband had a conference to attend in Stockholm and afterwards he would stay on and look at some new design trends in Europe, but he would be back in time to support her when she gave evidence. He was happy that he could travel and meet new people, his time occupied. When he returned, this would be just another matter to be dealt with. They could begin again after that.

By the time he got back the young man had died in a prison fight and the trial was called off. The DNA results had come through and it seemed that someone else might well have used the knife on the night of the killing in the city.

His weeping mother was pictured in the newspaper. 'I don't know how it all come about,' she said. Geraldine believed she did, and wished it wasn't so. The history of it all, the death of a boy. These things would haunt her.

ORBIS TERRARUM

— Witi Ihimaera

I.

Why did old Mrs. Travers wake so early nowadays? She would like to have slept for another three hours at least. But no, every morning at almost precisely the same time, at half-past four, she was wide awake. For — nowadays, again — she woke always in the same way, with a slight start, a small shock, lifting her head from the pillow with a quick glance as if she fancied someone had called her, or as if she were trying to remember for certain whether this was the same wallpaper, the same window she had seen last night before Warner switched off the light.

Mrs. Travers frowned. It was still so dark outside, still and dark. If it weren't for the night light beside her bed and the crack of light from the door, ajar, to the fluorescent glare of corridor outside, she could almost believe she was alone in the living, breathing dark; indeed, the only person alive in the entire world. Did the thought scare her? No; at ninety-two, it was such a presumption to be afraid of anything. One was too tired to be scared, if the truth be known, and had no energy to waste on such a silly, vain and superfluous emotion. At this age one just wanted to *go*.

But there was a slight delay. 'He won't be long,' Staff Nurse Warner had shouted in her ear. 'Your son Elliot is on his way from England to New Zealand now.'

Elliot was the youngest of Mrs. Travers' four children and the only boy. The others were Molly, Kate and Joan, all dutifully taking turns to visit her in her pensioner flat every week to pester her with questions about how was she feeling and was there anything she needed from the supermarket.

Why did Warner shout all the time? Although her sight was going, Mrs. Travers could hear perfectly well. When she was a very young girl of thirteen, her father, Cyprian, had jested, 'You must have been a bat in an earlier life, eh, Essie, my girl?'

And of course she was never alone. She heard every footfall of the nurses as they walked past her room, every piece of gossip they shared during night shift, every sigh of irritation when Mr. Winchester in the next room called out, 'Nurse! Nurse!' (he called out *all* the time, the insufferable man), and every silly giggle when they went off in the mornings and back to their boyfriends or whoever they lived with.

All except Warner, of course. She never had a boyfriend. Or any sort of friend. Warner was dedicated to her job. She was the nurse as a career woman. Now that was a scary thought.

It was her middle daughter, Kate, who had found Mrs. Travers, two weeks ago, where she'd collapsed in the kitchen of her flat while making herself a cup of tea: a stroke brought on by *diabetes mellitus*. Kate called an ambulance and Mrs. Travers was whisked off to hospital. The medical team 'brought her back', as Warner put it, and she had been making a good recovery. Then she took a turn for the worse: her kidneys stopped functioning.

'Your mother has acute renal failure,' Dr. Paterson told her daughters. 'If she was younger we might have considered a kidney transplant but, given her advanced age, and the long waiting list for cadaver donors, well . . .'

His voice trailed off. He expected them to get the drift.

'You mean there's no chance Mummy will get better?' Joan asked him, her eyes moistening.

'What we are talking about is end-stage renal disease,' Dr. Paterson continued. 'But we would keep her on dialysis until you're comfortable, ready, and have had the opportunity to say goodbye.'

Molly exchanged glances with her sisters. 'And there's no hope of any recovery?'

'It's now a matter of your choosing a time to say farewell,' Dr. Paterson said. 'Do you have any other family you would like to join you at her bedside? Apart from yourselves?'

'Our brother Elliot,' Kate told him. 'He lives in London. He would certainly want to come to see Mummy before she . . . before we . . . before . . . after all, he was her favourite.'

'How long would it take for him to get here?'

'Two days. Three at the most.'

'Perhaps you should telephone him and tell him to come as soon as he can.'

Mrs. Travers' daughters looked at each other. 'After all, Mummy's had a very good life,' Kate said.

And so they were all waiting for Elliot. Perhaps, for once in his life, he would be prompt. He would join the other children in Auckland and then, thank goodness, they would let her die.

Children? Ha! Molly was seventy, Kate sixty-eight, Joan sixty-six, and Elliot was the 'baby' at fifty-eight — another scary thought. And where on earth had Kate got the idea that Elliot was Mrs. Travers' favourite? He'd been a nasty little boy, and as an adult had become a mean little man whose only interest was making money.

And what was all this sentimentality about keeping her alive so the family could gather to say goodbye? Mrs. Travers' father, with his precise scientific approach, would not have been pleased. If he had been here he would have said to the children, 'Waiting for Elliot? Does an old elephant wait for the whole herd to shake its trunk before it dies? Or a sperm whale for a sentimental rub from the other whales before it makes its final sounding? Does a dying albatross, at its colony, take a last fly-by salute before its eyes glaze over? No! They die when they die. It's only humans who prolong life — and it's all vanity, you hear? Charles Darwin would not have approved.'

Father had been a disciple of the author of *On the Origin of Species by Means of Natural Selection*. Mr. Darwin's observations as a geologist, botanist, zoologist and general man of science underwent a startling transformation when he joined the *Beagle*, an expeditionary vessel that the admiralty sent on an extended voyage to the South Seas. The *Beagle* visited the Galapagos Islands, just off the coast of Ecuador, and that was where Darwin's decisive breakthrough occurred.

Father was always defending Mr. Darwin. At a public meeting he got into a fiery argument with the local bishop on Darwin's theory of evolution. 'The church's teachings from Genesis,' Cyprian shouted, 'that every species has been created whole and has come through the ages unchanged, can no longer be sustained.' Mrs. Travers had adored watching him in full, passionate flight. 'Read Mr. Darwin, Bishop! He will give you your answer: evolution by natural selection. The strongest survive, the weak die. Species are born, live and they respond to their environment by evolving. Hopefully, for us, mankind will evolve from strength to strength. And the sooner we evolve out of our religious conditioning, the better.'

They die when they die. Suddenly, thinking of her father, Mrs. Travers heard a sound that was new, that was different. Not Mr. Winchester calling yet again, or the nurses going back and forth along the corridor.

No, this sound was coming from beyond the windowframe — far, far beyond. It was a low, deep sigh, haunting, otherworldly, sibilant, low, somewhere between a deep hiss and moan. Not a sound to be scared of; rather, one that filled her with breathless anticipation.

Someone was calling her.

When Molly, Kate and Joan arrived later that day, Warner was only too ready to tell them about the 'incident'.

'Your mother was a little unsettled this morning,' Warner said. 'She pulled out her catheter. It was probably an accident.'

'But she was so good when we left her last night,' Kate answered.

'Good' was when Mrs. Travers was drugged and unconscious; 'bad' was when the drugs wore off and Mummy indulged herself in inchoate sighs and screams and incoherent ramblings.

'You mustn't worry about it,' Warner said. She lowered her voice to a whisper. 'It's what happens.'

But did it have to happen before their own eyes? Nervous, Mrs. Travers' daughters settled down with their knitting, magazines and boiled lollies to keep the watch.

II.

Half past four again. Why half past four?

Mrs. Travers sighed to herself. The drugs du jour had worn off; ah, clarity for a while! And with it came the urge to be up and about.

Not that there was much chance of that. Even as she shifted slightly she felt a tightening at her abdomen. That's where the catheter was for the contraption that stood beside the bed, winking at her and giving her the glad eye. She was hooked up to the silly thing — her own personal artificial kidney — continuously pumping into her a special solution to cleanse away all the waste fluids, drain them out and replace with fresh solution. Otherwise the toxins built up in her blood. And the children didn't want them to do *that*. Not quite yet.

Yesterday had been a good day, lucidly speaking. Mrs. Travers drifted in and out of consciousness, always aware of Molly, Kate and Joan sitting around her bed talking, knitting and reading women's magazines. She realised she startled them when she occasionally 'woke up' to create mayhem in their timid lives; it was almost as if she had said 'Boo!', and they would hurriedly ring for Warner to settle her down again. Every hour on the hour other medical staff would come into the room, check her pulse and the dialysis machine, do whatever else they did and then write a report on the bedclip: 'still alive', or words to that effect, presumably.

Dr. Paterson popped in regularly to check on her. 'Have you heard from your brother?' he asked Molly.

'There's been a delay,' she answered. 'He couldn't get out of an urgent board meeting. He won't be arrived for another two days.'

Money before Mummy. Sounded just like Elliot. Really, he was a disappointment. As for Molly, Kate and Joan, they were dutiful daughters but why, oh, why had they never possessed a life of the mind? 'Expanding our knowledge,' Father would have scolded them, 'and using it to advance humankind is what justifies our retaining our niche as a species.'

Actually, some time in the afternoon, while Mrs. Travers' daughters were having a light lunch in the room — Warner had given them some nougat to have with their tea — she was prompted by the memory of her father to tell them about him and, in particular, the great moment of her adolescent life when she joined him in the Galapagos Islands.

At least that's what she thought she was doing. To them she was as usual rambling on, speaking in tongues through the ravaged face that had collapsed during her stroke.

'Father was the leading herpetologist — an expert on reptiles — at the Schwimmer Aquarium,' she began. 'Mother, my sister Gloria and I were accustomed to his periods away on various expeditions and we were thrilled for him when he was appointed to lead a scientific expedition to study one of the most intriguing of all reptiles: the giant tortoise, *Geochelone elephantopus*. Our pleasure turned to dismay when we discovered he'd be away for a year.

'"But every three months the *Artemisia* will be coming back here with specimens," Father told us, "and I have arranged for you" — he was referring to Merle, my mother — "to come out for a fortnight. You'd have to make arrangements for Essie and Gloria to stay with relatives but please, Merle, do say you'll come."

'The trouble was that Mother became reluctant. She talked to Father by ship-to-shore telephone in the Galapagos. "I really can't make it, dear," she shouted. "Gloria is sickly again and Essie doesn't make matters any better. She keeps harassing her sister. The best option would be for me to send Essie out to you and I will stay home with Gloria. I'll come later."

'I couldn't believe my luck,' Mrs. Travers continued. 'I was thirteen and Gloria was eleven, and I skipped around the house, delighted that I was going. To make absolutely sure that Gloria stayed sickly — she had a bad heart — I kept on harassing her, especially at night, when she would weep because she wanted to go to sleep. I only stopped pinching and poking her the night before I left and knew, with absolute certainty, that nobody could stop me. Wasn't I a naughty girl?'

Mrs. Travers sighed happily — her daughters hovered between their nougat, wondering whether to call Warner — and lay back among the pillows, letting herself be taken off by the sedating fluid into her memories.

The *Artemisia* approached the Galapagos archipelago over a pearly sea. Morning mist led to sweeping showers of light rain. It was windy and cold, the clouds hanging low over black porous volcanic rock and jagged cliff formations. Along the shoreline fragmented boulders, lava flows, spatter cones, pit craters, columns of gas-driven steam, blowholes, fissures and uplifted blocks cracked against each other. Every height was crowned with the crater of a shield volcano.

'And the birds were everywhere,' Mrs. Travers remembered. 'I had never seen so many before, crowding the blue vault of the sky — frigate birds, swallow-tailed gulls, waved albatrosses, lava gulls, brown pelicans, red-billed tropicbirds — tribes upon limitless tribes of them. And all so beautiful, so free, that I wanted to fly with them.'

She lifted her hands, trying to follow the flights of the seabirds. Alarmed, Joan asked Molly, 'Look at Mummy. What is she doing? What is she seeing? Do you think she will last long enough for Elliot to say goodbye to her?'

Waiting for her at an impressive campsite right at the collapsed caldera of an island volcano was Father.

'Essie! Essie, my girl!' he waved.

The Galapagos was the Eden you found at world's end.

'Poor Cyprian,' Mrs. Travers murmured. 'You would have preferred Mother, wouldn't you?'

All the same, Father was happy to see her and she soon got to know his team of three assistants and four Ecuadorian seamen. The seamen gave her a name: they called her Mi Hija, the child. She was never too sure why.

It was the mating season for the seabirds, and Father straightaway took Mrs. Travers to an albatross colony at the top of a sheer sea cliff; albatrosses were balancing on the wind, coming in or leaving to feed on the fish shoals that broiled below. 'They mate for life,' Father told her, 'and see how their courtship is elaborately choreographed.' Indeed, the albatross birds courted for *ages*, repetitively going over the same patterned ritual. Their long bills circled each other, they made loud, castanet-like clicking sounds and high-pitched vocalisations, their necks arched and they performed very funny sideways rocking movements — and then they would start again. She could have watched the courting birds forever.

Father also took her to spy on a colony of blue-footed boobies. It was a different kind of wooing to the albatrosses: the male showed off his nest-building skills to attract a mate. The silly thing was that they didn't use the sticks and twigs to build a nest; instead, they incubated their eggs on the bare ground. Both parents took turns brooding and sitting on the eggs out in the heat of the sun. Two chicks were hatched, two days apart.

'Father showed me Mr. Darwin's natural selection in operation,' Mrs. Travers recalled. 'The mother hatched two chicks: the second chick was the "just in case" egg. Once the older chick was hatched, its function was to get stronger, establish domination, and then, cruelly peck the younger chick, prevent it from obtaining any food and push it further and further from the nest. The booby parents did not intervene.'

Was this what Mrs. Travers had done to her sister Gloria?

The thought bothered her, so she plunged quickly back into her shifting, swirling memories.

Her first swim was unforgettable.

The sea was so chill, fed by the cold Peru current sweeping north from the Antarctic. It was green and so clear you could see to the end of forever.

At first she was too scared (aha, at least she wasn't afraid to admit it) to go into deep water. She preferred to stay close by the rocks, where she came across a herd of sea turtles, munching away on sunlit seaweed.

'Don't be timid like Gloria,' Father teased.

That made her venture deeper. And there, the true magic opened up to her. She was as astonished at the fish life as she had been at the bird life. The sea was just a liquid sky, and tribes and tribes of fish were in dominion — angelfish, creole fish, grunts, Moorish idols, blue parrotfish, concentric pufferfish, yellow-tailed surgeonfish, yellow-bellied triggerfish and wahoo scintillating in huge, teeming shoals.

With a gasp she saw a whole group of seals swimming swiftly towards her. She blew bubbles of fear but all they wanted to do was gambol and play, sliding their skins along her body and flirting with her.

Then, suddenly, all around her the sea was speared by diving seabirds, particularly the blue-footed piqueros. Diving like bullets steeply into the water, their long tails like rudders, they hit the surface with tremendous force. One of them, on the way back to the surface with a fish in its beak, looked at her, cocking a curious eye, *What are you doing here?*

Far below her a school of manta rays slipped through the dark sea like disturbing dreams.

And so Mrs. Travers floated in and out of consciousness in her sea of memories. Before she realised it, night came upon her, and her daughters went home.

She lifted her head and looked out the window. Why, she felt quite light-headed.

What on earth had happened to the view? It wasn't the usual one at all: not the cityscape, dark, sprinkled with lights, and the familiar volcanic cone of Mt Eden. Rather, what was out there was a darker, altogether wilder landscape, greying with the morning. A road ran right through the middle of it. Something was moving right at the horizon, coming towards her. She couldn't make out what it was saying, whether it was saying anything at all, because she wasn't sure if it was human. How very strange!

Excited, she sat up.

'Yes?' she asked. 'Is anybody there?'

'We found your mother trying to get out of her bed this morning, the naughty girl,' Staff Nurse Warner told Mrs. Travers' daughters. 'Debbie was on duty, and when the alarm sounded she instantly came to investigate. Your mother was already halfway out of bed. Of course Debbie scolded her: 'What are you doing, Mrs. Travers?' She answered, "There's somebody outside who's calling to me." It was quite a struggle to get her back into bed and to quieten her down.'

Molly, Kate and Joan looked at each other. 'We noticed Mother doing some rather odd things yesterday. She was looking into the air as if there were people around her. She was talking to them — or at least her lips were moving.'

'And do you remember?' Kate asked Molly. 'She started to grope at the air and point and follow things that were flying around the room.'

'She's hallucinating,' Warner explained. 'It's what happens. I'll tell Dr. Paterson. He may increase her medication.'

'No, please don't do that, no,' Mrs. Travers tried to say. 'I'll be a good girl now.'

Warner peered into her eyes. 'We wouldn't want you to do any harm to yourself now, lovie, would we? Not before your son gets here, eh?'

III.

Half past four in the morning, on the dot, and Mrs. Travers was awake again.

For a moment she panicked. Warner had indeed advised Dr.

Paterson of her behaviour. As he increased her sedation she had tried to struggle and to plead with him, 'No, I don't want extra painkillers,' but he didn't hear her.

Had the medication eradicated the memories that had opened up to her about . . . about . . . ?

Mrs. Travers moaned into the pillow. It was the same wallpaper and same window, and Auckland was outside, as she knew it was supposed to be. But she didn't want it to be Auckland. She wanted it to be that other place. Where was it? What was its name again?

She sobbed with frustration. She thrashed around in her bed, and suddenly she ripped out the tube feeding the sedating fluids into her left arm. Another lunge and the tower holding her drip twirled away from her in a crazy dance, taking the tube with it. Oh, she didn't even care when Debbie came running in, not at all, because in the interim she remembered —

'You *are* there, aren't you?' she called through the window.

Thrillingly, she heard the sound again, the low, deep sigh, haunting, otherworldly, sibilant, low, somewhere between a deep hiss and moan.

The sound was closer. Whoever was calling her had arrived almost outside the window.

And she was back again in that place of endless sky and endless sea.

Father could not supervise her all the time. 'Time for you to leave the nest,' he jested. Even so, he assigned one of the young Ecuadorian crew to look after her. His name was Felipe and he showed her sealions lying on the gritty sand and among the rocks. The animals were so close at hand and surprisingly unconcerned by humans.

'They won't hurt,' Felipe told her. 'You can go right up to them with a club and, bang, you have them before they even know.'

Not far from the sealions were the lizards of the Galapagos: the marine iguanas. Mrs. Travers found them hilarious. They kept on sneezing, excreting salt through special nasal glands. Their heads were encrusted with white salt crowns. They huddled in huge colonies on the rocks to keep each other warm. They were nothing to be frightened of but they might have been were they larger. How amusing to realise that they only ate seaweed!

Then, near the end of Mrs. Travers' visit, the campsite was shifted to another island. Cyprian told her they would be there for the next four days and, after that, the *Artemisia* would be fully laden, and she would return with it to mother and Gloria.

Two days later Father had to lead an expedition inland, and he left her at the campsite. 'You have some sandwiches, there's lots to see, I'll be back in the late afternoon, okay, Essie, my girl?'

'Can't I come with you?'

'No, it's better that you don't,' he said. 'You'd be in the way.' There was an evasive tone in his voice; he was hiding something from her. 'And Felipe has a surprise for you.'

A surprise?

Felipe led her on a half-day walk. They arrived below the rim of a tall volcano. She saw a wide flat canyon studded with candelabra cactuses.

'Look,' Felipe said.

Far in the distance clouds of dust were being unsettled. Through the dust came creatures that looked as it they were advancing from out of the eye of Time. Mrs. Travers felt the psychic power emanating from them.

Giant tortoises, five feet tall, slowly lumbered in a herd towards her.

'They're on their way to bathe in dew ponds that form as a result of the Garua mist,' Felipe said.

He suggested that they sit cross-legged in the paths of the herd. Mrs. Travers wasn't too sure about doing *that* but she wasn't about to be bested by a boy, and a native boy at that.

The giant tortoises advanced unbelievingly slowly. 'They can live till they are 200 years old,' Felipe continued. 'There are over 10,000 here, but once there were 200,000.'

Mrs. Travers recalled hearing that they developed from one species — probably an ancestor who had made an incredible journey from the South American mainland — into fourteen different races or subspecies; the most startling fact was that each island had its own subspecies. They were a prime example of Darwin's theory of adaptive radiation, the process whereby several species evolved from a common ancestor over a relatively short period of evolutionary time to fill available ecological niches.

'You are lucky,' Felipe suddenly said to her. 'I know this herd. They are the oldest on the island. And look! El Rey is leading them.'

'El Rey?' Mrs. Travers asked, puzzled.

'The King,' Felipe said in a hushed voice. 'We are keeping him till last.'

Mrs. Travers strained to see. Perspiration from the hot sun had dripped into her eyes and they stung. She took out a handkerchief and wiped the sweat away. Ah, that was better. When she looked at the giant tortoises again they had grown larger. Their faces had a timeless quality, age-worn, and their shells were smooth saddleback carapaces.

But which one was El Rey? They all looked the same to her.

Two hundred yards away from Mrs. Travers the herd stopped. Just like that. The dust swirled like a cyclone. They moved apart to form a pathway. As soon as Mrs. Travers saw the ancient tortoise approaching in processional through their midst, she knew why he was called The King.

He was at least seven feet tall. He must have been six feet across the curvature of his shell. His face was incredibly wizened, his eyes huge and black. When he reached the front of the herd he opened the gash of his mouth and gave a loud, guttural roar.

He came nearer and nearer. From Mrs. Travers' sitting perspective he became a being that blotted out the rest of the world.

'He'll trample me!' Mrs. Travers cried to Felipe.

Then an extraordinary thing occurred. El Rey sighted her, gave a deep sigh and then, *thud*, down came his shell, enclosing him within, slamming tight around him and sealing him to the ground.

Mrs. Travers couldn't help thinking with glee, 'And I am only a girl!'

When El Rey did that the other giant tortoises in the front rank did the same. Eyes wide with amazement, Mrs. Travers stood up, wiped her dress and looked at Felipe.

Felipe nodded at her. 'That's what they do! Isn't it funny?' He began to run within the herd, yelling and flapping his hands, and one by one they sighed, *thudded*, and down they went. They looked like huge tortoiseshell cowpats.

'But if we approach them from behind,' Felipe said, 'we can have a lot of fun. I show you.'

He sneaked up to a giant tortoise and jumped onto its back. And it didn't even know! He motioned to Mrs. Travers that she should pick one of the giant tortoises and ride it.

With great deliberation she walked back through the herd.

'No, not El Rey,' Felipe shouted.

It was too late. Eyes bright and shining, Mrs. Travers hopped on The King's back. She laughed in triumph as El Rey's carapace elevated and he walked on, blissfully unaware that he had a passenger. Or was he? The sun had made his shell hot and the underneath of her thighs were burning. His saddle wasn't comfortable at all. Nevertheless, Mrs. Travers stayed on him for a few miles, riding El Rey through the sunlight.

After a while Felipe became bored. 'Let's go back to the shore,' he said as he dismounted. 'There's still so much I can show you.'

'Okay,' she answered. She slid off El Rey. For some reason that was beyond her, she did a little curtsey. Then she peered into his left eye and said, 'Thank you.'

And El Rey answered her, *You are not the first and I expect you will not be the last to ride on me.*

Mrs. Travers stepped back with shock and fell into the dust.

'What did you say?'

El Rey stopped and looked at her. *Humans come, humans go. There have been many like yourself, child, but taller than you, who have walked among us.*

'Like my father,' Mrs. Travers answered proudly. 'He's a scientist. He's come to collect herpetological specimens.'

El Rey's eyes were dark, black as eternity and inscribed with turbulent memories.

I met a scientist once. He was a young Englishman. He also rode on me and, afterwards, like you, child, he thanked me. He was so polite that I granted him the gift that only tortoises like myself can offer. We can look back into the past. We can also look at the present and into the future. It is the gift of foresight, and I told him to choose a question and I would answer it. He sat where you are sitting now and he pondered for a long time before asking it. And when he did, the question was — El Rey suddenly withdrew his head and, *thump,* down came his shell. But his voice echoed from beneath the carapace — *so simple but so terrible that I sobbed at the enormity of it. He should never have asked it.*

The dust swirled and drifted around Mrs. Travers. 'What did you tell him?'

After a long while El Rey rose, his head appeared and began to weave back and forth.

I told him that I would visit him at the moment of his death. And then I would show him the answer.

El Rey moved past Mrs. Travers quickly, as if trying to get away from her. But she walked swiftly after him and hopped on him again. Felipe was a speck far away, waving to her. She waved back and he shrugged, continuing down to the beach.

I didn't think I would lose you so easily, child, El Rey sighed. *All you humans have such an insatiable hunger. For everything. It will be your downfall, and many who live with you in the world have been wiped out by it. It won't be long before the rest of us follow.*

Mrs. Travers wasn't about to be put off by a silly old tortoise, even if he was a giant — and a king. 'The rest of us?'

We who live in Orbis Terrarum, El Rey explained. *The Inhabited World — all the birds of the air, the plants and flowers and creatures of the land, and the inhabitants of the sea, sharing our world with you, the greatest predator the universe has ever known.*

'Predator?' Mrs. Travers pondered the word, lifting it, weighing it and looking underneath it as if it were a stone.

Did you know, child, El Rey continued, grazing within the canyon, *that by the beginning of the 19th century, ten million of us had been lifted from our islands, mainly by buccaneers, whalers and other sailors? The sailors would come in gangs, some up to eight men, to lift us one by one into their ships. Each ship would take between 500 and 600 tortoises at a time. Our capacity to survive without water or food for many months was our downfall. In the days before refrigeration we provided an inexhaustible supply of fresh meat for the many months that the ships were at sea. We were apparently a delicacy in our own right, and greatly preferred to the standard fare of salted pork and hard tack. And then, of course, our population was also devastated by what the sailors brought to our islands: their own* familiars — *dogs, cats, pigs and goats — ravaged our vegetative food supply. The black rat pounced gladly on our tortoise hatchlings. Since then there have been poachers and . . . others . . . it's the old, old story, my child.*

'But then Darwin came,' Mrs. Travers said proudly. 'He saved you all, surely.'

Yes, the young Englishman came, El Rey acknowledged, *and then he went. And after him came other scientists. They took hundreds more of us for their museums and zoos. One scientist no better or worse than the rest.*

Mrs. Travers was offended. 'My father is not like that,' she said. 'You should apologise,' she ordered. 'Didn't you hear me? Say you're sorry!'

But El Rey was silent.

In a temper, Mrs. Travers kicked him. Hard. She bunched up her fists, pulled her sunhat tightly over her head and began to walk away. 'In that case, good*bye*.'

She was halfway along the canyon, heading toward the beach, when she stopped. A venal, greedy look, one tinged with the scent of revenge, came into her eyes. Turning, she stormed her way back to the herd. As she swept by, the giant tortoises *thudded* and *fell*, making obeisance to her. When she reached the front of the herd she turned and waited for El Rey to approach.

'Stop,' she commanded. She looked hard at him. 'I have a question,' she said.

The sun ceased its passage across the sky. The whole universe breathed in.

No, child, El Rey answered.

Mrs. Travers stamped her foot. 'I am entitled to it,' she said crossly. 'And I am not a child.'

El Rey pondered Mrs. Travers. *Ah well,* he began arrogantly, *I suppose it won't hurt to tell you what Father Christmas will leave you under the Christmas tree. You may ask your question.*

But when Mrs. Travers whispered her question into his ear El Rey was shocked. He stared at Mrs. Travers, horrified. *I underestimated you, child. It's the most terrible question of all. No inhabitant of Orbis Terrarum — no bird or animal or sea creature — would ever ask it. Only a human would ever dare to ask the unaskable.*

'I demand my answer,' Mrs. Travers said, compressing her lips.

Grief stricken, El Rey nodded. *I suppose I will have to promise you what I promised the young Englishman. I couldn't answer him at the time because to have done so would have pushed him into a madness from which he would not be able to return. When you are dying, I will come and show you the answer.*

'I'm dying now,' Mrs. Travers shouted, petulantly.

Not quite yet.

'Oh . . .' Mrs. Travers whispered, putting her wrinkled and veined hands to her face, 'but I can't remember the question now.'

Alas, but I do, El Rey sighed. *I remember everything. My cross is never to forget.*

IV.

Half past four, half past four.

There was a fluttering sound and suddenly a host of doves and finches settled on the window — and then proceeded to come through and perch on Mrs. Travers' bed.

Are you coming with us now? they chirped.

'All right,' she said.

What had father taught her about the finches? Oh yes, they were another example of Darwin's theory of adaptive radiation, evolving into thirteen species.

Mrs. Travers felt very strange, very strange indeed. She looked around the hospital room and saw that her daughters were there. And who was the male stranger with them? Why, it looked like Father!

No, it was Elliot. He'd finally arrived. He'd had his little cry with his sisters and dutifully sat by the bedside and looked into Mrs. Travers' eyes. He could never hide anything from her. She saw into his soul, and it wasn't love that she saw there but horror. Was this old woman really his mother? Is this what death looked like?

The silly boy was *scared*. Even as a boy he had always been scared of his own shadow.

'We will let Mummy go now,' he said.

But there was another delay. Joan insisted that a priest come to perform Mrs. Travers' last rites. Once that was done, Elliot, with a nod, approved the turning off of the dialysis machine.

And the toxins began to flood freely through her body, poisoning her to death. One by one the organs keeping her going shut down. Her bodily functions began to fail. Pumped full of drugs to alleviate the pain, she passed in and out of consciousness.

Mrs. Travers looked at her children one by one without any sense of emotion: Molly, Kate, Joan and Elliot. She wished they would go home, put up their feet and watch a bit of telly, and leave her to get on with it.

Oh, and now she did feel quite queasy, and her body was itching all over. She felt sluggish, extraordinarily tired, and she was aware of her heart going thunkety-thunk and the blood banging around her body like old pipes when the winter comes around and they start to freeze.

Time was running out. She'd better get going, and follow the finches.

Come along then, they called to her.

She sat up. At least she *thought* she sat up, but nobody in the room seemed to take any notice of her. And when she pushed down the bed covers and got out of bed, why, they didn't seem to care. Warner didn't even call her 'lovie' and scold her.

Then somebody did bar her way. It was Cyprian.

She wanted to scream at him, just scream and scream.

He hadn't told her what he was doing in the Galapagos Islands. She only discovered it for herself when she was on the way back home on the *Artemisia*. She liked exploring, and found the passageway leading to the hold.

It was filled with father's herpetological and other specimens. All nicely tagged and tabulated: birds, fishes, botanical plants. Stacked to the very top of the hold, upside down, were hundreds of giant tortoises. Most had been killed; some were still alive, kicking and moving their arms and legs, slowly, thrashing about.

Right at the top was El Rey.

'We are keeping him till last,' Felipe had said.

Don't fret, child, El Rey sighed. *It had to happen one day. And don't blame your father. He is no better or worse than all the rest.*

Mrs. Travers *did* scream then. Oh, she supposed she had been wanting to scream for years at her father because he was supposed to be better, he really was.

'You told me you didn't believe in intervention,' she accused him. 'You were just as bad and as culpable as the buccaneers, the whalers and sailors before you.'

Humanity had indeed evolved to fill every available niche, even if that niche was already filled by others; humanity, the greatest predator.

Then she heard the sound calling to her again. It came, not now from beyond the window frame but from the other side of it. It was low, deep, haunting, otherworldly, sibilant — somewhere between a deep hiss and moan. Not a sound to be scared of;

rather, one for which you waited with breathless anticipation.

Mrs. Travers floated — yes, floated — over the sill of the window and out of the room, away from them all, away.

She found it difficult to breathe and gave a huge inward gasp.

Outside, the landscape wasn't the usual one at all: not the cityscape, dark, sprinkled with lights, and the familiar volcanic cone of Mt Eden. Rather, it was a darker, altogether wilder landscape, greying with the morning. A road ran right through the middle of it. Something was moving right at the horizon, coming towards her.

The sky widened and whitened and, far away, she could see the sea. Running gaily, she made her way down among the rocks and saw scarlet-grey lizards sunning themselves. Then some of the lizards did an extraordinary thing: they leapt into the water, making humorous plopping noises, and when she peered into the water to look, Mrs. Travers could see them feeding on underwater seaweed. The seaweed looked so delicious that she couldn't help herself.

Nightdress and all, she dived into the sea and joined the feeding lizards. Shoals of scintillating fish surrounded her. Suddenly they changed into seabirds returning to their colony. Mrs. Travers walked among them and, without thinking, sprang upon a chick harassing her to her death.

'Oh, I'm so sorry, Gloria, I'm so sorry.'

She wanted to weep.

Hello, a voice said.

El Rey had arrived. He had kept his promise.

When Mrs. Travers looked up, she saw she was on his island, below the rim of a volcano, in a pass studded with candelabra cactuses.

'I knew it was you,' Mrs. Travers said, smoothing her nightdress.

El Rey looked at her. Around him, a herd of giant tortoises

was waiting. Strangely, there was a window sill, and on the other side of it she could see her grieving children beside a bed in which lay an old woman.

Time to go, El Rey said.

She nodded, lifted up the hem of her dressing gown and slid onto his carapace. She turned to the children on the other side of the window. 'Goodbye.' Then she gasped, 'I can't remember the question.'

Alas, I can, El Rey sighed. *Lean down and I'll whisper it in your ear.*

Mrs. Travers heard El Rey's voice and nodded when he told her. 'Yes, I remember it now.'

Come along then, child, El Rey said. He gave a guttural roar and, at his command, the herd made way for him and the old woman who was riding him. A dark dust cloud rose, radiant, glistening.

There was a moment in the Galapagos, Mrs. Travers remembered, just before the sun went down and the waves were darkening, when the horizon went smoky grey, as if many fires were being lit along it. The smoke billowed through oranges and reds, which became pastel shades of cerise, vermilion, blushes of pink within a vault of celestial blue. The reds lasted for a long time. It was the sea that darkened quickly, advancing to the rim of red, and above, one by one, the stars began to appear.

As El Rey turned to face the darkness, Mrs. Travers felt a cool wind chilling her. It was just a little, well, *scary.*

'Will it hurt?' she asked.

'It's only life that hurts,' El Rey answered.

'Will it *hurt*?' Mrs. Travers asked again, sharply.

'Just a little bit,' he said.

KATHERINE MANSFIELD'S UNFINISHED STORIES

A MARRIED MAN'S STORY

I.

It is evening. Supper is over. We have left the small, cold dining-room, we have come back to the sitting-room where there is a fire. All is as usual. I am sitting at my writing-table which is placed across a corner so that I am behind it, as it were, and facing the room. The lamp with the green shade is alight; I have before me two large books of reference, both open, a pile of papers . . . All the paraphernalia, in fact, of an extremely occupied man. My wife, with her little boy on her lap, is in a low chair before the fire. She is about to put him to bed before she clears away the dishes and piles them up in the kitchen for the servant girl to-morrow morning. But the warmth, the quiet, and the sleepy baby, have made her dreamy. One of his red woollen boots is off, one is on. She sits, bent forward, clasping the little bare foot, staring into the glow, and as the fire quickens, falls, flares again, her shadow — an immense *Mother and Child* — is here and gone again upon the wall.

Outside it is raining. I like to think of that cold drenched window behind the blind, and beyond, the dark bushes in the garden, their broad leaves bright with rain, and beyond the fence, the gleaming road with the two hoarse little gutters singing against each other, and the wavering reflections of the lamps, like fishes' tails. While I am here, I am there, lifting my face to the dim sky, and it seems to me it must be raining all over the world — that the whole earth is drenched, is sounding with a soft, quick patter or hard, steady drumming, or gurgling and something that is like sobbing and laughing mingled together, and that light, playful splashing that is of water falling into still lakes and flowing rivers. And all at one and the same moment I am arriving in a strange city, slipping under the hood of the cab while the driver whips the cover off the breathing horse, running from shelter to shelter, dodging someone, swerving by someone else. I am conscious of tall houses, their doors and shutters sealed against the night, of dripping balconies and sodden flower-pots. I am brushing through deserted gardens and falling into moist smelling summer-houses (you know how soft and almost crumbling the wood of a summer-house is in the rain); I am standing on the dark quayside giving my ticket into the wet, red hand of the old sailor in an oilskin. How strong the sea smells! How loudly the tied-up boats knock against one another! I am crossing the wet stackyard, hooded in an old sack, carrying a lantern, while the house-dog, like a soaking doormat, springs, shakes himself over me. And now I am walking along a deserted road — it is impossible to miss the puddles, and the trees are stirring — stirring.

But one could go on with such a catalogue for ever — on and on — until one lifted the single arum lily leaf and discovered the tiny snails clinging, until one counted . . . and what then? Aren't those just the signs, the traces of my feeling? The bright green streaks made by someone who walks over the dewy grass? Not the feeling itself. And as I think that a mournful, glorious voice begins to sing in my bosom. Yes, perhaps that is nearer what I mean. What a voice! What power! What velvety softness! Marvellous!

Suddenly my wife turns round quickly. She knows — how long has she known? — that I am not 'working'. It is strange that with her full, open gaze she should smile so timidly — and that she should say in such a hesitating voice, 'What are you thinking?'

I smile and draw two fingers across my forehead in the way I have. 'Nothing,' I answer softly.

At that she stirs and, still trying not to make it sound important, she says, 'Oh, but you must have been thinking of something!'

Then I really meet her gaze, meet it fully, and I fancy her face quivers. Will she never grow accustomed to these simple — one might say — everyday little lies? Will she never learn not to expose herself — or to build up defences?

'Truly, I was thinking of nothing.'

There! I seem to see it dart at her. She turns away, pulls the other red sock off the baby, sits him up, and begins to unbutton him behind. I wonder if that little soft rolling bundle sees anything, feels anything? Now she turns him over on her knee, and in this light, his soft arms and legs waving, he is extraordinarily like a young crab. A queer thing is I can't connect him with my wife and myself — I've never accepted him as ours. Each time when I come into the hall and see the perambulator I catch myself thinking: 'H'm, someone has brought a baby!' Or, when his crying wakes me at night, I feel inclined to blame my wife for having brought the baby in from outside. The truth is, that though one might suspect her of strong maternal feelings, my wife doesn't seem to me the type of woman who bears children in her own body. There's an immense difference! Where is that . . . animal ease and playfulness, that quick kissing and cuddling one has been taught to expect of young mothers? She hasn't a sign of it. I believe that when she ties its bonnet she feels like an aunt and not a mother. But of course I may be wrong; she may be passionately devoted . . . I don't think so. At any rate, isn't it a trifle indecent to feel like this about one's own wife? Indecent or not, one has these feelings. And one other thing. How can I reasonably expect my wife, *a broken-hearted woman*, to spend her time tossing the baby? But that is beside the mark. She never even began to toss when her heart was whole.

And now she has carried the baby to bed. I hear her soft, deliberate steps moving between the dining-room and the kitchen, there and back again, to the tune of the clattering dishes. And now all is quiet. What is happening now? Oh, I know just as surely as if I'd gone to see — she is standing in the middle of the kitchen facing the rainy window. Her head is bent, with one finger she is tracing something — nothing — on the table. It is cold in the kitchen; the gas jumps; the tap drips; it's a forlorn picture. And nobody is going to come behind her, to take her in his arms, to kiss her soft hair, to lead her to the fire and to rub her hands warm again. Nobody is going to call her or to wonder what she is doing out there. And she knows it And yet, being a woman, deep down, deep down, she really does expect the miracle to happen; she really could embrace that dark, dark deceit, rather than live — like this.

II.

To live like this . . . I write those words very carefully, very beautifully. For some reason I feel inclined to sign them, or to write underneath — Trying a New Pen. But, seriously, isn't it staggering to think what may be contained in one innocent-looking little phrase? It tempts me — it tempts me terribly.

Scene: The supper-table. My wife has just handed me my tea. I stir it, lift the spoon, idly chase and then carefully capture a speck of tea-leaf, and having brought it ashore, I murmur, quite gently, 'How long shall we continue to live — like — this?' And immediately there is that famous 'blinding flash and deafening roar. Huge pieces of débris (I must say I like débris) are flung into the air . . . and when the dark clouds of smoke have drifted away . . .' But this will never happen; I shall never know it. It will be found upon me 'intact', as they say. 'Open my heart and you will see . . .'

Why? Ah, there you have me! There is the most difficult question of all to answer. Why do people stay together? Putting aside 'for the sake of the children', and 'the habit of years' and 'economic reasons' as lawyers' nonsense — it's not much more — if one really does try to find out why it is that people don't leave each other, one discovers a mystery. It is because they can't; they are bound. And nobody on earth knows what are the bonds that bind them except those two. Am I being obscure? Well, the thing itself isn't so frightfully crystal clear, is it? Let me put it like this. Supposing you are taken, absolutely, first into his confidence and then into hers. Supposing you know all there is to know about the situation. And having given it not only your deepest sympathy but your most honest impartial criticism, you declare, very calmly (but not without the slightest suggestion of relish — for there is — I swear there is — in the very best of us — something that leaps up and cries 'A-ahh!' for joy at the thought of destroying), 'Well, my opinion is that you two people ought to part. You'll do no earthly good together. Indeed, it seems to me, it's the duty of either to set the other free.' What happens then? He — and she — agree. It is their conviction too. You are only saying what they have been thinking all last night. And away they go to act on your advice, immediately . . . And the next time you hear of them they are still together. You see — you've reckoned without the unknown quantity — which is their secret relation to each other — and that they can't disclose even if they want to. Thus far you may tell and no further. Oh, don't misunderstand me! It need not necessarily have anything to do with their sleeping together . . . But this brings me to a thought I've often half entertained. Which is that human beings, as we know them, don't choose each other at all. It is the owner, the second self inhabiting them, who makes the choice for his own particular purposes, and — this may sound absurdly far-fetched — it's the second self in the other which responds. Dimly — dimly — or so it has seemed to me — we realise this, at any rate to the extent that we realise the hopelessness of trying to escape. So that, what it all amounts to is — if the impermanent selves of my wife and me are happy — *tant mieux pour nous* — if miserable — *tant pis* . . . But I don't know, I don't know. And it may be that it's something entirely individual in me — this sensation (yes, it is even a sensation) of how extraordinarily *shell-like* we are as we are — little creatures, peering out of the sentry-box at the gate, ogling through our glass case at the entry, wan little servants, who never can say for certain, even, if the master is out or in . . .

The door opens . . . My wife. She says, 'I am going to bed.'

And I look up vaguely, and vaguely say, 'You are going to bed.'

'Yes.' A tiny pause. 'Don't forget — will you? — to turn out the gas in the hall.'

And again I repeat, 'The gas in the hall.'

There was a time — the time before — when this habit of mine — it really has become a habit now — it wasn't one then — was one of our sweetest jokes together. It began, of course, when on several occasions I really was deeply engaged and I didn't hear. I emerged only to see her shaking her head and laughing at me, 'You haven't heard a word!'

'No. What did you say?'

Why should she think that so funny and charming? She did — it delighted her. 'Oh, my darling, it's so like you! It's so — so —' And I knew she loved me for it. I knew she positively looked forward to coming in and disturbing me, and so — as one does — I played up. I was guaranteed to be wrapped away every evening at 10.30 p.m. But now? For some reason I feel it would be crude to stop my performance. It's simplest to play on. But what is she waiting for to-night? Why doesn't she go? Why prolong this? She is going. No, her hand on the door-knob, she turns round again, and she says in the most curious, small, breathless voice, 'You're not cold?'

Oh, it's not fair to be as pathetic as that! That was simply damnable. I shuddered all over before I managed to bring out a slow 'No-o!' while my left hand ruffles the reference pages.

She is gone; she will not come back again to-night. It is not only I who recognise that — the room changes too. It relaxes, like an old actor. Slowly the mask is rubbed off; the look of strained attention changes to an air of heavy, sullen brooding. Every line, every fold breathes fatigue. The mirror is quenched; the ash whitens; only my sly lamp burns on . . . But what a cynical indifference to me it all shows! Or should I perhaps be flattered? No, we understand each other. You know those stories of little children who are suckled by wolves and accepted by the tribe, and how for ever after they move freely among their fleet, grey brothers? Something like that has happened to me. But wait! That about the wolves won't do. Curious! Before I wrote it down, while it was still in my head, I was delighted with it. It seemed to express, and more, to suggest, just what I wanted to say. But written, I can smell the falseness immediately and the . . . source of the smell is in that word fleet. Don't you agree? Fleet, grey brothers! 'Fleet'. A word I never use. When I wrote 'wolves' it skimmed across my mind like a shadow and I couldn't resist it. Tell me! Tell me! Why is it so difficult to write simply — and not simply only but *sotto voce*, if you know what I mean? That is how I long to write. No fine effects — no bravura. But just the plain truth, as only a liar can tell it.

III.

I light a cigarette, lean back, inhale deeply — and find myself wondering if my wife is asleep. Or is she lying in her cold bed, staring into the dark, with those trustful, bewildered eyes? Her eyes are like the eyes of a cow that is being driven along a road. 'Why am I being driven — what harm have I done?' But I really am not responsible for that look; it's her natural expression. One day, when she was turning out a cupboard, she found a little old photograph of herself, taken when she was a girl at school. In her confirmation dress, she explained. And there were the eyes, even then. I remember saying to her, 'Did you always look so sad?' Leaning over my shoulder, she laughed lightly, 'Do I look sad? I think it's just . . . me.' And she waited for me to say something about it. But I was marvelling at her courage at having shown it to me at all. It was a hideous photograph! And I wondered again if she realised how plain she was, and comforted herself with the idea that people who loved each other didn't criticise but accepted everything, or if she really rather liked her appearance and expected me to say something complimentary.

Oh, that was base of me! How could I have forgotten all the numberless times when I have known her turn away to avoid the light, press her face into my shoulders. And, above all, how could I have forgotten the afternoon of our wedding-day when we sat on the green bench in the Botanical Gardens and listened to the band; how, in an interval between two pieces, she suddenly turned to me and said in the voice in which one says, 'Do you think the grass is damp?' or 'Do you think it's time for tea?' . . . 'Tell me, do you think physical beauty is so very important?' I don't like to think how often she had rehearsed that question. And do you know what I answered? At that moment, as if at my command, there came a great gush of hard, bright sound from the band, and I managed to shout above it cheerfully, 'I didn't hear what you said.' Devilish! Wasn't it? Perhaps not wholly. She looked like the poor patient who hears the surgeon say, 'It will certainly be necessary to perform the operation — but not now!'

IV.

But all this conveys the impression that my wife and I were never really happy together. Not true! Not true! We were marvellously, radiantly happy. We were a model couple. If you had seen us together, any time, any place, if you had followed us, tracked us down, spied, taken us off our guard, you still would have been forced to confess, 'I have never seen a more ideally suited pair.' Until last autumn.

But really to explain what happened then I should have to go back and back — I should have to dwindle until my two hands clutched the banisters, the stair-rail was higher than my head, and I peered through to watch my father padding softly up and down. There were coloured windows on the landings. As he came up, first his bald head was scarlet, then it was yellow. How frightened I was! And when they put me to bed, it was to dream that we were living inside one of my father's big coloured bottles. For he was a chemist. I was born nine years after my parents were married. I was an only child, and the effect to produce even me — small, withered bud I must have been — sapped all my mother's strength. She never left her room again. Bed, sofa, window, she moved between the three.

Well I can see her, on the window days, sitting, her cheek in her hand, staring out. Her room looked over the street. Opposite there was a wall plastered with advertisements for travelling shows and circuses and so on. I stand beside her, and we gaze at the slim lady in a red dress hitting a dark gentleman over the head with her parasol, or at the tiger peering through the jungle while the clown, close by, balances a bottle on his nose, or at a little golden-haired girl sitting on the knee of an old black man in a broad cotton hat . . . She says nothing. On sofa days there is a flannel dressing-gown that I loathe and a cushion that keeps on slipping off the hard sofa. I pick it up. It has flowers and writing sewn on. I ask what the writing says, and she whispers, 'Sweet Repose!' In bed her fingers plait, in tight little plaits, the fringe of the quilt and her lips are thin. And that is all there is of my mother, except the last queer 'episode' that comes later.

My father . . . Curled up in the corner on the lid of a round box that held sponges, I stared at my father so long, it's as though his image, cut off at the waist by the counter, has remained solid in my memory. Perfectly bald, polished head, shaped like a thin egg, creased, creamy cheeks, little bags under the eyes, large pale ears like handles. His manner was discreet, sly, faintly amused and tinged with impudence. Long before I could appreciate it I knew the mixture . . . I even used to copy him in my corner, bending forward, with a small reproduction of his faint sneer. In the evening his customers were, chiefly, young women; some of them came in every day for his famous fivepenny pick-me-up. Their gaudy looks, their voices, their free ways fascinated me. I longed to be my father, handing them across the counter the little glass of bluish stuff they tossed off so greedily. God knows what it was made of. Years after I drank some, just to see what it tasted like, and I felt as though someone had given me a terrific blow on the head; I felt stunned.

One of those evenings I remember vividly. It was cold; it must have been autumn, for the flaring gas was lighted after my tea. I sat in my corner and my father was mixing something; the shop was empty. Suddenly the bell jangled and a young woman rushed in, crying so loud, sobbing so hard, that it didn't sound real. She wore a green cape trimmed with fur and a hat with cherries dangling. My father came from behind the screen. But she couldn't stop herself at first. She stood in the middle of the shop and wrung her hands and moaned; I've never heard such crying since. Presently she managed to gasp out, 'Give me a pick-me-up!' Then she drew a long breath, trembled away from him and quavered, 'I've had *bad news*!' And in the flaring gaslight I saw the whole side of her face was puffed up and purple; her lip was cut and her eyelid looked as though it was gummed fast over the wet eye. My father pushed the glass across the counter, and she took the purse out of her stocking and paid him. But she couldn't drink; clutching the glass, she stared in front of her as if she could not believe what she saw. Each time she put her head back the tears spurted out again. Finally she put the glass down. It was no use. Holding the cape with one hand, she ran in the same way out of the shop again. My father gave no sign. But long after she had gone I crouched in my corner, and when I think back it's as though I felt my whole body vibrating — 'So that's what it is outside,' I thought. 'That's what it's like out there.'

V.

Do you remember your childhood? I am always coming across these marvellous accounts by writers who declare that they remember 'everything'. I certainly don't. The dark stretches, the blanks, are much bigger than the bright glimpses. I seem to have spent most of my time like a plant in a cupboard. Now and again, when the sun shone, a careless hand thrust me out on to the window-sill, and a careless hand whipped me in again — and that was all. But what happened in the darkness — I wonder? Did one grow? Pale stem . . . timid leaves . . . white reluctant bud. No wonder I was hated at school. Even the masters shrank from me. I somehow knew that my soft, hesitating voice disgusted them. I knew, too, how they turned away from my shocked, staring eyes. I was small and thin and I smelled of the shop; my nickname was Gregory Powder. School was a tin building, stuck on the raw hillside. There were dark red streaks like blood in the oozing clay banks of the playground. I hide in the dark passage, where the coats hang, and am discovered there by one of the masters. 'What are you doing there in the dark?' His terrible voice kills me; I die before his eyes. I am standing in a ring of thrust-out heads; some are grinning, some look greedy, some are spitting. And it is always cold. Big crushed-up clouds press across the sky; the rusty water in the school tank is frozen; the bell sounds numb. One day they put a dead bird in my overcoat pocket. I found it just when I reached home. Oh, what a strange flutter there was at my heart when I drew out that terribly soft, cold little body, with the legs thin as pins and the claws wrung. I sat on the back door step in the yard and put the bird in my cap. The feathers round the neck looked wet and there was a tiny tuft just above the closed eyes that stood up too. How tightly the beak was shut! I could not see the mark where it was divided. I stretched out one wing and touched the soft, secret down underneath; I tried to make the claws curl round my little finger. But I didn't feel sorry for it — no! I wondered. The smoke from our kitchen chimney poured downwards, and flakes of soot floated — soft, light in the air. Through a big crack in the cement yard a poor-looking plant with dull, reddish flowers had pushed its way. I looked at the dead bird again . . . And that is the first time that I remember singing — rather . . . listening to a silent voice inside a little cage that was me.

VI.

But what has all this to do with my married happiness? How can all this affect my wife and me? Why — to tell what happened last autumn — do I run all this way back into the Past? The Past — what is the Past? I might say the star-shaped flake of soot on a leaf of the poor-looking plant, and the bird lying on the quilted lining of my cap, and my father's pestle and my mother's cushion belong to it. But that is not to say they are any less mine than they were when I looked upon them with my very eyes and touched them with these fingers. No, they are more — they are a living part of me. Who am I, in fact, as I sit here at this table, but my own past? If I deny that, I am nothing. And if I were to try to divide my life into childhood, youth, early manhood and so on, it would be a kind of affectation; I should know I was doing it just because of the pleasantly important sensation it gives one to rule lines and to use green ink for childhood, red for the next stage, and purple for the period of adolescence. For, one thing I have learnt, one thing I do believe is, Nothing Happens Suddenly. Yes, that is my religion, I suppose.

My mother's death, for instance. Is it more distant from me to-day than it was then? It is just as close, as strange, as puzzling, and, in spite of all the countless times I have recalled the circumstances, I know no more now than I did then, whether I dreamed them, or whether they really occurred. It happened when I was thirteen and I slept in a little strip of a room on what was called the half-landing. One night I woke up with a start to see my mother, in her nightgown, without even the hated flannel dressing-gown, sitting on my bed.

But the strange thing which frightened me was, she wasn't looking at me. Her head was bent; the short, thin trail of hair lay between her shoulders; her hands were pressed between her knees and my bed shook; she was shivering. It was the first time I had ever seen her out of her own room. I said, or I think I said, 'Is that you, Mother?' And as she turned round, I saw in the moonlight how queer she looked. Her face looked small — quite different. She looked like one of the boys at the school baths, who sits on a step, shivering just like that, and wants to go in and yet is frightened.

'Are you awake?' she said. Her eyes opened; I think she smiled. She leaned towards me. 'I've been poisoned,' she whispered. 'Your father's poisoned me.' And she nodded. Then, before I could say a word, she was gone; I thought I heard the door shut. I sat quite still, I couldn't move, I think I expected something else to happen. For a long time I listened for something; there wasn't a sound. The candle was by my bed, but I was too frightened to stretch out my hand for the matches. But even while I wondered what I ought to do, even while my heart thumped — everything became confused. I lay down and pulled the blankets round me. I fell asleep, and the next morning my mother was found dead of failure of the heart.

Did that visit happen? Was it a dream? Why did she come to tell me? Or why, if she came, did she go away so quickly? And her expression — so joyous under the frightened look — was that real? I believed it fully the afternoon of the funeral, when I saw my father dressed up for his part, hat and all. That tall hat so gleaming black and round was like a cork covered with black sealing-wax, and the rest of my father was awfully like a bottle, with his face for the label — *Deadly Poison*. It flashed into my mind as I stood opposite him in the hall. And Deadly Poison, or old D. P., was my private name for him from that day.

VII.

Late, it grows late. I love the night. I love to feel the tide of darkness rising slowly and slowly washing, turning over and over, lifting, floating, all that lies strewn upon the dark beach, all that lies hid in rocky hollows. I love, I love this strange feeling of drifting — whither? After my mother's death I hated to go to bed. I used to sit on the window-sill, folded up, and watch the sky. It seemed to me the moon moved much faster than the sun. And one big, bright green star I chose for my own. My star! But I never thought of it beckoning to me or twinkling merrily for my sake. Cruel, indifferent, splendid — it burned in the airy night. No matter — it was mine! But, growing close up against the window, there was a creeper with small, bunched-up pink and purple flowers. These did know me. These, when I touched them at night, welcomed my fingers; the little tendrils, so weak, so delicate, knew I would not hurt them. When the wind moved the leaves I felt I understood their shaking. When I came to the window, it seemed to me the flowers said among themselves, 'The boy is here.'

As the months passed there was often a light in my father's room below. And I heard voices and laughter. 'He's got some woman with him,' I thought. But it meant nothing to me. Then the gay voice, the sound of the laughter, gave me the idea it was one of the girls who used to come to the shop in the evenings — and gradually I began to imagine which girl it was. It was the dark one in the red coat and skirt who once had given me a penny. A merry face stooped over me — warm breath tickled my neck — there were little beads of black on her long lashes, and when she opened her arms to kiss me there came a marvellous wave of scent! Yes, that was the one.

Time passed, and I forgot the moon and my green star and my shy creeper — I came to the window to wait for the light in my father's window, to listen for the laughing voice, until one night I dozed and I dreamed she came again — again she drew me to her, something soft, scented, warm and merry hung over me like a cloud. But when I tried to see, her eyes only mocked me, her red lips opened and she hissed, 'Little sneak! Little sneak!' But not as if she were angry, — as if she understood, and her smile somehow was like a rat — hateful!

The night after, I lighted the candle and sat down at the table instead. By and by, as the flame steadied, there was a small lake of liquid wax, surrounded by a white, smooth wall. I took a pin and made little holes in this wall and then sealed them up faster than the wax could escape. After a time I fancied the candle flame joined in the game; it leapt up, quivered, wagged; it even seemed to laugh. But while I played with the candle and smiled and broke off the tiny white peaks of wax that rose above the wall and floated them on my lake, a feeling of awful dreariness fastened on me — yes, that's the word. It crept up from my knees to my thighs, into my arms; I ached all over with misery. And I felt so strangely that I couldn't move. Something bound me there by the table — I couldn't even let the pin drop that I held between my finger and thumb. For a moment I came to a stop, as it were.

Then the shrivelled case of the bud split and fell, the plant in the cupboard came into flower. 'Who am I?' I thought. 'What is all this?' And I looked at my room, at the broken bust of the man called Hahnemann on top of the cupboard, at my little bed with the pillow like an envelope. I saw it all, but not as I had seen before . . . Everything lived, everything. But that was not all. I was equally alive and — it's the only way I can express it — the barriers were down between us — I had come into my own world!

VIII.

The barriers were down. I had been all my life a little outcast; but until that moment no one had "accepted" me; I had lain in the cupboard — or the cave forlorn. But now I was taken, I was accepted, claimed. I did not consciously turn away from the world of human beings; I had never known it; but I from that night did beyond words consciously turn towards my silent brothers . . .

THE DOVE'S NEST

I.

After lunch Milly and her mother were sitting as usual on the balcony beyond the salon admiring for the five-hundredth time the stocks, the roses, the small, bright grass beneath the palms, and the oranges against a wavy line of blue, when a card was brought them by Marie. Visitors at the Villa Martin were very rare. True, the English clergyman, Mr. Sandiman, had called, and he had come a second time with his wife to tea. But an awful thing had happened on that second occasion. Mother had made a mistake. She had said 'More tea, Mr. Sandybags?' Oh, what a frightful thing to have happened! How could she have done it? Milly still flamed at the thought. And he had evidently not forgiven them; he'd never come again. So this card put them both into quite a flutter.

Mr. Walter Prodger, they read. And then an American address, so very much abbreviated that neither of them understood it. Walter Prodger? But they'd never heard of him.

Mother looked from the card to Milly.

'Prodger, dear?' she asked mildly, as though helping Milly to a slice of never-before-tasted pudding.

And Milly seemed to be holding her plate back in the way she answered 'I — don't — know, Mother.'

'These are the occasions', said Mother, becoming a little flustered, 'when one does so feel the need of our dear English servants. Now if I could just say, "What is he like, Annie?" I should know whether to see him or not. But he may be some common man, selling something — one of those American inventions for peeling things, you know, dear. Or he may even be some kind of foreign sharper.' Mother winced at the hard, bright little word as though she had given herself a dig with her embroidery scissors.

But here Marie smiled at Milly and murmured, '*C'est un très beau Monsieur.*'

'What does she say, dear?'

'She says he looks very nice, Mother.'

'Well, we'd better —' began Mother. 'Where is he now, I wonder.'

Marie answered 'In the vestibule, Madame.'

In the hall! Mother jumped up, seriously alarmed. In the hall, with all those valuable little foreign things that didn't belong to them scattered over the tables.

'Show him in, Marie. Come, Milly, come, dear. We will see him in the salon. Oh, why isn't Miss Anderson here?' almost wailed Mother.

But Miss Anderson, Mother's new companion, never was on the spot when she was wanted. She had been engaged to be a comfort, a support to them both. Fond of travelling, a cheerful disposition, a good packer and so on. And then, when they had come all this way and taken the Villa Martin and moved in, she had turned out to be a Roman Catholic. Half her time, more than half, was spent wearing out the knees of her skirts in cold churches. It was really too . . .

The door opened. A middle-aged, clean-shaven, very well-dressed stranger stood bowing before them. His bow was stately. Milly saw it pleased Mother very much; she bowed her Queen Alexandra bow back. As for Milly, she never could bow. She smiled, feeling shy, but deeply interested.

'Have I the pleasure', said the stranger very courteously, with a strong American accent, 'of speaking with Mrs. Wyndham Fawcett?'

'I am Mrs. Fawcett', said Mother graciously, 'and this is my daughter, Mildred.'

'Pleased to meet you, Miss Fawcett.' And the stranger shot a fresh, chill hand at Milly, who grasped it just in time before it was gone again.

'Won't you sit down?' said Mother, and she waved faintly at all the gilt chairs.

'Thank you, I will,' said the stranger.

Down he sat, still solemn, crossing his legs and, most surprisingly, his arms as well. His face looked at them over his dark arms as over a gate.

'Milly, sit down, dear.'

So Milly sat down, too, on the Madame Récamier couch and traced a filet lace flower with her finger. There was a little pause. She saw the stranger swallow; Mother's fan opened and shut.

Then he said, 'I took the liberty of calling, Mrs. Fawcett, because I had the pleasure of your husband's acquaintance in the States when he was lecturing there some years ago. I should like very much to renoo our — well — I venture to hope we might call it friendship. Is he with you at present? Are you expecting him out? I noticed his name was not mentioned in the local paper. But I put that down to a foreign custom, perhaps — giving precedence to the lady.'

And here the stranger looked as though he might be going to smile.

But as a matter of fact it was extremely awkward. Mother's mouth shook. Milly squeezed her hands between her knees, but she watched hard from under her eyebrows. Good, noble little Mummy! How Milly admired her as she heard her say, gently and quite simply, 'I am sorry to say my husband died two years ago.'

Mr. Prodger gave a great start. 'Did he?' He thrust out his under lip, frowned, pondered. 'I am truly sorry to hear that, Mrs. Fawcett. I hope you'll believe me when I say I had no idea your husband had . . . passed over.'

'Of course.' Mother softly stroked her skirt.

'I do trust', said Mr. Prodger, more seriously still, 'that my inquiry didn't give you too much pain.'

'No, no. It's quite all right,' said the gentle voice.

But Mr. Prodger insisted. 'You're sure? You're positive?' At that Mother raised her head and gave him one of her still, bright, exalted glances that Milly knew so well. 'I'm not in the least hurt,' she said, as one might say it from the midst of the fiery furnace.

Mr. Prodger looked relieved. He changed his attitude and continued. 'I hope this regrettable circumstance will not deprive me of your —'

'Oh, certainly not. We shall be delighted. We are always so pleased to know anyone who —' Mother gave a little bound, a little flutter. She flew from her shadowy branch on to a sunny one. 'Is this your first visit to the Riviera?'

'It is,' said Mr. Prodger. 'The fact is I was in Florence until recently. But I took a heavy cold there —'

'Florence so damp,' cooed Mother.

'And the doctor recommended I should come here for the sunshine before I started for home.'

'The sun is so very lovely here,' agreed Mother enthusiastically.

'Well, I don't think we get too much of it,' said Mr. Prodger dubiously, and two lines showed at his lips. 'I seem to have been sitting around in my hotel more days than I care to count.'

'Ah, hotels are so very trying,' said Mother, and she drooped sympathetically at the thought of a lonely man in an hotel . . . 'You are alone here?' she asked gently, just in case . . . one never knew . . . it was better to be on the safe, the tactful side.

But her fears were groundless.

'Oh yes, I'm alone,' cried Mr. Prodger, more heartily than he had spoken yet, and he took a speck of thread off his immaculate trouser leg. Something in his voice puzzled Milly. What was it?

'Still, the scenery is so very beautiful', said Mother, 'that one really does not feel the need of friends. I was only saying to my daughter yesterday I could live here for years without going outside the garden gate. It is all so beautiful.'

'Is that so?' said Mr. Prodger soberly. He added, 'You have a very charming villa.' And he glanced round the salon. 'Is all this antique furniture genuine, may I ask?'

'I believe so,' said Mother. 'I was certainly given to understand it was. Yes, we love our villa. But, of course, it is very large for two, that is to say three, ladies. My companion, Miss Anderson, is with us. But unfortunately she is a Roman Catholic and so she is out most of the time.'

Mr. Prodger bowed as one who agreed that Roman Catholics were very seldom in.

'But I am so fond of space,' continued Mother, 'and so is my daughter. We both love large rooms and plenty of them — don't we, Milly?'

This time Mr. Prodger looked at Milly quite cordially and remarked, 'Yes, young people like plenty of room to run about.'

He got up, put one hand behind his back, slapped the other upon it and went over to the balcony.

'You've a view of the sea from here,' he observed.

The ladies might well have noticed it; the whole Mediterranean swung before the windows.

'We are so fond of the sea,' said Mother, getting up too.

Mr. Prodger looked towards Milly. 'Do you see those yachts, Miss Fawcett?'

Milly saw them.

'Do you happen to know what they're doing?' asked Mr. Prodger.

What they were doing? What a funny question! Milly stared and bit her lip.

'They're racing!' said Mr. Prodger, and this time he did actually smile at her.

'Oh yes, of course,' stammered Milly. 'Of course they are.' She knew that.

'Well, they're not always at it,' said Mr. Prodger goodhumouredly. And he turned to Mother and began to take a ceremonious farewell.

'I wonder,' hesitated Mother, folding her little hands and eyeing him, 'if you would care to lunch with us? — if you would not be too dull with two ladies. We should be so very pleased.'

Mr. Prodger became intensely serious again. He seemed to brace himself to meet the luncheon invitation. 'Thank you very much, Mrs. Fawcett. I should be delighted.'

'That will be very nice,' said Mother warmly. 'Let me see. To-day is Monday — isn't it, Milly? Would Wednesday suit you?'

Mr. Prodger replied, 'It would suit me excellently to lunch with you on Wednesday, Mrs. Fawcett. At *mee-dee*, I presume, as they call it here.'

'Oh no! We keep our English times. At one o'clock,' said Mother.

And that being arranged, Mr. Prodger became more and more ceremonious and bowed himself out of the room.

Mother rang for Marie to look after him, and a moment later the big glass hall-door shut.

'Well!' said Mother. She was all smiles. Little smiles, like butterflies, alighting on her lips and gone again. 'That was an adventure, Milly, wasn't it, dear? And I thought he was such a very charming man, didn't you?'

Milly made a little face at Mother and rubbed her eyes.

'Of course you did. You must have, dear. And his appearance was so satisfactory — wasn't it?' Mother was obviously enraptured. 'I mean he looked so very well kept. Did you notice his hands? Every nail shone like a diamond. I must say I do like to see . . .'

She broke off. She came over to Milly and patted her big collar straight.

'You do think it was right of me to ask him to lunch — don't you, dear?' said Mother pathetically.

Mother made her feel so big, so tall. But she was tall. She could pick Mother up in her arms. Sometimes, rare moods came when she did. Swooped on Mother who squeaked like a mouse and even kicked. But not lately. Very seldom now . . .

'It was so strange,' said Mother. There was the still, bright, exalted glance again. 'I suddenly seemed to hear Father say to me "Ask him to lunch." And then there was some — warning . . . I think it was about the wine. But that I didn't catch — very unfortunately,' she added mournfully. She put her hand on her breast; she bowed her head. 'Father is still so near,' she whispered.

Milly looked out of the window. She hated Mother going on like this. But, of course, she couldn't say anything. Out of the window there was the sea and the sunlight silver on the palms, like water dripping from silver oars. Milly felt a yearning — what was it? — it was like a yearning to fly.

But Mother's voice brought her back to the salon, to the gilt chairs, the gilt couches, sconces, cabinets, the tables with the heavy-sweet flowers, the faded brocade, the pink-spotted Chinese dragons on the mantelpiece and the two Turks' heads in the fire-place that supported the broad logs.

'I think a leg of lamb would be nice, don't you, dear?' said Mother. 'The lamb is so very small and delicate just now. And men like nothing so much as plain roast meat. Yvonne prepares it so nicely, too, with that little frill of paper lace round the top of the leg. It always reminds me of something — I can't think what. But it certainly makes it look very attractive indeed.'

II.

Wednesday came. And the flutter that Mother and Milly had felt over the visiting-card extended to the whole villa. Yes, it was not too much to say that the whole villa thrilled and fluttered at the idea of having a man to lunch. Old, flat-footed Yvonne came waddling back from market with a piece of gorgonzola in so perfect a condition that when she found Marie in the kitchen she flung down her great basket, snatched the morsel up and held it, rustling in its paper, to her quivering bosom.

'*J'ai trouvé un morceau de gorgonzola*,' she panted, rolling up her eyes as though she invited the heavens themselves to look down upon it. '*J'ai un morceau de gorgonzola ici pour un prr-ince, ma fille*.' And hissing the word '*prr — ince*' like lightning, she thrust the morsel under Marie's nose. Marie, who was a delicate creature, almost swooned at the shock.

'Do you think,' cried Yvonne scornfully, 'that I would ever buy such cheese *pour ces dames*? Never. Never. *Jamais de ma vie*.' Her sausage finger wagged before her nose, and she minced in a dreadful imitation of Mother's French, 'We have none of us large appetites, Yvonne. We are very fond of boiled eggs and mashed potatoes and a nice, plain salad. Ah-Bah!' With a snort of contempt she flung away her shawl, rolled up her sleeves, and began unpacking the basket. At the bottom there was a fiat bottle which, sighing, she laid aside.

'*De quoi pour mes cors*,' said she.

And Marie, seizing a bottle of Sauterne and bearing it off to the dining-room, murmured as she shut the kitchen door behind her, '*Et voilà pour les cors de Monsieur!*'

The dining-room was a large room panelled in dark wood. It had a massive mantelpiece and carved chairs covered in crimson damask. On the heavy, polished table stood an oval glass dish decorated with little gilt swags. This dish, which it was Marie's duty to keep filled with fresh flowers, fascinated her. The sight of it gave her a *frisson*. It reminded her always, as it lay solitary on the dark expanse, of a little tomb. And one day, passing through the long windows on to the stone terrace and down the steps into the garden, she had the happy thought of so arranging the flowers that they would be appropriate to one of the ladies on a future tragic occasion. Her first creation had been terrible. *Tomb of Mademoiselle Anderson* in black pansies, lily-of-the-valley and a frill of heliotrope. It gave her a most intense, curious pleasure to hand Miss Anderson the potatoes at lunch and at the same time to gaze beyond her at her triumph. It was like (*O ciel!*) — it was like handing potatoes to a corpse.

The *Tomb of Madame* was, on the contrary, almost gay. Foolish little flowers, half yellow, half blue, hung over the edge, wisps of green trailed across and in the middle there was a large scarlet rose. *Coeur saignant*, Marie had called it. But it did not look in the least like a *coeur saignant*. It looked flushed and cheerful, like Mother emerging from the luxury of a warm bath.

Milly's, of course, was all white. White stocks, little white rose-buds, with a sprig or two of dark box edging. It was Mother's favourite.

Poor innocent! Marie, at the sideboard, had to turn her

back when she heard Mother exclaim, 'Isn't it pretty, Milly? Isn't it sweetly pretty? Most artistic. So original.' And she had said to Marie, '*C'est très joli, Marie. Très original.*'

Marie's smile was so remarkable that Milly, peeling a tangerine, remarked to Mother, 'I don't think she likes you to admire them. It makes her uncomfortable.'

But to-day — the glory of her opportunity made Marie feel quite faint as she seized her flower scissors. *Tombeau d'un beau Monsieur*. She was forbidden to cut the orchids that grew round the fountain basin. But what were orchids for if not for such an occasion? Her fingers trembled as the scissors snipped away. They were enough; Marie added two small sprays of palm. And back in the dining-room she had the happy idea of binding the palm together with a twist of gold thread deftly torn off the fringe of the dining-room curtains. The effect was superb. Marie almost seemed to see her *beau Monsieur*, very small, very small, at the bottom of the bowl, in full evening dress with a ribbon across his chest and his ears white as wax.

What surprised Milly, however, was that Miss Anderson should pay any attention to Mr. Prodger's coming. She rustled to breakfast in her best black silk blouse, her Sunday blouse, with the large, painful-looking crucifix dangling over the front. Milly was alone when Miss Anderson entered the dining-room. This was unfortunate, for she always tried to avoid being left alone with Miss Anderson. She could not say exactly why; it was a feeling. She had the feeling that Miss Anderson might say something about God, or something fearfully intimate. Oh, she would sink through the floor if such a thing happened; she would expire. Supposing she were to say 'Milly, do you believe in our Lord?' Heavens! It simply didn't bear thinking about.

'Good morning, my dear,' said Miss Anderson, and her fingers, cold, pale, like church candles, touched Milly's cheeks.

'Good morning, Miss Anderson. May I give you some

coffee?' said Milly, trying to be natural.

'Thank you, dear child,' said Miss Anderson, and laughing her light, nervous laugh, she hooked on her eyeglasses and stared at the basket of rolls. 'And is it to-day that you expect your guest?' she asked.

Now why did she ask that? Why pretend when she knew perfectly well? That was all part of her strangeness. Or was it because she wanted to be friendly? Miss Anderson was more than friendly; she was genial. But there was always this something. Was she spying? People said at school that Roman Catholics spied . . . Miss Anderson rustled, rustled about the house like a dead leaf. Now she was on the stairs, now in the upstairs passage. Sometimes, at night, when Milly was feverish she woke up and heard that rustle outside her door. Was Miss Anderson looking through the keyhole? And one night she actually had the idea that Miss Anderson had bored two holes in the wall above her head and was watching her from there. The feeling was so strong that next time she went into Miss Anderson's room her eyes flew to the spot. To her horror a large picture hung there. Had it been there before? . . .

'Guest?' The crisp breakfast roll broke in half at the word.

'Yes, I think it is,' said Milly vaguely, and her blue, flowerlike eyes were raised to Miss Anderson in a vague stare.

'It will make quite a little change in our little party,' said the much-too-pleasant voice. 'I confess I miss very much the society of men. I have had such a great deal of it in my life. I think that ladies by themselves are apt to get a little — h'm — h'm . . .' And helping herself to cherry jam, she spilt it on the cloth.

Milly took a large, childish bite out of her roll. There was nothing to reply to this. But how young Miss Anderson made her feel! She made her want to be naughty, to pour milk over her head or make a noise with a spoon.

'Ladies by themselves', went on Miss Anderson, who realised

none of this, 'are very apt to find their interests limited.'

'Why?' said Milly, goaded to reply. People always said that; it sounded most unfair.

'I think', said Miss Anderson, taking off her eyeglasses and looking a little dim, 'it is the absence of political discussion.'

'Oh, politics!' cried Milly airily. 'I hate politics. Father always said —' But here she pulled up short. She crimsoned. She didn't want to talk about Father to Miss Anderson.

'Oh! Look! Look! A butterfly!' cried Miss Anderson, softly and hastily. 'Look, what a darling!' Her own cheeks flushed a slow red at the sight of the darling butterfly fluttering so softly over the glittering table.

That was very nice of Miss Anderson — fearfully nice of her. She must have realised that Milly didn't want to talk about Father and so she had mentioned the butterfly on purpose. Milly smiled at Miss Anderson as she never had smiled at her before. And she said in her warm, youthful voice, 'He is a duck, isn't he? I love butterflies. I think they are great lambs.'

III.

The morning whisked away as foreign mornings do. Mother had half decided to wear her hat at lunch.

'What do you think, Milly? Do you think as head of the house it might be appropriate? On the other hand, one does not want to do anything at all extreme.'

'Which do you mean, Mother? Your mushroom or the jampot?'

'Oh, not the jampot, dear.' Mother was quite used to Milly's name for it. 'I somehow don't feel myself in a hat without a brim. And to tell you the truth, I am still not quite certain whether I was wise in buying a jampot. I cannot help the feeling that if I were to meet Father in it he would be a little too surprised. More than once lately,' went on Mother quickly, 'I have thought of taking off the trimming, turning it upside down and making it into a nice little work-bag. What do you think, dear? But we must not go into it now, Milly. This is not the moment for such schemes. Come on to the balcony. I have told Marie we shall have coffee there. What about bringing out that big chair with the nice, substantial legs for Mr. Prodger? Men are so fond of nice, substantial . . . No, not by yourself, love! Let me help you.'

When the chair was carried out Milly thought it looked exactly like Mr. Prodger. It *was* Mr. Prodger admiring the view.

'No, don't sit down on it. You mustn't,' she cried hastily, as Mother began to subside. She put her arm through Mother's and drew her back into the salon.

Happily, at that moment there was a rustle and Miss Anderson was upon them. In excellent time, for once. She carried a copy of the *Morning Post.*

'I have been trying to find out from this', said she, lightly tapping the newspaper with her eyeglasses, 'whether Congress is sitting at present. But unfortunately, after reading my copy right through, I happened to glance at the heading and discovered it was five weeks old.'

Congress! Would Mr. Prodger expect them to talk about Congress? The idea terrified Mother. Congress! The American parliament, of course, composed of senators — grey-bearded old men in frock-coats and turn-down collars, rather like missionaries. But she did not feel at all competent to discuss them.

'I think we had better not be too intellectual,' she suggested timidly, fearful of disappointing Miss Anderson, but more fearful still of the alternative.

'Still, one likes to be prepared,' said Miss Anderson. And after a pause she added softly, 'One never knows.'

Ah, how true that was! One never does. Miss Anderson and Mother seemed both to ponder this truth. They sat silent, with head bent, as though listening to the whisper of the words.

'One never knows,' said the pink-spotted dragons on the mantelpiece and the Turks' heads pondered. Nothing is known — nothing. Everybody just waits for things to happen as they were waiting there for the stranger who came walking towards them through the sun and shadow under the budding plane trees, or driving, perhaps, in one of the small, cotton-covered cabs . . . An angel passed over the Villa Martin. In that moment of hovering silence something timid, something beseeching seemed to lift, seemed to offer itself, as the flowers in the salon, uplifted, gave themselves to the light.

Then Mother said, 'I hope Mr. Prodger will not find the scent of the mimosa too powerful. Men are not fond of flowers in a room as a rule. I have heard it causes actual hay-fever in some cases. What do you think, Milly? Ought we perhaps —' But there was no time to do anything. A long, firm trill sounded from the hall door. It was a trill so calm and composed and unlike the tentative little push they gave the bell that it brought them back to the seriousness of the moment. They heard a man's voice; the door clicked shut again. He was inside. A stick rattled on the table. There was a pause, and then the door handle of the salon turned and Marie, in frilled muslin cuffs and an apron shaped like a heart, ushered in Mr. Prodger.

Only Mr. Prodger, after all? But whom had Milly expected to see? The feeling was there and gone again that she would not have been surprised to see somebody quite different, before she realised this wasn't quite the same Mr. Prodger as before. He was smarter than ever: all brushed, combed, shining. The ears that Marie had seen white as wax flashed as if they had been pink enamelled. Mother fluttered up in her pretty little way, so hoping he had not found the heat of the day too trying to be out in . . . but happily it was a little early in the year for dust. Then Miss Anderson was introduced. Milly was ready this time for that fresh hand, but she almost gasped; it was so very chill. It was like a hand stretched out to you from the water. Then together they all sat down.

'Is this your first visit to the Riviera?' asked Miss Anderson graciously, dropping her handkerchief.

'It is,' answered Mr. Prodger composedly, and he folded his arms as before. 'I was in Florence until recently, but I caught a heavy cold —'

'Florence so —' began Mother, when the beautiful brass gong, that burned like a fallen sun in the shadows of the hall, began to throb. First it was a low muttering, then it swelled, it quickened, it burst into a clash of triumph under Marie's sympathetic fingers. Never had they been treated to such a performance before. Mr. Prodger was all attention.

'That's a very fine gong,' he remarked approvingly.

'We think it is so very oriental,' said Mother. 'It gives our little meals quite an Eastern flavour. Shall we . . .'

Their guest was at the door bowing.

'So many gentlemen and only one lady,' fluttered Mother. 'What I mean is the boot is on the other shoe. That is to say — come, Milly, come, dear.' And she led the way to the dining-room.

Well, there they were. The cold, fresh napkins were shaken out of their charming shapes and Marie handed the omelette. Mr. Prodger sat on Mother's right, facing Milly, and Miss Anderson had her back to the long windows. But after all — why should the fact of their having a man with them make such a difference? It did; it made all the difference. Why should they feel so stirred at the sight of that large hand outspread, moving among the wine glasses? Why should the sound of that loud, confident 'Ah-hm!' change the very look of the dining-room? It was not a favourite room of theirs as a rule — it was overpowering. They bobbed uncertainly at the pale table with a curious feeling of exposure. They were like those meek guests who arrive unexpectedly at the fashionable hotel and are served with whatever may be ready, while the real luncheon, the real guests lurk important and contemptuous in the background. And although it was impossible for Marie to be other than deft, nimble and silent, what heart could she have in ministering to that most uninspiring of spectacles — three ladies dining alone?

Now all was changed. Marie filled their glasses to the brim as if to reward them for some marvellous feat of courage. These timid English ladies had captured a live lion, a real one, smelling faintly of eau-de-Cologne, and with a tip of handkerchief showing, white as a flake of snow.

'He is worthy of it,' decided Marie, eyeing her orchids and palms.

Mr. Prodger touched his hot plate with appreciative fingers. 'You'll hardly believe it, Mrs. Fawcett,' he remarked, turning to Mother, 'but this is the first hot plate I've happened on since I left the States. I had begun to believe there were two things that just weren't to be had in Europe. One was a hot plate and the other was a glass of cold water. Well, the cold water one can do without; but a hot plate is more difficult. I'd got so discouraged with the cold wet ones I encountered everywhere that when I was arranging with Cook's Agency about my room here I explained to them "I don't mind where I go to. I don't care what the expense may be. But for mercy's sake find me an hotel where I can get a hot plate by ringing for it."'

Mother, though outwardly all sympathy, found this a little bewildering. She had a momentary vision of Mr. Prodger ringing for hot plates to be brought to him at all hours. Such strange things to want in any numbers.

'I have always heard the American hotels are so very well equipped,' said Miss Anderson. 'Telephones in all the rooms and even tape machines.'

Milly could see Miss Anderson reading that tape machine.

'I should like to go to America awfully,' she cried, as Marie brought in the lamb and set it before Mother.

'There's certainly nothing wrong with America,' said Mr. Prodger soberly. 'America's a great country. What are they? Peas? Well, I'll just take a few. I don't eat peas as a rule. No, no salad, thank you. Not with the hot meat.'

'But what makes you want to go to America?' Miss Anderson ducked forward, smiling at Milly, and her eyeglasses fell into her plate, just escaping the gravy.

Because one wants to go everywhere, was the real answer. But Milly's flower-blue gaze rested thoughtfully on Miss Anderson as she said, 'The ice-cream. I adore ice-cream.'

'Do you?' said Mr. Prodger, and he put down his fork; he seemed moved. 'So you're fond of ice-cream, are you, Miss Fawcett?'

Milly transferred her dazzling gaze to him. It said she was.

'Well,' said Mr. Prodger quite playfully, and he began eating again, 'I'd like to see you get it. I'm sorry we can't manage to ship some across. I like to see young people have just what they want. It seems right, somehow.'

Kind man! Would he have any more lamb?

Lunch passed so pleasantly, so quickly, that the famous piece of gorgonzola was on the table in all its fatness and richness before there had been an awkward moment. The truth was that Mr. Prodger proved most easy to entertain, most ready to chat. As a rule men were not fond of chat as Mother understood it. They did not seem to understand that it does not matter very much what one says; the important thing is not to let the conversation drop. Strange. Even the best of men ignored that simple rule. They refused to realise that conversation is like a dear little baby that is brought in to be handed round. You must rock it, nurse it, keep it on the move if you want it to keep on smiling. What could be simpler? But even Father . . .

Mother winced away from memories that were not as sweet as memories ought to be.

All the same, she could not help hoping that Father saw what a successful little lunch party it was. He did so love to see Milly happy, and the child looked more animated than she had done for weeks. She had lost that dreamy expression, which, though very sweet, did not seem natural at her age. Perhaps what she wanted was not so much Easton's Syrup as taken out of herself.

'I have been very selfish,' thought Mother, blaming herself as usual. She put her hand on Milly's arm; she pressed it gently as they rose from the table. And Marie held the door open for the white and the grey figure; for Miss Anderson, who peered shortsightedly, as though looking for something; for Mr. Prodger, who brought up the rear, walking stately, with the benign air of a Monsieur who had eaten well.

IV.

Beyond the balcony, the gardens, the palms and the sea lay bathed in quivering brightness. Not a leaf moved; the oranges were little worlds of burning light. There was the sound of grasshoppers ringing their tiny tambourines, and the hum of bees as they hovered, as though to taste their joy in advance, before burrowing close into the warm wide-open stocks and roses. The sound of the sea was like a breath, was like a sigh.

Did the little group on the balcony hear it? Mother's fingers moved among the black and gold coffee-cups; Miss Anderson brought the most uncomfortable chair out of the salon and sat down. Mr. Prodger put his large hand on to the yellow stone ledge of the balcony and remarked gravely, 'This balcony rail is just as hot as it can be.'

'They say', said Mother, 'that the greatest heat of the day

is at about half-past two. We have certainly noticed it is very hot then.'

'Yes, it's lovely then,' murmured Milly, and she stretched out her hand to the sun. 'It's simply baking!'

'Then you're not afraid of the sunshine?' said Mr. Prodger, taking his coffee from Mother. 'No, thank you. I won't take any cream. Just one lump of sugar.' And he sat down balancing the little, chattering cup on his broad knee.

'No, I adore it,' answered Milly, and she began to nibble the lump of sugar . . .

SIX YEARS AFTER

I.

It was not the afternoon to be on deck — on the contrary, it was exactly the afternoon when there is no snugger place than a warm cabin, a warm bunk. Tucked up with a rug, a hot-water bottle and a piping hot cup of tea she would not have minded the weather in the least. But he — hated cabins, hated to be inside anywhere more than was absolutely necessary. He had a passion for keeping, as he called it, above board, especially when he was travelling. And it wasn't surprising, considering the enormous amount of time he spent cooped up in the office. So, when he rushed away from her as soon as they got on board and came back five minutes later to say he had secured two deck-chairs on the lee side and the steward was undoing the rugs, her voice through the high sealskin collar murmured 'Good'; and because he was looking at her, she smiled with bright eyes and blinked quickly, as if to say, 'Yes, perfectly all right — absolutely.' And she meant it.

'Then we'd better —' said he, and he tucked her hand inside his arm and began to rush her off to where their chairs stood. But she just had time to breathe, 'Not so fast, Daddy, please,' when he remembered too and slowed down.

Strange! They had been married twenty-eight years, and it was still an effort to him, each time, to adapt his pace to hers.

'Not cold, are you?' he asked, glancing sideways at her.

Her little nose, geranium pink above the dark fur, was answer enough. But she thrust her free hand into the velvet pocket of her jacket and murmured gaily, 'I shall be glad of my rug.'

He pressed her tighter to his side — a quick, nervous pressure. He knew, of course, that she ought to be down in the cabin; he knew that it was no afternoon for her to be sitting on deck, in this cold and raw mist, lee side or no lee side, rugs or no rugs, and he realised how she must be hating it. But he had come to believe that it really was easier for her to make these sacrifices than it was for him. Take their present case, for instance. If he had gone down to the cabin with her, he would have been miserable the whole time, and he couldn't have helped showing it. At any rate, she would have found him out. Whereas, having made up her mind to fall in with his ideas, he would have betted anybody she would even go so far as to enjoy the experience. Not because she was without personality of her own. Good Lord! She was absolutely brimming with it. But because . . . but here his thoughts always stopped. Here they always felt the need of a cigar, as it were. And, looking at the cigar-tip, his fine blue eyes narrowed. It was a law of marriage, he supposed . . . All the same, he always felt guilty when he asked these sacrifices of her. That was what the quick pressure meant. His being said to her being: 'You do understand, don't you?' and there was an answering tremor of her fingers, 'I *understand*.'

Certainly the steward — good little chap — had done all in his power to make them comfortable. He had put up their chairs in whatever warmth there was and out of the smell. She did hope he would be tipped adequately. It was on occasions like these (and her life seemed to be full of such occasions) that she wished it was the woman who controlled the purse.

'Thank you, steward. That will do beautifully.'

'Why are stewards so often delicate-looking?' she wondered, as her feet were tucked under. 'This poor little chap looks as though he'd got a chest, and yet one would have thought . . . the sea air . . .'

The button of the pigskin purse was undone. The tray was tilted. She saw sixpences, shillings, half-crowns.

'I should give him five shillings,' she decided, 'and tell him to buy himself a good nourishing —'

He was given a shilling, and he touched his cap and seemed genuinely grateful.

Well, it might have been worse. It might have been sixpence. It might, indeed. For at that moment Father turned towards her and said, half apologetically, stuffing the purse back, 'I gave him a shilling. I think it was worth it, don't you?'

'Oh, quite! Every bit!' said she.

It is extraordinary how peaceful it feels on a little steamer once the bustle of leaving port is over. In a quarter of an hour one might have been at sea for days. There is something almost touching, childish, in the way people submit themselves to the new conditions. They go to bed in the early afternoon, they shut their eyes and 'it's night' like little children who turn the table upside down and cover themselves with the table-cloth. And those who remain on deck — they seem to be always the same, those few hardened men travellers — pause, light their pipes, stamp softly, gaze out to sea, and their voices are subdued as they walk up and down. The long-legged little girl chases after the red-cheeked boy, but soon both are captured; and the old sailor, swinging an unlighted lantern, passes and disappears . . .

He lay back, the rug up to his chin, and she saw he was

breathing deeply. Sea air! If anyone believed in sea air it was he. He had the strongest faith in its tonic qualities. But the great thing was, according to him, to fill the lungs with it the moment you came on board. Otherwise, the sheer strength of it was enough to give you a chill . . .

She gave a small chuckle, and he turned to her quickly. 'What is it?'

'It's your cap,' she said. 'I never can get used to you in a cap. You look such a thorough burglar.'

'Well, what the deuce am I to wear?' He shot up one grey eyebrow and wrinkled his nose. 'It's a very good cap, too. Very fine specimen of its kind. It's got a very rich white satin lining.' He paused. He declaimed, as he had hundreds of times before at this stage, 'Rich and rare were the gems she wore.'

But she was thinking he really was childishly proud of the white satin lining. He would like to have taken off his cap and made her feel it. 'Feel the quality!' How often had she rubbed between finger and thumb his coat, his shirt cuff, tie, sock, linen handkerchief, while he said that.

She slipped down more deeply into her chair.

And the little steamer pressed on, pitching gently, over the grey, unbroken, gently moving water, that was veiled with slanting rain.

Far out, as though idly, listlessly, gulls were flying. Now they settled on the waves, now they beat up into the rainy air and shone against the pale sky like the lights within a pearl. They looked cold and lonely. How lonely it will be when we have passed by, she thought. There will be nothing but the waves and those birds and rain falling.

She gazed through the rust-spotted railing along which big drops trembled, until suddenly she shut her lids. It was as if a warning voice inside her had said, 'Don't look!'

'No, I won't,' she decided. 'It's too depressing, much too depressing.'

But, immediately, she opened her eyes and looked again. Lonely birds, water lifting, white pale sky — how were they changed?

And it seemed to her there was a presence far out there, between the sky and the water; someone very desolate and longing watched them pass and cried as if to stop them — but cried to her alone.

'Mother!'

'Don't leave me,' sounded in the cry. 'Don't forget me! You are forgetting me, you know you are!' And it was as though from her own breast there came the sound of childish weeping.

'My son — my precious child — it isn't true!'

Sh! How was it possible that she was sitting there on that quiet steamer beside Father and at the same time she was hushing and holding a little slender boy — so pale — who had just waked out of a dreadful dream?

'I dreamed I was in a wood — somewhere far away from everybody — and I was lying down and a great blackberry vine grew over me. And I called and called to you — and you wouldn't come — you wouldn't come — so I had to lie there for ever.'

What a terrible dream! He had always had terrible dreams. How often, years ago, when he was small, she had made some excuse and escaped from their friends in the dining-room or the drawing-room to come to the foot of the stairs and listen. 'Mother!' And when he was asleep, his dream had journeyed with her back into the circle of lamplight; it had taken its place there like a ghost. And now —

Far more often — at all times — in all places — like now, for instance — she never settled down, she was never off her guard for a moment but she heard him. He wanted her. 'I am coming as fast as I can! As fast as I can!' But the dark stairs have no ending, and the worst dream of all — the one that is always the same — goes for ever and ever uncomforted.

This is anguish! How is it to be borne? Still, it is not the idea of her suffering which is unbearable — it is his. Can one do nothing for the dead? And for a long time the answer had been — Nothing!

. . . But softly without a sound the dark curtain has rolled down. There is no more to come. That is the end of the play. But it can't end like that — so suddenly. There must be more. No, it's cold, it's still. There is nothing to be gained by waiting.

But — did he go back again? Or, when the war was over, did he come home for good? Surely, he will marry — later on — not for several years. Surely, one day I shall remember his wedding and my first grandchild — a beautiful dark-haired boy born in the early morning — a lovely morning — spring!

'Oh, Mother, it's not fair to me to put these ideas into my head! Stop, Mother, stop! When I think of all I have missed, I can't bear it.'

'I can't bear it!' She sits up breathing the words and tosses the dark rug away. It is colder than ever, and now the dusk is falling, falling like ash upon the pallid water.

And the little steamer, growing determined, throbbed on, pressed on, as if at the end of the journey there waited . . .

DAPHNE

I had been in Port Willin six months when I decided to give a one-man show. Not that I was particularly keen, but little Field, the picture-shop man, had just started a gallery and he wanted me — begged me, rather — to kick off for him. He was a decent little chap; I hadn't the heart to refuse. And besides, as it happened, I had a good deal of stuff that I felt it would be rather fun to palm off on any one who was fool enough to buy it. So with these high aims I had the cards printed, the pictures framed in plain white frames, and God knows how many cups and saucers ordered for the Private View.

What was I doing in Port Willin? Oh well — why not? I'll own it does sound an unlikely spot, but when you are an impermanent movable, as I am, it's just those unlikely spots that have a trick of holding you. I arrived, intending to stay a week and go on to Fiji. But I had letters to one or two people, and the morning of my arrival, hanging over the side of the ship while we were waiting in the stream, with nothing on earth to do but stare, I took an extraordinary fancy to the shape — to the look of the place.

It's a small town, you know, planted at the edge of a fine deep harbour like a lake. Behind it, on either side, there are hills. The houses are built of light painted wood. They have iron roofs coloured red. And there are big dark plumy trees massed together, breaking up those light shapes, giving a depth — warmth — making a composition of it well worth looking at . . . Well, we needn't go into that — But it had me that fine morning. And the first days after my arrival, walking, or driving out in one of the big swinging, rocking cabs, I took an equal fancy to the people.

Not to quite all of them. The men left me cold. Yes, I must say, colonial men are not the brightest specimens. But I never struck a place where the average of female attractiveness was so high. You can't help noticing it, for a peculiarity of Port Willin is the number of its teashops and the vast quantity of tea absorbed by its inhabitants. Not tea only — sandwiches, cream cakes, ices, fruit salad with fresh pine-apples. From eleven o'clock in the morning you meet with couples and groups of girls and young married women hurrying off to their first tea. It was a real eleven o'clock function. Even the business men knocked off and went to a café. And the same thing happened in the afternoon. From four until half-past six the streets were gay as a garden. Which reminds me, it was early spring when I arrived and the town smelled of moist earth and the first flowers. In fact, wherever one went one got a strong whiff, like the whiff of violets in a wood, which was enough in itself to make one feel like lingering . . .

There was a theatre too, a big bare building plastered over with red and blue bills which gave it an oriental look in that blue air, and a touring company was playing 'San Toy'. I went my first evening. I found it, for some reason, fearfully exciting. The inside smelled of gas, of glue and burnt paper. Whistling draughts cut along the corridors — a strong wind among the orchestra kept the palms trembling, and now and again the curtain blew out and there was a glimpse of a pair of large feet walking rapidly away. But what women! What girls in muslin dresses with velvet sashes and little caps edged with swansdown! In the intervals long ripples of laughter sounded from the stalls, from the dress-circle. And I leaned against a pillar that looked as though it was made of wedding-cake icing — and fell in love with whole rows at a time . . .

Then I presented my letters, I was asked out to dine, and I met these charmers in their own homes. That decided it. They were something I had never known before — so gay, so friendly, so impressed with the idea of one's being an artist! It was rather like finding oneself in the playground of an extremely attractive girls' school.

I painted the Premier's daughter, a dark beauty, against a tree hung with long, bell-like flowers as white as wax. I painted a girl with a pigtail curled up on a white sofa playing with a pale-red fan . . . and a little blonde in a black jacket with pearl grey gloves . . . I painted like fury.

I'm fond of women. As a matter of fact I'm a great deal more at my ease with women than I am with men. Because I've cultivated them, I suppose. You see, it's like this with me. I've always had enough money to live on, and the consequence is I have never had to mix with people more than I wished. And I've equally always had — well, I suppose you might call it — a passion for painting. Painting is far and away the most important thing in life — as I see it. But — my work's my own affair. It's the separate compartment which is me. No strangers allowed in. I haven't the smallest desire to explain what it is I'm after — or to hear other men. If people like my work I'm pleased. If they don't — well, if I was a shrugging person, I'd shrug. This sounds arrogant. It isn't; I know my limitations. But the truth about oneself always sounds arrogant, as no doubt you've observed.

But women — well, I can only speak for myself — I find the

presence of women, the consciousness of women, an absolute necessity. I know they are considered a distraction, that the very Big Pots seal themselves in their hives to keep away. All I can say is work without women would be to me like dancing without music or food without wine or a sailing boat without a breeze. They just give me that . . . what is it? Stimulus is not enough; inspiration is far too much. That — well, if I knew what it is, I should have solved a bigger problem than my own! And problems aren't in my line.

I expected a mob at my Private View, and I got it, too . . . What I hadn't reckoned on was that there would be no men. It was one thing to ask a painter fellow to knock you up something to the tune of fifty guineas or so, but it was quite another to make an ass of yourself staring. The Port Willin men would as soon have gazed into shops. True, when you came to Europe, you visited the galleries, but then you shop-gazed too. It didn't matter what you did in Europe. You could walk about for a week without being recognised.

So there were little Field and I absolutely alone among all that loveliness; it frightened him out of his life, but I didn't mind, I thought it rather fun, especially as the sightseers didn't hesitate to find my pictures amusing. I'm by no means an out-and-out modern, as they say; people like violins and landscapes of telegraph poles leave me cold. But Port Willin is still trying to swallow Rossetti, and Hope by Watts is looked upon as very advanced. It was natural my pictures should surprise them. The fat old Lady Mayoress became quite hysterical. She drew me over to one drawing; she patted my arm with her fan.

'I don't wonder you drew her slipping out,' she gurgled. 'And how depressed she looks! The poor dear never could have sat down in it. It's much too small. There ought to be a little cake of Pears' Soap on the floor.' And overcome by her own joke, she flopped on the little double bench that ran down the middle of the room, and even her fan seemed to laugh.

At that moment two girls passed in front of us. One I knew, a big fair girl called May Pollock, pulled her companion by the sleeve. 'Daphne!' she said. 'Daphne!' And the other turned towards her, then towards us, smiled and was born, christened part of my world from that moment.

'Daphne!' Her quick, beautiful smile answered . . .

Saturday morning was gloriously fine. When I woke up and saw the sun streaming over the polished floor I felt like a little boy who has been promised a picnic. It was all I could do not to telephone Daphne. Was she feeling the same? It seemed somehow such a terrific lark that we should be going off together like this, just with a couple of rucksacks and our bathing suits. I thought of other week-ends, the preparation, the emotional tension, the amount of managing they'd needed. But I couldn't really think of them; I couldn't be bothered, they belonged to another life . . .

It seemed to me suddenly so preposterous that two people should be as happy as we were and not be happier. Here we were, alone, miles away from everybody, free as air, and in love with each other. I looked again at Daphne, at her slender shoulders, her throat, her bosom, and, passionately in love, I decided, with fervour: Wouldn't it be rather absurd, then, to behave like a couple of children? Wouldn't she even, in spite of all she had said, be disappointed if we did? . . .

And I went off at a tremendous pace, not because I thought she'd run after me, but I did think she might call, or I might look round . . .

It was one of those still, hushed days when the sea and the sky seem to melt into one another, and it is long before the moisture dries on the leaves and grasses. One of those days when the sea smells strong and, there are gulls standing in a row on the sand. The smoke from our wood fire hung in the air and the smoke of my pipe mingled with it. I caught myself staring at nothing. I felt dull and angry. I couldn't get over the ridiculous affair. You see, my *amour propre* was wounded.

Monday morning was grey, cloudy, one of those mornings peculiar to the seaside when everything, the sea most of all, seems exhausted and sullen. There had been a very high tide, the road was wet — on the beach there stood a long line of sickly-looking gulls . . .

When we got on board she sat down on one of the green benches and, muttering something about a pipe, I walked quickly away. It was intolerable that we should still be together after what had happened. It was indecent. I only asked — I only longed for one thing — to be free of this still, unsmiling and pitiful — that was the worst of it — creature who had been my playful Daphne.

For answer I telephoned her at once and asked if I might come and see her that evening. Her voice sounded grave, unlike the voice I remembered, and she seemed to deliberate. There was a long pause before she said, 'Yes — perhaps that would be best.'

'Then I shall come at half-past six.'

'Very well.'

And we went into a room full of flowers and very large art photographs of the Harbour by Night, A Misty Day, Moonrise over the Water, and I know I wondered if she admired them.

'Why did you send me that letter?'

'Oh, but I had to,' said Daphne. 'I meant every word of it. I only let you come to-night to . . . No, I know I shall disappoint you. I'm wiser than you are for all your experience. I shan't be able to live up to it. I'm not the person for you. Really I'm not!' . . .

FATHER AND THE GIRLS

I.

At midday, Ernestine, who had come down from the mountains with her mother to work in the vineyards belonging to the hotel, heard the faint, far-away *chuff-chuff* of the train from Italy. Trains were a novelty to Ernestine; they were fascinating, unknown, terrible. What were they like as they came tearing their way through the valley, plunging between the mountains as if not even the mountains could stop them? When she saw the dark, flat breast of the engine, so bare, so powerful, hurled as it were towards her, she felt a weakness — she could have sunk to the earth. And yet she must look. So she straightened up, stopped pulling at the blue-green leaves, tugging at the long, bright-green, curly suckers, and, with eyes like a bird, stared. The vines were very tall. There was nothing to be seen of Ernestine but her beautiful, youthful bosom buttoned into a blue cotton jacket and her small, dark head covered with a faded cherry-coloured handkerchief.

Chiff-chuff-chaff. Chiff-chuff-chaff, sounded the train. Now a wisp of white smoke shone and melted. Now there was another, and the monster itself came into sight and snorting horribly drew up at a little, toy-like station five minutes away. The railway ran at the bottom of the hotel garden which was perched high and surrounded by a stone wall. Steps cut in the stone led to the terraces where the vines were planted. Ernestine, looking out from the leaves like a bright bird, saw the terrible engine and looked beyond it at doors swinging open, at strangers stepping down. She would never know who they were or where they had come from. A moment ago they were not here; perhaps by to-morrow they would be gone again. And looking like a bird herself, she remembered how, at home, in the late autumn, she had sometimes seen strange birds in the fir tree that were there one day and gone the next. Where from? Where to? She felt an ache in her bosom. Wings were tight-folded there. Why could she not stretch them out and fly away and away? . . .

II.

From the first-class carriage tall, thin Emily alighted and gave her hand to Father whose brittle legs seemed to wave in the air as they felt for the iron step. Taller, thinner Edith followed, carrying Father's light overcoat, his field-glasses on a strap and his new Baedeker. The blond hotel porter came forward. Wasn't that nice? He could speak as good English as you or me. So Edith had no trouble at all in explaining how, as they were going on by the morning train to-morrow, they would only need their suit-cases and what was left in the compartment. Was there a carriage outside? Yes, a carriage was there. But if they cared to walk there was a private entrance through the hotel gardens . . . No, they wouldn't walk.

'You wouldn't care to walk, would you, Father dear?'

'No, Edith, I won't walk. Do you girls wanna walk?'

'Why no, Father, not without you, dear.'

And the blond hotel porter leading, they passed through the little knot of sturdy peasants at the station gate to where the carriage waited under a group of limes.

'Did you ever see anything as big as that horse, Edith!' cried Emily. She was always the first to exclaim about things.

'It is a very big horse,' sang Edith, more sober. 'It's a farm horse, from the look of it, and it's been working. See how hot it is.' Edith had so much observation. The big, brown horse, his sides streaked with dark sweat, tossed his head and the bells on his collar set up a loud jangling.

'Hu-yup!' called the young peasant driver warningly, from his seat on the high box.

Father, who was just about to get in, drew back, a little scared.

'You don't think that horse will run away with us, do you, Edith?' he quavered.

'Why no, Father dear,' coaxed Edith. 'That horse is just as tame as you or me.' So in they got, the three of them. And as the horse bounded forward his ears seemed to twitch in surprise at his friend the driver. Call that a load? Father and the girls weighed nothing. They might have been three bones, three broomsticks, three umbrellas bouncing up and down on the hard seats of the carriage. It was a mercy the hotel was so close. Father could never have stood that for more than a minute, especially at the end of a journey. Even as it was his face was quite green when Emily helped him out, straightened him, and gave him a little pull.

'It's shaken you, dear, hasn't it?' she said tenderly.

But he refused her arm into the hotel. That would create a wrong impression.

'No, no, Emily. I'm all right. All right,' said Father, as

staggering a little he followed them through big glass doors into a hall as dim as a church and as chill and as deserted.

My! Wasn't that hall cold! The cold seemed to come leaping at them from the floor. It clasped the peaked knees of Edith and Emily; it leapt high as the fluttering heart of Father. For a moment they hesitated, drew together, almost gasped. But then out from the Bureau a cheerful young person, her smiling face spotted with mosquito bites, ran to meet them, and welcomed them with such real enthusiasm (in English too) that the chill first moment was forgotten.

'Aw-yes. Aw-yes. I can let you ave very naice rooms on de firs floor wid a lif. Two rooms and bart and dressing-room for de chentleman. Beautiful rooms wid sun but nort too hot. Very naice. Till to-morrow. I taike you. If you please. It is dis way. You are tired wid the churney? Launch is at half-pas tvelf. Hort worter? Aw-yes. It is wid de bart. If you please.'

Father and the girls were drawn by her cheerful smiles and becks and nods along a cloister-like corridor, into the lift and up, until she flung open a heavy, dark door and stood aside for them to enter.

'It is a suite,' she explained. 'Wid a hall and tree doors.' Quickly she opened them. 'Now I gaw to see when your luggage is gum.'

And she went.

'Well!' cried Emily.

Edith stared.

Father craned his thin, old neck, looking, too.

'Did you — ever see the like, Edith?' cried Emily, in a little rush.

And Edith softly clasped her hands. Softly she sang 'No, I never did, Emily. I've never seen anything just like this before.'

'Sims to me a nice room,' quavered Father, still hovering. 'Do you girls wanna change it?'

Change it! 'Why, Father dear, it's just the loveliest thing we've ever set eyes on, isn't it, Emily? Sit down, Father dear, sit down in the arm-chair.'

Father's pale claws gripped the velvet arms. He lowered himself; he sank with an old man's quick sigh.

Edith still stood, as if bewitched, at the door. But Emily ran over to the window and leaned out, quite girlish . . .

For a long time now — for how long? — for countless ages — Father and the girls had been on the wing. Nice, Montreux, Biarritz, Naples, Mentone, Lake Maggiore, they had seen them all and many, many more. And still they beat on, beat on, flying as if unwearied, never stopping anywhere for long. But the truth was — Oh, better not inquire what the truth was. Better not ask what it was that kept them going. Or why the only word that daunted Father was the word — home . . .

Home! To sit around, doing nothing, listening to the clock, counting up the years, thinking back . . . thinking! To stay fixed in one place as if waiting for something or somebody. No! no! Better far to be blown over the earth like the husk, like the withered pod that the wind carries and drops and bears aloft again.

'Are you ready, girls?'

'Yes, Father dear.'

'Then we'd better be off if we're to make that train.'

But oh, it was a weariness, it was an unspeakable weariness. Father made no secret of his age; he was eighty-four. As for Edith and Emily — well, he looked now like their elder brother. An old, old brother and two ancient sisters, so the lovely room might have summed them up. But its shaded brightness, its beauty, the flutter of leaves at the creamy stone windows seemed only to whisper 'Rest! Stay!'

Edith looked at the pale, green-panelled walls, at the doors that had lozenges and squares of green picked out in gold. She made the amazing discovery that the floor had the same pattern in wood that was traced on the high, painted ceiling. But the colour of the shining floor was marvellous; it was like tortoiseshell. In one corner there was a huge, tilted stove, milky white and blue. The low wooden bed, with its cover of quilted yellow satin, had sheaves of corn carved on the bed-posts. It looked to fanciful, tired Edith — yes — that bed looked as if it were breathing, softly, gently breathing. Outside the narrow, deep-set windows, beyond their wreaths of green, she could see a whole, tiny landscape bright as a jewel in the summer heat.

'Rest! Stay!' Was it the sound of the leaves outside? No, it was in the air; it was the room itself that whispered joyfully, shyly. Edith felt so strange that she could keep quiet no longer.

'This is a very old room, Emily,' she warbled softly. 'I know what it is. This hotel has not always been a hotel. It's been an old château. I feel as sure of that as that I'm standing here.' Perhaps she wanted to convince herself that she was standing there. 'Do you see that stove?' She walked over to the stove. 'It's got figures on it. Emily,' she warbled faintly, 'it's 1623.'

'Isn't that too wonderful!' cried Emily.

Even Father was deeply moved.

'1623? Nearly three hundred years old.' And suddenly, in spite of his tiredness, he gave a thin, airy, old man's chuckle. 'Makes yer feel quite a chicken, don't it?' said Father.

Emily's breathless little laugh answered him; it, too, was gay.

'I'm going to see what's behind that door,' she cried. And half running to the door in the middle wall she lifted the slender steel catch. It led into a larger room, into Edith's and her bedroom. But the walls were the same and the floor, and there were the same deep-set windows. Only two beds instead of one stood side by side with blue silk quilts instead of yellow. And what a beautiful old chest there was under the windows!

'Oh,' cried Emily, in rapture. 'Isn't it all too perfectly

historical for words, Edith! It makes me feel —' She stopped, she looked at Edith who had followed her and whose thin shadow lay on the sunny floor. 'Queer!' said Emily, trying to put all she felt into that one word. 'I don't know what it is.'

Perhaps if Edith, the discoverer, had had time she might have satisfied Emily. But a knock sounded at the outer door; it was the luggage boy. And while he brought in their suit-cases there came from downstairs the ringing of the luncheon bell. Father mustn't be kept waiting. Once a bell had gone he liked to follow it up right then. So without even a glance at the mirror — they had reached the age when it is as natural to avoid mirrors as it is to peer into them when one is young — Edith and Emily were ready.

'Are you ready, girls?'

'Yes, Father dear.'

And off they went again, to the left, to the right, down a stone staircase with a broad, worn balustrade, to the left again, finding their way as if by instinct — Edith first, then Father, and Emily close behind.

But when they reached the *salle à manger*, which was as big as a ballroom, it was still empty. All gay, all glittering, the long French windows open on to the green and gold garden, the *salle à manger* stretched before them. And the fifty little tables with the fifty pots of dahlias looked as if they might begin dancing with . . .

ALL SERENE!

I.

At breakfast that morning they were in wonderfully good spirits. Who was responsible — he or she? It was true she made a point of looking her best in the morning; she thought it part of her duty to him — to their love, even, to wear charming little caps, funny little coats, coloured mules at breakfast time, and to see that the table was perfect as he and she — fastidious pair! — understood the word. But he, too, so fresh, well-groomed and content, contributed his share . . . She had been down first, sitting at her place when he came in. He leaned over the back of her chair, his hands on her shoulders; he bent down and lightly rubbed his cheek against hers, murmuring gently but with just enough pride of proprietorship to make her flush with delight, 'Give me my tea, love.' And she lifted the silver teapot that had a silver pear modelled on the lid and gave him his tea.

'Thanks . . . You know you look awfully well this morning!'

'Do I?'

'Yes. Do that again. Look at me again. It's your eyes. They're like a child's. I've never known anyone have such shining eyes as you.'

'Oh, dear!' She sighed for joy. 'I do love having sweet things said to me!'

'Yes, you do — spoilt child! Shall I give you some of this?'

'No, thank you . . . Darling!' Her hand flew across the table and clasped his hand.

'Yes?'

But she said nothing, only 'Darling!' again. There was the look on his face she loved — a kind of sweet jesting. He was pretending he didn't know what she meant, and yet of course he did know. He was pretending to be feeling 'Here she is — trust a woman — all ready for a passionate love scene over the breakfast table at nine o'clock in the morning.' But she wasn't deceived. She knew he felt just the same as she did. That amused tolerance, that mock despair was part of the ways of men — no more.

'May I be allowed to *use* this knife please, or to put it down?'

Really! Mona had never yet got accustomed to her husband's smile. They had been married for three years. She was in love with him for countless reasons, but apart from them all, a special reason all to itself, was because of his smile. If it hadn't sounded nonsense she would have said she fell in love at first sight over and over again when he smiled. Other people felt the charm of it, too. Other women, she was certain. Sometimes she thought that even the servants watched for it . . .

'Don't forget we're going to the theatre to-night.'

'Oh, good egg! I had forgotten. It's ages since we went to a show.'

'Yes, isn't it? I feel quite thrilled.'

'Don't you think we might have a tiny small celebration at

dinner?' ('Tiny small' was one of her expressions. But why did it sound so sweet when he used it?)

'Yes, let's. You mean champagne?' And she looked into the distance, and said in a far-away voice: 'Then I must revise the sweet.'

At that moment the maid came in with the letters. There were four for him, three for her. No, one of hers belonged to him, too, rather a grimy little envelope with a dab of sealing-wax on the back.

'Why do you get all the letters?' she wailed, handing it across. 'It's awfully unfair. I love letters and I never get any.'

'Well, I do like that!' said he. 'How can you sit there and tell such awful bangers? It's the rarest thing on earth for me to get a letter in the morning. It's always you who get those mysterious epistles from girls you were at college with or faded aunts. Here, have half my pear — it's a beauty.' She held out her plate.

The Rutherfords never shared their letters. It was her idea that they should not. He had been violently opposed to it at first. She couldn't help laughing; he had so absolutely misunderstood her reason.

'Good God! my dear. You're perfectly welcome to open any letters of mine that come to the house — or to read any letters of mine that may be lying about. I think I can promise you . . .'

'Oh no, no, darling, that's not what I mean. I don't suspect you.' And she put her hands on his cheeks and kissed him quickly. He looked like an offended boy. 'But so many of Mother's old friends write to me — confide in me — don't you know? — tell me things they wouldn't for the world tell a man. I feel it wouldn't be fair to them. Don't you see?'

He gave way at last. But 'I'm old-fashioned,' he said, and his smile was a little rueful. 'I like to feel my wife reads my letters.'

'My precious dear! I've made you unhappy.' She felt so repentant; she didn't know quite about what. 'Of course I'd love to read . . .'

'No, no! That's all right. It's understood. We'll keep the bond.' And they had kept it.

He slit open the grimy envelope. He began to read. 'Damn!' he said and thrust out his under lip.

'Why, what is it? Something horrid?'

'No — annoying. I shall be late this evening. A man wants to meet me at the office at six o'clock.'

'Was that a business letter?' She sounded surprised.

'Yes, why?'

'It looked so awfully unbusinesslike. The sealing-wax and the funny writing — much more like a woman's than a man's.'

He laughed. He folded the letter, put it in his pocket and picked up the envelope. 'Yes,' he said, 'it is queer, isn't it. I shouldn't have noticed. How quick you are! But it does look exactly like a woman's hand. That capital R, for instance' — he flipped the envelope across to her.

'Yes, and that squiggle underneath. I should have said a rather uneducated female . . .'

'As a matter of fact,' said Hugh, 'he's a mining engineer.' And he got up, began to stretch and then stopped. 'I say, what a glorious morning! Why do I have to go to the office instead of staying at home and playing with you?' And he came over to her and locked his arms round her neck. 'Tell me that, little lovely one.'

'Oh,' she leaned against him, 'I wish you could. Life's arranged badly for people like you and me. And now you're going to be late this evening.'

'Never mind,' said he. 'All the rest of the time's ours. Every single bit of it. We shan't come back from the theatre to find —'

'Our porch black with mining engineers.' She laughed. Did

other people — could other people — was it possible that anyone before had ever loved as they loved? She squeezed her head against him — she heard his watch ticking — precious watch!

'What are those purple floppy flowers in my bedroom?' he murmured.

'Petunias.'

'You smell exactly like a petunia.'

And he raised her up. She drew towards him. 'Kiss me,' said he.

II.

It was her habit to sit on the bottom stair and watch his final preparations. Strange it should be so fascinating to see someone brush his hat, choose a pair of gloves and give a last quick look in the round mirror. But it was the same when he was shaving. Then she loved to curl upon the hard little couch in his dressing-room; she was as absorbed, as intent as he. How fantastic he looked, like a pierrot, like a mask, with those dark eyebrows, liquid eyes and the brush of fresh colour on his cheek-bones above the lather! But that was not her chief feeling. No, it was what she felt on the stairs, too. It was, 'So this is my husband, so this is the man I've married, this is the stranger who walked across the lawn that afternoon swinging his tennis racket and bowed, rolling up his shirt-sleeves. This is not only my lover and my husband but my brother, my dearest friend, my playmate, even at times a kind of very perfect father too. And here is where we live. Here is his room — and here is our hall.' She seemed to be showing their house and him to her other self, the self she had been before she had met him. Deeply admiring, almost awed by so much happiness, that other self looked on . . .

'Will I do?' He stood there smiling, stroking on his gloves.

But although he wouldn't like her to say the things she often longed to say about his appearance, she did think she detected that morning just the very faintest boyish showing-off. Children who know they are admired look like that at their mother.

'Yes, you'll do . . .' Perhaps at that moment she was proud of him as a mother is proud; she could have blessed him before he went his way. Instead she stood in the porch thinking, 'There he goes. The man I've married. The stranger who came across the lawn.' The fact was never less wonderful . . .

It was never less wonderful, never. It was even more wonderful if anything, and the reason was — Mona ran back into the house, into the drawing-room and sat down to the piano. Oh, why bother about reasons — She began to sing,

See, love, I bring thee flowers
To charm thy pain!

But joy — joy breathless and exulting thrilled in her voice, on the word 'pain' her lips parted in such a happy — dreadfully unsympathetic smile that she felt quite ashamed. She stopped playing, she turned round on the piano stool facing the room. How different it looked in the morning, how severe and remote. The grey chairs with the fuchsia-coloured cushions, the black and gold carpet, the bright green silk curtains might have belonged to anybody. It was like a stage setting with the curtain still down. She had no right to be there, and as she thought that a queer little chill caught her; it seemed so extraordinary that anything, even a chair, should turn away from, should not respond to her happiness.

'I don't like this room in the morning, I don't like it at all,' she decided, and she ran upstairs to finish dressing. Ran into their big, shadowy bedroom . . . and leaned over the starry petunias . . .

A BAD IDEA

Something's happened to me — something bad. And I don't know what to do about it. I don't see any way out for the life of me. The worst of it is, I can't get this thing into focus — if you know what I mean. I just feel in a muddle — in the hell of a muddle. It ought to be plain to anyone that I'm not the kind of man to get mixed up in a thing like this. I'm not one of your actor Johnnies, or a chap in a book. I'm — well, I knew what I was all right until yesterday. But now — I feel helpless, yes, that's the word, helpless. Here I sit, chucking stones at the sea like a child that's missed its mother. And everybody else has cut along home hours ago and tea's over and it's getting on for time to light the lamp. I shall have to go home too, sooner or later. I see that, of course. In fact, would you believe it? at this very moment I wish I was there in spite of everything. What's she doing? My wife, I mean. Has she cleared away? Or has she stayed there staring at the table with the plates pushed back? My God! when I think that I could howl like a dog — if you know what I mean . . .

I should have realised it was all U.P. this morning when

she didn't get up for breakfast. I did, in a way. But I couldn't face it. I had the feeling that if I said nothing special and just treated it as one of her bad headache days and went off to the office, by the time I got back this evening the whole affair would have blown over somehow. No, that wasn't it. I felt a bit like I do now, 'helpless'. What was I to do? Just go on. That was all I could think of. So I took her up a cup of tea and a couple of slices of thin bread and butter as per usual on her headache days. The blind was still down. She was lying on her back. I think she had a wet handkerchief on her forehead. I'm not sure, for I couldn't look at her. It was a beastly feeling. And she said in a weak kind of voice, 'Put the jug on the table, will you?' I put it down. I said, 'Can I do anything?' And she said, 'No. I'll be all right in half an hour.' But her voice, you know! It did for me. I barged out as quick as I could, snatched my hat and stick from the hall-stand and dashed off for the tram.

Here's a queer thing — you needn't believe me if you don't want to — the moment I got out of the house I forgot that about my wife. It was a splendid morning, soft, with the sun making silver ducks on the sea The kind of morning when you know it's going to keep hot and fine all day. Even the tram bell sounded different, and the little school kids crammed between people's knees had bunches of flowers. I don't know — I can't understand why — I just felt happy, but happy in a way I'd never been before, happy to beat the band! That wind that had been so strong the night before was still blowing a bit. It felt like her — the other — touching me. Yes, it did. Brought it back, every bit of it. If I told you how it took me, you'd say I was mad. I felt reckless — didn't care if I was late for the office or not and I wanted to do every one a kindness. I helped the little kids out of the tram. One little chap dropped his cap, and when I picked it up for him and said, 'Here, sonny!' . . . well, it was all I could do not to make a fool of myself.

At the office it was just the same. It seemed to me I'd never known the fellows at the office before. When old Fisher came over to my desk and put down a couple of giant sweet peas as per usual with his 'Beat 'em, old man, beat 'em!' — I didn't feel annoyed. I didn't care that he was riddled with conceit about his garden. I just looked at them and I said quietly, 'Yes, you've done it this time.' He didn't know what to make of it. Came back in about five minutes and asked me if I had a headache.

And so it went on all day. In the evening I dashed home with the home-going crowd, pushed open the gate, saw the hall-door open as it always is and sat down on the little chair just inside to take off my boots. My slippers were there, of course. This seemed to me a good sign. I put my boots into the rack in the cupboard under the stairs, changed my office coat and made for the kitchen. I knew my wife was there. Wait a bit. The only thing I couldn't manage was my whistling as per usual, 'I often lie awake and think, "What a dreadful thing is work . . ."' I had a try, but nothing came of it. Well, I opened the kitchen door and said, 'Hullo! How's everybody?' But as soon as I'd said that — even before — I knew the worst had happened. She was standing at the table beating the salad dressing. And when she looked up and gave a kind of smile and said 'Hullo!' you could have knocked me down! My wife looked dreadful — there's no other word for it. She must have been crying all day. She'd put some white flour stuff on her face to take away the marks — but it only made her look worse. She must have seen I spotted something, for she caught up the cup of cream and poured some into the salad bowl — like she always does, you know, so quick, so neat, in her own way — and began beating again. I said, 'Is your head better?' But she didn't seem to hear. She said, 'Are you going to water the garden before or after supper?' What could I say? I said, 'After,' and went off to the dining-room, opened the evening paper and sat by the open window — well, hiding behind that paper, I suppose.

I shall never forget sitting there. People passing by, going down the road, sounded so peaceful. And a man passed with some cows. I — I envied him. My wife came in and out. Then she called me to supper and we sat down. I suppose we ate some cold meat and salad. I don't remember. We must have. But neither of us spoke. It's like a dream now. Then she got up, changed the plates, and went to the larder for the pudding. Do you know what the pudding was? Well, of course, it wouldn't mean anything to you. It was my favourite — the kind she only made me on special occasions — honeycomb cream . . .

A MAN AND HIS DOG

To look at Mr. Potts one would have thought that there at least went someone who had nothing to boast about. He was a little, insignificant fellow with a crooked tie, a hat too small for him and a coat too large. The brown canvas portfolio that he carried to and from the Post Office every day was not like a business man's portfolio. It was like a child's school satchel; it did up even with a round-eyed button. One imagined there were crumbs and an apple core inside. And then there was something funny about his boots, wasn't there? Through the laces his coloured socks peeped out. What the dickens had the chap done with the tongues? 'Fried 'em,' suggested the wit of the Chesney bus. Poor old Potts! 'More likely buried 'em in his garden.' Under his arm he clasped an umbrella. And in wet weather when he put it up he disappeared completely. He was not. He was a walking umbrella — no more — the umbrella became his shell.

Mr. Potts lived in a little bungalow on Chesney Flat. The bulge of the water tank to one side gave it a mournful air, like a little bungalow with the toothache. There was no garden.

A path had been cut in the paddock turf from the gate to the front door, and two beds, one round, one oblong, had been cut in what was going to be the front lawn. Down that path went Potts every morning at half-past eight and was picked up by the Chesney bus; up that path walked Potts every evening while the great kettle of a bus droned on. In the late evening, when he crept as far as the gate, eager to smoke a pipe — he wasn't allowed to smoke any nearer to the house than that — so humble, so modest was his air, that the big, merrily shining stars seemed to wink at each other, to laugh, to say, 'Look at him! Let's throw something!'

When Potts got out of the tram at the Fire Station to change into the Chesney bus he saw that something was up. The car was there all right, but the driver was off his perch; he was flat on his face half under the engine, and the conductor, his cap off sat on a step rolling a cigarette and looking dreamy. A little group of business men and a woman clerk or two stood staring at the empty car; there was something mournful, pitiful about the way it leaned to one side and shivered faintly when the driver shook something. It was like someone who'd had an accident and tries to say: 'Don't touch me! Don't come near me! Don't hurt me!'

But all this was so familiar — the cars had only been running to Chesney the last few months — that nobody said anything, nobody asked anything. They just waited on the off chance. In fact, two or three decided to walk it as Potts came up. But Potts didn't want to walk unless he had to. He was tired. He'd been up half the night rubbing his wife's chest — she had one of her mysterious pains — and helping the sleepy servant girl heat compresses and hot-water bottles and make tea. The window was blue and the roosters had started crowing before he lay down finally with feet like ice. And all this was familiar, too.

Standing at the edge of the pavement and now and again changing his brown canvas portfolio from one hand to the other Potts began to live over the night before. But it was vague, shadowy. He saw himself moving like a crab, down the passage to the cold kitchen and back again. The two candles quivered on the dark chest of drawers, and as he bent over his wife her big eyes suddenly flashed and she cried:

'I get no sympathy — no sympathy. You only do it because you have to. Don't contradict me. I can see you grudge doing it.'

Trying to soothe her only made matters worse. There had been an awful scene ending with her sitting up and saying solemnly with her hand raised: 'Never mind, it will not be for long now.' But the sound of these words frightened her so terribly that she flung back on the pillow and sobbed, 'Robert! Robert!' Robert was the name of the young man to whom she had been engaged years ago, before she met Potts. And Potts was very glad to hear him invoked. He had come to know that meant the crisis was over and she'd begin to quieten down . . .

By this time Potts had wheeled round; he had walked across the pavement to the paling fence that ran beside. A piece of light grass pushed through the fence and some slender silky daisies. Suddenly he saw a bee alight on one of the daisies and the flower leaned over, swayed, shook, while the little bee clung and rocked. And as it flew away the petals fluttered as if joyfully . . . Just for an instant Potts dropped into the world where this happened. He brought from it the timid smile with which he walked back to the car. But now everybody had disappeared except one young girl who stood beside the empty car reading.

At the tail of the procession came Potts in a cassock so much too large for him that it looked like a night-shirt and you felt that he ought to be carrying not a hymn and a prayer book but a candle. His voice was a very light plaintive tenor. It surprised everybody. It seemed to surprise him, too. But it was so plaintive that when he cried 'for the wings, for the wings of a dove', the ladies in the congregation wanted to club together and buy him a pair.

Lino's nose quivered so pitifully, there was such a wistful, timid look in his eyes, that Potts' heart was wrung. But, of course, he would not show it. 'Well,' he said sternly, 'I suppose you'd better come home.' And he got up off the bench. Lino got up, too, but stood still, holding up a paw.

'But there's one thing', said Potts, turning and facing him squarely, 'that we'd better be clear about before you do come. And it's this.' He pointed his finger at Lino, who started as though he expected to be shot. But he kept his bewildered wistful eyes upon his master. 'Stop this pretence of being a fighting dog,' said Potts more sternly than ever. 'You're not a fighting dog. You're a watch dog. That's what you are. Very well. Stick to it. But it's this infernal boasting I can't stand. It's that that gets me.'

In the moment's pause that followed while Lino and his master looked at each other it was curious how strong a resemblance was between them. Then Potts turned again and made for home.

And timidly, as though falling over his own paws, Lino followed after the humble little figure of his master . . .

SUCH A SWEET OLD LADY

Why did old Mrs. Travers wake so early nowadays? She would like to have slept for another three hours at least. But no, every morning at almost precisely the same time, at half-past four, she was wide awake. For — nowadays, again — she woke always in the same way, with a slight start, a small shock, lifting her head from the pillow with a quick glance as if she fancied someone had called her, or as if she were trying to remember for certain whether this was the same wallpaper, the same window she had seen last night before Warner switched off the light . . . Then the small, silvery head pressed the white pillow again, and just for a moment, before the agony of lying awake began, old Mrs. Travers was happy. Her heart quietened down, she breathed deeply, she even smiled. Yet once more the tide of darkness had risen, had floated her, had carried her away; and once more it had ebbed, it had withdrawn, casting her up where it had found her, shut in by the same wall-paper, stared at by the same window — still safe — still *there!*

Now the church clock sounded from outside, slow, languid, faint, as if it chimed the half-hour in its sleep. She felt under the pillow for her watch; yes, it said the same: half-past four. Three and a half hours before Warner came in with her tea. Oh dear, would she be able to stand it? She moved her legs restlessly. And, staring at the prim, severe face of the watch, it seemed to her that the hands — the minute hand especially — knew that she was watching them and held back — just a very little — on purpose . . . Very strange, she had never got over the feeling that watch hated her. It had been Henry's. Twenty years ago, when standing by poor Henry's bed she had taken it into her hands for the first time and wound it, it had felt cold and heavy. And two days later, when she undid a hook of her crape bodice and thrust it inside, it had lain in her bosom like a stone . . . It had never felt at home there. Its place was — ticking, keeping perfect time, against Henry's firm ribs. It had never trusted her, just as he had never trusted her in those ways. And on the rare occasions when she had forgotten to wind it, she had felt a pang of almost terror, and she had murmured as she fitted the little key: 'Forgive me, Henry!'

Old Mrs. Travers sighed and pushed the watch under the pillow again. It seemed to her that lately this feeling that it hated her had become more definite. . . . Perhaps that was because she looked at it so often, especially now that she was away from home. Foreign clocks never go. They are always stopped at twenty minutes to two. Twenty minutes to two! Such an unpleasant time, neither one thing nor the other. If one arrived anywhere lunch was over and it was too early to expect a cup of tea . . . But she mustn't begin thinking about tea. Old Mrs. Travers pulled herself up in the bed and, like a tired baby, she lifted her arms and let them fall on the eiderdown.

The room was gay with morning light. The big french window on to the balcony was open and the palm outside flung its quivering spider-like shadow over the bedroom walls. Although their hotel did not face the front, at this early hour you could smell the sea, you could hear it breathing, and flying high on golden wings sea-gulls skimmed past. How peaceful the sky looked, as though it was tenderly smiling! Far away — far away from this satin-stripe wall-paper, the glass-covered table, the yellow brocade sofa and chairs, and the mirrors that showed you your side view, your back view, your three-quarters view as well.

Ernestine had been enthusiastic about this room.

'It's just the very room for you, Mother! So bright and attractive and non-depressing! With a balcony, too, so that on wet days you can still have your chair outside and look at those lovely palms. And Gladys can have the little room adjoining, which makes it so beautifully easy for Warner to keep her eye on you both . . . You couldn't have a nicer room, could you, Mother? I can't get over that sweet balcony! So nice for Gladys! Cecil and I haven't got one at all . . .'

But all the same, in spite of Ernestine, she never sat on that balcony. For some strange reason that she couldn't explain she hated looking at palms. Nasty foreign things, she called them in her mind. When they were still they drooped, they looked draggled like immense untidy birds, and when they moved they reminded her always of spiders. Why did they never look just natural and peaceful and shady like English trees? Why were they for ever writhing and twisting or standing sullen? It tried her even to think of them, or in fact of anything foreign . . .

HONESTY

I.

There was an expression Rupert Henderson was very fond of using: 'If you want my *honest* opinion . . .' He had an honest opinion on every subject under the sun, and nothing short of a passion for delivering it. But Archie Cullen's pet phrase was 'I cannot *honestly* say . . .' Which meant that he had not really made up his mind. He had not really made up his mind on any subject whatsoever. Why? Because he could not. He was unlike other men. He was minus something — or was it plus? No matter. He was not in the least proud of the fact. It depressed him — one might go so far as to say — terribly at times.

Rupert and Archie lived together. That is to say, Archie lived in Rupert's rooms. Oh, he paid his share, his half in everything; the arrangement was a purely, strictly business arrangement. But perhaps it was because Rupert had invited Archie that Archie remained always — his guest. They each had a bedroom — there was a common sitting-room and a largish bathroom which Rupert used as a dressing-room as well. The first morning after his arrival Archie had left his sponge in the bathroom, and a moment after there was a knock at his door and Rupert said, kindly but firmly, 'Your sponge, I fancy.' The first evening Archie had brought his tobacco jar into the sitting-room and placed it on a corner of the mantelpiece. Rupert was reading the newspaper. It was a round china jar, the surface painted and roughened to represent a sea-urchin. On the lid was a spray of china seaweed with two berries for a knob. Archie was excessively fond of it. But after dinner, when Rupert took out his pipe and pouch, he suddenly fixed his eyes on this object, blew through his moustaches, gasped, and said in a wondering, astonished voice, 'I say! Is that yours or Mrs. Head's?' Mrs. Head was their landlady.

'It's mine,' said Archie, and he blushed and smiled just a trifle timidly.

'I *say*!' said Rupert again — this time very meaningly.

'Would you rather I . . .' said Archie, and he moved in his chair to get up.

'No, no! Certainly not! On no account!' answered Rupert, and he actually raised his hand. 'But perhaps' — and here he smiled at Archie and gazed about him — 'perhaps we might find some spot for it that was a trifle less conspicuous.'

The spot was not decided on, however, and Archie nipped his sole personal possession into his bedroom as soon as Rupert was out of the way.

But it was chiefly at meals that the attitude of host and guest was most marked. For instance, on each separate occasion, even before they sat down, Rupert said, 'Would you mind cutting the bread, Archie?' Had he not made such a point of it, it is possible that Archie in a moment of abstractedness might have grasped the bread knife . . . An unpleasant thought! Again, Archie was never allowed to serve. Even at breakfast, the hot dishes and the tea, both were dispensed by Rupert. True, he had half apologised about the tea; he seemed to feel the necessity of some slight explanation, there.

'I'm rather a fad about my tea,' said he. 'Some people, females especially, pour in the milk first. Fatal habit, for more reasons than one. In my opinion, the cup should be filled just *so* and the tea then coloured. Sugar, Archie?'

'Oh, please,' said Archie, almost bowing over the table, Rupert was so very impressive.

'But I suppose,' said his friend, 'you don't notice any of these little things?'

And Archie answered vaguely, stirring: 'No, I don't suppose I do.'

Rupert sat down and unfolded his napkin.

'It would be very inconsistent with your character and disposition', said he genially, 'if you did! Kidneys and bacon? Scrambled eggs? Either? Both? Which?'

Poor Archie hated scrambled eggs, but, alas! he was practically certain that scrambled eggs were expected of him too. This 'psychological awareness', as Rupert called it, which existed between them might after a time make things a trifle difficult. He felt a little abject as he murmured, 'Eggs, please.' And he saw by Rupert's expression that he had chosen right. Rupert helped him to eggs largely.

II.

Psychological awareness . . . perhaps it was that which explained their intimacy. One might have been tempted to say it was a case of mutual fascination. But whereas Archie's reply to the suggestion would have been a slow 'Poss-ibly!' Rupert would have flouted it at once.

'Fascination! The word's preposterous in this connection. What on earth would there be in Cullen to fascinate me even if I was in the habit of being fascinated by my fellow creatures; which I certainly am not. No, I'll own I am deeply interested. I confess my belief is, I understand him better than anybody else. And if you want my honest opinion, I am certain that my — my — h'm — influence over — sympathy for — him — call it what you like, is all to the good. There is a psychological awareness . . . Moreover, as a companion, instinctively I find him extremely agreeable. He stimulates some part of my mind which is less active without him. But fascination — wide of the mark, my dear — wide!'

But supposing one remained unconvinced? Supposing one still played with the idea. Wasn't it possible to see Rupert and Archie as the python and the rabbit keeping house together? Rupert that handsome, well-fed python with his moustaches, his glare, his habit of uncoiling before the fire and swaying against the mantelpiece, pipe and pouch in hand. And Archie, soft, hunched, timid, sitting in the lesser arm-chair, there and not there, flicking back into the darkness at a word but emerging again at a look — with sudden wholly unexpected starts of playfulness (instantly suppressed by the python). Of course, there was no question of anything so crude and dreadful as the rabbit being eaten by his housemate. Nevertheless, it was a strange fact, after a typical evening the one looked immensely swelled, benign and refreshed, and the other, pale, small and exhausted . . . And more often than not Rupert's final comment was — ominous this — as he doused his whisky with soda:

'This has been very absorbing, Archie.' And Archie gasped out, 'Oh, *very*!'

III.

Archie Cullen was a journalist and the son of a journalist. He had no private money, no influential connections, scarcely any friends. His father had been one of those weak, disappointed, unsuccessful men who see in their sons a weapon for themselves. He would get his own back on life through Archie. Archie would show them the stuff he — his father was made of. Just you wait till my son comes along! This, though highly consoling to Mr. Cullen *père*, was terribly poor fun for Archie. At two and a half his infant nose was put to the grindstone and even on Sundays it was not taken off. Then his father took him out walking and improved the occasion by making him spell the shop signs, count the yachts racing in the harbour, divide them by four and multiply the result by three.

But the experiment was an amazing success. Archie turned away from the distractions of life, shut his ears, folded his feet, sat over the table with his book, and when the holidays came he didn't like them; they made him uneasy; so he went on reading for himself. He was a model boy. On prize-giving days his father accompanied him to school, carried the great wad of stiff books home for him and, flinging them on the dining-room table, he surveyed them with an exultant smile. My prizes! The little sacrifice stared at them, too, through his spectacles as other little boys stared at puddings. He ought, of course, at this juncture to have been rescued by a doting mother who, though cowed herself, rose on the . . .

SUSANNAH

Of course there would have been no question of their going to the exhibition if Father had not had the tickets given to him. Little girls cannot expect to be given treats that cost extra money when only to feed them, buy them clothes, pay for their lessons and the house they live in takes their kind generous Father all day and every day working hard from morning till night — 'except Saturday afternoons and Sundays', said Susannah.

'Susannah!' Mother was very shocked. 'But do you know what would happen to your poor Father if he didn't have a holiday on Saturday afternoons and Sundays?'

'No,' said Susannah. She looked interested. 'What?'

'He would die,' said their Mother impressively.

'Would he?' said Susannah, opening her eyes. She seemed astounded, and Sylvia and Phyllis, who were four and five years older than she, chimed in with 'Of course' in a very superior tone. What a little silly-billy she was not to know that! They sounded so convinced and cheerful that their Mother felt a little shaken and hastened to change the subject . . .

'So that is why,' she said a little vaguely, 'you must each thank Father separately before you go.'

'And then will he give us the money?' asked Phyllis.

'And then I shall ask him for whatever is necessary,' said their Mother firmly. She sighed suddenly and got up. 'Run along, children, and ask Miss Wade to dress you and get ready herself and then to come down to the dining-room. And now, Susannah, you are not to let go Miss Wade's hand from the moment you are through the gates until you are out again.'

'Well — what if I go on a horse?' inquired Susannah.

'Go on a horse — nonsense, child! You're much too young for horses! Only big girls and boys can ride.'

'There're roosters for small children,' said Susannah, undaunted. 'I know, because Irene Heywood went on one and when she got off she fell over.'

'All the more reason why you shouldn't go on,' said her Mother.

But Susannah looked as though falling over had no terrors for her. On the contrary.

About the exhibition, however, Sylvia and Phyllis knew as little as Susannah. It was the first that had ever come to their town. One morning, as Miss Wade, their lady help, rushed them along to the Heywoods', whose governess they shared, they had seen carts piled with great long planks of wood, sacks, what looked like whole doors, and white flagstaffs, passing through the wide gate of the Recreation Ground. And by the time they were bowled home to their dinners there were the beginnings of a high, thin fence, dotted with flagstaffs, built all round the railings. From inside came a tremendous noise of hammering, shouting, clanging; a little engine, hidden away, went *Chuff-chuff-chuff. Chuff!* And round, woolly balls of smoke were tossed over the palings.

First it was the day after the day after to-morrow, then plain day after to-morrow, then to-morrow, and at last, the day itself.

When Susannah woke up in the morning there was a little gold spot of sunlight watching her from the wall; it looked as though it had been there for a long time, waiting to remind her: 'It's to-day — you're going to-day — this afternoon. Here she is!'

(Second Version)

That afternoon they were allowed to cut jugs and basins out of a draper's catalogue, and at tea-time they had real tea in the doll's tea-set on the table. This was a very nice treat, indeed, except that the doll's teapot wouldn't pour out even after you'd poked a pin down the spout and blown into it.

But the next afternoon, which was Saturday, Father came home in high feather. The front door banged so hard that the whole house shook, and he shouted to Mother from the hall.

'Oh, how more than good of you, darling!' cried Mother, 'but how unnecessary too. Of course, they'll simply love it. But to have spent all that money! You shouldn't have done it, Daddy dear! They've totally forgotten all about it. And what is this! Half a crown?' cried Mother. 'No! Two shillings, I see,' she corrected quickly, 'to spend as well. Children! Children! Come down, downstairs!'

Down they came, Phyllis and Sylvia leading, Susannah holding on. 'Do you know what Father's done?' And Mother held up her hand. What was she holding? Three cherry tickets and a green one. 'He's bought you tickets. You're to go to the circus, this very afternoon, all of you, with Miss Wade. What do you say to that?'

'Oh, Mummy! Lovely! Lovely!' cried Phyllis and Sylvia.

'Isn't it?' said Mother. 'Run upstairs. Run and ask Miss Wade to get you ready. Don't dawdle. Up you go! All of you.'

Away flew Phyllis and Sylvia, but still Susannah stayed where she was at the bottom of the stairs, hanging her head.

'Go along,' said Mother. And Father said sharply, 'What the devil's the matter with the child?'

Susannah's face quivered. 'I don't want to go,' she whispered.

'What! Don't want to go to the Exhibition! After Father's — You naughty, ungrateful child! Either you go to the Exhibition, Susannah, or you will be packed off to bed at once.'

Susannah's head bent low, lower still. All her little body bent forward. She looked as though she was going to bow down, to bow down to the ground, before her kind generous Father and beg for his forgiveness . . .

SECOND VIOLIN

A February morning, windy, cold, with chill-looking clouds hurrying over a pale sky and chill snowdrops for sale in the grey streets. People look small and shrunken as they flit by; they look scared as if they were trying to hide inside their coats from something big and brutal. The shop doors are closed, the awnings are furled, and the policemen at the crossings are lead policemen. Huge empty vans shake past with a hollow sound; and there is a smell of soot and wet stone staircases, a raw, grimy smell . . .

Flinging her small scarf over her shoulder again, clasping her violin, Miss Bray darts along to orchestra practice. She is conscious of her cold hands, her cold nose and her colder feet. She can't feel her toes at all. Her feet are just little slabs of cold, all of a piece, like the feet of china dolls. Winter is a terrible time for thin people — terrible! Why should it hound them down, fasten on them, worry them so? Why not, for a change, take a nip, take a snap at the fat ones who wouldn't notice? But no! It is sleek, warm, cat-like summer that makes the fat one's life a misery. Winter is all for bones . . .

Threading her way, like a needle, in and out and along, went Miss Bray, and she thought of nothing but the cold. She had just come out of her kitchen, which was pleasantly snug in the morning, with her gas-fire going for her breakfast and the window closed. She had just drunk three large cups of really boiling tea. Surely, they ought to have warmed her. One always read in books of people going on their way warmed and invigorated by even one cup. And she had had three! How she loved her tea! She was getting fonder and fonder of it. Stirring the cup, Miss Bray looked down. A little fond smile parted her lips, and she breathed tenderly, 'I love my tea.'

But all the same, in spite of the books, it didn't keep her warm. Cold! Cold! And now as she turned the corner she took such a gulp of damp, cold air that her eyes filled. *Yi-yi-yi*, a little dog yelped; he looked as though he'd been hurt. She hadn't time to look round, but that high, sharp yelping soothed her, was a comfort even. She could have made just that sound herself.

And here was the Academy. Miss Bray pressed with all her might against the stiff, sulky door, squeezed through into the vestibule hung with pallid notices and concert programmes, and stumbled up the dusty stairs and along the passage to the dressing-room. Through the open door there came such shrill loud laughter, such high, indifferent voices that it sounded like a play going on in there. It was hard to believe people were not laughing and talking like that . . . on purpose. 'Excuse me — pardon — sorry,' said Miss Bray, nudging her way in and looking quickly round the dingy little room. Her two friends had not yet come.

The First Violins were there; a dreamy, broad-faced girl leaned against her 'cello; two Violas sat on a bench, bent over a music book, and the Harp, a small grey little person, who only came occasionally, leaned against a bench and looked for her pocket in her underskirt . . .

'I've a run of three twice, ducky,' said Ma, 'a pair of queens make eight, and one for his nob makes nine.'

With an awful hollow groan Alexander, curling his little finger high, pegged nine for Ma. And 'Wait now, wait now,' said she, and her quick short little hands snatched at the other cards. 'My crib, young man!' She spread them out, leaned back, twitched her shawl, put her head on one side. 'H'm, not so bad! A flush of four and a pair!'

'Betrayed! Betrayed!' moaned Alexander, bowing his dark head over the cribbage board, 'and by a woo-man.' He sighed deeply, shuffled the cards and said to Ma, 'Cut for me, my love!'

Although, of course, he was only having his joke like all professional young gentlemen, something in the tone in which he said 'my love!' gave Ma quite a turn. Her lips trembled as she cut the cards, she felt a sudden pang as she watched those long slim fingers dealing.

Ma and Alexander were playing cribbage in the basement kitchen of number 9 Bolton Street. It was late, it was on eleven, and Sunday night, too — shocking! They sat at the kitchen table that was covered with a worn art serge cloth spotted with candle grease. On one corner of it stood three glasses, three spoons, a saucer of sugar lumps and a bottle of gin. The stove was still alight and the lid of the kettle had just begun to lift, cautiously, stealthily, as though there was someone inside who wanted to have a peep and pop back again. On the horse-hair sofa against the wall by the door the owner of the third glass lay asleep, gently snoring. Perhaps because he had his back to them, perhaps because his feet poked out from the short overcoat covering him, he looked forlorn, pathetic and the long, fair hair covering his collar looked forlorn and pathetic, too.

'Well, well,' said Ma, sighing as she put out two cards and

arranged the others in a fan, 'such is life. I little thought when I saw the last of you this morning that we'd be playing a game together to-night.'

'The caprice of destiny,' murmured Alexander. But, as a matter of fact, it was no joking matter. By some infernal mischance that morning he and Rinaldo had missed the train that all the company travelled by. That was bad enough. But being Sunday, there was no other train until midnight, and as they had a full rehearsal at 10 o'clock on Monday it meant going by that, or getting what the company called the beetroot. But God! what a day it had been. They had left the luggage at the station and come back to Ma's, back to Alexander's frowsy bedroom with the bed unmade and water standing about. Rinaldo had spent the whole day sitting on the side of the bed swinging his leg, dropping ash on the floor and saying, 'I wonder what made us lose that train. Strange we should have lost it. I bet the others are wondering what made us lose it, too.' And Alexander had stayed by the window gazing into the small garden that was so black with grime even the old lean cat who came and scraped seemed revolted by it, too. It was only after Ma had seen the last of her Sunday visitors . . .

MR. AND MRS. WILLIAMS

I.

That winter Mr. and Mrs. Williams of The Rowans, Wickenham, Surrey, astonished their friends by announcing that they were going for a three weeks' holiday to Switzerland. Switzerland! How very enterprising and exciting! There was quite a flutter in Wickenham households at the news. Husbands coming home from the city in the evening were greeted immediately with:

'My dear, have you heard the news about the Williams?'

'No! What's up now?'

'They're off to Switzerland.'

'Switzerland! 'What the dickens are they going there for?'

That, of course, was only the extravagance of the moment. One knew perfectly well why people went. But nobody in Wickenham ever plunged so far away from home at that time of year. It was not considered 'necessary' — as golf, bridge, a summer holiday at the sea, an account at Harrods' and a small car as soon as one could afford it, were considered necessary . . .

'Won't you find the initial expenditure very heavy?' asked stout old Mrs. Prean, meeting Mrs. Williams quite by chance at their nice obliging grocer's. And she brushed the crumbs of a sample cheese biscuit off her broad bosom.

'Oh, we shall get our kit over there,' said Mrs. Williams.

'Kit' was a word in high favour among the Wickenham ladies. It was left over from the war, of course, with 'cheery', 'wash-out', 'Hun', 'Boche', and 'Bolshy'. As a matter of fact, Bolshy was post-war. But it belonged to the same mood. ('My dear, my housemaid is an absolute little Hun, and I'm afraid the cook is turning Bolshy . . .') There was a fascination in those words. To use them was like opening one's Red Cross cupboard again and gazing at the remains of the bandages, body-belts, tins of anti-insecticide and so on. One was stirred, one got a far-away thrill, like the thrill of hearing a distant band. It reminded you of those exciting, busy, of course anxious, but tremendous days when the whole of Wickenham was one united family. And, although one's husband was away, one had for a substitute three large photographs of him in uniform. One in a silver frame on the table by the bed, one in the regimental colours on the piano, and one in leather to match the dining-room chairs.

'Cook strongly advised us to buy nothing here,' went on Mrs. Williams.

'*Cook!*' cried Mrs. Prean, greatly astounded. 'What can —'

'Oh — *Thomas* Cook, of course, I mean,' said Mrs. Williams, smiling brightly. Mrs. Prean subsided.

'But you will surely not depend upon the resources of a little Swiss village for clothes?' she persisted, deeply interested, as usual, in other people's affairs.

'Oh no, certainly not.' Mrs. Williams was quite shocked. 'We shall get all we need in the way of clothes from Harrods'.'

That was what Mrs. Prean had wished to hear. That was as it should be.

'The great secret, my dear' (she always knew the great secret), 'the great secret' — and she put her hand on Mrs. Williams' arm and spoke very distinctly — 'is plenty of long-sleeved woven combies!'

'Thank you, m'm.'

Both ladies started. There at their side was Mr. Wick, the nice grocer, holding Mrs. Prean's parcel by a loop of pink string. Dear me — how very awkward! He must have . . . he couldn't possibly not have . . . In the emotion of the moment Mrs. Prean, thinking to gloss it over tactfully, nodded significantly at Mrs. Williams and said, accepting the parcel, 'And that is what I always tell my dear son!' But this was too swift for Mrs. Williams to follow.

Her embarrassment continued and, ordering the sardines, she just stopped herself from saying 'Three large pairs, Mr. Wick, please,' instead of 'Three large tins.'

II.

As a matter of fact it was Mrs. Williams' Aunt Aggie's happy release which had made their scheme possible. Happy release it was! After fifteen years in a wheel-chair passing in and out of the little house at Ealing she had, to use the nurse's expression, 'just glided away at the last'. Glided away . . . it sounded as though Aunt Aggie had taken the wheel-chair with her. One saw her, in her absurd purple velvet, steering carefully among the stars and whimpering faintly, as was her terrestrial wont, when the wheel jolted over a particularly large one.

Aunt Aggie had left her dear niece Gwendolen two hundred and fifty pounds. Not a vast sum by any means but quite a nice little windfall. Gwendolen, in that dashing mood that only women know, decided immediately to spend it — part of it on the house and the rest on a treat for Gerald. And the lawyer's letter happening to come at tea-time together with a copy of the *Sphere* full of the most fascinating, thrilling photographs of holiday-makers at Mürren and St. Moritz and Montana, the question of the treat was settled.

'You would like to go to Switzerland, wouldn't you, Gerald?'

'Very much.'

'You're — awfully good at skating and all that kind of thing — aren't you?'

'Fairly.'

'You do feel it's a thing to be done — don't you?'

'How do you mean?'

But Gwendolen only laughed. That was so like Gerald. She knew, in his heart of hearts, he was every bit as keen as she was. But he had this horror of showing his feelings — like all men. Gwendolen understood it perfectly and wouldn't have had him different for the world . . .

'I'll write to Cook's at once and tell them we don't want to go to a very fashionable place and we don't want one of those big jazzy hotels! I'd much prefer a really small out-of-the-way place where we could really go in for the sports seriously.' This was quite untrue, but, like so many of Gwendolen's statements, it was made to please Gerald. 'Don't you agree?'

Gerald lit his pipe for reply.

As you have gathered, the Christian names of Mr. and Mrs. Williams were Gwendolen and Gerald. How well they went together! They sounded married. Gwendolen-Gerald. Gwendolen wrote them, bracketed, on bits of blotting-paper, on the backs of old envelopes, on the Stores' catalogue. They looked married. Gerald, when they were on their honeymoon, had made an awfully good joke about them. He had said one morning, 'I say, has it ever struck you that both our names begin with *G*? Gwendolen-Gerald. You're a *G*', and he had pointed his razor at her — he was shaving — 'and I'm a *G*.

Two *G*s. Gee-Gee. See?'

Oh, Gwendolen saw immediately. It was really most witty. Quite brilliant! And so — sweet and unexpected of him to have thought of it. Gee-Gee. Oh, *very* good! She wished she could have told it to people. She had an idea that some people thought Gerald had not a very strong sense of humour. But it was a little too intimate. All the more precious for that reason, however.

'My dear, did you think of it at this moment? I mean — did you just make it up on the spot?'

Gerald, rubbing the lather with a finger, nodded. 'Flashed into my mind while I was soaping my face,' said he seriously. 'It's a queer thing' — and he dipped the razor into the pot of hot water — 'I've noticed it before. Shaving gives me ideas.' It did, indeed, thought Gwendolen . . .

WEAK HEART

Although it sounded all the year round, although it rang out sometimes as early as half-past six in the morning, sometimes as late as half-past ten at night, it was in the spring, when Bengel's violet patch just inside the gate was blue with flowers, that that piano . . . made the passers-by not only stop talking, but slow down, pause, look suddenly — if they were men — grave, even stern, and if they were women —dreamy, even sorrowful.

Tarana Street was beautiful in the spring; there was not a single house without its garden and trees and a plot of grass big enough to be called 'the lawn'. Over the low painted fences, you could see, as you ran by, whose daffys were out, whose wild snowdrop border was over and who had the biggest hyacinths, so pink and white, the colour of coconut ice. But nobody had violets that grew, that smelled in the spring sun like Bengel's. Did they really smell like that? Or did you shut your eyes and lean over the fence because of Edie Bengel's piano?

A little wind ruffles among the leaves like a joyful hand looking for the finest flowers; and the piano sounds gay, tender, laughing. Now a cloud, like a swan, flies across the sun, the violets shine cold, like water, and a sudden questioning cry rings from Edie Bengel's piano.

. . . Ah, if life must pass so quickly, why is the breath of these flowers so sweet? What is the meaning of this feeling of longing, of sweet trouble — of flying joy? Good-bye! Farewell! The young bees lie half awake on the slender dandelions, silver are the pink-tipped arrowy petals of the daisies; the new grass shakes in the light. Everything is beginning again, marvellous as ever, heavenly fair. 'Let me stay! Let me stay!' pleads Edie Bengel's piano.

It is the afternoon, sunny and still. The blinds are down in the front to save the carpets, but upstairs the slats are open and in the golden light little Mrs. Bengel is feeling under her bed for the square bonnet box. She is flushed. She feels timid, excited, like a girl. And now the tissue paper is parted, her best bonnet, the one trimmed with a jet butterfly, which reposes on top, is lifted out and solemnly blown upon.

Dipping down to the glass she tries it with fingers that tremble. She twitches her dolman round her slender shoulders, clasps her purse and before leaving the bedroom kneels down a moment to ask God's blessing on her 'goings out'. And as she kneels there quivering, she is rather like a butterfly herself, fanning her wings before her Lord. When the door is open the sound of the piano coming up through the silent house is almost frightening, so bold, so defiant, so reckless it rolls under Edie's fingers. And just for a moment the thought comes to Mrs. Bengel and is gone again, that there is a stranger with Edie in the drawing-room, but a fantastic person, out of a book, a — a — villain. It's very absurd. She flits across the hall, turns the door handle and confronts her flushed daughter. Edie's hands drop from the keys. She squeezes them between her knees, her head is bent, her curls are fallen forward. She gazes at her mother with brilliant eyes. There is something painful in that glance, something very strange. It is dusky in the drawing-room, the top of the piano is open. Edie has been playing from memory; it's as though the air still tingles.

'I'm going, dear,' said Mrs. Bengel softly, so softly it is like a sigh.

'Yes, Mother,' came from Edie.

'I don't expect I shall be long.'

Mrs. Bengel lingers. She would very much like just a word of sympathy, of understanding, even from Edie, to cheer her on her way.

But Edie murmurs, 'I'll put the kettle on in half an hour.'

'Do, dear!' Mrs. Bengel grasped at that even. A nervous little smile touched her lips. 'I expect I shall want my tea.'

But to that Edie makes no reply; she frowns, she stretches out a hand, quickly unscrews one of the piano candlesticks, lifts off a pink china ring and screws all tight again. The ring has been rattling. As the front door bangs softly after her mother Edie and the piano seem to plunge together into deep dark water, into waves that flow over both, relentless. She plays on desperately until her nose is white and her heart beats. It is her way of getting over her nervousness and her way too of praying. Would they accept her? Would she be allowed to go? Was it possible that in a week's time she would be one of Miss Farmer's girls, wearing a red and blue hat-band, running up the broad steps leading to the big grey painted house that buzzed, that hummed as you went by? Their pew in Church faced Miss Farmer's boarders. Would she at last know the names of the girls she had looked at so often? The pretty pale one with red hair, the dark one with a fringe, the fair one who held Miss Farmer's hand during the sermon? . . . But after all . . .

It was Edie's fourteenth birthday. Her father gave her a silver brooch with a bar of music, two crotchets, two quavers and a minim headed by a very twisted treble clef. Her mother gave her blue satin gloves and two boxes for gloves and handkerchiefs, hand-painted the glove box with a sprig of gold roses tying up the capital G and the handkerchief box with a marvellously lifelike butterfly quivering on the capital H. From the aunts in . . .

There was a tree at the corner of Tarana Street and May Street. It grew so close to the pavement that the heavy boughs stretched over, and on that part of the pavement there was always a fine sifting of minute twigs.

But in the dusk, lovers parading came into its shade as into a tent. There, however long they had been together, they greeted each other again with long kisses, with embraces that were sweet torture, agony to bear, agony to end.

Edie never knew that Roddie 'loved' it, Roddie never knew that it meant anything to Edie.

Roddie, spruce, sleek with water, bumped his new bike down the wooden steps, through the gate. He was off for a spin, and looking at that tree, dark in the glow of evening, he felt the tree was watching him. He wanted to do marvels, to astonish, to shock, to amaze it.

Roddie had a complete new outfit for the occasion. A black serge suit, a black tie, a straw hat so white it was almost silver, a dazzling white straw hat with a broad black band. Attached to the hat there was a thick guard that somehow reminded one of a fishing line and the little clasp on the brim was like a fly . . . He stood at the graveside, his legs apart, his hands loosely clasped, and watched Edie being lowered into the grave — as a half-grown boy watches anything, a man at work, or a bicycle accident, or a chap cleaning a spring-carriage wheel — but suddenly as the men drew back he gave a violent start, turned, muttered something to his father and dashed away, so fast that people looked positively frightened, through the cemetery, down the avenue of dripping clay banks into Tarana Road, and started pelting for home. His suit was very tight and hot. It was like a dream. He kept his head down and his fists clenched, he couldn't look up, nothing could have made him look higher than the tops of the fences — What was he thinking of as he pressed along? On, on until the gate was reached, up the steps, in at the front door, through the hall, up to the drawing-room.

'Edie!' called Roddie. 'Edie, old girl!'

And he gave a low strange squawk and cried 'Edie!' and stared across at Edie's piano.

But cold, solemn, as if frozen, heavily the piano stared back at Roddie. Then it answered, but on its own behalf, on behalf of the house and the violet patch, the garden, the velvet tree at the corner of May Street, and all that was delightful: 'There is nobody here of that name, young man!'

WIDOWED

They came down to breakfast next morning absolutely their own selves. Rosy, fresh, and just chilled enough by the cold air blowing through the bedroom windows to be very ready for hot coffee.

'Nippy.' That was Geraldine's word as she buttoned on her orange coat with pink-washed fingers. 'Don't you find it decidedly nippy?' And her voice, so matter-of-fact, so natural, sounded as though they had been married for years.

Parting his hair with two brushes (marvellous feat for a woman to watch) in the little round mirror, he had replied, lightly clapping the brushes together, 'My dear, have you got enough *on*?' and he, too, sounded as though well he knew from the experience of years her habit of clothing herself underneath in wisps of chiffon and two satin bows . . . Then they ran down to breakfast, laughing together and terribly startling the shy parlour-maid who, after talking it over with Cook, had decided to be invisible until she was rung for.

'Good morning, Nellie, I think we shall want more toast than *that*,' said the smiling Geraldine as she hung over the breakfast table. She deliberated — 'Ask Cook to make us four more pieces, please.'

Marvellous, the parlour-maid thought it was. And as she closed the door she heard the voice say, 'I do so hate to be short of toast, don't you?'

He was standing in the sunny window. Geraldine went up to him. She put her hand on his arm and gave it a gentle squeeze. How pleasant it was to feel that rough man's-tweed again. Ah, how pleasant! She rubbed her hand against it, touched it with her cheek, sniffed the smell.

The window looked out on to flower beds, a tangle of Michaelmas daisies, late dahlias, hanging heavy, and shaggy little asters. Then there came a lawn strewn with yellow leaves with a broad path beyond and a row of gold-fluttering trees. An old gardener, in woollen mitts, was sweeping the path, brushing the leaves into a neat little heap. Now, the broom tucked in his arm, he fumbled in his coat pocket, brought out some matches, and, scooping a hole in the leaves he set fire to them.

Such lovely blue smoke came breathing into the air through those dry leaves; there was something so calm and orderly in the way the pile burned that it was a pleasure to watch. The old gardener stumped away and came back with a handful of withered twigs. He flung them on and stood by, and little light flames began to flicker.

'I do think', said Geraldine, 'I do think there is nothing nicer than a real satisfactory fire.'

'Jolly, isn't it,' he murmured back, and they went to their first breakfast.

Just over a year ago, thirteen months, to be exact, she had been standing before the dining-room window of the little house in Sloane Street. It looked over the railed gardens. Breakfast was over, cleared away and done with . . . she had a fat bunch of letters in her hand that she meant to answer, snugly, over the fire. But before settling down, the autumn sun, the freshness had drawn her to the window. Such a perfect morning for the Row. Jimmie had gone riding.

'Good-bye, dear thing.'

'Good-bye, Gerry mine.' And then the morning kiss, quick and firm. He looked so handsome in his riding kit. She imagined him as she stood there . . . riding. Geraldine was not very good at imagining things. But there was mist, a thud of hooves and Jimmie's moustache was damp. From the garden there sounded the creak of a gardener's barrow. An old man came into sight with a load of leaves and a broom lying across. He stopped; he began to sweep. 'What enormous tufts of irises grew in London gardens,' mused Geraldine. 'Why?' And now the smoke of a real fire ascended.

'There is nothing nicer', she thought, 'than a really satisfactory fire.'

Just at that moment the telephone bell rang. Geraldine sat down at Jimmie's desk to answer it. It was Major Hunter.

'Good morning, Major. You're a very early bird!'

'Good morning, Mrs. Howard. Yes. I am.' (Geraldine made a little surprised face at herself. How odd he sounded!) 'Mrs. Howard, I'm coming round to see you . . . now . . . I'm taking a taxi . . . Please don't go out. And — and —' the voice stammered, 'p-please don't let the servants go out.'

'*Par*-don?' This last was so very peculiar, though the whole thing had been peculiar enough, that Geraldine couldn't believe what she heard. But he was gone. He had rung off. What on earth — and putting down the receiver, she took up a pencil and drew what she always drew when she sat down before a piece of blotting-paper — the behind of a little cat with whiskers and tail complete. Geraldine must have drawn that little cat hundreds of times, all over the world, in hotels, in clubs, at steamer desks, waiting at the bank. The little cat was her sign, her mark. She had copied it from a little girl at school when she thought it most wonderful. And she never tried anything else. She was . . . not very good at drawing. This particular cat was drawn with an extra firm pen and even its whiskers looked surprised.

'Not to let the servants go out!' But she had never heard anything so peculiar in her life. She must have made a mistake. Geraldine couldn't help a little giggle of amusement. And why should he tell her he was taking a taxi? And why — above all — should he be coming to see her at that hour of the morning?

Then — it came over her — like a flash she remembered Major Hunter's mania for old furniture. They had been discussing it at the Carlton the last time they lunched together. And he had said something to Jimmie about some — Jacobean or Queen Anne — Geraldine knew nothing about these things — something or other. Could he possibly be bringing it round? But of course. He must be. And that explained the remark about the servants. He wanted them to help getting it into the house. What a bore! Geraldine did hope it would tone in. And really, she must say she thought Major Hunter was taking a good deal for granted to produce a thing that size at that hour of the day without a word of warning. They hardly knew him well enough for that. Why make such a mystery of it too? Geraldine hated mysteries. But she had heard his head was rather troublesome at times ever since the Somme affair. Perhaps this was one of his bad days. In that case, a pity Jimmie was not back. She rang. Mullins answered.

'Oh, Mullins, I'm expecting Major Hunter in a few moments. He's bringing something rather heavy. He may want you to help with it. And Cook had better be ready too.'

Geraldine's manner was slightly lofty with her servants. She enjoyed carrying things off with a high hand. All the same, Mullins did look surprised. She seemed to hover for a moment before she went out. It annoyed Geraldine greatly. What was there to be surprised at? What could have been simpler? she thought, sitting down to her batch of letters, and the fire, and the clock and her pen began to whisper together.

There was the taxi — making an enormous noise at the door. She thought she heard the driver's voice too, arguing. It took her a long moment to clasp her writing-case and to get up out of the low chair. The bell rang. She went straight to the dining-room door —

And there was Major Hunter in his riding kit, coming quickly towards her, and behind him, through the open door at the bottom of the steps, she saw something big, something grey. It was an ambulance.

'There's been an accident,' cried Geraldine sharply.

'Mrs. Howard.' Major Hunter ran forward. He put out his icy cold hand and wrung hers. 'You'll be brave, won't you?' he said, he pleaded.

But of course she would be brave.

'Is it serious?'

Major Hunter nodded gravely. He said the one word 'Yes.'

'Very serious?'

Now he raised his head. He looked her full in the eyes. She'd never realised until that moment that he was extraordinarily handsome though in a melodrama kind of way. 'It's as bad as it can be, Mrs. Howard,' said Major Hunter simply. 'But — go in there,' he said hastily, and he almost pushed her into her own dining-room. 'We must bring him in — where can we —'

'Can he be taken upstairs?' asked Geraldine.

'Yes, yes, of course.' Major Hunter looked at her so strangely — so painfully.

'There's his dressing-room,' said Geraldine. 'It's on the first floor. I'll lead the way,' and she put her hand on the Major's arm. 'It's quite all right, Major,' she said, 'I'm not going to break down —' and she actually smiled, a confident brilliant smile.

To her amazement, as Major Hunter turned away he burst

out with, 'Ah, my God! I'm so sorry.'

Poor man. He was quite overcome. 'Brandy afterwards,' thought Geraldine. 'Not now, of course.'

It was a painful moment when she heard those measured deliberate steps in the hall. But Geraldine, realising this was not the moment, and there was nothing to be gained by it, refrained from looking.

'This way, Major.' She skimmed on in front, up the stairs, along the passage; she flung open the door of Jimmie's gay, living, breathing dressing-room and stood to one side — for Major Hunter, for the two stretcher-bearers. Only then she realised that it must be a scalp wound — some injury to the head. For there was nothing to be seen of Jimmie; the sheet was pulled right over . . .

CONTRIBUTORS

Catherine Chidgey's novels have been published to international acclaim. Her first, *In a Fishbone Church*, won Best First Book at the Montana New Zealand Book Awards, where it was also runner-up for the Deutz Medal. It won the Betty Trask Award in the UK and Best First Book at the Commonwealth Writers' Prize (Asia–Pacific section). It was nominated for the Orange Prize in the UK. Her second novel, *Golden Deeds*, was runner-up for the Deutz Medal at the Montana New Zealand Book Awards and has been serialised by Radio New Zealand. It was chosen by *Time Out* magazine, London, as a book of the year, and was a notable book of 2002 in both the *New York Times Review of Books* and the *LA Times*. Her third novel, *The Transformation*, was chosen by US bookstore chain Barnes & Noble as one of their Discover Picks of 2005. The *Times Literary Supplement* called it 'a perfect novel'. It has been translated into Turkish.

Catherine has held the Burns Fellowship at the University of Otago, the Ursula Bethell Fellowship at the University of Canterbury, the Katherine Mansfield Memorial Fellowship to Menton, France, the Sargeson Fellowship, and the Todd New Writers' Bursary. In 2002 she won the inaugural Prize in Modern Letters, New Zealand's richest single literary prize. In 2003 she was named by a *Listener* panel of writers, critics and booksellers as the best New Zealand novelist under forty. She has translated three German picture books into English, is a member of the Sargeson Trust, and has sat on the Literature Committee for Creative New Zealand. Catherine is the 2008 recipient of the Rathcoola Residency to Cork, Ireland.

Marilyn Duckworth OBE is a Wellington novelist who spent her childhood in England. Her first novel, *A Gap in the Spectrum*, was published in London when she was twenty-three. She went on to write fourteen more novels, including *Disorderly Conduct*, which won a New Zealand Book Award in 1984, and *Leather Wings*, shortlisted for a Commonwealth Writers' Prize. Her novel *Playing Friends* was released in 2007.

Prominent among the fellowships she has held are the 1980 Katherine Mansfield Memorial Fellowship, which took her to Menton where she lived in the room below the terrace of Isola Bella. There she wrote her sixth published novel, *Rest for the Wicked*, part of which is set in Mansfield's Garavan; and also a poem, 'At Isola Bella with Fleur'.

Fiona Farrell is a novelist and poet who lives on Banks Peninsula. Fiona writes: 'My childhood was totally colonised by fiction from Britain and the United States. I read Mansfield's "The Doll's House" when I was about sixteen and it was a revelation: fiction could actually be set in my own country! I asked for her *Collected Stories* as a school prize that year. (I still have it, with the school crest on the cover.) To be honest, I found it a disappointment. I expected all the stories to be like "The Doll's House", set in Wellington and about children. The delicate sexual savagery of her European stories repelled and frightened me. I was young. Now that I am old, it is the tough-minded brilliance of the stories and the youthfulness of their creator that strike me as unbearably poignant. I read them sensing the febrile brilliance of a mind hyperstimulated by disease and the terror of imminent death, and I am in awe.

'I lived in Menton in 1995 as one of the Mansfield Fellows, though I did not work in the room in Garavan. The roof had been leaking and when I opened the door it was to find everything coated in white mould like the winter dacha in Dr. Zhivago. I sat below the terrace where Mansfield had been photographed, coughing uncontrollably myself, and deciding that tradition would have to be ignored. I'd write in the apartment we were renting, where the table might wobble but my lungs would survive.

'Mansfield wasn't in Garavan anyway, any more than she is in Thorndon. She lives in the New Zealand imagination as one of those distinctive regional icons: one of us, like Ed Hillary or Peter Jackson, who "did very well overseas". She is revered as we revere Janet Frame, for the poignancy of a creative life expressed in the shadow of devastating ill-health. She is that classical heroine: young, beautiful, wayward, supremely gifted, and doomed to an early death.'

James George is a novelist, short story writer, biographer and creative writing tutor. His second novel, *Hummingbird*, was shortlisted for both the Deutz Medal for Fiction at the New Zealand Book Awards and for the Tasmania Pacific Fiction Prize. His third novel, *Ocean Roads*, was shortlisted for both the Deutz Medal and the Commonwealth Writers' Prize (Asia–Pacific section.) His short stories have appeared in anthologies in both New Zealand and France and have won awards in New Zealand. He is also the author of *Showband*, the story of Mahora and the Maori Volcanics.

James was born in Wellington of Maori (iwi — Ngapuhi), English and Irish whakapapa, and considers Northland (where two of his novels are set) his spiritual home. These days he fights the traffic jams in Auckland and dreams of Ninety Mile Beach.

For the last two years he has chaired Te Ha, the Writers' Committee of Toi Maori Aotearoa, and has organised and taken part in many events. James was the 2007 Buddle Findlay Sargeson Writing Fellow, and has also been awarded two writer's grants from Creative New Zealand. He has taught creative writing for many years in various forums in New Zealand and Australia.

James' next novel, *Theme from an Imaginary Western*, is scheduled for publication in mid-2008. He is working on a fifth novel, *Two Rivers*, which is expected to be completed in 2009.

Charlotte Grimshaw is the author of three novels and one collection of short stories. She has held the Buddle Findlay Sargeson Fellowship, has been a double finalist and prizewinner in the *Sunday Star-Times* Short Story Competition, a winner of a 2007 Book Council *Six Pack* prize, and won the 2006 Katherine Mansfield Award for Short Fiction. Her story collection, *Opportunity*, was shortlisted for the 2007 Frank O'Connor International Short Story Award.

She comments: 'When I was asked to contribute to *Second Violins*, and given, as a starter, Katherine Mansfield's unfinished story 'The Doves' Nest', I had to think carefully how to proceed. It seemed a difficult task, to 'finish' a story that was long, and possibly almost complete. I wanted to avoid simply filling in where Katherine Mansfield had left off, and also, in terms of style, to avoid an imitation of her tone that would amount to mere pastiche. With this in mind, I have incorporated the first paragraph of "The Doves' Nest" in my story in spirit rather than exactly, and have adapted it to my own original scenario. I have included various nods to Mansfield's style in tone and imagery, and also in subject matter. My story is a child's-eye view. It concerns a child's emerging perception of the adult world, the protean nature of personality, shifting identities, and masks. These are ideas which I think Mansfield was interested in, in her own work. And I have set the story in Menton, where Mansfield lived for a time, and where I lived and went to school as a child, when my father held the Katherine Mansfield Fellowship.'

Witi Ihimaera is a novelist, short story writer and librettist. He has written six short story collections, including *Dear Miss Mansfield* (1989), a homage to Katherine Mansfield. The story in this collection, 'Orbis Terrarum', was written following a trip with friends to the Galapagos Islands in July 2008. His latest book is *Ask the Posts of the House* (2008).

Annamarie Jagose is Professor of Film, Television and Media Studies at the University of Auckland. She is the author of three novels, most recently *Slow Water*, which won the Deutz Medal for Fiction at the Montana New Zealand Book Awards and the Vance Palmer Prize for Fiction at the Victorian Premier's Literary Awards. 'Kittenelle' is part of her current project in which she is rewriting a series of Katherine Mansfield short stories.

Stephanie Johnson is the author of three collections of short stories, two volumes of poetry and seven novels. She has also written for stage, radio, television and film and has been the recipient of awards and fellowships, including the Deutz Medal for Fiction in the Montana Book Awards (for *The Shag Incident*, 2003), the Bruce Mason Memorial Playwrights

Award, the Auckland University Fellowship and the Katherine Mansfield Fellowship. Several of her books have been published in the United States, Britain and Australia. Stephanie is the co-founder and co-creative director of the Auckland Writers and Readers Festival.

Fiona Kidman writes mainly novels, short stories and poetry, and also works as an anthologist from time to time. She has written more than 20 books, and edited the first three collections of Vintage's *Best New Zealand Fiction* series. In 2006 she was the Meridian Energy Katherine Mansfield Fellow, resident in Menton, France, where she worked regularly at Villa Isola Bella, home to Katherine Mansfield in 1920. That same year she toured France at the invitation of the French government as part of Les Belles Étrangères tour, promoting New Zealand literature in France. Her most recent novel, *The Captive Wife* (Vintage, 2005), won the Readers' Choice Award at the Montana New Zealand Book Awards, and is published in French translation as *Rescapée*. Her latest book is a memoir, *At the End of Darwin Road* (Vintage, 2008). Fiona has a DCNZM and OBE for services to literature.

Bill Manhire directs the creative writing programme at Victoria University. His most recent book is the Montana Award winner *Lifted*, mostly written while he held the Katherine Mansfield Fellowship in Menton during 2004. He has published several prize-winning collections of poetry and a volume of short stories, *Songs of My Life*, which contains the choose-your-own-adventure story, 'The Brain of Katherine Mansfield'. He has also edited a number of best-selling anthologies, including *Some Other Country: New Zealand's Best Short Stories*, *Soho Square*, and *121 New Zealand Poems*. He is one of the few poets ever to reach the South Pole.

Carl Nixon is a novelist and playwright. He is the current holder of the Bank of New Zealand Katherine Mansfield Award, having won it for his short story 'My Beautiful Balloon'. His first book, *Fish 'n' Chip Shop Song and other stories* (Vintage, 2006), topped the New Zealand bestseller list for fiction. It was shortlisted for the Commonwealth Writers' Prize Best First Book (Asia–Pacific section). His novel, *Rocking Horse Road* (Vintage, 2007), saw him described as 'a major talent' (*North and South* magazine). His latest play, *The Raft*, premiered at the Court Theatre in Christchurch. Carl lives in Christchurch with his wife and two young children.

Vincent O'Sullivan is a poet, fiction writer, playwright and biographer who lives in Wellington. He has published extensively on Katherine Mansfield's life and work, and has edited with Margaret Scott the five-volume edition of *The Collected Letters of Katherine Mansfield*. The final volume will be published later this year.

Sarah Quigley was the inaugural recipient of the Creative New Zealand Berlin Writers' Fellowship in 2000–2001. Since then she has divided her time between Europe and New Zealand. She has published a collection of short stories, two poetry collections, and three novels, the most recent of which is *Fifty Days* (Virago, 2004). She is also the author of *Write: A Thirty Day Guide to Creative Writing*. Her short fiction has won many prizes, including the *Sunday Star-Times* Short Story Award and the Commonwealth (Pacific Rim) Short Story Prize. She has a DPhil in English Literature from the University of Oxford.

Tracey Slaughter's short story 'Her First' won the Novice Writers' Section of the BNZ Katherine Mansfield Awards in 2001, and in 2004 she went on to receive the Supreme Award with the story 'Wheat'. *Her Body Rises*, her first collection of short stories and poems, was published in 2005 by Vintage. Recent stories have been featured in *The Six Pack Two* (2007), *Best New Zealand Fiction Volume 4*, *Landfall* and *Myth of the 21st Century*. She lives on the Coromandel Peninsula with her partner and two young children.

Alice Tawhai comments that her 'latest book of short stories, *Luminous*, is very, very good, and people should purchase it immediately from her publisher's website www.huia.co.nz, because selling lots of copies will mean that her publisher will allow her to keep working on her third book of short stories, which is already half completed, and which she is already in love with, instead of making her work on a novel, which she isn't ready to do until after the short stories in her next collection are finished. If people bought her first collection, *Festival of Miracles*, that would help as well. It, of course, is very, very good too.'

Peter Wells won the New Zealand and Reed awards for fiction with his first short story collection, *Dangerous Desires* (1991), about which *The Oxford Companion to New Zealand Literature* wrote: 'Extraordinary for the lucid and passionate eloquence of the writing as well as their sexual (mostly homosexual) explicitness, the stories combine emotional intensity with psychological insight and a rare wit . . . Though he is committedly and publicly a gay writer, his range of subject, setting and style is greater than any such definition can suggest. [In *The Duration of a Kiss*] some of the best writing deals with non-gay subjects.' Peter's short stories have been published internationally and widely anthologised. He has also written three novels, the second of which was runner-up in the Montana New Zealand Book Awards. Wells was joint winner (with C.K. Stead) of the 1999 Landfall essay competition. His memoir, *Long Loop Home* (2001), won the Biography Award in the 2002 Montana Book Awards.

He is equally known as a film and television director and scriptwriter, most notably for 'A Death in the Family' (1986) and for the feature film 'Desperate Remedies' (co-written and directed with Stewart Main), selected to screen at the 1993 Cannes Film Festival. In 2006 Peter was made a Member of the New Zealand Order of Merit for services to literature and film.

On Mansfield, he writes: 'I was commissioned to write a play based on K.M.'s "Prelude" and "At the Bay" for the New Zealand Festival of the Arts. I had always loved these two stories above all of her stories. But they are more inherently filmic than dramatic. Nevertheless I managed, under the directorship of Colin McColl, to produce a strange and rather richly visual mini-operatic play called *Ricordi!* (Ricordi was the enigmatic word D.H. Lawrence wrote on the back of a postcard when his ship called in at Wellington. He sent it to K.M., with whom he had bitterly fallen out.)'

Albert Wendt has been the Citizens' Chair in the English Department of the University of Hawaii for the past four years. He will be returning to Auckland and his home in Ponsonby in July 2008. While in Hawaii he has been working on three novels, a full-length feature-film script and a collection of poetry. He has also been painting, and had his first public exhibition of paintings in Honolulu in August–September 2007.

While Albert was at high school in New Plymouth, years ago, Katherine Mansfield dominated the New Zealand literature taught in his English classes. This led him to read most of her stories when he went to university.